Jules Hardy grew up in London and is no~~~~ ~~~~ carpenter and has recently completed a Ph~~~~ ~~~~ *Blue Earth* is her third novel following *Alt~~~~*

Acclaim for *MISTER CANDID*

'A powerful, compelling, yet uncomfortable read that explores the moral issues surrounding murder, in an intriguing and masterfully woven story. You'll be hooked from page one' *COMPANY*

'In prose that is both graceful and hard-hitting, Jules Hardy nudges us towards the truth at the heart of a terrifyingly dysfunctional family. It gets darker as it progresses, playing across the fuzzy lines that separate good from bad deeds and morality from law' *THE TIMES*

'Impressive foray into the pathology of revenge . . . which you might expect from the gifted Jules Hardy. The writing is poetic. Excellent' *UNCUT*

'The book takes you on a journey from the affluent, cosseted world of East Hampton, to Harvard, sleepy Florida and down town New York, this is a true page turner' *SHE*

'A seductive, shadowy novel . . . described in prose that is sweet and sinister as funeral lilies' *ZEMBLA*

'A gripping story . . . she is a talented writer' *SUNDAY TIMES*

'For once, it seems to me, "stunning" is an entirely appropriate description. I love its originality, the near-poetic quality of some of its passages. Above all, I love its bravery – its delicious darkness. A brilliant, breathtaking achievement' PAUL EDDY, author of *FLINT*

'A brilliant and unputdownable read that throws everything you believe into question' *B*

ALSO BY JULES HARDY

Altered Land

Mister Candid

JULES HARDY

BLUE EARTH

POCKET
BOOKS

LONDON • SYDNEY • NEW YORK • TORONTO

First published in Great Britain by Simon & Schuster UK Ltd, 2005
This paperback edition published by Pocket Books, 2006
An imprint of Simon & Schuster UK Ltd
A Viacom company

1 3 5 7 9 10 8 6 4 2

Simon & Schuster UK Ltd
Africa House
64–78 Kingsway
London WC2B 6AH

www.simonsays.co.uk

Simon & Schuster Australia
Sydney

A CIP catalogue record for this book
is available from the British Library

ISBN 0 7434 9567 5
EAN 97807432495677

Typeset by M Rules
Printed and bound in Great Britain by
Cox & Wyman Ltd, Reading, Berks

ACKNOWLEDGEMENTS

This novel has taken so long to write that it has driven nearly everyone around me to despair. Not true. It *has* driven everyone around me to despair. Over the years, I have duped so many people into donating their time and sharing their expertise, it's difficult to remember them all; anyway, how to thank a cast of hundreds?

I must mention: Mary-Ellen Butkus, who hauled textbooks across the Caribbean for me (and, I've just realized, paid for them too); Mark Jones, who *does* love geology, who, in fact, loves it so much he checked the typescript for geographical accuracy; Louise O'Neill (and her mother), who drank my gin and then set me straight on the finer points of Irish culture and customs; Sheila Roles, who searched for unpleasant medical conditions, without flinching; Amanda Suart, who brought me cold beers and arcane information; and John Pratt, who told me all about correct radio communication protocol between pilots. I'd particularly like to thank Phil Bergman of Vancouver Island Air for answering so many dull questions about floatplanes, and for being there at the end of an email address when the tropical storms kicked in and the doors were bolted and windows shut. Marie Dilworth has the patience of a saint; I know, because she had the pleasure of listening to me ranting twice a day for three months, as we walked the dogs. Thank you. Tim Binding at Simon & Schuster made incisive comments and the ever-lovely Nigel Stoneman listened to my endless whinging without batting an eyelid. Obviously, I should also thank my mother and my godmother, who put up with many tantrums, but I think they've been thanked enough. Anyway, that's what they're here for.

I must also acknowledge my debt to other writers, whose books enthralled and informed me: John Gardey's *Alaska: The Sophisticated*

Wilderness; Dee Brown's *Bury My Heart at Wounded Knee*; Joe McGinniss's *Going to Extremes*; and the incomparable Jonathan Raban's *Passage to Juneau*. I'd like to thank the Alaskan Native Knowledge Network's education programme for information provided. I would also like to acknowledge the financial support of the Arts and Humanities Research Board.

As I said, many people helped me in very different ways and there is not space here to thank them all. But I can hardly ignore two of them: my agent, Maggie Phillips, who last year waited until I was 4000 miles away before contacting me, to announce that I should throw half the manuscript which existed at the time straight in the bin. She was, as always, right. And, of course, my editor, Melissa Weatherill. Where would I be without her? Well, probably down the pub, enjoying a normal life.

For Moosey

'Tribes are made up of individuals and are no better than they. Men come and go like the waves of the sea. A tear, a *tanamawus*, a dirge, and they are gone from our longing eyes for ever. Even the white man, whose God walked and talked with him, as friend to friend, is not exempt from the common destiny.'

From a speech made by the Suquamish Leader,
Great Chief Seattle, 1854

She has two names: Sedna and Arnaknagsak. Sedna – a short name with shades of a Dravidian heritage; her other name hard and guttural, hints of Viking abounding, so many Ks like fish hooks snagging in a speaker's mouth. Some say she married a dog, a husky, a wild thing; others say she married a raptor. What is known is that her father killed her husband, the manner of whose death is unrecorded or has perhaps been forgotten. The father left the husband to die on the drifting floes, blood turning ice diamonds to rubies, and dragged his daughter to his boat, bundling her over the side of the smooth-edged kayak. The kayak departed for the father's home as a storm slammed in from the west, rocking the flimsy craft, tossing it on spume-capped waves. The girl was pitched over the side as the wind howled and waters raged, yet still she managed to cling to the kayak with her delicate hands, calling for help as the ocean dragged at her heels. What is also unrecorded – or forgotten – in this story is why her father chose not to pull her aboard. What was he thinking? Why travel so far to retrieve his first-born child, only to abandon her in her moment of need? As it happened, rather than grabbing her wrists and heaving her out of the maelstrom, he reached for his axe and chopped at his daughter's hands, severing the fingers. The girl disappeared into the mad whirls of freezing water as her bloodied fingers slithered down the hide sides of the kayak and came to rest at the father's feet. Imagine, then, his surprise as the fingers took shape, became walrus, whale and seal. Even more, his surprise when the walrus attacked and devoured him. The kayak, scene of so much blood and violence, sank and the whale, seal and walrus slid into arctic seas. Meanwhile, Arnaknagsak (or Sedna) had sunk deep into the waters, where she became the Great Sea Spirit, the provider of quarry, food and sport on the waves. Her abyssal, sapphire domain is known as Adlivun, and when she is angry, insufficiently propitiated, she will send a dead spirit, a malignant tupilaq *to unsettle the mortals living on the ice shelf.*

This was the story told by Inuit mothers and fathers to Inuit children to explain why the world they lived in was as it was. Perhaps the story varied a little in the different tellings but always Arnaknagsak (or Sedna) sank fingerless into the abyss. The children sat in their iglus or hide-bound tents, surrounded by ice fields or tundra, and listened to the world being made by the Moon Spirit and the Air Spirit. What were they doing there, these smooth-cheeked, brown-eyed babies, with their dark, straight hair, stark against the ice fields? How had they arrived at the edge of the world, hearing the tale of a fingerless spirit, a spirit whose hands became mere flippers, seal-like? A spirit apparently suffering from phocomelia.

The story of the arrival of the Native Americans in Alashka is far simpler than tales of raptors disguising themselves as human or bear to make off with young Inuit women. Indeed, it is a very simple story – they walked. They walked from Siberia across an ice bridge. When the temperatures began to fall thousands of years ago, the oceans were sucked to the poles where they froze, where they became ice sheets hundreds of feet thick, and the world was changed. The tribes of Siberia headed east, crossed the glittering ice bridge which was bedded in the shallow Bering Sea, and arrived in a land much like the one they had left. Some – the Aleuts and Eskimos – stayed; others kept moving, moving south, searching for heat. Eventually the temperatures began to rise again, the glaciers melted and retreated and the waters rushed back over the land. The Siberians were lucky – they had discovered two vast, watery continents. They kept walking, shedding clothes as they travelled south, swapping furs for loincloths. Some tribes came to rest on the coast of the Pacific, some ventured into the great plain lands in the middle of the continent: the Sioux, Cheyenne, Comanche. Others kept moving south, travelling the length of the land to find that their journey ended in the mountainous archipelago of Tierra del Fuego, at the other end of the earth, another ice dome fluxing over the horizon, mirroring the one they had left behind. Mayan and Incan civilizations burgeoned, the Codex Borbonicus was written, gold was fashioned into jewellery as the Aztecs awaited the return of Quetzalcoatl.

Meanwhile the stragglers, the Inuit, island-hopped their way from Siberia twenty thousand years later. Some arrived via the shrinking, ever more fragile ice bridge, some in shallow boats. Once in their new land – now named Alashka, the Great Land – they fanned out east, leaving other tribes to build cities in the sun. The Inuit spread as far as Greenland, strung out like water beads across taiga and tundra. They settled or they moved, built iglus or were nomads. The Inuit survived – they kept their heads down, chewed the dried meat of caribou, whale, seal and fish, and they survived. As the Algonquin, Cherokee and Navajo, their distant cousins, found time to decorate themselves, to build and create, the Inuit survived. Their bodies changed to accommodate the demands of the Air Spirit and the Great Sea Spirit, their blood running faster, their need for plant food diminishing. They survived earthquakes, volcanoes, the great thaw, the frozen waters, ice cracks, crevasses. The Inuit even survived the arrival of the white man, for a while at least.

As the Inuit hunkered down on their white earth, other tribes settled the glittering, wild coastline of Alashka. The Tlingit, Tsimshian, Haida, Nootka and Chinook tribes waited thousands of years for the sea to settle, waited for the land and sea to stop shifting, and then they swarmed over the narrow strip of land between ocean and mountains. Beyond the mountains, in the interior, the Inuit were scanning a featureless, albino horizon, sensing movement others could not see. But on the coast the Pacific tribes looked out on a world streaked with aquamarine, azure, midnight, plum and cobalt beneath a sky of lapis lazuli and violet. The Inuit chewed dried seal meat as the Tlingit threw elaborate potlatches, feasting on elk, sheep, salmon and halibut, root vegetables and berries. The Haida traded with Asia, discovered that iron could be used to carve elaborate effigies. The Chinook and Tsimshian built villages, long huts and drying sheds. They sang, they wore costumes and danced to celebrate a new moon, a newborn child, a death. All the tribes created sea-going craft – kayak and oomiak – and they spent their days on the oceans, fearing the earth, the mountains and forests behind the villages, where bears took young women, and the water's edge where the glaciers cracked, calved and tumbled, where fire flared. The Raven, the Eagle and the Wolf were their guardian spirits, evoked to save them from the perils of the land. The Inuits' Pacific cousins had music, iron, art and time – all luxuries.

For more than thirty thousand years these tribes survived or flourished. Tenochtitlán and Cuzco, the fabulous cities of Mesoamerica, were birthed and still the Inuit chewed as they scanned their white, unsullied landscape;

still the Tlingits ensured their survival by pleasing the spirits of the ocean and wind and air. How were any of them to know about the birth of a weaver's son in the city state of Genoa?

Forty-one years after his birth Cristoforo Colombo boarded the Santa Maria, *waved to well-wishers standing on the dock in Palos, South-east Spain, hitched up his breeches, weighed anchor and set sail. A little over two months later the* Santa Maria *arrived at the island of Guanahaní, in the Bahamas. Cristoforo stepped ashore and addressed a large gathering of natives, possibly Caribs, claiming their island for Spain, and renaming it San Salvador. One wonders what the Caribs made of this. It must have seemed rather a presumption on the part of a visitor – particularly one who had been there such a short time. More than this, there was the small matter that Cristoforo, standing on the baking sand dressed in leather jerkin and breeches, tropical sun beating down, thought he was in Asia, near India. A mistake anyone could make. For three months the* Santa Maria *hightailed it up and down the newly named West Indies, claiming land hand over fist, and Colombo then turned east to head back to Palos. No doubt the Caribs were glad to see the back of him.*

What the Caribs, the Apaches, Comanches, Incas, Aztecs, Inuit and Aleuts – all the hundreds of tribes whose odyssey began with a trek across a glittering ice bridge – did not realize was that Cristoforo was not the last white man, rather he was the first. There were ninety million people living on the continents before Cristoforo weighed anchor in Palos harbour. Five hundred years later there were two million left in the northern continent. Conquistadores rode the coastal ranges on their dappled horses, riding tall, beards sharp as blades, eyes cold as snow, and were hailed by some as gods. The white man came and he brought with him pox and plague, guns and horses, rape and enslavement – all of it made legal, rendered virtuous even, by the papal bulls emanating from the Vatican. The Thunderbird, the Great Lynx, the Raven, Wolf and Eagle were no match for the Papal Bull – even the Sun God, Huitzilopochtli himself, couldn't have stopped that maddened beast.

1960

The Convent of the Immaculate Virgin squatted on a bluff near the town of Louisburgh, Co. Mayo, Éire. The benefactor of the order – a merchant of metals – had funded the building in the late nineteenth century, a commitment born not of religious fervour but, rather, an attempt to buy a place in heaven, a gamble which, had it been possible, would indeed have been a good bet since he was unlikely to reach Paradise, given his outrageous philandering. The buildings, reached only by negotiating a gravel track, were hidden by the thick trunks and crowns of old English oak trees, planted at the same time as those at Old Head, and fenced by stout wrought iron. The site of the convent was spectacular: to the north lay the island of Achill and the drumlin-studded waters of Clew Bay, to the west was Clare Island and to the south the Atlantic waters ate away at the islands of Inishturk and Inishbofin. But these violent, intoxicating vistas were denied the nuns; the walls had no windows other than those facing east, so the sole view from the interior was that of Croagh Patrick, the Mountain of St Patrick, where, it was said, he had spent forty days and forty nights. The iron fencing surrounding the buildings had, of course, been supplied, designed and wrought by the convent's founder. The poles were tipped with arrowed finials, each facet serrated to discourage the world from climbing in, serrated both to impale and disembowel intruders, who might or might not be intent on violating the brides of Christ within. Local granite formed the walls, thick as a man's waist, hard as a man's heart, flecked with flashing mica. The windows, leaded and inadequate, were arched, framed in pale freestone, as if blond eyebrows were permanently raised in surprise. The slate floors, worn now in places, had been smoothed by the pounding of thousands of paces, each step taken in bare feet, skin meeting cold stone, each step wearing the slate down, each step eroding hexagonal carbon molecules. The paces were taken with bare feet because the convent was of the Order of Discalced Carmelites, nuns whose lives passed in prayer, penance, hard work and silence. They ate no meat, and from the day of the Exaltation of the Cross until Easter they ate no cheese or eggs either, nor did they drink milk.

The convent was a dour, loveless and isolated place, hunched over, clutching at itself, yet even the women who spent their lives penned behind the spiked railings could not escape the winds of change howling across the world. Pope John XXIII had, in January, issued various decrees in an attempt to bring his flock back into line – Catholics were banned from watching corrupting television programmes and films, priests forbidden to smoke, the sacrament denied to women in male clothing or displaying bare arms. The Mother Superior smiled thinly when she heard these things and determined that she would batten down the hatches, slam them so tightly shut that nothing could worm its way in and disrupt the smooth running of the convent. How she tried, reinforcing the stipulation of the vows, repeating the evangelical counsels, overseeing a steely, hard-edged silence in the refectory, taking aside those novitiates who wept quietly over bowls of soup and whipping them into shape. The Mother Superior ran an airtight ship. Yet . . . yet . . . even she could not silence those who came in from outside, hard as she tried, and corruption still crept in, insidious as the salt spray.

At the rear of the convent, behind the school, hidden, almost, by the walls of the battered, wind-swept vegetable garden, was a small cottage hospital, a single-storey, breeze-block building, lined with asbestos, darkened by thin curtains hanging in the east-facing windows. The patients in the hospital were the Fallen, those girls who had done the easiest thing in the world. Young country girls from the towns and farms, who'd gone to a Saturday night dance and been swirled around bare, dusty floorboards before being taken outside by gangling, desperate youths. Once outside, unsure of what was happening to them, they had either squirmed or lain unresisting as skirts were lifted and drawers removed. Stunned into silence, either by shame or confusion, they had said nothing for months, said nothing even when their mothers' eagle eyes had seen them leaning against the sink in a certain way, or bending awkwardly over a laundry basket. Some were thrown out of the family home, left to fend for themselves; others were sent to far-distant relatives for a while, returning empty handed. The truly unfortunate were sent to the convent, where their spiritual rebirth was overseen by the Mother Superior, as was the birth of their children. The lowest of the low were those who'd been to the convent school, whose hearts and minds had been forged by the nuns, whose knowledge of the scriptures was second to none. How was it, then, that they returned? Carrying their parts of shame and their fecund bellies before them? How could this be? The Mother Superior flattered herself that she could spot a potential returnee as young as four years old. She believed she could look a small girl in the eye and see her future, as innocent or reprobate.

The prattle of the Fallen was what the Mother Superior could not control, for they brought with them news from Outside. To be sure, the expectant mothers had but a tenuous grasp of what they were describing and events were garbled in the retelling. Those who could, brushed and scrubbed the refectory and corridor floors, dusted down the dormitories, wiped clean the small hospital, and they talked as they pushed buckets with oedemic feet and rubbed sore backs. Those who were too bovine, too heavy slung to move, lay in their hard beds and jabbered. The nuns who moved silently among these pregnant girls shushed and frowned, but they could not stop the tumult of words. Nor could they help overhearing. The nuns gleaned a great deal about brothers and sisters, about drunken fathers, about who had said what to whom; they heard complaints about worn clothes handed down, loving memories of mothers who kissed goodnight, they heard a great deal about family life. But snippets of the Outside also flew in, snagging on the nuns' minds – garbled stories of black riots, girls falling in love with beetles, smallpox epidemics, men flying around the earth and pigs fighting with bombs. No surprise, then, that the brides of Christ were glad to be protected by their serrated barrier; the world was going to the dogs.

*

There was no privacy in the hospital, no thick walls within it to absorb the screams and shouts of young women and girls who felt their bodies distending past breaking point, as blood and plasma oozed between their legs. A birth was the only time the Fallen fell silent, the only time they turned on their sides in their beds, closed their eyes and pulled grey woollen blankets over their ears. Behind a flimsy curtain, which hung in loops from rings rusted by the salt air, the Mother Superior, looking grim, looking disapproving, looking like an angel of death, would draw each mucus-cauled baby away from its mother and savour the moment. She held in her hands, if only for a short time, the truly innocent. Two knots, a snip and the Mother Superior would be off, the infant swaddled in clean linen, leaving the novitiates to clean up the girl and remove all traces of what had happened. After she had left, the whispers would start again, rolling from bed to bed, like wind-blown grasses. But if, as sometimes happened, there was silence behind the curtain after the infant had gone, if the silence was as deep as open water, as deep as a limestone cave, then there were no whispers. The girls and young women would cross themselves and cry quietly, hopelessly, fearful that they, too, might soon die in childbirth.

That was what happened on the second Sunday of October that year, as a storm blew itself out across the cliffs and rias of Mayo. Even with the windows and doors closed and firmly bolted, the curtains drifted in thin curls of wind that wormed their way into the hospital. The Mother Superior scooped up the child after sketching a cross on her chest and glanced at the mother – a returnee. Typical of *that* one to go giving birth on a Sunday, throwing the convent into confusion, disrupting the run of the Lord's day. And the priest hadn't arrived in time, of course, to give extreme unction – which was a shame, because if ever it was needed, that girl needed it. The baby roared, its eyes creased shut in fat folds, feet kicking, and the Mother Superior motioned to Sister Mary to carry on, before forcing open the door against a spiteful, capricious wind, allowing it to slam behind her. The whimpers of the pregnant girls behind the curtain fell into the ensuing silence, the only sound in the ward, other than the whispers of wind.

*

The Mother Superior, had she been born in a different time and place, might have been an entrepreneur, for she had a firm grasp of the market economy, an innate understanding of the principles of capitalism. It is doubtful the Mother Superior could have articulated her understanding, could have described her actions in terms of resource use and control, but that was exactly what it was. She would not have described the pregnant girls, mewling babies and post-natal young women as capital goods, but that is exactly what they were. Her other capital asset was the fabric and land of the convent itself. In order to maintain one she had to exploit the other. The pregnant arrivals were fattened on a diet of mass and liturgy, then their offspring were farmed out, in return for a percentage of the eventual sale price, and the newly bereaved girls were frequently sent to the mainland to work in service, again for a fee. (Was there nothing people wouldn't buy? Nothing they wouldn't sell?) The Mother Superior slept well each night, lying down after lengthy prayers with a clear conscience and a quiet grunt – for the money raised by this dabbling in the market economy was used to refurbish the church, the nave, the roof, used to enrich the capital assets of the order. And the Mother Superior was determined that she would leave a legacy of sound buildings and watertight roofs, rectitude and obedience, as well as a penitential flock of the barefoot and pregnant.

1957

He sailed from New York City on the day Sputnik 2 was launched from the wastes of the Siberian hinterland. Unknown to him, at the very moment he leaned on the railings of the liner to watch Manhattan slip away, Laika, the Russian dog sent to orbit the earth, died in her modified R-7 rocket. As Laika was overwhelmed by temperatures running to hundreds of degrees Centigrade, he watched the sun sliding like a melting butter pat behind distant scrapers and he shivered, tugged at the collar of his flecked overcoat and then, surprising himself, waved briefly at the disappearing city-scape. It was, perhaps, an unconscious homage of sorts for the first mammal to die in space. The wind kicked up the Atlantic, tossed it skywards as the *Queen Mary* laboured away from New York, and he pulled his coat closer, buttoning it against the cold. He scanned the horizon, searching for the Wave, convinced it was still circling the globe, hunting him down. Once the liner made deep, open water it began to buck in the storm moving in from the east, bowling the wave trains along, but the waves were shallow and fractured, too ill disciplined to worry about.

He made his way down to the observation lounge on the promenade deck, settled in an empty booth and ordered an Indian pale ale (having no idea what it was like). He watched the barman steadying himself, moving among glass, appreciating the economy of movement, the grace of the man. Having drunk his first beer and ordered a second, he looked around and caught sight of himself in the etched mirror behind the ranked bottles, penned against the swell by brass fittings – a head of thick, tousled blond hair setting off a face of Nordic symmetry. A face that still surprised him, a face that belonged to someone else.

A slender, dark-haired woman in a figure-hugging black dress and wavering stilettos weaved her way towards him, near-falling as the liner shuddered and listed to starboard. He stood to help her as she lurched and fell awkwardly on to the banquette next to him.

'Why, thank you.' The woman smoothed her hair and touched her cheek. 'It's a little rougher than I thought it would be.'

'It's certainly getting interesting out there. You look pale – would you like a drink?'

'Yes, I certainly would.' Again she touched her cheek. 'A brandy would be marvellous.'

He motioned to the barman, gave the order and sat back on the red, plush seat. 'Allow me to introduce myself: Billy-Ray Rickman.' Billy-Ray held out his hand and the woman touched his fingertips for a moment.

'Jacqueline Cooper.'

'Apparently a storm's building up. Spinning out of the Azores, being pushed by a depression sheering north. Problem is, the air's very warm coming in from the south, straight off the Sahara I guess.' The drinks arrived and Billy-Ray took a sip of ale. 'It's very unusual for November. We may be in for some rough weather.'

'It sounds, Mr Rickman, as if you know what you're talking about.' Jacqueline dipped a finger into the brandy glass and wet her lips with a forefinger dripping with Courvoisier. Licked her lips.

Billy-Ray watched her, his eyes riveted by the slowly moving finger.

'I said, you sound as if you know something about the weather, Mr Rickman.'

'Not enough to change it,' said Billy-Ray.

Jacqueline smiled. 'Well, that's a shame. So what exactly is it that you do, Mr Rickman?'

'It sounds quite dull but I can tell you it's not. I'm a geophysical prospector.'

Jacqueline Cooper frowned slightly, dabbed more brandy on her lips, then drank from the glass, her tongue moving over her lips as she mulled this over. 'A geophysical prospector? What does that involve?'

'I work for Karbo Inc. I'm an oil man.'

The great ship was suddenly hoisted up the wall of a towering wave, rising and tilting slowly, achingly slowly, until it teetered and lurched bow to stern, shimmying from side to side, before slithering down the wave's other cheek. It was as if the ocean itself were protesting its future rape.

'What a waste,' said Jacqueline, dabbing at the brandy spilled in her lap, and the two of them smiled. 'An oil man, Mr Rickman?'

'Billy-Ray, please. Everyone calls me Billy-Ray.'

That evening Billy-Ray and Jacqueline were seated as neighbours at the captain's table. The captain, sitting opposite, smiled and introduced them: 'Lady Cooper, may I introduce Mr Wilhelm Reichmann? Mr Reichmann, Lady Cooper.'

'We've already had the pleasure of meeting,' said Jacqueline, her finger moving to touch her lips as Billy-Ray watched. 'We braved the bar earlier.'

'I applaud you,' said the captain, raising his glass. 'Mad dogs and Englishmen may go out in the midday sun, but it would seem that only Americans have the stomach for Atlantic storms.' The sommelier appeared at the captain's elbow. 'Do excuse me.'

Billy-Ray offered Jacqueline an untipped Chesterfield, lit it with a worn brass Zippo.

'Thank you, Wilhelm Reichmann.'

'Wilhelm-Rajmund Reichmann. Bit of a mouthful – product of a German father and a Polish mother. When I went to college I changed it to Billy-Ray Rickman. The old name must be the one on the manifest. I just got my first passport and that's what's on my birth papers.' Billy-Ray stopped a passing waiter and ordered a double vodka on the rocks.

'So, Billy-Ray, where do you look for your oil?'

'In Alaska, around the Kenai and Katmai. I guess you probably don't know it.'

Jacqueline laughed. 'I barely know anywhere north of East Eighty-second in Manhattan. And that's only because I have family living there. I've been visiting with them for a month.'

Jacqueline's disconcerting habit of touching her full, red lips had Billy-Ray mesmerized. The entrée arrived, three delicate slivers of smoked salmon, laced with dill: gravadlax, one of Billy-Ray's favourite dishes. He pushed it aside and asked the waiter for another vodka. With ice – to cool the delicious, familiar heat he could feel rising through him. Mercury expanding.

'Lady Cooper—'

'Jacqueline, please call me Jacqueline. "Lady Cooper" makes me feel about a hundred years old.'

'Um . . . Jacqueline, I was going to ask where the title came from? We don't have lords and ladies and all that kind of stuff.'

Jacqueline cut a sliver of fish, chewed and swallowed before saying, 'I'm married to an Englishman, Sir Sidney Cooper. You may have heard of him. He's big in hardware.'

'Military hardware?'

Jacqueline laughed and touched her lips again. 'God, no. Nuts, bolts, screws and nails. That sort of hardware. Good old Granddaddy Cooper saw the housing boom coming at the end of the war – the First World War – and bought in whilst he could. Then along came Hitler and it happened all over again. Lucky old Sidney.' Again she laughed. 'Lucky old me,' she added, staring straight into Billy-Ray's blue eyes, which the wave of heat spreading through him had so far left untouched.

Four days and nights Billy-Ray Rickman spent with Jacqueline Cooper on the *Queen Mary* that first week of November 1957; four days of sybaritic pleasure funded by her absent husband. They had managed, for the sake of appearances, to last out the meal at the captain's table that first night, before Lady Cooper mentioned a headache, brushed Billy-Ray's hand and left. Twenty minutes and three large vodkas later, Billy-Ray made his apologies and slipped away.

Jacqueline's stateroom was vast yet still not spacious enough to contain Billy-Ray's lust. Jacqueline opened the door on his first quiet knock and he slammed it behind himself, pushed her against the wall by the door. Reaching down, he pulled up her Dior skirt, crushing it, tore at the satin panties beneath her garters, tearing them open, before pushing himself into her. Jacqueline, whose husband was sixty-three and big only in hardware, tried to ignore the pain as

Billy-Ray thudded her against the wall, squeezing at her breasts, grabbing at her ass. She wrapped her arms around Billy-Ray's thick, muscular, son-of-a-farmer's neck, felt the tension in his jaw as he hissed through his teeth, and wondered whether her back was broken as he shuddered and gripped her buttocks, if possible, even tighter. As Billy-Ray made a noise like a lung puncturing, Jacqueline considered, fleetingly, whether she could have stopped him had she wished to; wondered whether he would have stopped had she asked.

Billy-Ray withdrew from her as she lowered her feet back to the ground and rested his forehead against the wall, panting. He looked wounded, looked like the victim of a catastrophe.

Jacqueline slipped away from him, stepped out of the torn panties and walked towards the bathroom, shedding clothes and jewellery. Lying in scalding water scented with essence of vanilla, a steaming flannel covering her face, she felt her pubic bone, tender now to the touch, bruised. Jacqueline was aroused, unfinished.

Billy-Ray, meanwhile, searched the bar for ice and vodka, found both and stood at a porthole which the night sky had made a mirror. His brother, Siggy, stared back at him. Forcing his vision beyond the glass, he watched spume being whipped by waves, watched the wave train rolling into the distance. Sipping, firing himself again. When Billy-Ray's blood reached boiling point, he stripped and went to the bathroom, to find Jacqueline showering the vanilla foam away. Again he took her, standing in the jets of water, more slowly this time, water blinding them, the shower taps digging into the soft flesh of her side, water flattening them, filling their eyes and mouths. Billy-Ray shuddered and Jacqueline said, 'Next time it's the goddam bed.' Still she was unfinished.

They dried themselves, lit cigarettes and climbed into the bed, taking a bottle of Krug with them. Neither spoke. Then Jacqueline took Billy-Ray's hand, slid it beneath the sheets and raised an eyebrow. Billy-Ray smiled, threw back the sheet and knelt at the end of the bed, pulled her towards him, opening her legs.

'Doesn't he care, your husband? Doesn't he care about how you spend his money?' Billy-Ray asked one night, as Jacqueline lay with her head on his chest.

'Old Daddy Cooper doesn't know *how* I spend it, only that I do. He gives me an allowance, and a good one. It was something I insisted on before we married, as well as having my own checking account. His first wife didn't, apparently. All I ask is that he puts money into the account, which he does. He's not a bad guy, he's just old. And English.'

Billy-Ray frowned. 'Have you done this before?'

'Done what?'

'Cheated on him?'

Jacqueline slipped from the bed and fetched the bottle. 'That's not a very nice question, Mr Rickman.'

Billy-Ray shrugged. 'It's a logical one.'

'You haven't been to England before, have you?'

'No. Never been out of the States before.'

'The English are different. In high society, as they call it, everyone relies on manners to get them through, to get them through anything. Death, birth, divorce, adultery. There are codes that you learn and you follow them. The English always look so proper, so goddam buttoned up. But don't make the mistake of thinking it's all Queen and country, Empire and honour. They can be as down-dirty as the rest of us.'

'That so?'

'Yeah – especially the aristocracy, the moneyed class. They got the strictest rules of all, but as long as you follow them no one seems to care what else you do. Wear the right clothes, use the right knife and fork, speak with the right accent, well, shit, you can do anything. Get away with most everything, except perhaps murder. Unless you're killing foxes and pheasants.'

Billy-Ray laughed. 'What?'

'And even then, you got to dress in the right clothes. You can't just go out in a pair of jeans, or bibs or something. God, no. You have to wear pinks.'

'Pinks?'

'Yeah – only, of course, they mean red. Red jackets, and you have to wear the jacket with a pair of tight white trousers. And long leather boots. And a black suede hat with this crazy peak. Then you can kill foxes.'

Billy-Ray was laughing, wine spilling from the glass he rested on his stomach. For half an hour he listened as Jacqueline Cooper, who had a fine ear for imitation and a keen eye for hypocrisy (both of which attributes had been extremely useful in her time as an adopted member of Society), instructed him in the finer points of etiquette.

'But the fact is, Billy-Ray,' she concluded, 'if I could give you only one piece of advice, it's this: marry money. Even better, marry old money. Best of all, marry old English money. It's all invested in dull, risk-free land and property, some gold, maybe a little steel and construction. Things people always need. That money isn't going anywhere.' She watched as Billy-Ray finished his wine. 'Except down your throat.'

Karbo Inc., the second-largest oil company in North America, sent Billy-Ray Rickman to London in November 1957 because the company knew the global oil business was about to explode. Across Europe and the Middle East, through Russia and the Caucasus, the black gold was flowing and the world could not drink it quickly enough. The executives in Anchorage, Alaska, held many meetings to discuss what they should do, and reached the same conclusion as every other oil company: dig deeper, explore farther and expand. Expand and merge or die on your knees.

Billy-Ray Rickman was considered to have many qualities: as well as having degrees in geophysics and petrochemical engineering he also had a gift for languages, speaking seven in total. To the executives in Anchorage, this seemed miraculous, for they were men with business degrees from Harvard, whose grasp of foreign tongues extended as far as kissing European prostitutes. But more than all these things, during the eight years he had been with Karbo, Billy-Ray had worked like a dog, like a maniac. He was a man driven by ambition, or so it seemed. Out on the rigs, in the offices, in the labs – no matter where he worked, Billy-Ray worked like a man possessed – by what, no one could say. So when the company was looking to appoint a negotiator, Billy-Ray was invited to Anchorage and asked whether he would take up a three-year contract, based in London, England, where his office would be in Waterloo and where he would, of course, have a luxury house rented for him in South Kensington. There, he would work with a team of experts identifying and buying up the burgeoning, ever-fracturing European petroleum and gas concerns. He was to be involved in the birth of a conglomerate. Billy-Ray Rickman, who had never been out of the States, who had no wife, no children, who had been running from the Wave all his life, agreed to the proposal then and there.

'D'you ever look in the mirror sometimes and get surprised?' Billy-Ray asked Jacqueline on their last night together, as the liner nudged its way towards the battered chalk cliffs of England. 'You know? The face looking back at you isn't quite how you think of yourself. Not quite how you thought you remembered.'

Jacqueline considered this. 'Yeah – I know what you mean. Not a stranger, more like almost you, but not quite. Not what you expected.'

'And that thing – you know? When you're in the bathroom or whatever, and you're standing behind someone you know who's looking in a mirror, and you see what they think of as their face. You see the reflection they see and it's all a bit out of whack? The wrong way round. The same face but the wrong way round. But that's what they think they look like. They think – all their life – they think that's what they look like and they don't.'

Jacqueline frowned. 'Is mine different?'

'Yah – of course it is. That's what made me think of it. Just then, I could see your face in the mirror and it was like I was with someone else. Someone who was you but not you. A sister or a twin maybe.'

Jacqueline lit a cigarette, pondered the notion of being herself-but-not. Asked, 'Do you have any brothers or sisters?'

Billy-Ray rattled ice, drank vodka, stared at the ceiling and drank more vodka. Touched his thigh. 'No.' He left the bed, went to the bathroom.

Jacqueline heard the lock being turned and lay still, wondering about Billy-Ray Rickman. He had told her about the farm in Blue Earth County, Minnesota, where his German father had raised hogs, while his mother, a Polish-Russian woman, ran the home. The farm where Billy-Ray had worked the summers of his childhood, lifting bales, cleaning out pens, sorting feed, hosing yards. Winching swine carcasses. The farm where his childhood bedroom, cluttered with the boyhood paraphernalia of football pennants, hockey sticks, school books, postcards, rocks and fossils, had eventually become his refuge. The farmhouse where a crucifix hung in every room, where, as he ate or slept or read, he tried to avoid looking at the gaunt man whose head hung loosely as blood flowed down his face. The farm he and his mother left every Sunday morning to attend mass, as his father ranted in the yard about Papists and blood, miracles and superstitions. Ranted because of his own loss of faith. The farm Wilhelm-Rajmund had left eleven years before when he was eighteen and to which he had never returned.

What else did Jacqueline know about Billy-Ray? That he had never been abroad before. That he was intelligent, ambitious. That he spoke seven languages – she could now say 'Make love to me' in Polish, German, Russian, Czech, Swedish and Latin. That he was an accomplished lover. That he changed when he drank vodka, that he became someone else: the man in the mirror who was Billy-Ray-but-not.

The lock of the bathroom door turned again and Billy-Ray walked out, climbed back into bed and lay staring at the ceiling once more. Jacqueline Cooper, who used time well, who understood how to use it, let it pass. Waited for Billy-Ray Rickman to make the next move. But Billy-Ray said nothing. He just rubbed at the deep, old scar on his thigh and stared at the ceiling.

Bitte, Gott, lass es Dieter sein.

Jacqueline's journey into London from the Southampton docks was hellish: the traffic was heavier even than the rain; roads in Hampshire were flooded and the chauffeur was forced into detours that took them through small, congested villages of half-timbered houses, thatched roofs and flinted walls. Jacqueline, sitting bolt upright in the rear seat, smoked and tried not to chew her nails. It took the driver five and a half hours to reach Jarman House, the Coopers' London home. Jacqueline ran up the steps to the open door and tossed her coat to Miss O'Toole, the housekeeper, before trotting up one side of the sweeping double stairs leading to her suite. She undressed and headed for the bathroom. The taps wheezed and spat brown water, seized, rumbled and finally dribbled boiling water – both of them – and Jacqueline cursed as she recalled her airy, efficient duplex on East 73rd. Where the shower pelted, where the bath filled quickly, where the garbage disappeared down the building's throat, where the refrigerator was the size of her closets, where the heating worked. As she slipped out of her robe there was a knock on her door. Cursing again, she threw the robe back on, called, 'Come.'

Miss O'Toole sidled in, sly, unattractive and efficient as ever. 'Good afternoon, Lady Cooper. I trust you enjoyed your trip?'

'Yes, thank you.' Jacqueline opened a mahogany cigarette case, selected a cigarette, smelled it, rolled it between her fingers. 'These are stale.'

'Ah, well, yes.' Miss O'Toole shifted her shoulders in a way that infuriated Jacqueline. 'I'm sorry to be bursting in on you like this, and of course, in the normal run of things, I wouldn't. But I have a few matters I need to discuss.'

Jacqueline was fighting many desires: to yell, to drink, to smoke, to get in the goddam tub. To call Billy-Ray Rickman. 'Go ahead.'

Miss O'Toole closed her eyes momentarily. Americans really did not know how to treat the help. 'You're expected at the French embassy at seven for seven thirty tonight. Sir Sidney will meet you there.'

Jacqueline sighed as the evening loomed – too close. 'And? What else?'

'Siobhan left ten days ago. Upped sticks and left without a word. That's why the cigarettes are stale. We are understaffed.'

'Well, just do whatever it is you do. Contact your sister and get someone as soon as possible.' Jacqueline sighed, lit the stale cigarette.

Miss O'Toole permitted herself a smile, augmented by a roll of her crossed, lunatic eyes. 'I took the liberty, ma'am, of doing just that whilst you were gone.'

Jacqueline blew smoke ceilingward, touched her lips. 'And how much this time?' she asked, moving to a stout oak bureau in the corner. 'How much this time?'

Miss O'Toole crossed her hands at her waist. 'Sixty pounds,' she said.

'Sixty?' Jacqueline tried to catch one of Miss O'Toole's eyes. 'Sixty? Wasn't it forty-eight last time? For Siobhan?'

Jacqueline, who knew not only the value of time and how to spend it but also the value of money and how to keep it, took out a cheque book and filled a slip. She held the cheque as it dried, flapping it in the cold air. 'Miss O'Toole, wouldn't it be better, you know, just easier, to ask an employment agency for help? I see signs all over town advertising agencies, most of my friends use the service. Do we have to go through all this hassle and expense?'

'The first Lady Cooper wouldn't have had it otherwise.' Mrs O'Toole readjusted the ring of keys at her belt. 'It's what we do.'

Jacqueline Cooper, who was twenty-six, who was, originally, from Albany, NY, who was not academically inclined but 'had smarts,' as they said in her home town, took stock of the situation and then gave Miss O'Toole the cheque. She shrugged. When all was said and done, it wasn't her money she was giving away. 'Just get a girl who knows what she's doing, OK?'

Mrs O'Toole looked at the cheque, scanned it for errors, put it in a pocket. 'That will be helping towards the new roof. God bless you.'

'So what do I get out of it?'

Miss O'Toole straightened, shook herself a little, the keys at her waist clinking. 'The new girl should be here tomorrow. I took the liberty of . . .'

'Miss O'Toole, instead of taking liberties, why don't you just fetch me some fresh cigarettes?' Jacqueline was slipping the robe from her shoulders as she turned and headed for her bathroom. 'And lay out the blue Givenchy.'

1957

Most childhoods meander to an end and segue uneventfully into adulthood, but the end of Maggie Regan's childhood was stark, sudden and undeniable. She stood outside the hand-worn door of her family home, cardboard suitcase at her feet, and kissed her mother and her childhood goodbye. Annie, Maggie's mother, thrust an envelope into one of her hands and a paper bag containing two bacon soda-bread sandwiches, a homemade potato pie and a curranty cake in the other. Maggie Regan was fifteen and confused – why was she going? *Where* was she going?

'Now, Maggie,' said her mother, 'you'd better behave now. No more moping and dreaming. You'd better be behaving yourself and not having such a bad influence. I'd come with you but with the babby . . .' Annie glanced over her shoulder as Noël began to whinge. 'Now, too, we'll be expecting you to forward a little money when you can. Only when you can, mind.'

Maggie looked at her mother's plump, uncaring face. Watched the face as it emptied of ideas, emptied like a tidal basin, leaving endless flat sands. Annie Regan could think of nothing more to say to her daughter. Maggie put the paper bag in the case, slipped the envelope in the pocket of her coat as a car horn sounded and her father's jalopy of a van came to a stop.

'Off you go now. Make sure you write.' Maggie scanned her mother's face for the last time but Annie was looking over her daughter's shoulder, watching the pavement to see who was passing by, who was going where. 'And be good,' Annie shouted, as Maggie clambered into the cab of the van.

Sean Regan forced the protesting gear stick into first and the old Bedford groaned as it moved away from the house. Father and daughter said nothing as they made their way out of Ballysod, south along the coast road, Maggie looking out at the foaming waters of Blacksod Bay, the sheer cliffs of granite on Achill Island, littered with the flashing white breasts of guillemots and razor-bills. Maggie looked, trying to commit the panorama to memory, but her mind was too busy worrying for her to see clearly. London – a place she had heard of, a place she had learned about in school. But she had never thought to see it. Maggie felt sick. She drew the envelope out of her pocket and ripped it open, stared at the contents: one English ten-shilling note, a map, a card and a letter from her mother.

Dear Maggie,
    I am sure you will be all right. I now your upset now but in time you will see this is For the Best. Danny Maconnell is not a Nice Boy. He would of been Bad News. This way you can't see him and you will learn a good trade. Behave yourself and be good my lovely girl. Come back and see us.
    You're Loving Mother

Maggie reread the note. Loving mother? If so, why was she sending Maggie away?
    'Are you all right?' Sean asked.
    Maggie nodded, stuffed the envelope back in her pocket. She'd read the card so often since it had arrived at the house in Ballysod a week before that she knew it off by heart. Instructions, written on thick, textured card, headed with a dark blue address, printed in cursive script:

Jarman House
54 Thurloe Square
Kensington
London

Maggie Regan –
    When you get to Liverpool, take a taxi to Lime Street station. Go to the ticket man in the reservations booth and he has a ticket

reserved in your name to Euston station in London. You do not
have to change trains. When you get to Euston, ask a porter
where the Underground is and take the Victoria line to South
Kensington – ask for help if you get lost. The map shows you
where to go from there. It is about a ten-minute walk. The
money is for you to buy some food and for the taxi and
Underground fares. I shall expect you here at about six o'clock
on Wednesday, if everything is on time.

Miss O'Toole,
Housekeeper

Maggie didn't understand why she had to go under the ground –
what would she find there? Still she felt sick. The familiar smell of
the van didn't help, what with the faint stink of fish guts and the
strangely metallic tang of Ballysod earth.

The journey to Castlebar took an hour, the van grinding over
steep hills and then dropping down, past the loughs and peat bogs,
November rain obscuring the distant mountains, washing green to
grey. Sean parked the van as close to the train station as possible, and
he and Maggie walked, still not speaking, to the ticket booth. Sean
bought a single ticket to Dublin, took his change and turned to see
Maggie standing by her case, head down. She looked lonely, very
lonely, and already a long, long way from home. On impulse Sean
turned back to the ticket booth and bought a return ticket for himself. It cost a startling amount of money and for a moment Sean
wavered – perhaps he should not do this? But he paid and he went
to his daughter, showed her the tickets.

'Come on, the train leaves in five minutes.'

Maggie smiled, slipped her hand through his arm.

They found two window seats in the third-class carriage, facing
each other, Sean's bony knees brushing occasionally against
Maggie's. The motion of the wheels on the track rocked Sean – who
had been up since five that morning, tending the smoking hut – into
an early sleep, so he didn't see Maggie rereading her mother's letter,
didn't see her tearing it to pieces and dropping the fragments on the
dirty floor, was unaware of Maggie leaving her seat to be sick. When
she returned, she stared at her father as he slept, his mouth slightly

open, his poor, weathered hands resting on his thighs. She looked at his extraordinary face and knew that he didn't believe in God.

'What's that?' Sean jerked awake, wiped his mouth with the back of his hand, wondered where he was.

'I was just thinking, Da, about the Fish God. Remember? When I was a little girl and you told me there was a Fish God?'

Sean smiled. 'That's right. Something about putting them to sleep before I caught them.'

'You said you prayed to the Fish God whenever you took out your line, and then he'd make sure that you only caught fish that were asleep. Remember? I didn't want them to hurt.'

'Did I ever tell you where I got the idea of the Fish God from?'

Maggie shook her head.

'A farmer, Donnie Loaghton, you don't know him but it doesn't matter. I was talking to him one day and he told me a story about Red Indians, you know, out in America. He told me that when they want to fell a tree, want to cut it down, they choose the one they want and then they all dance around another one, singing about killing it.'

Maggie frowned. 'That's an eejit thing to do.'

'Well, no, not really. The Red Indians believe that the trees faint away when they hear one of them is dying. And then, once they've fainted, the Indians cut into the one they want. D'you see? The one that thought it was going to die, lives. The one that dies doesn't know anything about it.'

'I thought,' and Maggie looked out at the still waters of Lough Ree, 'I thought the Fish God must live in the bay. But he doesn't, does he?'

'No, Maggie, he doesn't. Let's have a look at those sandwiches, why don't we?'

After they had eaten, Maggie dozed and it was Sean's turn to watch over her, to watch over his favoured daughter, his butterfly. *Pàilliun*. He watched her and he tried to imagine life in Ballysod without her, imagined working up at the big house without Maggie by his side, and it hurt him, caused Sean physical pain. He knew she was scared, that she didn't want to leave. He didn't want to let Maggie go but he had to – Ballysod was no place for her, with its privations and foul secrets, barren cliffs and sodden landscape. Maggie had to get away – and maybe this wasn't how he'd imagined her escape but it was an escape. Sean loved her and he didn't want her ever to come back. He woke her, shaking her shoulder gently, as the train pulled into Heuston station, Dublin.

The ferry was loading as they arrived at North Wall dockside, crowds milling, freight rumbling into the bowels of the boat.

'Da – why can't I stay here? Why can't I stay and keep working up at the house and stay with you?' The question was nearly drowned out by a blast from the ferry

Sean shook his head slightly. 'On you go now.' He hugged her tightly, as if he'd never let her go, then he let her go. 'On you go now,' said Sean Regan quietly, discomfited by the excesses of emotion around him: soldiers and sailors, navvies and husbands bidding wives, girlfriends and harlots goodbye. 'On you go,' he repeated gently, nearly overwhelmed by emotion himself.

Maggie picked up her suitcase and walked away, up the passenger ramp, disappeared into the crowds. Sean stayed until the ferry blasted three sonorous notes and slipped its moorings, scanning the decks, waving, trying to catch a glimpse of his child. His *child* – Maggie was too young to be doing this. 'Maggie!' her father shouted, forcing his way through the crowds, shoving at whores' plump bodies, trying to catch sight of her. 'Maggie! Maggie!' He waved and shouted as scummy water churned. Shouted until the ferry had left harbour.

Maggie sat in a window seat in the second-class lounge, watching the docks slip away, to be replaced by choppy water, gunmetal grey in twilight. In the glass she caught occasional glimpses of her own pale face and noticed the frown line between her eyes. She also noticed a man in a fawn gabardine overcoat staring at her, beginning to move towards her in a way she recognized, and she picked up the small suitcase, put it on her lap and feigned sleep.

Maggie's journey to Jarman House was a nightmare. Having managed finally to fall asleep, she was woken by the sound of vomiting. The ferry, she realized, was listing violently, and the sounds of retching echoed in the small lounge.

'Don't worry yourself,' said the man in the gabardine, who had sat next to her as she slept. 'It's often this rough, especially this time of year.' He put a hand on her stockinged knee and patted it. Left it there.

Maggie swept his hand away. 'I'm not worried,' she said, standing and walking away, steadying herself, hand on the wall.

Eleven hours the crossing took, and she didn't reach Liverpool until six o'clock the following morning. The port was packed, hands waving, shouts flying, people running into open arms. Maggie stood uncertainly in the arrivals area, measuring her choices. She had ten shillings – what could it buy her? An escape?

'You all right there?' asked a thin, high-pitched voice. Maggie looked round to see a gaunt, filthy man, breathing heavily behind her. 'I may be able to help you, my darling, in exchange fer a cup. Pretty girl like you, um, pretty girl.' Maggie recognized the stale whisky wreathing the man's heavy breath just as she recognized the fawn coat heading straight for her.

The taxi ride cost four shillings and threepence, a ride through a city so big, so noisy even at that time, that Maggie's head hurt. The ticket man at Lime Street was surly and unhelpful, but did eventually give her the ticket Miss O'Toole had reserved for her.

'Platform nine. Nine seventeen.'

'Platform nine seventeen?'

The man ignored her.

'Platform nine seventeen?' Maggie asked again. 'I don't understand.'

The man sighed. 'Where are you from?'

'Ballysod in County Mayo.'

'Don't they have clocks there?'

Maggie stared at him. Collected her ticket from the counter and walked away.

'Hey, hey, miss!' he called after her. 'An hour's time – platform nine. The train leaves at seventeen minutes past nine!' Maggie kept walking and the man shrugged, returned to his paper. Bloody Irish girls, they were all the same – pig-shit ignorant. Came over here causing trouble. Especially when they looked like that. He looked up again and watched Maggie. *Particularly* when they looked like that.

There was nowhere open to buy food in the station and by the time she finally sat on the London train, Maggie was ravenous. Yet still she refused the offer of food from fellow passengers – all of them bleary-eyed men. Even when a brown-eyed, lanky young man, who reminded her of Danny Maconnell, asked whether she'd share a bap with him, she refused bluntly. It was sleep which finally saved her from hunger pangs.

If Maggie had found the dim, cavernous dimensions of Lime Street station overwhelming, she was completely unprepared for the filthy place, throbbing with sound, grit, smoke and people, that was Euston station. Maggie looked for an Underground – but what would it look like? She stood by her case, the map in her hand, and stared about herself. Ask someone. Three women ignored her, but eventually a man stopped.

'I'm looking for the Underground.'

'It's over there. Where you going, miss?'

Maggie handed the man the map and he explained where to catch her train.

'Will it be blue? Will the train be blue?'

The man laughed and walked away, leaving Maggie to find her own way to Thurloe Square. Of course, the train wasn't blue, it was red and grey, the wooden seats scuffed and grimed with human grease. The carriage smelled and no one spoke; instead they read newspapers or stared at the blank darkness beyond the windows. The sound and motion sickened Maggie and she swallowed repeatedly as the train wormed its way beneath London streets. She could have left the train at any of the stations – could have disembarked at Victoria, and disappeared into the throngs she had seen up there. Perhaps had a bite to eat before finding a boarding house and beginning a new life which would take her full circle back to Danny Maconnell. But Miss O'Toole had calculated carefully: Maggie had been travelling now for more than thirty hours since she left her parents' cottage in Ballysod, County Mayo; she was dirty and tired, thirsty and faint with hunger. In her purse she had only three shillings and eightpence. So she stayed underground, counting the stops, willing the journey to end.

Thurloe Square, when Maggie turned into it, her suitcase now lead heavy in her hand, her thin coat soaked through by cold, light rain, undid her finally. The confection of virgin white stucco and balconies, shutters, balustrades, palm trees and stone lions which was Jarman House nearly blinded her – she thought she had been sent to a *castle*. Maggie Regan had often dreamed of castles, had drawn them on rough sugar paper at school, had even imagined living in a castle in Czechoslovakia. But she had never dreamed of a castle like this – built in the middle of an infinite city, amongst other castles. Maggie Regan stood motionless in the evening rain, dumbstruck, as a chauffered car whispered past, bearing Billy-Ray Rickman to his luxurious London home, in Pelham Crescent.

THE REICHMANNS

Minnesota: land of sky-blue waters. A harsh land, an old land. Land that clung on to the edge of the oldest rocks in the world, the Laurentian Shield. Minnesota: a state that had been eroded and then sunk and finally drowned.

Blue Earth County, Minnesota, was still essentially frontier land when Wilhelm-Rajmund's parents moved in, bought a six-hundred-acre parcel and established their hog farm in 1921. Oliver Reichmann, Wilhelm-Rajmund's father, stood at the boundary of his new farm, which ran inevitably along a lake-side, and felt the danger of the future: both of the young men yet to come and the men who had been. He felt this danger as a clean white hand pushing against his chest. When he cleared the land, as he ploughed the soil and buried stakes for the fencing, marking out the sties, digging the foundations of the farmhouse, he found skulls and snapped femurs, large scraps of tanned hide and arrowheads. Often he thought he caught the scent of blood on the air. It was a scent he recognized: Oliver Reichmann was, after all, a German immigrant from Görlitz, a town in the foothills of the Sudety Ranges, who had landed at Ellis Island in 1919. He knew the scent of blood only too well, and each time he unearthed it he crossed himself. Oliver was Catholic so he crossed himself, but it was meant neither as apology nor benediction. He felt nothing for the men he ploughed under. Why, in Europe you couldn't move without stepping on someone's dreams, on someone's deathbed, on someone's grave. But he didn't tell his wife, Irochka, about what he sensed out in the fields for many years; didn't tell her what he unearthed on their land until the stench was all around them.

Oliver Reichmann and Irochka Frankiowiec first met in the

milling, rootless crowds of dispossessed on Ellis Island. Oliver, a tall, strong, proud man, saw Irochka over the heads of those around him; saw she was as tall as he, wide hipped and high cheeked, a Slav beauty from Boleslawiec, a mere twenty miles from his home town, almost facing him across the border in Poland. Oliver gravitated towards Irochka and was soon close enough to glance at her papers.

'It is very confusing here,' Oliver said to Irochka in Polish, gesturing at the queues. 'I keep joining the wrong one.' Her smile, prompted by the familiarity of the language, caused Oliver to smile in return. He noted the clarity of her sea-green eyes, which made him think of moss and aspen leaves. 'Oliver Reichmann,' he said, and held out his hand. Only much later, as they stood talking, waiting, waiting, waiting for their papers to be stamped, did he realize that the rivers on which they had lived, the Bobr and the Nysa (which seemed a world away – which *were* a world away), both emptied into the Oder, and he chose to take this as a sign.

They married within months, driven into each other's arms by language, by longing, by the absence of so much that was familiar. When they talked, when they lay together, the world they had left behind seemed closer. They spoke in German and Polish, combining the two to create their own language, Irochka embellishing this new tongue with the Russian of her childhood. They left New York and travelled north and west, stopping in towns for weeks or months, staying in segregated bunk houses on farms, working in orchards picking fruit and packing boxes. In winter they lived in tenement rooms in filthy cities and found their place on production lines in roaring factories. And all the time they were hoarding their money. Each night they sat out under the stars, Oliver chewing a wad of Sköl tobacco, Irochka smoking a corn pipe, and they talked, planned their lives. Oliver had been a timber man in Germany, had spent his days felling trees and sawing trunks; Irochka had been a pig farmer's daughter. Between them, they reckoned, they had the knowledge, the determination, to make something of themselves, to make something from the twisted wreckage that was all that was left of their pasts.

When they reached Minnesota they stopped moving, stopped moving west, and stayed with Oliver's Uncle Siegfried and his family on their farm outside Mankato. For more than a year they stayed there, as Oliver learned the pig farming business from Siegfried and Irochka helped out where she could in the fields and in the farmhouse. The two of them had a small room in the eaves, furnished only with two ladderback chairs, a wooden rail on which to hang their clothes and a small, lumpy bed, but they felt they had found heaven of a kind. There were dormer windows at either end of the room, looking north and south over a vista of gentle rolling hills and crystal lakes. Irochka woke each morning to the sharp, ammoniac stink of pigs and she smiled – it was the smell of home.

Each evening nine of them sat at the kitchen table, Oliver and Irochka, Siegfried and his wife, Eva, and the five children, and ate together. Homemade, home-slaughtered food, thick and sanguine: *kiełbasa z krwi*, with *kluski*, or *barszcz* followed by *cielęcina*. Eva, who was also Polish, taught Irochka how to cook *czarina*, duck's blood soup, and *kołety z móżdżku cielęta*, calf's brain cutlets, rounded off with *chustciki*, which was Oliver's favourite meal. When the dishes were done and the children in bed, Oliver and Irochka took an evening stroll, or sat on the porch and watched the moon rise – planning. Always planning.

The Reichmann farm, south of Mankato, near the small town of Bow Regard by the border with Faribault County, prospered over the years. It was a fine plot of land, fertile and well drained, fed by numerous streams. Stands of elm and basswood created islands of shade. Oliver built the farmhouse behind a copse of ash and poplar, where the wind was broken but sunlight still filtered through. He chose the wood with his expert timber man's eye, and men from neighbouring farms helped him build the frame. Irochka and he designed the layout together, their blond heads nearly touching as they drew pencil lines on paper by the buttery light of the oil lamps in the small shack where they lived as the house took shape. Oliver staked out the pens and sties, built a paddock, three stables and a barn (ignoring the scent of blood meanwhile).

When the building was done, when the last detail had been attended to, Oliver sent a letter to his Uncle Siegfried and invited him to stay with them for a week. Uncle Siegfried spent the first of those seven days admiring the beauty of the land and the finish of the farmhouse, taking note of the fertility of the till-soil (rubbing handfuls between his palms, watching it fall) and its efficient drainage. He commented on the ways in which Oliver had improved on his own farm set-up; remarked on the layout of the pens and their sturdiness. Siegfried examined the barns and the gleaming machinery housed in them and wished they were his own.

That evening, once Irochka had cleaned the dishes, made coffee and set a bottle of vodka and two glasses before them, she bid them goodnight and left the men to talk pigs. Oliver's five-star hog hotel was ready for occupants – but which? That night and subsequent nights, the men talked for hours, downing shots of vodka and drinking thick, tepid coffee. Siegfried lamented the fact that he had invested in too many Tamworth – thin-rind, muscular-top swine with dished faces. He'd calculated that the world would want muscle – meat, bacon, pork – when in fact it had wanted lard.

'But the world *will* want meat,' Oliver argued. 'Lard is just fat, oil. There are other sources of oil – maybe from vegetables. *Then* the world will want bacon – and pork, livers, bratwurst, schnitzel too. The world cannot eat oil.'

'Lard is selling for the same as muscle,' Siegfried replied, lighting a small, bitter cigar.

'Have you seen the pamphlets from Hormel's? The packing company out Austin way?'

'Nah.'

'The head hog buyer, Lew Reeves – you know him?'

Siegfried shrugged.

'He says to buy Yorkshire – Large White—'

'Nah,' said Siegfried again. 'You need to have lard. And the Yorkshire – too much Middle and Small White. And slow growing.'

'But Siegfried! So much length, so much frame and scale. You know how big the litters are? Once they are multiparous—'

Siegfried blew out a cloud of evil-smelling smoke. 'What about Hampshires? Good hogs – trim jowl, depth of side – and look at the lean meat in the carcass if that's the way you want to go, although I still think lard . . .'

And so it went on, night after night. Foraging ability, vigour,

carcass quality, rate of gain and feed conversion. The essential senti-
mentality of choosing *České bílé uslechtilé prase* – the Czech Improved
White – which both their families had reared in the old country. The
suitability of the Landrace, the Hampshire. Every morning Irochka
would come down to the kitchen and find it foul with stale smoke,
the two men asleep in their chairs. The decision was made on the last
morning, when both Siegfried and Oliver were too hung over to
argue: Yorkshire, Large White – and maybe some Hampshire in a
few years.

Once Uncle Siegfried had left to return to his family and the
Yorkshires were snuffling and foraging in the fields and pens, Oliver
and Irochka spent their first weeks alone together in the pine-scented
farmhouse smiling, talking, making love. Nine months later
Siegfried (named for Oliver's uncle) was born. A year later Dieter
arrived. They grew into tall, handsome boys, Aryan delights, with
blond hair, blue eyes and strong, unwavering jaw lines. Trim jowls
indeed.

The plot next to the farm was put up for sale – seven hundred and
fifty acres of heavily wooded but potentially productive land, in the
middle of which was a lake full of walleye and trout. Oliver rode
through it and around it many times before deciding to buy –
imagine it, owning your own lake! Possessing water. He pictured the
land cleared, other houses and barns being built by his sons and
filled with their families. He imagined the birth of the Reichmann
dynasty – a vision he shared with Irochka. Once they had paid the
deposit for the land and secured it, arranged a mortgage for the out-
standing amount from the farmers' cooperative, they allowed
themselves to dream as well as plan as they worked to pay off the
debt. They played a game each night, as they lay in bed, creating
families for their young sons and naming their as yet unborn grandchildren, conferring on them professions.

'Jerzy will be a teacher of art,' Oliver might say.

Irochka would consider this. 'No – he will be a scientist. He will
discover things.'

'Salsia—'

'Which one is she?'

'She is Siegfried's fifth daughter.'

Irochka might laugh. 'Fifth? His *fifth*? Does he have sons as well?'

'Yes – five of those too,' Oliver would say firmly. 'And Salsia will be a dancer. She will be famous – she will dance in Paris and London.'

And both of them, although they never said it, would fall asleep marvelling at the future fertility of their sons, at the extent of their legacy, their dynasty.

Because of the mortgage on the new land, they waited four years before they birthed Wilhelm-Rajmund. Planning, always planning.

The Reichmann family was the envy of Blue Earth County. Women whose husbands drank every night, whose husbands stumbled up the stairs and beat them before raping them, would covertly watch Irochka in church, as they fingered their rosary beads, and ask forgiveness for the envy they felt. They looked at her – tall, blonde, always smiling – sitting next to Oliver, who was ever attentive to his family. These women who were raped (who did not think of it as rape but, rather, as an approximation of love) inevitably gave birth to yet another child, which meant more work, another gaping mouth, driving the men to drink all the more. But not Oliver Reichmann, who loved his wife and children. As for the men, they, too, watched Irochka and imagined taking her up against a wall, in the barley fields, in a bed (they, too, did not think of it as rape but, rather, an approximation of love).

It was the Reichmanns who organized the fund-raising for the new Church of St Teresa, the Reichmanns who arranged the barn dances and bake-outs, ice-boat races and pig derbies which paid for the materials to build the church. Oliver Reichmann turned the first sod for the foundations and Irochka designed the stained glass and arranged for it to be made in Warsaw, then shipped to Bow Regard. When the church was finished, during the first mass held to consecrate the building and the surrounding fenced land, the Reichmanns sat in the front pew, smiling proudly, and this pew became known as theirs. Rightly so, rightly so – for the Reichmanns were the heart beating at the centre of this small Polish-German Catholic community. They were the evidence, the proof that if one worked hard, if one loved one's family, if one practised restraint and abstinence, if one loved God, loved America and its bounties, its *possibilities*, then one would be blessed. And blessed the Reichmanns duly felt.

The Reichmann boys, Siegfried, Dieter and Wilhelm-Rajmund, were strong, handsome boys, living, as has been said, a blessed childhood. They swam in the lake, they rode the farm's horses (all named after American presidents), they fished, they hiked in the hills, camped in the woods on the farmland. Siegfried and Dieter, born only a year apart, spent their lives together. They learned to cycle, to swim, to play football together; they caught the school bus together, waiting at the end of the farm track every morning, talking and arguing. When Wilhelm-Rajmund joined them he always felt apart, slightly distanced, but still he loved his brothers. He admired Siegfried the more because he was older, seemed somehow braver. The three of them walked the track and they talked about teachers, other children, about what they wanted to do when they grew up. (The Reichmanns – planning; always planning.) They tussled each other to the ground, exchanged friendly punches, threw stones into the lake to see who could throw the farthest. Eventually, they began to talk about girls.

'I kissed her. I kissed Magde,' said Siegfried into the darkness of the bedroom he shared with Dieter, late one night after a barn dance.

'Nah – you didn't.'

'I damn well did.'

Dieter lit the candle on the chair between their beds, sat up and looked at his sixteen-year-old brother. 'You did? You really did?'

'Yah.'

'How?'

'What d'you mean – how?'

'How d'you even get a chance?'

'Saw her going outside for some air and told Ma I was going to get a root beer from the ice box.' Siegfried smiled. 'It was great.'

Dieter was raging with jealousy – Magde was the prettiest girl in the school. 'And she let you?'

'She didn't let me, she practically asked me. Boy, it was great.'

'So what's it like?'

'I can't tell you, you gotta do it. She put her tongue in my mouth.'

'She *what*?' Dieter was stunned by this.

'I know it sounds yucky but it ain't. Honest to God, it feels good.' Siegfried smiled at the memory. 'And she let me feel under her blouse.'

'You touched her there?'

'Yah. Felt her breasts.'

A silence fell between the brothers as Dieter tried to imagine feeling Magde's breasts. 'What did it feel like?'

'Like . . . like . . . I dunno. Like the softest thing you can think of.'

'Horse's underlip.'

Siegfried yelped. *'Horse's lip*? Maybe – but it weren't as hairy!'

The two of them wheezed with laughter, stuffed pillows into their mouths so as not to wake their parents. Dieter blew out the candle and the two of them lay saying nothing, both made erect by the thought of Magde's breasts.

'Deet?' Siegfried whispered some time later. 'Do you know what men and women do? Y'know, sex?'

Dieter wrestled with the fact of his ignorance, wondered whether to lie. Instead admitted he didn't. Siegfried told him as he gently rubbed himself. And of course the next day Dieter told Wilhelm-Rajmund the details as the two of them walked to school (Siegfried had graduated high school by then and was working on the farm). Wilhelm-Rajmund was appalled.

Dieter Reichmann, who was a jock, a bit of a lunk, a boy who thought with his body and let his brain relax, signed up to join the army in 1940, when he was eighteen. Oliver was proud of his son. Irochka, whose memory was perhaps clearer than her husband's, who recalled the ravaged wastelands of Silesia and Sudetenland, the mud fields of Ypres and the Somme, was proud but fearful too. The Reichmanns, indeed everyone in their community, listened to the radio and scanned the *Courier* for news of their homelands as Austria, Yugoslavia, Poland and Czechoslovakia smouldered, ignited and began to burn. Farmers met at the cattle markets or in bars and talked quietly, scratching beards, fiddling with keys and penknives, kicking the tyres of their trucks, turning bottles, talked about what was happening in Europe. They had difficulty with this, with this talking: many were German, many Austrian – what to say?

What were they? Americans? German Americans? Germans? Austrians? What, exactly, *were* they? And when their fellow Polish farmers joined them to talk, what should they say? Should they apologize? Should they sympathize? It was difficult. And more than that: should they be there? Should they be back home, in Europe, and if so, on which side should they fight? These things were never said but each man saw something in the other men's eyes and recognized it: guilt. But it was, when all was said and done, Europe's war, Europe's problem – and wasn't that why they'd left? Another beer would be bought, another toast drunk to the American flag. And always Oliver would mention Dieter and his accomplishments, proud as ever, knowing his son was safe.

But then, in December 1941, Japanese pilots flew to the Hawaiian islands and everything changed again. As the months passed and news trickled through of camps – in Germany, in California – as the American Japanese were rounded up and the German Jews filled the cattle carts, the European immigrant farmers loaded their own cattle carts and kept their heads down.

Dieter sent postcards home, from Maryland, from Tennessee, from Georgia – short, misspelled, funny messages about his life. He was no letter writer but the cards kept coming. Wilhelm-Rajmund collected all of them, stuck them up on the walls of his bedroom, and he would lie in bed at night and look at them, imagining being in Biloxi or Memphis. The excitement of the card from California, where Dieter had gone for a week's leave, unbalanced Wilhelm-Rajmund for a day. What was Dieter doing? Had he met Barbara Stanwyck? Or Vivien Leigh? What was he *doing*?

What Dieter was doing, of course, was escaping the faultless human being who was his brother Siegfried. That handsome, charming, accomplished sibling, who – what else? – got the prettiest girl in class, the highest grades, was the most valued player on the high school team, got the votes for the boy Most Likely to Succeed. Dieter knew he could never compete, so he joined the US Army and escaped.

Wilhelm-Rajmund was ten years old when his father decided to drill a new well at the north end of the farm. This was an undertaking which involved the hiring of heavy plant, the moving of pigs, the help of neighbours. Wilhelm-Rajmund was taken along on the day when the digging was done and told to watch so he might learn. The Dory Bore arrived, belching diesel fumes, and lumbered across the farmland to the point marked by Oliver with a red stake. Wilhelm-Rajmund watched, fascinated, as the giant awl was lifted, positioned and then dropped into the soft, giving topsoil. The machine's gears ground and squealed and the blade began to cut, peeling the earth away, driving into it, the drill bit spiralling, spewing up the earth's innards. Periodically the screw stopped turning to allow the debris to be cleared by the barrow-load and the men set to, shovelling and shifting soil and rock. Wilhelm-Rajmund wondered at the different colours of the earth, at the different sizes of the rocks, and he spent the day sifting through the waste land, picking out stones shot through with fool's gold, oxidized silica, ammonites, flinty blades. Later – much later – when he was in college, he looked back at that day and realized that the well-boring had triggered his fascination with rocks.

With Dieter gone, tramping dust squares, shouldering rifles in patterned sequences, Siegfried was Wilhelm-Rajmund's closest friend. Wilhelm-Rajmund now caught the school bus alone but sometimes, if Siegfried had chores to do in town, he'd drive down and take Willie into Bow Regard where he'd buy him a milkshake or soda and talk to him about the school day. One late summer's afternoon, the two of them met and went into town because Siegfried needed to buy some flour and collect eight sacks of Kentucky beans. Wilhelm-Rajmund sat in Munchssen's Milk Bar, toying with a malt float, and watched his brother on the street outside, just standing easy, smiling, slapping other men on the back. Siegfried made others smile, encouraged them to relax, he realized, and Wilhelm-Rajmund smiled too, just watching him. Once Siegfried had completed his business and loaded the beans in the truck, he waved to Wilhelm-Rajmund and the two of them set off back to the farm. As the old Dodge bounced along the back roads of Blue Earth County, Wilhelm-Rajmund sweated in the early evening sun – the temperature had nudged a hundred and three that day. Suddenly he grabbed his brother's arm, pointing.

'Hey – look – a lake!'

On the newly metalled and finished stretch of road a body of water glittered, flooding the blacktop.

Siegfried smiled. 'Ain't a lake. It's what they call a mirage – something that ain't really there. Looks like it is but it ain't.'

'I know that – I know the word. It means an optical illusion.'

'Sure it does – it's because of the heat. You can see things that ain't there. Cold does it too, so I've heard. 'Parently you can see ships and cities way out on ice fields. And you can get it out at sea sometimes. But they ain't there, these mirages, you just think they are. If you look hard you can see it ain't a lake – looks like it but not.'

Siegfried, who was, by that time, twenty, was still dating Magde and occasionally they took Wilhelm-Rajmund on Saturday afternoon picnics by the farm's lake, where Siegfried and Wilhelm-Rajmund rowed out in the tiny boat and fished for an hour or two. Then Siegfried would tell Wilhelm-Rajmund to get lost for a while. Wilhelm-Rajmund would walk off and get lost, only to creep back and watch his brother and Magde kissing and canoodling.

It was Siegfried who taught Wilhelm-Rajmund to ride a horse, to shoot and sled, to fly-fish. It was Siegfried who taught him how to drive, at the age of fourteen, Wilhelm-Rajmund sitting at the wheel, gripping it, white knuckled with concentration, veering and weaving over potholes and ruts as his brother laughed. Siegfried was the person Wilhelm-Rajmund told about his minor persecutions at school, his brilliant play during football training, his passion for a tenth-grade redhead who ignored him. It was Siegfried Wilhelm-Rajmund went to when he had his frequent, inexplicable nightmares. Wilhelm-Rajmund lived on the longitudinal line that marked the centre of North America, the Atlantic and the Pacific oceans equidistant from the solid, rooted, landlocked Reichmann farmhouse, and yet his sleep was flooded. He'd close his eyes and breathe deep and then the Wave came, hundreds of feet high, and the waters thundered over him. He'd wake and whimper, stumble to his brothers' room, and Siegfried, half asleep, would lift his sheet and hold Wilhelm-Rajmund through the night, keeping the waters at bay.

*

With Dieter gone, the similarities between Siegfried and Wilhelm-Rajmund were even more apparent; the six years between them meant little; it was as if Wilhelm-Rajmund was the *same* boy as Siegfried had been – they looked identical, thought the same way, shared the same passions. Oliver and Irochka would sit at the kitchen table, watching their sons eat, and have the same thought: that they had somehow replicated their first-born. Oliver watched his sons bending over an open tractor hood, wrestling with the distributor cap, and blinked, wondering whether Siegfried was the younger or the elder, wondering whether he was looking in a six-year-old mirror. Irochka would see them sitting in the stables soaping and waxing saddles, talking, always talking, and she would smile at their easy companionship, at their being so right. Smile at the snugness of their fit.

There was, however, one difference between the brothers: Wilhelm-Rajmund had a singular aptitude for languages. All the brothers spoke German, Polish and English – languages that intermingled, interbred around the fecund Reichmann farm. But Wilhelm-Rajmund had something his brothers did not: a mouth that could chew language as if it were ripe apricot flesh and swallow it without thought. Irochka taught him Russian, which he lapped up like a kitten downing milk. The Tridentine mass gave him Latin on a silver salver, and he began to worry at it, taking it apart. When he read, which was often, he would encounter words – submarine, umbrella, bibliophile, sacrosanct – and crack their meaning like a nut, like a walnut between the pincers of his understanding. Then he stumbled across the word 'etymology' and was lost in the labyrinthine corridors of language birth. It was the European languages which fascinated him. If beer was *bière*, *bier*, beer, then why was it also *cerveza* and *pivo*? If butter was *beurre*, *botor* and butter, then why was it *mantequilla*? Why was it *smör*? If love was love, why was it also *amore*, *älskar* and *beninnen*? Wilhelm-Rajmund asked Siegfried about this and his brother laughed and said he had no idea, which surprised the younger sibling because he thought his older brother god-like and infallible. Rocks and language – these were the only differences between them.

*

One winter morning, in late December, when Minnesota was frozen, when the elements were harassing the ancient land, forcing it apart and shattering it, Oliver and Wilhelm-Rajmund were out with the pigs, Oliver selecting the hogs ready for slaughter, daubing their backs with blue paint. Out back, behind the shed, on the corrugated roof of which snow lay heavy, hung the winch. The large, serrated hook swung in the freezing breeze, waiting for bait.

Oliver, having marked the hogs, motioned for Wilhelm to enter a sty with him, pointing to a sow with cobalt smeared on her spine. 'That one. We'll start with her. You take the front and hold her down, cross her legs and pull her head back.' The hog squinted at them, guessed what was about to happen and began to run in small, tight, porcine circles, trotters working in muck. Wilhelm-Rajmund, who was thirteen, who had lived on a hog farm all his life, second-guessed the pig, crouched, feinted right and then snatched at the skittering hoofs. Within moments the pig was hog-tied. Wilhelm-Rajmund grabbed at the pig's pale pink, tight throat and pulled it back. Piggy eyes stared right at him. *Carne*, carnal, carnage. *Lomo*, pork, *Schweinefleisch*. Wilhelm-Rajmund looked into the hog's eyes, with their white unmoving lashes, dark, pink-tinged irises and realized that death had no language and yet encompassed every language in the world. 'Lethe,' Wilhelm-Rajmund muttered, and his father slashed the hog's throat, starting the dance of death. As pearly trotters beat against Wilhelm-Rajmund's shins and blood flowed he thought of his brother Dieter shouldering rifles.

The wind, which had been blowing fiercely, kicked up another notch as Oliver and his son wrestled the dying hog on to a trolley, pushed it to the outhouse where the corpse would hang, the blood draining into a concrete gully. This one was earmarked for the Reichmanns' own larder. Wilhelm-Rajmund climbed on to the platform and began to haul the Yorkshire Large White, deadweight, as his father pushed and hefted. The blue dye ran in the melt water from the snow on the outhouse roof, dyeing Wilhelm-Rajmund's trousers. The hook, a fourteen-inch MeersKraum with a honed point, which had cost Oliver eighty-nine dollars to have shipped from Essen, was lifted by the wind, tossed in an unlikely arc and fell, impaling Wilhelm-Rajmund's left thigh, tearing open his flesh and muscles, pulling them apart. The dying, twitching hog pinned the bleeding boy down as his father roared, leaped on to the platform and flipped the six-hundred-pound pig aside, reached down and lifted his son in his arms.

Irochka nursed Wilhelm-Rajmund back to health, sitting with him during the day and sleeping in the chair at night, so she could wipe his brow, feed him oils and vitamins, change the dressings on the gaping, blood-filled wound. The wound did eventually heal, closed in on itself, but it took months and left Wilhelm-Rajmund with a dented thigh and a slight limp.

Siegfried came in to visit Wilhelm-Rajmund one morning, sat on the edge of the bed and mussed his brother's hair. 'How we doing, soldier?' he asked.

'Fine,' said Wilhelm-Rajmund. 'I can walk from there' – pointing at the door – 'to Ma and Pa's bedroom. Dr Frank reckons I'll be OK to go downstairs in a coupla days.'

'That's good, Willie. That's good. You had me worried for a while there.' Siegfried patted his pockets, brought out a pack of Lucky Strikes, began to smoke. 'Willie, I,' Siegfried searched for an ashtray, sat back on the bed, 'I have to ask you to do something,' he stood up again and looked out of the window at the endless view, 'for me. For all of us,' he sat down, drew heavily on his cigarette, 'I guess. I went in to Mankato today. I've signed up before I get drafted. I'm joining,' he stood up and rearranged the old hockey trophies on the shelves, 'the navy. Going next week. That's me,' he stubbed out his cigarette, grimacing, 'and Deet gone. I want you to look after Ma and Pa. I want you,' he walked over to the collection of Dieter's postcards stuck to the wall, touched the picture of the Hollywood sign, 'to look after Magde. Look after everyone. Sounds like a tall order, don't it?'

Wilhelm-Rajmund touched his damaged flesh beneath the sheet. 'You don't have to go, Siggy. You can stay here.'

'I can't, Willie. I can't do that. Deet's out there fighting to protect what we have and I have to do the same.' Siegfried smiled then, sat on Wilhelm-Rajmund's bed. 'Hey, it'll be fine. I'll bring you back . . . I dunno . . . a dictionary or something. Something European maybe. Something fancy. You'll like that.'

Lethe, thought Wilhelm-Rajmund. *Die Vergesslichkeit. Zapomnienie.*

THE REGANS

Maggie Regan was exceptional among the many Regan children –
the only child to be born in the summer; all her siblings, those who
died as well as those who lived, were born in winter. Maggie was,
although she didn't know it, Gemini, the butterfly of the zodiac,
butterfly of the universe. Her mother had no truck with this pagan-
ism, would cross her ample bosom if astrology was mentioned,
mutter a prayer. So how was Maggie to know that her planet was
Mercury, her flower narcissus? That she was both jewel and dung?
She was aware that at any given moment she might slip from jubi-
lation to despair, that she flitted across the emotional map, but she
did not know that this was preordained. It was the distant wheeling
of planets which caused her to be Janus-faced, something about
which she knew nothing and over which she had no control.

The Regan family was not a particularly happy one when Maggie
was born but, then, it hadn't been even before she saw the light of
day. Raising seven children in a two-bedroomed cottage was as easy
as stuffing rabid ferrets in a sack, and the strain showed, just as it did
on every parent's face in the village. Nine stomachs to be filled every
day, and if some days they were left empty, well, it wasn't for want
of trying. It was for want of money, alternatives, opportunities – all
of them in short supply in 1942. As the rest of Europe blazed, Éire
turned its back on the flames and tried to go about its business.

The Regan house, one of a squat row of cottages in the hamlet of
Ballysod, situated between the towns of Doohooma and Achill in
County Mayo, was a crowded house. Maggie, Mary and Clare slept
in their parents' room, whilst the boys, Padraig, Joseph, Sean and
Michael, had the other room. Downstairs was a kitchen and a

parlour. The kitchen housed an ancient peat-fired range, a Belfast sink with one cold tap, its glaze crazed with tannin stains, and a table with four odd hardback chairs. Shelves ran around two walls, stacked with mismatched crockery, saucepans and cutlery. Every day a pot simmered on the hob, chuckling malevolently, bubbles bursting with the smell of overcooked bacon and cabbage. In the parlour was one over-stuffed armchair, its lines suggesting an attempt at art deco design. The antimacassar on its back was stained with grease from hair oil, the arms dyed by the sweat of hands. This was Sean's chair – only Da could sit in it. A wireless squatted in the corner, each evening hissing and spitting out the numbers of dead across the Irish Sea. The only attempt at decoration was a crucifix over the fireplace (bought by Annie, Maggie's mother, when she went on a day trip to Ballina as a thirteen year old), and a sampler sewn by Clare. 'God Bless this Happy Home', the sampler instructed. When Maggie was older and had learned to read, she was of the opinion that the house needed more blessing than most. The spider-filled privy was at the end of a large garden, behind the vegetable plot, next to the sty, where two pigs rootled in muck; a crumbling wooden shed shored up the privy walls. Yet the house was blessed in one way – the tiny front windows looked out over the sea. On a clear day, if Maggie sat on the rough stone wall in front of the cottage, she could see the village of Blacksod across the bay, see the cliffs of Achill Island. Gulls and puffins soared and swooped as Atlantic waves pounded the rocky beach below. From the boys' bedroom in the back, if one stood on a bed and peered through the window, the roof slates of the main house of the Whyte estate two miles away glittered on sunny days.

This view of the sea battering the cliffs and islands was of no consequence to Sean and Annie Regan, for they had no time to sit on the wall and admire the watery panorama. Sean woke every morning at five, threaded his way through the crowded bedroom to the stairs, and went down to wash and dress at the kitchen sink. Annie would lie in bed, awake, for ten minutes and then follow him. She made thick, black tea and spread slices of bread with butter and jam on good days; on bad days there was no jam, on the worst no butter either. Sean sat at the table as Annie peeled and cut potatoes to throw into the stew, perhaps adding a knuckle or a trotter for taste. Sean rarely spoke, already too busy calculating what he might make that day, what he could steal from that day. He and Annie left the house by six, having loaded his old Bedford van with smoked fish and vegetables. He had altered the rear of the van himself, converting it into a makeshift shop, with rudimentary scales and uneven shelves, and he spent his mornings driving the rutted tracks and unmetalled roads in the hills around the bay, sometimes travelling as far south as Rosturk, other days east as far as Keenagh or north to Portacloy. He sold the potatoes, cabbages, leeks and onions he grew and the fish he caught, which were smoked or salted in the shed at the back of the garden. The land was ungiving, infertile, but Sean coaxed it into life with a potion of bones, paper, tea and rinds handed down by his father – whose fingers may have been arthritic but were also verdant green. Sean acted as a postman, delivery man, messenger, milkman and confessor to the area. People gave him letters to deliver over the hill and round the bay; they gave him eggs for relatives in Belmullet, smocks for a newborn baby in Gweesalia. And they gave him their secrets as well. Just gone noon he'd return to Ballysod and collect Annie from the Whyte House, where she cleaned every morning, except Sundays, and then he'd return to the estate where he spent the afternoons working as an odd-job man, clearing pathways, pruning trees, pointing walls, overhauling machinery. Annie worked the afternoons at home, taking in laundry and sewing, knitting traditional jumpers when she had time.

Annie Regan was an extraordinarily round woman, round as a butterball. Her eyes were round, her frizzy hair cut into the shape of a ball, her nose small and as spheroidal as a cherry, her eyes like buttons. When she fell pregnant – which was often – she swelled like a sunfish, her features disappearing into a surprised face. Sean Regan, however, was tall and gaunt, his black hair always greased back from a face creased and sharp as a skate wing. He spoke only when he had something to say, which was no bad thing, given that Annie barely paused for breath from the moment she woke to the moment she laid her head on the pillow at night. Sean could neither read nor write but that was fine; he could add and subtract which was, frankly, all he needed to be able to do. Somehow the subtraction always outweighed the addition, with the notable exception of their offspring, who multiplied.

Since their parents had already left the house by six o'clock, the Regan children roused, washed and dressed themselves before breakfasting on whatever was left on the table. Their clothes were intimately familiar to all of them – they were passed back and forth, interchanged, handed down, patched, resewn, tucked and, finally, torn up for cloths and dusters. Clare, the eldest, was nine when Maggie was born and it was assumed she would look after the little ones until her mother came home if the neighbour couldn't take them in, then Clare would go to school for the afternoon. When it was harvest or tillage, the boys stayed home to help in the fields; when one of the children was ill another would stay at home. Education was an optional extra, a way of passing time if there was nothing more profitable to be done.

Maggie grew up in a house without books, without stories, without pictures. Her mother might have told her legends and rhymes, myths and fairy tales had she not always been at some exhausting stage of breeding – antenatal, post-partum, gestating, miscarrying, still-birthing – her rotund body constantly being put through the wringer of reproduction. The babies just kept coming, some alive, some not. Some merely piscean suggestions of life, others smeared with blood, seemingly already bawling as they emerged into the cold air of the front bedroom. For they were all (all those that lived) born into bleak winter, with spume flying high above the cliffs of Achill. All but Maggie, the butterfly, the jewel, who emerged on a fine June day.

One delirious summer's day, when Maggie was seven, the entire Regan family went into Ballina to visit a fair and she saw a push-penny machine for the first time. A coin was rolled down a shute into a pile of other coins resting on a moving wooden shelf, where it rolled to a halt. Sometimes another penny, or perhaps even three pennies or more, were shunted off, to fall on to a trough below, and the player kept these. Maggie watched, fascinated, for hours as the shelf moved regularly back and forth, taking one penny and dropping another. It was like home – a brother or sister left and another baby arrived; there always seemed to be the same number of pennies on the shelf as there always seemed to be the same number of people in the house in Ballysod. In the house in Ballysod there was never a surplus, an excess of anything – food, clothes, comfort, space. There was always the same amount of everything, stretched so thin it was transparent, tugged this way and that to cover them all. So it was that whenever the schoolteacher talked about the miracle of life Maggie was nonplussed: how could the miraculous also be the mundane? Silence, second helpings, new socks – now those *were* miracles.

Maggie Regan, who had no excess of food, space or privacy, did, however, have imagination in abundance. She'd sit on the front wall, on a stony beach, on soft, peaty grass, gazing at the distant horizon, and make up stories for herself – of talking dogs, walking fish, seas that disappeared, rivers that ran gold. Sometimes she told her sisters, Clare and Mary, and later Teresa and Kathleen, these stories. Mary, who was a serious, literal girl, thought Maggie was lying and told their mother so.

Although this fertile imagination may have comforted Maggie it also had serious repercussions. Mrs Coughlan, the schoolmistress, was a stout, grey-haired woman who had more in common with Mary than Maggie, because she, too, frowned on any act of imagination for the simple reason that she mistook it for inattention. Maggie was caned, detained and sent home so many times it was barely worth her going to school at all. The problem, of course, was that the reading lessons provided her with material to dream with: warriors, cromlechs, Firbolgs, Cu Chulainn, black bulls and leopards, golden sheep and elephants (although, of course, she already knew about snakes and their duplicity). It was after a particularly frustrating arithmetic lesson – during which Maggie fought at Boru's side in Clontarf, sending the Vikings off with a flea in their collective ear – that Mrs Coughlan sent her home with a letter for her parents.

When Annie returned from the bakery to find Maggie waiting outside the house, sunning herself on the wall, holding a letter in her hand, she panicked. To guard against all eventualities she gave Maggie a clip in the ear before reading the letter aloud.

'"Dear Mr and Mrs Regan",' read Annie, squinting in the bright light, '"I am sorry to have to tell you that Maggie is not welcome at school as from today, Thursday. She is a disob . . . disobedient and rude girl and is having a bad influence on other girls. The Convent of the Immaculate Virgin outside Louisburgh might be a good idea. Yours, Mrs Coughlan".'

'But I wasn't rude, Mam. I—'

Annie smacked Maggie across the cheek, fingered the gold cross hanging on her remarkable breasts, puffed, smacked Maggie again and began to mutter, 'What have we done to deserve this? Jesus, Mary and Joseph, what have we done to deserve this? Now we have a girl running round being a bad influence as if we haven't got enough to be doing with. The convent? Do you know how much money that will be? How much food you'll be taking away from the babby?'

On and on Annie babbled but Maggie wasn't listening. She was already taking her vows of poverty, chastity and obedience, looking demure in her habit, a smear of ash on her forehead.

When the storm had died down, when the shouting and praying were over, then Maggie was permitted back into the bosom of her family, having spent a day locked in her parents' bedroom with only bread and water for nourishment. A deal was struck with the Mother Superior over the fees (something to do with her father supplying fish and vegetables – Maggie was never sure), and Maggie was packed off to the convent school, in the hope she would achieve her Inter-Cert and perhaps go on to the vocational school in Doohooma. But, more than that, Annie Regan wanted the nuns to knock the stuffing out of her daughter – 'She's having a bad influence so you do whatever you think is right. We have faith, of course we have faith, that you know best,' she told the Mother Superior. The Mother Superior looked at Maggie, noted the impertinent tilt of her chin and made a mental note to have a word with Sister Immaculata.

So began four years of Maggie waking at dawn to eat hard bread and tepid porridge, four years of praying, sewing, chanting and learning responses. Hours of Latin and arithmetic, Irish history and laborious calligraphy, all overseen by the despotic Sister Immaculata, all designed to break her spirit. Maggie was caned, starved, spent weeks in isolation, was bidden to be silent for days on end – yet nothing changed. Four years later, when Maggie was fourteen, Sister Immaculata watched her one morning, unobserved, and thought that even the way Maggie Regan *stood* was insolent. This saddened the sister, who had never before encountered a girl like Maggie Regan – a girl whose spirit she couldn't break.

What no one understood was that this life, which consisted mainly of enforced solitude and contemplation, was ideally suited to Maggie. Contemplation was what she did best; to slip away from the dormitory or solitary cell to be an inspired leader at the Battle of the Boyne, or to sit wild-haired and filthy around a campfire with a Nemedian tribe, was all she wanted to do. So the punishments passed unnoticed; indeed, became solace. What she came to dread were the holidays when she returned to Ballysod, to the push-penny house which was awash with humanity, Padraig, Joseph, Sean, Michael and Clare having moved on and out, to be replaced by Matthew, Eamonn, Brigid and Ceile. Mary and Maggie were then the eldest and were expected to help with raising funds to keep their stomachs full, as well as looking after the little ones.

The last Christmas Maggie was at the convent, she returned to Ballysod to discover that Ceile had arrived, a mewling, pink turd machine. As Maggie stood by the vat boiling on the stove, stirring and gagging occasionally as the soiled towelling nappies were tossed in the water, she glanced over at Mary, serious, literal Mary, who was frowning with concentration as she folded paper, trying to make a card to give to Annie and Sean.

'I'm not going to have any children,' said Maggie. 'When I grow up, I'm not having babies.'

Mary didn't look at her. 'Don't be silly.'

'I am not. I'm going to live in a big house on my own. A house like a castle.' Maggie stared out at the distant sea, dropped the wooden stirring pin in the water and sat at the table. 'Bigger than Whyte House.'

'Maggie Regan, you're lying again.'

'No, I am not. I'm going to meet a rich, handsome man and marry him and we'll live in . . . in Czechoslovakia.' Maggie had discovered Czechoslovakia the week before during a history lesson and had thought the name impossibly romantic.

'Where?'

'Czechoslovakia. It's in Europe.'

Dazzled by this piece of information, Mary said nothing, simply sighed and shook her head.

'Mary – have you started?'

Maggie's sister looked up from the collapsing card, exasperated. 'Started what?'

'You know.'

'No, I don't know.'

'You do know.' Maggie brushed her lap as if flicking crumbs from her skirt.

'Maggie Regan, you're mad.'

Maggie leaned over the table. 'You do know – blood every month.'

Mary blushed and crossed herself. 'Maggie – not at the table.'

'Where, then?'

Where indeed? Where exactly was Maggie supposed to go to be told about love and affection? Where exactly was Margaret Louise Sorcha Regan, fourteen years old, from Ballysod, County Mayo, supposed to *go* to be told about Eros and Agape, about kindness and chivalry? Or even, God forbid (and He did), romance and sexual congress?

'It's a punishment,' said Mary, after a few moments.

Maggie stared at her sister's pale parting as Mary bent over the collapsing paper. 'What for?'

Mary looked up and shrugged, and in that shrug there was more helplessness than Maggie ever wanted to see.

Of course, Maggie didn't last at the convent until the Inter-Cert. She nearly made it, nearly made it to the summer term of her fifteenth year, but not quite. One dreamy acquiescence too many, one unconsciously sultry pout too many, and she was out. Sister Immaculata, for all her faults (and she had many), had persevered with the breaking of the girl but it was not to be. The sister snapped at the beginning of Maggie's last term and Maggie was sent back to the Regan home in Ballysod in disgrace.

1957

When Billy-Ray Rickman arrived in London, he was nervous and a little confused as to what, exactly, was expected of him. Feeling as gauche as the Minnesotan farm boy he was, he went into downtown London on his first day, walked the streets around Piccadilly, scanning shop windows, trying to find a suit and shirt that might fit. He noted the prices, converted the cost to dollars, and his nervousness increased. In the end, he bought an off-the-peg dark blue suit and a number of white shirts and dark ties. He noticed a sleek black leather briefcase in a luggage shop and bought that too. London in November was warm and wet, a constant drizzle falling on crowded pavements. He watched the men as he walked, trying to work out how to blend in, and noticed that everyone was dowdy, dressed in greys and browns, even the women. But the buildings, the arcades, were like nothing he'd ever seen. He went into a pub off Bond Street and was stunned by the warm air and smoke, the noise, the flatness of the beer.

Billy-Ray caught a cab back to his new home in Pelham Crescent, watching the city-scape pass by; the boulevards, the tiny cars, rumbling red buses, black cabs, Harrods, the museums, street vendors, newspaper boys yelling, police on horseback. Billy-Ray closed his front door behind him and breathed deeply. He hadn't thought about this, of how it would be to be in London, alone. Hadn't thought of what he was going to do in an office. He drew a hot bath and lay in it as the day dimmed, lay in it until the only light was cast by the street lamp outside. Billy-Ray didn't want to sleep because he knew the Wave would come looking for him.

Months later, Billy-Ray looked back on that night, the night before he began work in the Waterloo offices, and he smiled a little when he thought about how nervous he'd been. Why had he worried? Months later he had a closet full of Savile Row suits, racks of hand-made shoes, silk ties, Jermyn Street shirts. He'd thrown away the ready-made clothes he'd bought that day and dumped the brief-case. Months later, Billy-Ray felt he was on top of the world.

Billy-Ray spent some of his days in the Waterloo office, where he met with accountants who had sifted through the end-of-years and bank-ruptcy filings of small European concerns, and with field surveyors and engineers, who came to his office touting maps and blueprints. Billy-Ray talked and he analysed and he thought and then he pounced. The days he wasn't in the office, Billy-Ray Rickman trav-elled around Europe, negotiating with small, independent petrol companies, buying up expired leases, and identifying potentially pro-ductive fields. His job was simple: to expand Karbo's interests by buying up leases and exploration rights, and to provide outlets for the Libyan oil that was gushing from wounds in the desert. Standard Oil of California, New York and New Jersey, Gulf, Texaco, Royal Dutch Shell and British Anglo-Persian – the Seven Sisters – were also in the race, and Billy-Ray flew to the Hebrides, Rotterdam, Dublin, Stavanger and Oslo to try to outbid or outmanoeuvre the competitors. Billy-Ray was ruthless – his grasp of languages, his grasp of the prin-ciples of acquisition (that is, his understanding of the importance of not being found out), ensured he kept up with the big boys. Oil refineries across Europe were supplied by Karbo Inc.; schoolchildren in Hanover, Trømso, London and Geneva were kept warm in winter by heating systems fired by Karbo Inc.; maternity wards and crema-toria were kept alive by the oil flowing through the veins of Karbo Inc.

Often, in the late afternoons, as the sun sank, when his door was closed and the office was silent, Billy-Ray would stand at his window watching the traffic crawling over the bridge, and he would imagine himself away. Imagined pulling on jeans, boots and water-proofs, carrying a hard hat under his arm, and going out to the rigs. Being dockside and climbing down into the crew boat, travelling choppy water, then being hauled up to the platform in the basket. This he could imagine: the stacks of down-hole tools, pipe, cable, storage tanks, the shape of the rotary table, drill collars, fractured drill-string sleeves. And everywhere the vivid yellow chevrons and red-and-white steel beams, stacked cabins for offices and rec rooms, and the rec rooms all smelled the same, all over the world – stale coffee and cigarette smoke, wet rubber and meat grease. The spindly legs of jack-ups, the faint motion of anchored semi-subs, all of it so familiar. The labs where sampling and analysis were done – where Billy-Ray would spend his time, poring over the breakdown and analysis of crude samples. API, specific gravity, sulphur, pour point, viscosity – he built the figures into pictures, into a feeling rolled between his thumb and forefinger.

But Billy-Ray was, once again, landlocked. Each morning he shucked on a suit, knotted a tie and spent his days suggesting the purchase of share options, or merging of interests, the securing of field leases and exploration rights. He'd roll up one map and unfurl another because the thick black gold was haemorrhaging from the seabed, over desert sands, over marshy flatlands, welling up in drowned deltas and basins, and still it kept coming. Rigs, derricks and processing plants bloomed like sarcoma in Libya, Saudi Arabia, Angola, Yemen and Russia; pipelines ran like blind worms for hundreds of miles. Continental shelves were explored and prodded, and then the oil companies began to buy up the ocean itself. Men were everywhere sniffing the earth like dogs, like pigs hunting truffles, hoping to catch the scent of oil.

Cars were rolling off the production lines, power stations were belching fumes, freighters slopped oil in their vast tanks – where could Billy-Ray go wrong? He earned money that his English friends gawped at. Everyone around him struggled to hide their impecunity, struggled to disguise old suits, threadbare carpets, defective heating (if indeed they had heating). But Billy-Ray's wallet was as thick as the Bible, endless as the oilfields, bottomless as the Aleutian Trench. As well as all this, he had a delectable lover to boot. He met Jacqueline often, in country hotels in Surrey, Oxfordshire, Royal Berkshire; sometimes she visited his house but was circumspect about this because Billy-Ray lived only a few minutes' walk from Jarman House. He liked Jacqueline's company – she was sassy, sharp and sexy and they understood each other only too well. Occasionally he thought of the gauche Minnesotan farm boy, thought of the farm itself – what would his father say if he could see him now? What would all the kids he graduated with say if they could see his chauffeured car, his house, see him dining at the Ritz, drinking at Ed's Bar? So why was all this not enough? Why did he still feel hollow? Why did he still feel a presence, a shadow, at his back?

When Billy-Ray received the telegram at his office, in June 1958, announcing that Karbo Inc. had finally struck oil in the Middle Shoals area of the Kenai Peninsula in Alaska, he left work early, for once loathing the cars and trucks streaming over Waterloo Bridge. He ordered a vodka in the Savoy American Bar, although it was only two in the afternoon, and he drank until evening. He kept staring at his suit; he looked like an office man, like everyone else there, because he was. He sat in the bar and knew he should be elsewhere, that he should be at the edge of the world, tearing it apart. He sat there playing out silvery blue dreamscapes in his mind as two blond heads touched in the foreground of a panorama of ice-covered mountain peaks.

That night Billy-Ray stood in his black-and-white marble bathroom in Pelham Crescent, looking in the mirror as he loosened his tie, and he watched Siegfried undress, watched him brush his hair. An older Siegfried than he had ever known. As vodka washed through him, he closed his eyes and the Wave broke over him.

Bitte, Gott, lass es Dieter sein.

THE REGANS

Maggie Regan was inching towards the lip of the push-penny shelf. She was too old, too big, too *hungry* to stay idly in the Regan house where she might, in any case, be a bad influence. She had missed the opportunity to better herself, as she was constantly reminded by her mother. Maggie's misdemeanours, the shame she had brought on the Regan house, fuelled Annie's flapping tongue for months. Annie woke every morning and, almost before her eyes had adjusted to the gloom of the packed bedroom, her tongue was off and running, chasing down Maggie wherever she might be.

'So, being thrown out of the school by Mrs Coughlan was not enough for you? You have to go farther – get thrown out of the convent as well! And the good Sister Immaculata saying you were the worst, the *worst*, she had ever taken. The worst girl. How can you stand there and not be ashamed! What kind of daughter have we raised? Blessed Mary, help us with this sinner.' This would be said with some heat and vigour as Annie readied herself for work at the House, as she buttered bread, pushing back the bubble of hair from her sunfish face. It would be said over the bowls of stew in the evening. And repeated each night as the heap of bodies in the bedroom settled down. Annie had been given a new conversational bone to gnaw and she was worrying it to shards.

Maggie, for her part, was rather baffled by the venom of her mother's verbal onslaught, and somewhat bored by its unchanging tone. She could not, for the life of her, work out what she had done wrong.

Sean Regan bore the burden of his wife's constant prattling with fortitude. Each morning, as the two of them bounced their way in the old Bedford van over to the Whyte House, Annie would witter endlessly. First a five-minute prate about Maggie's faults, followed by comments on the cleanliness or otherwise of the neighbours' houses they passed. Then on to the talk and gossip from below stairs at the House, which did at least vary a little. Sean would grunt occasionally as he calculated his possible takings for the day.

'Now, old Miss Grehan went into Ballina Thursday last to buy a new hat. What will she be wanting that for? At her age? Don't forget to collect the cardigan from Eleanor Doyle out Strahmore way if you get there, Padraig will be needing it soon as the old one is too worn at the elbows. Now, Michael Flynn tipped his tractor the other day – did you hear that? Broke his leg, it did, and he's at home for at least six weeks with the potatoes ready and so who'll be doing that? I'll go to O'Malley's this morning to get a hock if we can afford it but he'll fleece us all the same so I might as well not bother.'

Sean grunted – it was about time he ought to.

Annie delved suddenly into her handbag, rooted around looking for a comb, dragged it through her frizzy hair. 'Then there's all the talk about Constance Wycherley – have you heard? Well, she's been having new curtains and a new rug in the kitchen. And there's even been talk of an icebox. Now, where's she getting the money, that's what we'd like to know? Used to be poor as a church mouse, all crusts and rainwater. And now it's full-cream milk and best side of bacon. She must have come into something – but we'd know if anyone had died. Unless it was up Dublin way, a cousin or something. But she's not been away to a wake, so probably not. And now she's painting the door and having a gate hung in the garden. Used to look like a cross between a hovel and a kennel, and now Constance Wycherley thinks she deserves a castle. Why? *That's* what I want to know.' Annie thrust the comb back into her handbag and pouted (perhaps not quite as successfully as her raven-haired daughter).

One of the tragedies of Annie Regan's life, although she never knew it, was that her husband, ersatz confessor, sham shaman to women from Portacloy to Killadoon, was privy to more secrets and confidences than Annie could even dream of. When he appeared at the doors and gates of the isolated houses across the peninsula, gaunt and silent, dressed always in a black jacket, dark trousers, black waistcoat and white, collarless shirt, the women began to babble – about themselves, their husbands, their thoughts, their desires. And Sean Regan would stand in drizzle or sunlight, his hypnotic dark eyes watching them as the bags of fish or bread grew heavy in his hands. Because the women never heard their tales being repeated, never heard a whisper or rumour of what they had told, they knew their secrets were safe, locked away in Sean's head or, perhaps, his heart. Shaman or priest? They didn't care. Annie could have spent days gorging at the table groaning with Sean's secret pile of intimacies. But she never thought to ask him, which was a shame because he could have solved so many mysteries, answered so many vexed questions. Not, of course, that he would have done.

Annie fingered the crucifix hanging between her breasts as the House came into view. 'Well, Marie said she was going over to Constance Wycherley's last night for a visit. We'll see what she has to say. She'll have found out something – like a ferret that girl.' Annie clambered out of the truck and waddled down the path.

Sean's skate-wing face was impassive as he drove on, towards Inver where, he'd heard, crates from a wreck had washed up. Maybe there was salvage? As the truck rattled along the potholed road, the weighing scales in the back shifting and clanking, he thought of the imminent Easter weekend. He didn't have much time for the religious convictions his wife enjoyed – he'd rather have a morning of hurling, thumping the slitter end to end across mud, followed by a few pints of Guinness, than a morning spent on his knees on a stone floor. What good the confessional if all these secrets and desires still oozed out? How many Hail Marys did it take for absolution when all was not confessed? Maybe there wasn't salvage? Sean smiled thinly at the thought.

Passing a sign for Bunnahowen, on the hills behind which Constance Wycherley's nascent castle was to be found, he thought of the woman who was the cause of so much speculation. A stick of a woman, a bamboo cane of a woman, her joints and knuckles as prominent as her cheekbones. Pale, dusty skin covered in copper freckles. Thin hair, thin lips, ravaged by poverty since her Ulster-born husband went down in 1944 off the coast of Normandy. But now she had found a foothold, a ladder that would lead her out of the well-hole of her misery. Yes, she was indeed considering a new icebox, as she had told Sean. Even a car! Because she had become a farmer, and a very successful one. She didn't farm sugar beet or turnips or potatoes – all those tubers, so prone to damp, blight and rot. No, she farmed something far more reliable, something that was in endless supply and which didn't suffer at the mercy of the seasons. A sturdy, self-maintaining stock (with a fine rate of feed and gain conversion, as Oliver Reichmann and his uncle Siegfried would have noted). Constance Wycherley farmed babies.

At fifteen Maggie Regan was simply breathtaking. A glimpse of her could make a heart skip or stop, a man draw breath, a woman contemplate the unfairness of the universe. It was as if, in the womb, Maggie had sifted through the genetic smorgasbord of generations, picking and choosing, like a hawk-eyed jeweller at an antiques fair. At fifteen Maggie was tall and broad shouldered, with meat on her finely formed, long bones. Her skin was pale, her hair thick and blue-black, her eyes quite small yet keen, coloured the shades of sphagnum moss in spring sunlight. Her lips were full, her jaw sharp as her neck was long. Her breasts sat high and inviting on her long torso. Visitors to County Mayo who tramped the coastal path might catch glimpses of her leaning against the stone wall of the house in Ballysod, wearing thin, over-washed, too-short cotton dresses in the summer evenings. She stood scanning the waters of the bay, her arms crossed, her full lips moving, as the visitors wondered and glanced back at the young woman who looked like a goddess, a faerie, a consort of Finn mac Cumhail.

But, as has been said, Maggie was too old to be sitting around in the Regan house listening to Annie's daily rants. So it was soon agreed that she would spend the mornings watching the little ones, Brawny and Brigid, and then, when her mammy was home from the morning shift, she would go up to the House with her father in the afternoons. Sean went to the lady of the house, cap in hand, and asked for permission to bring his daughter to the estate.

'But what on earth will she do?' asked the lady. 'Surely, we already have enough staff.'

'I could do with some help, m'am. She can help me load the truck, maybe do some clipping. She's a strong girl, a mucker.' As Sean spoke he looked at the woman's shoes.

'Well, if you must. We'll see how she gets on.' The door closed.

So every afternoon Maggie went with her father in the Bedford, the two of them bouncing silently, in harmony with the worn suspended leaf springs. Sean enjoyed these journeys – simply sitting in the cab with company that was silent. Maggie was indeed a mucker and proved to be a great help to her father. She hauled cut branches to pyres of dead wood, shovelled the lichen he scraped from pathways, wheeled barrow-loads of leaves and weeds to compost heaps. She'd tuck her worn dress into her long knickers, revealing shapely legs, and heave loads of debris, cut down striplings, trim bushes, rub down peeling paint, scrub pavings. Maggie enjoyed physical labour, loved being outdoors, the sweat rolling from her armpits, the smell of chopped, bleeding greenery around her, loved the heft of an adze. And she could do all of this while dreaming. She could labour up a rutted slope with a barrow-load of stones and broken brick whilst imagining herself sitting at the feet of Turlough O'Carolan, listening to the blind harpist play.

Sean Regan watched Maggie with something approaching pride as she laboured. For the life of him he couldn't understand what Maggie had done that was so bad that the powers of state and Church had come down on her so hard. She was beautiful, she worked hard and she kept her mouth shut. And wasn't that some kind of recipe for success?

Summer arrived and Maggie was still working at the House. Annie complained that the work was hardly suitable for a young woman – showing her legs and growing muscles in her arms, arms that were brown now, from being too much in the sun – but Sean refused to let Maggie go.

'She's a help,' he growled over stew and dumplings. 'I get much more done and the lady's paying her now. Look at how much she brings into the house. An extra two pounds a week.'

The money helped, to be sure, but more than that, Sean liked having his daughter with him, silent and accommodating. The two of them barely needed to speak as they tackled a job, seemed to have a tacit understanding of what needed to be done. More than that, Maggie was happy. Sean's eternal near-silence did not signal a lack of caring that his children were so poor, so neglected as he and Annie struggled. He did care but he had so little time to stop and tell them so, to show them so. Seeing Maggie happy was some recompense.

'I could get her a place below stairs,' Annie replied, rubbing the mound of her latest pregnancy. 'Or maybe Marie ní Challanain over Doohooma way could teach her a little sewing – not that she'll be any good for it. Too flighty as we know too well. Head in the clouds and not on the Lord's earth.'

'She's a good worker.'

'She's a good *eater* – will you look at her, wolfing it down like it's her first meal in a month.'

Maggie looked up from her plate, watched her mother, wiping the worn surfaces, rolling round the tired, old kitchen like a ball bearing. 'I'm hungry, Mammy,' she said mildly.

'And what's more,' Annie continued, puffing at her upper lip as the evening sun streamed through the open door, 'which man will have her? Looking like a navvy, all dirty and sunburned, with calluses on her hands. Which man would want that? Time she learned to be a lady, time she made up for what she's done so far with her life. Having a bad influence – that's all she's good for. I'll take her up to the House.'

Maggie looked up again, frowning.

'Maybe,' said Sean, lighting a reed-thin, hand-rolled cigarette, rubbing his tired eyes, 'she doesn't want to go. Why don't you ask her?'

Annie's little round eyes widened. 'Ask her?'

'Yes. She's sitting there, right in front of you. Ask her if she wants to go below stairs.'

'Jesus, Mary and Joseph – you think she knows her own mind?'

'As happens, I do.'

Annie folded her arms, bunched her breasts high under her chins. 'Well, little missy, know your own mind, do you? Now – do you want to go to the House and learn a proper woman's trade or keep running round like a navvy?'

'I don't want to work below stairs, Mammy. I want to work with Da.'

'Why can't you go off to the convent like good Mary – already a novitiate with the Carmelites, praying and paying her penance, as you should be.'

'For what?' asked Maggie.

Sean smiled faintly behind the acrid smoke cording his face.

Annie's eyes extended as far as they could, like little ebony buttons, like teddy bear's eyes. 'What did you say?'

Maggie laid down her spoon. 'What does Mary have to pay penance for? She's never done anything wrong. She's never really done anything at all.'

Annie's hand flew out, slapped the back of Maggie's head. 'She's paying penance for her sins, as you know.'

'*What* sins?' asked Maggie.

Annie crossed herself, looked down at her daughter. 'We are all born sinners.'

'I—' Maggie stopped. Cleared her throat. 'I don't think we are.'

Bedlam erupted as Annie flew at her daughter, and Sean kicked back his chair, walked over to grab his wife's flailing fists. Maggie, who stood a good foot taller than her rotund mother, held her easily at arms' length – arms with, as Annie had observed, beautifully sculpted muscles.

'I think it'd be best if you stayed away from Mammy for a while,' remarked Sean the next afternoon as he and Maggie headed for Whyte House.

Maggie nodded. Looked at the sun bouncing on the waters of the bay, thinking. Turned to Sean. 'Do *you* think we're born sinners, Da?'

'I think some are.'

'Do you think Mary was born a sinner?'

Sean considered the idea of poor, pale, insubstantial Mary as sinner. He sighed. 'I don't know, Maggie.'

'Do you believe in God?'

'Of course I do. And so should you.' But of course, he didn't. How could Sean Regan (priest or shaman?) travel the worn, tired peninsula every day and hear the tales that he was told – of stillbirth and incest, gangrene and rape – and still believe in a God? How could anyone have followed Europe's drama, heard the news from Russia, from Belsen, from Dachau, and still believe in a God? Yet still Sean thought it a wonderful thing to have faith, to be able to believe, when all was said and done, that there was a God. He didn't want Maggie to lose that. He looked over at his daughter and saw something in her face that told him she had lost it already. That somewhere, at some time during her fifteen years, she had lost her faith and had managed to conceal that loss from everyone. 'Don't you worry about Mammy – I'll deal with her. Sometimes I think maybe she has a little too *much* faith. You'll not be going to the convent. Or below stairs.'

Father and daughter smiled at each other.

When they reached the House, Sean led Maggie along a path behind the stables which led to a large octagonal, glazed summer house, stained glass ornamenting the fanlights. The roof was slate-covered, with a delicate arrow for a weathervane jutting from it. Inside there were window seats and a long cane settle. It was beautiful, Maggie thought, a hideaway, surrounded by huge azalea and laurel bushes, its small, overgrown garden dotted with leggy roses. As they walked closer, she could see that it was dilapidated, paint peeling, mildew on the window benches and on the settle's cushions, heaps of dried leaves piled in each of the eight corners.

Sean eyed the structure, calculating how much work needed to be done, how long it would take. 'Maggie, I'm going to leave you to do this.'

'To do what?'

'The lady wants it restored – you know, cleaned out, painted, pavings scrubbed and sealed. So the family can use it again. Hasn't been used for years, she told me.'

Maggie looked at the summer house again. 'Strange, isn't it, Da? It's bigger than our house but they don't even bother to use it.'

Sean kicked at a broken brick by his foot. 'No point thinking like that, Maggie – it doesn't get you anywhere. I should know.' He stuffed his hands in his pockets, trying not to think of how tired he was; he had been up since five (as always) and all the way over to Kilmeena that morning with a case of smoked mackerel. 'I'm not going to give you too much advice – I think you know what needs doing and how to do it. Clean first, then rub down, fill anything you can, wash with sugar soap and then we'll get you painting. Reckon you'll enjoy that. Anything you need, paper, brushes, all that, is in the workshop. I'll show you.'

The workshop was at the rear of the stables, a small, dark barn lit by a single light bulb. Shelf upon shelf of tools, racks of drivers and pliers, baskets and bottles of nails and screws. And an all-pervading smell Maggie hadn't encountered before – oil and grease, combined with dust and wood shavings, mingled with the smell from the stables, earthy and rich. Maggie gathered together buckets and scrubbing brushes, bars of soap, long, hard-bristled brushes.

'Do it well, Maggie. Do your best.'

'I will, Da.'

'We need the money.'

When don't we, thought Maggie as she watched her father walk away, his feet dragging slightly.

The first time Danny Maconnell saw Maggie Regan, she was at the top of a ladder, a claw hammer in one hand as the other grabbed hold of the weathervane for balance, and between her lips she held a brace of round-head tacks. She was levering a dislodged slate off the roof so she could reset and rehang it. Two weeks she'd been working on the summer house. She'd finished the preparation and now she was beginning to put it all back together again. It wasn't a labour of love – how could it be? – but she wanted to do it well for her da, who had kept Annie at bay for Maggie's sake. But Danny Maconnell thought at first she was *stealing* the roof.

Having stumbled across Maggie, Danny Maconnell stood and watched her, saw her calves straining as she balanced and hefted, saw the line of her long thighs against the thin cotton of her dress, nonplussed by the picture of a girl, a *girl*, wielding a hammer. He watched her as she tapped the slate into place, heard an oath as the hammer hit flesh, waited for her to come down the ladder and turn around. Maggie did just that and Danny Maconnell lost his heart.

Maggie didn't notice Danny; she was lost in a reverie about how it would be to take tea with her husband in the summer house on just such a day as this – hot and cloudless, gulls overhead, azaleas flaming.

'Hello,' said Danny.

Maggie looked up and saw a young, brown-haired man, wearing leather chaps, strange tools hanging at his belt. She said nothing.

'Sorry – didn't mean to frighten you.'

Maggie turned the claw hammer in her hand, still said nothing.

'I'm Danny Maconnell – Eamonn Maconnell's son.' Danny waved a hand in the direction of the stables, hidden behind the bushes. 'He's the farrier – I'm in apprenticeship to him. Learning the trade. Who might you be? I've not seen you before, but then I've been ill and haven't worked for a while.'

'Maggie Regan, daughter to Sean Regan.'

'Is he the tall, dark man? Drives a green truck and doesn't have much to say for himself?' Much like his daughter, thought Danny.

Maggie nodded.

Danny gestured at the slate roof. 'So what are you doing here?'

'I'm fixing the summer house.'

'All on your own?'

'Yes,' said Maggie, 'all on my own.' Again she turned the claw hammer over in her palm.

Danny smiled, and in the high August light his face crinkled just so. 'That's wonderful. There's not many girls who could do that.'

'Not many boys either.'

'That's true,' and he laughed again.

Four days later, when Eamonn Maconnell and his son returned to reshoe the hunters, Danny slipped away from his father and went in search of Maggie, who was sitting in a sun patch in the rose garden, taking a break, her tanned legs stretched out on the scrubby grass. The young man took courage and sat next to her and began to talk. Danny Maconnell had not so much kissed the Blarney stone as been to bed with it. He sat and talked about travelling with his father from Galway to Dublin to Cork, about the bars and hotels, about the races and the camaraderie of the equine world, the stables of the Curragh. He showed Maggie his tools – the flat-end tampers and hooks, the curved knife used to trim the hoof. Danny sat there in the sun, his strong, knotted forearms hooked over his knees, rocking slightly on his buttocks as he talked. He thought Maggie was the most beautiful thing he had ever seen, and he was right.

Maggie, for her part, had never met anyone like Danny – someone who talked with a purpose, to tell a story, to recount an event, to describe things he had seen. Unlike her mother, who merely droned and prattled, Danny talked because he loved it, because there was so much to say, so much enjoyment to be had in simply telling a tale. Maggie had spent her life concocting her own stories from thin pickings, unable to share them without being accused of lying by her self-righteous siblings. In the convent, silence had been expected, even enforced. And now here was this young man waving his expressive hands, which moved to illustrate each point in his narrative, who laughed and slapped his knees and just kept talking. It was when Danny regaled her with the origins of thoroughbreds, described the three great stallions, the Byerly Turk, the Darley Arabian and the Godolphin Barb, that Maggie fell into his trap. It seemed to her he was talking about myths, legends, which of course, he was. Those horses were mythical but they had existed. It was language that snared Maggie: the sound of Danny Maconnell's mouth saying the word 'Godolphin'.

The gazebo was a perfect location for their trysts – Maggie dragged the cane settle back into the still-shabby interior and it was on that creaking, mildew-spotted furniture that Danny made love to her. Slowly at first, holding her and kissing, stroking her arm as they lay and talked. Then he began to touch her elsewhere, talking, always talking, soothing her doubts. One day he took her callused hand and guided it to the place between his chaps, where Maggie found a strange, hard lump. When he took her virginity, on the last day of summer, as the sky lowered beyond the stained glass of the fanlights, Danny was surprised to find Maggie clinging to him, moaning, pulling him into her with her navvy-toned muscles. As she came she bit his shoulder, stifling a yelp, and Danny was shocked.

How did they manage to meet for so long without being discovered? Maggie drew out the project of the summer house until the last week of September, telling her father that she wanted to finish it as best she could – everything as fine and careful as it might be. Danny, who usually visited the Whyte estate only every couple of weeks with his father, would cadge a ride to Ballysod and meet Maggie whenever they could manage. Maggie's absences were not remarked upon; after all, she was known for her solitary walks. Maggie felt that she was, at last, within reach of one of her fantasies: the taking of tea with her husband as the lozenges of hand-blown glass cast a rainbow of colours no matter what the season.

So it was surprising that Annie discovered her daughter and Danny Maconnell not in the delicious summer house but in the dark, earthy workshop. Eamonn had sent Danny to the estate to pick up a toolbox he had left behind by mistake. When Danny arrived, chapless, in the workshop, it was to find Maggie bent over tins of creosote in a dim corner. Her vulnerable position was not the spark that lit Danny's fire – it was the sight of her hands in fingerless gloves to protect them against the October chill.

Annie – who had walked the two miles to the Whyte estate to tell Sean that one of the pigs was ailing and needed attention – was puffing heavily as she blundered into the small workshop, squinting in the gloom. At first she mopped her face with a handkerchief, propping herself on a bench to rest her heavy belly, trying to make out shapes in the darkness. She became aware of a strange smell, of oil and horses, creosote and rust. She had never been up to the workshop before and she found she liked the smell, liked the strangeness of the place – all the unfathomable tools, the masculinity of them. Annie became aware of a curious sound, a rhythmic tinkling and rattling, of glass and something else. She shuffled forward uncertainly, peering into the gloom, until she saw a bank of shelves moving, the glass jars full of nails and pins glinting as they rocked slightly. Annie frowned, puzzled. She moved forward cautiously; there might be a dangerous animal back there. And indeed there was – the animal her daughter became when Danny Maconnell was inside her. Even in the sunless barn Annie could see Danny Maconnell's white buttocks, so pale, almost blue-white, as to be luminous.

Annie gasped and covered her mouth with her handkerchief. It was only when Danny managed to slow himself and glance over his shoulder that Annie realized that the woman being bounced against the shelves was Maggie. Maggie, who opened her eyes with irritation when Danny slid out of her, only to see her mother's teddy-bear eyes staring right back at her.

When, a month later, as Billy-Ray and Jacqueline sailed the Atlantic, Noël, Maggie's eleventh sibling, arrived on the same day as a proposal from Sister Immaculata that she go to London to work in service, Maggie's fate was sealed. She fell headlong off the pushpenny shelf, fell so far and so fast that it took her breath away.

THE REICHMANNS

Minnesota, being in the middle of the North American continent, was as far from the battle between the Axis and the Allies as it was possible to be, and yet the farmers and miners, lumber men and mill workers felt squeezed by it. Felt that the breath was being squeezed from them. The steel mills and iron foundries increased productivity, churning out hundreds of tons of metal that would be fashioned into destroyers, bullets and tanks. The farmers tried to raise the yield – they had, after all, to feed an army. And despite their distance from the massacres, they were aware of their homelands being strangled.

Oliver and Wilhelm-Rajmund were in the fields, stopping gopher holes, when Irochka rode up one broiling day in June 1942, wide eyed and breathless.

'What? What is it?' Oliver stood stock still, as Wilhelm-Rajmund closed his eyes, knowing this was the moment he dreaded every day.

Irochka dismounted, held the reins in her hands, pointed north-west. 'On the radio – the Japanese – they've landed in Alaska. They landed on two islands in the Aleutians. They're here.'

Oliver swivelled and looked in the direction of Irochka's pointing finger, as Wilhelm-Rajmund opened his eyes and muttered a prayer of thanks that this was the news Irochka had brought. Then he, too, looked north-west, across Blue Earth, across Brown, Redwood, Yellow Medicine, across the rainbow counties of Minnesota. Imagined flying over Saskatchewan and Alberta, across the Gulf of Alaska to the islands of Kiska and Attu. He moved, then, towards his father, who put an arm around the boy's shoulders.

'It's a long way away, isn't it, Pa?' Wilhelm-Rajmund's voice sounded like a wet pebble, small and hard.

'Sure is. Thousands of miles.'

Irochka let the reins drop and the horse whinnied, began to crop at clumps of grass. She moved into the ambit of her husband's other arm, and the three of them stared at the horizon, sweating in the midday sun. Wilhelm-Rajmund shaded his eyes, saw an improbable island wavering in the mid-distance, surrounded by water.

'Can you see that? That island?' he asked his mother.

'Yah, Willie, it's a mirage, that's all. It's a trick of the light.'

Wilhelm-Rajmund began to cry then. 'I thought, when you came on the horse, I thought that—'

'I know,' said Irochka, and dried his cheeks roughly with her callused thumbs before hugging him close.

With both Siggy and Deet gone, Oliver tried to make up for their absence in Wilhelm-Rajmund's life. He asked his youngest son to help him in the fields, taught him what he knew about fixing engines, showed him how to help the runts in the litters suckle. When Wilhelm-Raymund's leg was stronger, his limp almost unnoticeable, the two of them hiked in the woods of Faribault, through stands of prairie oak and elm, Oliver pointing out woodchuck, muskrat and pine marten. He taught Wilhelm-Rajmund to be wary of garter snakes, redbelly snakes and snapping turtles. Some late evenings when the day's chores were done, he and Wilhelm-Rajmund would go down to the lake, which they had never named, which they simply called Home Lake, and take the small rowing boat out to fish as the sun sank. Irochka never joined them by the lake; she hated deep water, scared by its darkness, by the void it masked. In the long summer evenings father and son sat immobile at the lake's edge, watching for leopard frogs and tiger salamanders as muskellunge jumped for flies, creating ripples on the surface. On Fall evenings they sat and watched families of river otters playing in a feeder stream, as Canadian geese and gadwall flew overhead, travelling the Mississippi Flyway which crossed the state. Sometimes father and son would sit in the tall grass, Oliver chewing a wad of tobacco, Wilhelm-Rajmund smoking Lucky Strike (a habit he'd adopted when Siggy had left), Oliver talking about the way Minnesota had been before the farmers arrived, before the forests and woodlands and tall prairie grasses had been cleared to make way for the hog and beef farms and the endless corn belt. There were black bear and timber wolves still prowling the counties of Kitsch and Roseau, he said, deer and moose wandering in the woodlands of Clay and Becker, but Wilhelm-Rajmund would never see them because their habitat had been wiped out in Blue Earth County.

'The world is changing,' mused Oliver, during one of their lakeside vigils. 'Won't ever be the same again. We cut things down and we don't replace them. We take things away and we'll never find them again.'

Wilhelm-Rajmund ferreted at a loose stone buried in sandy shale, held it up for his father's inspection. 'Obviously igneous, Pa. But what's it doing here? It shouldn't be here.'

'I don't know, Willie. I don't know.'

'It's out of place.'

Which was exactly how Dieter felt, dressed in filthy khakis, waving his rifle like a crucifix, hoping it would save him. Scrambling his way through the Italian town, or what was left of it, he saw words he didn't understand painted on a ruined wall: Macceleria Scolaria. He crawled forward on his elbows, perhaps hoping to find something familiar, perhaps scenting something familiar, perhaps scenting pig's blood? Dieter rested against a wooden door, cradling his gun and scanning the streets and alleyways, unnerved by the silence, when he heard a faint sound behind the door. He strained to hear: a baby crying, a woman moaning. The noise stopped. Then began again, the baby's crying stifled now. Dieter pushed gently at the door and then flattened himself against the wall, waited for repercussions. There were none. He edged forward slowly, peered around the door jamb and saw a woman, saw the blood on her face. Saw her look at him. Dieter put his finger to his lips and it was at that moment he noticed the young blond man in the dark grey uniform, crouched behind the table, gun aimed at Dieter's chest, at Dieter's heart. There was just enough time for Dieter to think how familiar the young man looked, how in a different time they might have met and shared a beer in Mettler's bar.

*

Wilhelm-Rajmund admired his parents' belief in God, respected his mother for the depth of her faith, but this admiration and respect were the same he felt for his father's ability to flip a mature Yorkshire Large White boar on its back and his mother's ability to bake corn bread. In fact, it seemed to him that when his mother pulled open the stove, reached in with a gloved hand and produced a steaming, brown-crusted loaf, this was a more miraculous event than eating the body of Christ. A thought that occurred to him whenever he took the communion wafers on his tongue: the wafer itself was not miraculous but the fact that it was there at all was.

Wilhelm-Rajmund had doubts. He had doubts because he knew the earth had not been made in seven days, and if Genesis was flawed, if the story of the earth's *birth* was founded on a fallacy, then what of the rest of the Bible? If he couldn't be certain about the beginnings, then what? Because Wilhelm-Rajmund knew that the earth was millions of years old, that the Laurentian Shield had once been a massive mountain range and time and ice had eroded it. Lots of time and lots of ice had first worn and then washed the great peaks away. He knew that the reason the Yorkshires, Tamworths and Hampshires fattened on the land (Oliver had been right all along – the world wanted lean meat almost as much as it wanted blood) was because the land was rich till, formed from glacial deposits and nurtured under long prairie grass. It was not the hand of God which had done this, it was the earth itself.

The geography teacher at the high school, a Mr Svensson, encouraged Wilhelm-Rajmund in his studies, lent him books from his own private library. Talked to the boy about continental drift, sial and sima, the Morohovičić Discontinuity line, the crust, mantle and core of the globe. Wilhelm-Rajmund sat every evening in his room and read about igneous and sedimentary rocks, about deposition and erosion, brea fields and polar deserts – amazing deserts of sand sitting in ice. Mr Svensson also gave him a geological table as a present – an overview, almost a biography, of the earth's life so far. Wilhelm-Rajmund learned about the major eras, read the footnotes, discovered carbon in all its forms, and knew that either God or Mr Svensson was lying.

Yet by the time he was fourteen, Wilhelm-Rajmund did have *some* idea why people might need faith. He'd stand at his dormer window

and look at the earth below, at the fields, woods, lakes and hills –
floating, all floating on the surface of the mantle. America was floating away from Europe, tearing itself apart as Baja sought the
companionship of the Pacific Ocean plate, which was hunkering
down, nosing its way beneath Alaska. Anyone might need faith to
live on a thin, brittle crust, floating for eternity on a lake of elements
boiling at five thousand degrees.

Oliver and Irochka no longer played the game of creating lives and
professions for their grandchildren. Neither said it, but they both
looked back on those times – when the farmhouse was so new it
smelled of sawn timber and the two of them lay in their bed giggling
at the future fecundity of their sons – as being at the edge of their
memories, almost as if two other people had lived it. What surprised
them when they recalled the game they had played was that they
had never given a thought to what Siggy and Deet would do. Why
not? Because Siggy and Deet would stay on the farm, buy more
land, build houses for their children. And later the brothers would sit
on the porch with Oliver and Irochka (old, now, but hale and hearty)
and reminisce about the time Deet caught a fourteen-pounder in
Home Lake, when Siggy threw a fifty-eight-yard pass for a touchdown against St Peter's in Nicollet, when Deet fell through
ice-fishing and Siggy saved him, when the hook caught Willie's leg.
Yes, Siggy and Deet would stay on the farm, so what was the point
in creating lives for them? Their lives were empty rooms simply
waiting for the boys to move in. But neither Irochka nor Oliver had
ever thought that their sons would volunteer, and had certainly
never thought that their sons would see Europe. To be sure, Siggy
and Deet may not have seen Europe at its best, but they did see it.

Every Saturday morning Wilhelm-Rajmund was allowed to sleep in
a little later than the rest of the week, because he didn't have school
and he went to mass on Sundays. He'd drift, hovering in a dreamy
state, half hallucinating volcanic eruptions, touchdown passes, kissing a girl, scenes that began as fantasy then slid into deep sleep. What
always woke him was the smell of frying bacon – bacon from the
deep-sided Tamworths on the farm, home-slaughtered, home-dry-

cured. Washed and dressed in jeans and a soft flannel shirt, he'd walk into the kitchen to find his father and mother talking, Irochka flicking hot oil over eggs and slicing her miraculous bread. In winter the range and wood-burning stove kept the kitchen toasty, in summer the doors and windows would be wide open to catch the breezes cooled by Home Lake. This was Wilhelm-Rajmund's favourite part of the week: Saturday mornings, when the three of them sat and ate eggs, links and bacon with *placki kartoflane*, small, savoury potato pancakes. They'd talk about the week past – the problems with drainage in a boggy field, a failed delivery of feed, a sow that had rejected her litter. Irochka would gossip mildly about church acquaintances and Wilhelm-Rajmund told them about his studies and his sport. They'd talk about the week to come – Wilhelm-Rajmund's football training on Tuesday, Oliver going to Mankato on Thursday for market, Irochka's attempts to persuade the editor of the Bow Regard newsletter to include a Polish recipe page. Wilhelm-Rajmund sat there, safe, loved, and felt himself growing, felt his shoulders and neck thickening, his beard ever rougher, his hands stronger, and he was content.

Wilhelm-Rajmund never wasted any of his time trying to figure out what he would look like when he was older – all he had to do was think of Siegfried, his doppelgänger, and he knew. He knew what his voice would sound like, how tall he would be, how long in the thigh. There were differences – the dent in his thigh, for instance, or the twist in his left canine – but these were minor. Wilhelm-Rajmund did, however, waste some time worrying that he wasn't as good, as caring, as *moral* as Siegfried. One spring morning, before Siggy volunteered, when the two of them were in the stables cleaning and polishing the bits and stirrups, Wilhelm-Rajmund took courage and told Siggy he'd stolen two candy bars from Munchssen's.

Siggy looked at Wilhelm-Rajmund for a moment and then returned to buffing the leather of a harness. 'Well, that ain't right, Willie, and y'know it.'

Wilhelm-Rajmund felt relieved that someone else knew what he'd done, and especially because that person was Siggy. 'Don't know why I did it. Had enough money to buy 'em.'

'Lotsa kids do it. Some of them keep doing it and that's when it gets serious.' Siggy dropped the harness and lit a cigarette, leaned back against the rough boards of the barn's walls. 'I did it once. Took a box of hooks from Krankowiec's in Mankato. And I don't know why I did it. Didn't need the darn things – just took 'em because I could.'

'What happened?'

'Pa found it, found the box in my room. He asked me if I'd taken it and I told him yes.'

'Did he give you a whipping?'

Siggy laughed. 'Pa's never given any of us a whipping, Willie. Nah – he just looked sad, kinda . . . hurt. He took me back the next day and I had to hand over the hooks and apologize. Never did it again. Never wanted to.'

'Why not? Because you're scared of being found out?'

Siggy smoked for a while, thinking. 'I don't think it's that. I think it's maybe because I got all I want anyway. And, too, I don't want to make Pa look like that again.' He stood, brushed the muck from his jacket. 'And I know it's wrong and so do you. Come on.'

Wilhelm-Rajmund looked up from the bit he was polishing. 'Where we going?'

'Munchssen's. Go get the candy bars. You still got 'em?'

'Yah. Didn't want to eat 'em somehow.'

Wilhelm-Rajmund often thought about that morning; how they'd made some excuse to take the truck and drive into Bow Regard. How Siggy had made him go into the milk bar on his own to give the candy back and apologize to Karl Munchssen. But what worried Wilhelm-Rajmund was that, if he were honest, the only reason he hadn't done it again was the fear of being found out.

The smell of frying pork fat permeated Wilhelm-Rajmund's half-dream of doing things to Magde and he woke with a start, feeling guilty. Siegfried had asked him, after all, to watch out for her, not to feel her breasts. He dressed quickly, trying to move away from the dream, and trotted down the stairs. He kissed his mother, smiled at his father and stole a potato pancake from the plate on the table, chewing as he poured a glass of milk.

'Hot today,' remarked Oliver. 'Already eighty-two in the shade.

Reckon it's going to be the hottest yet. Wouldn't be surprised if this isn't a record-breaker of a summer.' Wilhelm-Rajmund noted that they were speaking German that day.

'You say that every summer,' said Irochka, putting a plate of bacon in front of Wilhelm-Rajmund.

'This year feels different – not as much moisture in the air. Bad for pigs, good for snakes.'

'You say that every summer too.'

Wilhelm-Rajmund ate as his parents bantered, as they did most mornings. It was a ritual, they both knew the script. But then the script changed.

'What's that?' Oliver looked up from his pancakes. The sound of an engine approaching on the long, hard-packed dirt track leading from the local road to the farm. Oliver wiped his mouth and hands. 'That fool Wojciek Jancker told me he was coming at noon – you know, to deliver the feed pellets. Now what – he wants to ruin my breakfast?' Oliver, still holding his fork, napkin tucked in his collar, went to the open door and out on to the porch. Said nothing.

Irochka, sensing the unexpected, took the pan of eggs off the range, set it down and, wiping her hands on her apron, went to join her husband. The jeep rolled to a halt by the porch steps as Wilhelm-Rajmund, treading very carefully, treading very slowly, trying to slow time, trying even to put time in reverse, watched from the doorway.

The captain climbed out of the car, slipped his cap under his arm and looked at the family on the porch. Sighed quietly. This he hated – deciding who to give the telegram to, who to choose as the recipient of the wafer-thin, double-folded message. He nearly always chose the man, but something about Irochka – her height perhaps? – made him hesitate.

Wilhelm-Rajmund saw the man hesitate, saw him falter for a moment, then walk heavily up the steps, and ask, 'Mr Oliver Reichmann?'

'Yah.'

And Wilhelm-Rajmund hated himself then, because as he stood in the doorway, he heard a mantra in his mind, *Bitte, Gott, lass es Dieter sein. Bitte, Gott, lass es Dieter sein. Bitte, Gott, lass es Dieter sein.*

God must have been listening that fine June morning because it was.

1958

Each night Miss O'Toole lay in her bed, her crazy, crossed eyes flicking around her large, comfortable attic room in Jarman House, her mind locked on the problem of Maggie Regan. How could she break the girl? Nearly a year it had been and still Maggie Regan was as impertinent as ever. Not that it was anything that she did or said – oh no, that would have been easy to correct. It was simply that she had about her an air of impertinence, nothing you could put your finger on. She didn't have to do anything, she just had to *be* in order to anger Miss O'Toole. Of course, Miss O'Toole could perhaps have murmured a few words in Lady Jacqueline's ear and Maggie would have been out on the streets in moments. But Miss O'Toole had the feeling that the American had a soft spot for the girl. Anyway, that was not the point: no minion had ever encountered Miss O'Toole who had not been snapped like a reed. So, every night, Miss O'Toole lay sleepless in her room, plotting Maggie's downfall, her hands opening and closing as she gripped and released the bedspread.

The reason Miss O'Toole could not unsettle Maggie, of course, was because her private world, peopled by fantasy friends with whom she lived a fabulous life, had become more vivid than the world in which she actually lived. Maggie now had access to a wealth of new material with which to weave her fantasies – Jacqueline had long since realized that when Maggie served at dinner, male guests were generally more animated. So Maggie would stand in the shadows of the sumptuous dining room for hours, watching the great and good at play, noting the fashions of the women, the demeanour of the men. Many times, as she leaned over the table to remove plates or replenish water jugs, a man's hand would rest for a moment on the back of her thigh. Maggie noted the warmth but felt nothing about the action. (The only time she had been surprised yet flattered was when the hand had been a woman's.)

Over the months after her arrival at Jarman House, Maggie moved from a state of fear to a state of near-terminal boredom. The work she was expected to do – cleaning, polishing, preparing food for the cook, waiting at the dining table – was arduous but dull. The only relief from the boredom came at weekends when Maggie was given time off, and for the first few weeks she spent these days sitting on the bed in her room, her hands folded in her lap, wondering whether this was life and, if so, could she bear it? But her fear of going out alone on to the streets of London, which she guessed to be dark and unfamiliar, trapped her. She passed the hours between meals taken in the kitchen trying to recall in every detail her encounters with Danny Maconnell – the feel of his skin, the smell of his shirt. Tried to recall the sensations occasioned by his kisses, his fondling of her breasts. But these musings only amplified the boredom.

This peneplain of tedium was also broken by the occasional weekend trips to Sherston Park, the Coopers' country house. The kitchens there were ancient and ill equipped and Maggie was sent up on Thursdays to help prepare the guests' food for the weekend. She enjoyed the journey up there, on a slow train to Oxford and then change for Charlbury, where she was collected. The rocking of the train, the motion of the wheels, lulled her as she drifted, between kisses and cliffs, the butchered gardens of the Whyte House and pebbled beaches. She could conjure the sound of razorbills, the smell of tatties and bacon, the feel of her sister Mary's breath on her neck as they tried to sleep in a jumble of bodies. Maggie discovered that if she drifted in a certain way, if she breathed slow and deep, her eyes closed, she could imagine herself into her father's van, could spend an afternoon with him, rocking and bouncing across the roads of Mayo.

Gradually, Maggie learned to live a new life as she shed the old. She began to venture out and walk the streets and parks of London; she no longer went to mass, she thought about Danny Maconnell less and less often; she barely remembered the view over Blacksod Bay. Instead, all week Maggie hoarded her memories of the suppers and the cocktail parties, kept them clean and sharp so she could slot them razor-like, without damage, into the moving images that played themselves out every weekend as she strolled through Hyde Park. Come winter, when London was sleek with rain, cold as death, she visited the museums, seeking out warm spots where she could sit and watch Londoners shuffle past, overawed by history. She sat, in a near-swoon, dreaming, dreaming of how things could be different, surrounded by minerals, fading ball gowns and stuffed ocelots.

Sir Sidney Cooper was an eejit, Maggie thought; cheerful and harmless but an eejit none the less. At first she couldn't imagine why a woman as young and beautiful as Jacqueline Cooper was married to him. The old man had a hacking cough, thin grey hair and a bulging stomach. To be sure, Sir Sidney was always nice, but why had Jacqueline, with her seductive American accent, hourglass figure and knowing look, agreed to marry him? It didn't take Maggie long to unravel this problem, for she, like her employer, had smarts. Money – pure and simple. Money and opportunity. It took Maggie a while longer to work out what the opportunities were. Occasionally she entered a room to find Lady Cooper on the phone, smiling in a certain way. Other times Lady Cooper left the house unexpectedly, for a couple of hours, and returned without evidence of having been shopping, nor having met a lady friend for lunch. And when she returned from these sudden forays, she seemed different. It took Maggie a while, but she soon deduced that Lady Cooper had a lover, perhaps even more than one. It took Maggie a while longer to realize that Sir Sidney was not the eejit she had thought.

One October evening, when she had been in service for nearly a year, Maggie served an informal supper for the Coopers in the garden room and half listened to the usual dull talk over the table that passed for conversation when servants were present.

'The point is, my dear,' said Sir Sidney, spearing a carrot, 'English business simply won't compete unless it diversifies.'

'That so?' Jacqueline lazily heaped her plate with salad, picked at it.

'Take nuts.' Sir Sidney chewed and swallowed, swigged from his glass. 'How much easier if there were global calibrations.'

'Quite so,' murmured Jacqueline, who had by then lived in England for seven years and learned a number of conversational tics.

'Energy – that's what we need.'

Jacqueline watched her ageing husband as he pursued a lone pea around his dinner plate. Giving up the chase, Sir Sidney placed his knife and fork down carefully, eyeing the offending vegetable. 'Energy,' he repeated, and launched into a coughing fit as Maggie deftly cleared the table.

Jacqueline lit a cigarette and Maggie placed a lead-crystal glass ashtray at her elbow.

'Met a chap at the Reform today. Damned interesting – Yankee from somewhere, forget where. He was having lunch with . . . what's his name? . . . Reginald . . . Reginald – oh, it will come to me. Anyway, joined them for a couple of brandies and this Yankee, what he said, well! Had all the figures to go with it. Said that the number of cars in England would double in two years. That by the end of the century millions will have them, literally millions of people in England will have cars. Can you believe it? We'll need more roads, more petrol stations – gas stations, he called them. But what he said that was most interesting was that we'll also need more service stations, you know, where cars are serviced and mended. You know what that means?'

Jacqueline shaped the tip of her cigarette, glanced at Maggie, who was in profile, thought how beautiful the girl was, and replied, 'Tell me.'

'Spare parts – the whole world will need spare engine parts. Now, I'm wondering, I have been thinking since that conversation, can the Cooper company supply these? We do, after all, have the machinery, we have plant in Sheffield that can be modified, a workforce in place. Of course, people will always need a screw, but is there a larger market?'

Jacqueline smiled as she motioned for Maggie to refill her wine-glass. 'I have no doubt there will be.'

'Anyway, this Yankee has a lot to say for himself. Nice fellow, very bright. I've asked him up to Sherston next weekend.' Sir Sidney weathered another coughing fit. 'You'll like him. Thought it would be interesting for him to encounter another side of English life.'

Jacqueline sipped wine before she asked the question to which she suspected she already knew the answer. 'What was this Yank's name?'

'A Mr Rickman. I'd like to introduce him to Isobel. I can see those two hitting it off.'

Jacqueline shifted in her chair, stubbed out the cigarette. 'To be honest, Sidney, we have a full house next weekend. It might be better to invite him some other time.'

'I have invited Mr Rickman and he'll be there. He has already accepted.'

'Has he indeed?'

'There is no room for discussion, my dear. This is business. I need to talk to him in a . . . a . . . congenial atmosphere.'

'All I'm suggesting—'

Maggie Regan, who was stacking crockery, was arrested in her movements by the tone of Sir Sidney's next utterance.

'Mr Rickman will visit Sherston Park next weekend. And you will make him feel welcome.'

Jacqueline gathered together her cigarettes and lighter, stood. 'Maggie, no coffee for me. Goodnight, Sidney.'

'*Where* did you say it was?' asked Billy-Ray, incredulously, as he lay in bed next to Jacqueline.

'Slaughter on the Water.'

'You're kidding me. You've got to be kidding me.'

Jacqueline laughed. 'I'm not – the Brits have some very weird place names. Slaughter on the Water isn't the craziest one I've heard, but it comes close.'

'How do I get there?'

'Well, your driver will know. It's not far, just in Oxfordshire.'

'I'm coming from Dover – I'm in Brussels the day before, but that's fine. It'll be interesting anyhow.'

'I doubt it. You're in for a dull weekend of kedgeree and billiards. Can you shoot?'

'Sure I can.'

'Sidney's setting up a clay-pigeon shoot on Sunday before lunch. I think he'll expect you to tag along.'

'Clay pigeons?'

'Well, they don't look like pigeons. I mean, they're not like little pigeon statues. They're clay discs that are thrown up in the air and you shoot them.'

A silence fell as Billy-Ray considered the English concept of slaughter, on the water or otherwise. 'OK.'

Hours later Billy-Ray screamed, three, four, five times, before Jacqueline swam out of her deep sleep. They were staying in a discreet, expensive hotel near Bray and the hammering at the door shocked her.

'What?' she yelled, looking around wildly. 'What?' She recognized her lover, screaming, remembered she was in a hotel, spoke through the door to the night porter, and returned to the bed. Wrapping her arms around Billy-Ray, she rocked him as he whimpered. 'What's up? Billy-Ray? What's up? You had a bad dream?'

Billy-Ray nodded, whimpered once more.

Jacqueline kept her arms locked around him, rocked him for the best part of an hour, until her neck was stiff, her fingers aching. She felt him grow suddenly, as if his body were spreading like jelly, and she knew he was unfurling. Letting him go by degrees, she settled back, rubbed her hands, flexed her neck. 'What was that about? You must have had a nightmare.'

'Yes.' Billy-Ray's voice sounded different: flattened, smaller. 'I often have them. I've had them since I was a kid.' The image of a sheet being yanked back like a fore-sail made him whimper again, a tiny yip, so small it escaped unnoticed.

'You want to talk about it?'

'No.'

'OK. No problem.' Jacqueline leaned over to reach for a cigarette. 'Look, I tried to change the plans for the weekend, but I can't. You'll have to come. But behave yourself – OK? Don't drink too much. And don't forget – we never met.'

Billy-Ray said nothing, reached for Jacqueline's hand and placed it on the dent in his thigh, held it there.

Sherston Park seemed unimaginably old to Billy-Ray when his car pulled into the driveway of the Coopers' Jacobean mansion; grey

lichen was spattered in dime-size spots on the walls, moss clumped
on the roof slates. But there was no denying it was impressive: tall
chimney stacks, gables, gargoyle gutters, mullioned, diamond-
leaded windows, ochre freestone – this, then, was England?
Billy-Ray climbed out of the car and looked at the surrounding
fields, which were painted in dun and pale brown, grey and black,
rolling fields of thin soil, with no rivers visible. Billy-Ray pulled his
overcoat tighter – the November wind was cutting – turned back to
the house and there was Jacqueline, standing at a long window on
the second floor of the house, in a scarlet dress. She hadn't noticed
Billy-Ray and she was smoking pensively, occasionally touching her
lips with her fingertip. She looked so out of place, so dislocated, a
splash of fresh blood stark against the weight of ages, that he could
not look away. Evidently someone came into the room, spoke to her
and she replied, stubbed out her cigarette, adjusted her cardigan
and walked away from the ancient, bubbled glass.

Once he was in his room, Billy-Ray spent a while lying on his
bed, drinking vodka from the bottle, thinking of how displaced,
how *exiled*, Jacqueline had looked, framed by pock-marked
Cotswold stone. A long, long way from home was how she had
looked.

'Splendid of you to make the effort to visit, Mr Rickman. I know you
must be a busy man – just back from Brussels, I hear? Never been
there myself but I'm told it's a dismal place.' Sir Sidney looked grey
and wan but as paunchy as ever.

'Please, sir, call me Billy-Ray. Everyone does.'

'Well, thank you, I will. Now Billy-Ray, would you like a top-up
there? What is it? Gin and tonic?'

Billy-Ray registered a slight. Did not realize that the 'sir' he had
uttered was not the 'Sir' that was heard. (If sir was sir, sir and sir,
then why was it also Sir?) 'Vodka on the rocks, please.'

'Good Lord, never heard of anyone drinking that. Well, well.' Sir
Sidney motioned and a waitress approached. He handed her his
glass. 'Top that up, please. And a . . . what was it?'

Billy-Ray noticed the girl's disturbing green eyes, the thickness of
her blue-black hair. 'Um . . . vodka on the rocks.'

'A vodka with ice, please.' Sir Sidney smiled faintly, as if congratulating himself on his grasp of all matters transatlantic. 'Now, Billy-Ray, been wanting to continue with the conversation at the Reform. Remember? Talked about the growth of business in . . . Ah, excuse me. May I introduce you to my wife, Lady Cooper? Jacqueline, Mr Billy-Ray Rickman.'

Billy-Ray turned and there she was in her scarlet finery, her dark hair now lifted and folded into a chignon, her flawless skin powdered, walking towards them, a smile on her lips, pale hand extended.

'Mr Rickman, I'm delighted to meet you.' Jacqueline shook Billy-Ray's hand for a moment and then moved towards her husband, smiling still.

Billy-Ray stared at her. The troubled exile had disappeared, to be replaced by this charming, mannered, Anglicized version of the woman who folded her arms around his neck and lowered herself on to him. The waitress reappeared with a tray of drinks and Billy-Ray smiled at her, took note of her eyes again, took the vodka and downed the lukewarm spirit. 'Thank you, Lady Cooper, for inviting me. You sure have a fine house here.'

'Thank you.'

'Another of those?' asked Sir Sidney, nodding at Billy-Ray's glass.

'Yah, that'd be great.'

'Jacqueline, my dear, do you recall I told you about a chap who talked about the future of the car industry?'

'Yes, I do.'

'Well, this is the very chap. Seems to know everything there is to know about oil and petrol. I need to pick his brains' – Sir Sidney laughed, showing yellow teeth – 'so make sure you keep him happy. Billy-Ray, I apologize but I have to mingle. We'll talk after lunch.' Sir Sidney bumbled off in his seemingly absent-minded fashion.

Jacqueline sipped at her sherry and smiled winningly. 'So, Mr Rickman, what do you think of the Cotswolds? Behave and stay off the vodka, OK, buddy?' Her smile didn't waver.

Three hours later Billy-Ray found himself back in the drawing room, drinking lukewarm vodka once again – why did the English hand out their ice cubes one at a time? – watching Jacqueline, dressed now in a black Chanel. It was a dress he recognized: the dress she'd been wearing when she weaved her way towards him on the *Queen Mary* a year before.

Billy-Ray noticed a thin, pale man edging towards him across the drawing room, smiling faintly in the way the English seemed to favour. The man was slope shouldered, hollow stomached, his pants loose on his hips. He held out his hand.

'Been meaning to say hello. Tried to find you after lunch but you'd disappeared. Michael Cunningham.'

'Billy-Ray Rickman.'

Michael Cunningham's hand was cold and damp with sweat. Billy-Ray, who was maintaining a state somewhere between drunkenness and sobriety, floating on a braided brook of vodka, resisted the impulse to squeeze the bird bones in Michael Cunningham's hand.

'Heard you were in oil and that excited my interest.' Michael Cunningham smiled, displaying crooked, discoloured teeth. 'Damned interesting.'

'Sure is.' Billy-Ray didn't know whether to play hokey Minnesotan farm boy or *über* urbanite, would make the decision soon. He looked over at Jacqueline, whose eyes slid past his.

'So, where does it come from?' Michael Cunningham took a glass of dry sherry from a passing tray, raised it. 'Cheers.'

'Excuse me?'

'Oil, petrol – where does it come from? How is it formed?'

Billy-Ray frowned. 'I'm sorry – I thought you were interested in oil.'

'I am.'

'So . . . I mean, why? You're not in the business?'

Michael Cunningham smiled again, no doubt amused by the American habit of implying the interrogative by inflection rather than construction. 'Good Lord, no. I read Classics at Cambridge, class of forty-one, as I believe you would say. I'm a civil servant, a mandarin, as we describe it. Recruited in forty-four, when we were needed. Sorry, old chap, no doubt that's all a foreign language to you. But, anyway, I believe one should dabble in many different disciplines. Renaissance man has much to teach us.' Michael Cunningham was a man who gathered white, glutinous deposits of age-old spittle at the corners of his mouth, some of which stretched slightly in thin stringy hair-like strands as he spoke, like baleen.

Billy-Ray Rickman, who was as sharp as an edge of sheered slate, who had seen carbon in all its forms, who knew the refractive index of a diamond, was revolted by this musty relic of empire. Billy-Ray Rickman, who knew how to speak seven languages, made his decision and the Minnesotan farm boy faded. 'Mr Cunningham, please excuse me if I sound a little didactic, but no doubt you would be the same should I ask you about Classics. Petroleum, as we call it, as we Americans call it – you call it crude oil – is a complex substance—'

'I'm sure it must be.' Michael Cunningham smiled complacently.

'Petroleum is an organic chemical compound, which is found in gaseous, liquid and solid states. There are three classes of crude oil: paraffin, asphalt and mixed-base. Petroleum forms under the earth's surface, as a result of the decomposition of marine and land organisms washed down into a quiet sea basin—'

'What a delightful phrase! "A quiet sea basin". I can imagine it.' The baleen mouth closes, as the baleen mind loses itself in images of capricious, tempestuous seas, having read too much Percy Bysshe Shelley.

'—that is, a sea which has not been subjected to seismic shifts. The organisms are deposited in an ever-thickening layer, and eventually the sediment thickens to the point where it begins to sink. Obviously as the pressure rises, so does the temperature—'

'Obviously? I'm not sure about that, old chap.'

'I guess you didn't study physics?'

'Well, I did, but it was a long time ago and—'

'Laws of physics haven't changed.'

'Well, I may be a bit rusty.'

Billy-Ray, improbably handsome in his dinner jacket, smiled a farm-boy smile. 'I guess I'll keep it simple, then. Anyway, the pressure rises and the temperatures rise hundreds of degrees as a result. The mud and sand from the river deposits become shale and sandstone, the carbonate precipitates and skeletal shells become limestone – whether it's Jurassic or Triassic doesn't bother us here.'

'No, of course not.'

'So, of course, the remains of the dead organisms, the fats, the hydrocarbons, become crude oil. Makes perfect sense, doesn't it?' Billy-Ray looked at the mandarin.

'With you so far,' lied Michael Cunningham, taking a gulp of sherry.

'So, as anyone knows, the molecular density of the brine in the sediments is heavier than crude oil, and the oil rises through the pores in the shale and so on, and keeps going. Until, that is,' Billy-Ray downed the remnants of his vodka and looked around the room for the girl with the dangerously green eyes, 'it hits an impermeable layer – could be clay, could be granite, whatever the earth comes up with. But then it stops. Can't go any farther – inhibited migration, we call it – and then you get a petroleum reservoir. Hiding under thousands of feet of sand or sea. '

Michael Cunningham frowned, actually put a finger to his spittle-laced lips and frowned. 'Fascinating, fascinating. But Mr . . . Rickman, was it? . . . how do you *find* it?'

'Oh, that's real simple. You just have to locate shales and sandstone rich in organic matter, lying in a sedimentary basin that was once a sea, or maybe a delta, that has been subjected to a narrow range of climatic and seismic pressures and variations over – say – twenty million years.'

'Ah.' Michael Cunningham – Renaissance man (CBE) – gestured at the door. 'Nature calls, old chap. Must go to the john, as I believe you call it.' With a flash of rotting teeth he was gone, leaving Billy-Ray to his empty glass and rising heat.

The dining room was vast, high ceilinged, lit by two wavering, fitful fires; those diners seated at the ends of the table were scorched, those in the middle shivered quietly: frozen or burned. Billy-Ray was seated in the middle; on his right was Lady Sybil Fletcher, on his left an empty chair awaiting a guest who had not yet arrived. Despite the cold, Billy-Ray was firing as the vodka flowed through his body. He scanned the room and found Jacqueline watching him from the end of the table. She shook her head slightly.

Sir Sidney tapped a lead-crystal glass with his knife. 'A toast.'

The waitresses hurried forward to ensure all glasses were full and

Billy-Ray had to resist the temptation to run his hand up the green-eyed waitress's close, firm thigh.

Sir Sidney stood, staggered a little. Raised his glass. 'Queen and country.'

The assembled company stood. 'Queen and country.'

Billy-Ray and Jacqueline, still seated, smiled at each other for the first time that evening.

Sir Sidney looked at the two of them, lurched slightly, put his hand on the edge of the table to steady himself. 'Apologies for Boston and all that. Propose a second toast: apologies for Boston.'

'Apologies for Boston.'

Fortunately, before Billy-Ray had the chance to say that he didn't give a fuck about Boston, the dining-room doors opened and the Hon. Isobel Chalfont-Webbe was announced.

A few minutes later Billy-Ray was lost. He was trying to do so many things: manage the cutlery, catch Jacqueline's eye, drink and eat. He was by then quite drunk. Gradually he noticed the hand resting on the tablecloth next to his. Stared at it. It was a *huge* hand, with prominent knuckles and long fingers, manicured nails and calluses. It belonged to a woman: the Hon. Isobel. He was aware that he had not made the best effort to be sociable with his neighbour.

'Hi there,' he said. 'Billy-Ray Rickman.'

'Mr Rickman, how do you do? Isobel Chalfont.'

Billy-Ray stared into a pair of eyes so blue they put his own to shame, made them appear almost muddy. 'You missed the cocktails.'

'Yes, unfortunately. I was unavoidably detained.' In fact, Isobel's favourite hunter had broken a leg in a bad fall and had been shot that afternoon.

Something about Isobel brought Billy-Ray round, made him wish he were sober. 'You live near here?'

'Yes. Just outside Stow-on-the-Wold. It's not far. Do you know the Cotswolds?'

'No. I only arrived this morning. Haven't had the opportunity to look around yet. Looks very interesting.'

'It's not, particularly.'

Billy-Ray laughed.

Isobel dabbed her lips, closed her knife and fork on her plate, leaving the food half eaten. 'Where in America are you from?'

'Minnesota, originally.'

'That's right. Americans never seem to stay in the same place, always moving, always from somewhere else originally. Are you here on holiday?'

'No, I work in Waterloo, in London, for Karbo Inc. It's an oil company.'

'I know that, Mr Rickman. I happen to own a substantial number of shares in it.'

Billy-Ray suppressed the desire to ask whether she was shitting him. Isobel Chalfont couldn't be more than twenty. 'Good investment.'

Isobel turned to talk to her other neighbour, giving Billy-Ray the opportunity to study her profile – she was what was called an English beauty. Fine blonde hair, smooth pale skin with full, bloody lips. Something about her snagged Billy-Ray; like a stocking on a nail, a thigh on a hook. He glanced up the table to find Jacqueline watching him again, a fingertip brushing her lips.

'So, Mr Rickman, what do you do in London?' The blue-blue eyes were trained on him again.

'Buy up independent European gas companies, check out prospective drilling sites.'

'You must travel a great deal.'

'Yah – I'm often away. In fact, got back from Brussels this morning.' Why was he trying to impress this woman?

'Do you enjoy it?'

'The travelling? Well,' Billy-Ray shrugged, not wanting to think about running, 'I guess I do.'

'I really meant do you enjoy what you do, your job?'

Billy-Ray frowned. 'Do I enjoy it?' He thought for a moment – no one had ever asked him this question. 'No, I don't.' He surprised himself.

'Why not?'

'I don't like cities much. That's not true. I like them, it's just . . .' The vodka had loosened Billy-Ray's tongue (that cultured, educated muscle). 'Well, I guess if I'm honest, I don't really like them. Don't get me wrong – London's OK, but sometimes I wish I was some-where else.'

'Where?'

'I wish I was in Alaska.'

'Alaska?'

'Yah. I lived there before I came out here. I didn't used to buy oil, I used to find it. Used to work out in the field, finding it. Around the Cook Inlet in the Kenai. Y'know, there was no one there, out towards the Swanson River, except us. Sometimes we took samples out in Tuxedni Bay, got near swamped by humpbacks. Or we'd fly out to Katmai, disturb the grizzlies.'

'Well, I can see Waterloo would be a little dull after that.'

'I heard a while ago they finally brought it up, in Middle Shoals. I should have been there. I spent three years surveying there, I should have been there when they hit pay dirt.' Billy-Ray was sur-prised by nostalgia, put it down to the vodka.

'Why don't you go back? Back to Alaska?'

Billy-Ray was staring at the flames of the fire, thinking of sitkas and salmon, replaying the sound of gunshot, the glimpse of an eagle's maddened golden eye. He turned to Isobel. 'I'm going to.'

Jacqueline, elegant and predatory as ever, drifted over to Billy-Ray the next morning as he was heaping his plate with kedgeree from a heated silver tureen. 'Had kedgeree before?' she asked.

'Nah. Is it good?'

'It's an acquired taste. What are your plans for the day?' Jacqueline lowered her voice. 'Thought maybe you'd like to meet up later.'

Billy-Ray felt the base tug of lust at the tail of his spine, felt blood run swiftly through his fingertips. 'Where?'

'After lunch people will sleep, or maybe go into town. No one will be around – it's like a ghost town after two o'clock. Come to my room. Top of the right-hand stairs, third door on the right. I was just saying to Billy-Ray that kedgeree is an acquired taste.'

Sir Sidney nodded absently. 'Certainly is. Billy-Ray, came to see if you were up for the shoot. Hope so, hope so. Cars are leaving in half an hour. Couldn't find you after lunch yesterday and want to have a word with you.'

It was a journey of less than two miles to the field where the traps were set, over slithering mud, crushed branches, past cows ruminating as they chewed, turning in unison to look at the convoy. The field was at the head of a low bluff and Billy-Ray could see the Cotswolds stretching to the distance, beige and dun, etched with the white lines of walls, scarred by the blacktop of roads. Twenty, maybe twenty-five people, dressed in a uniform of green Barbours and Hunter boots, were milling around a shooting brake, its back lowered to form a table for the flasks of coffee and tea. Beyond the car was a tall rack, filled with shotguns, ammunition in boxes on the ground. Although the silver sun was well up, the distant, low-lying mist and funereal drapes of the land made Billy-Ray shiver. He was wearing a red plaid wool jacket: a popinjay among a flock of starlings. A figure detached itself from the crowd and walked towards him, hands swinging, as Billy-Ray tried to remember exactly what he had said the night before.

'Hi there again,' he said.

'Good morning,' said Isobel. 'I didn't see you at breakfast.'

'Nah – I slept late.' Billy-Ray was looking straight into Isobel's robin's-egg eyes. She was six feet tall. He thought of his mother, heard gunshot, and quickly asked, 'The guns – what are they?'

'Trap guns, full-choke, twenty-eight-inch. Some are three-quarter-choke, and there's two sports, on tightest tube. I like your jacket, Mr Rickman.'

'Billy-Ray. Please call me Billy-Ray.'

Isobel sipped steaming coffee from a cup, scanned the view. 'Do you shoot?'

'Yah – when I lived on the farm we used to hunt. We had mallards and gadwalls all over. And, of course, wild turkeys, but you wouldn't waste the shot. Our farm was on the migration route, y'see, from Canada down to the south. They call it the Mississippi Flyway – like an interstate for birds. What's the set-up here?'

'I think Sir Sidney's arranged a down-the-line sporting – it's not pure but it's fun. Something he concocted. Sometimes we have skeet—'

'Shoot,' said Billy-Ray.

'I beg your pardon?'

'Skeet – it's Swedish for "shoot".'

'How interesting. I didn't know that.'

'What's this down-the-line sporting?' Billy-Ray wanted Isobel to talk, to keep talking, wanted Isobel to stop the tall, blonde woman raising the shotgun and firing over and over.

'It's really very simple, and very good for beginners – although somehow I don't think you'll count as a beginner.' Billy-Ray noticed Isobel was wearing no make-up, yet her lips were bright red, red as the blood of a pinprick. 'Right – down there,' she pointed with her strangely large-knuckled forefinger, 'is the trap. It's a machine that fires the clay targets in the air, ten feet from the ground at the lowest up to the highest point in their possible trajectory. In some ways it's easy because the targets always rise at a constant angle, but it is random across the horizontal plane and the maximum arc is forty-four degrees. So you have to be alert. We fire from five stations and five targets per station is what we'd call straight down the line, but Sir Sidney mixes it up with sporting, so two targets are released each time and you have two cartridges. One target is ten points, two targets twenty, so the maximum is five hundred points. Couldn't be more simple.'

'What's a station?'

'It's the point you shoot from. For beginners it's about sixteen yards from the trap but there are handicap distances, from seventeen to twenty-seven yards.'

Billy-Ray looked into Isobel's clear eyes, colour in a drab landscape. 'Where do *you* shoot from? I mean, how far is your station?'

'Twenty-seven yards, Mr Rickman.'

'Billy-Ray, please.'

'A word of advice – the cartridge load is twenty-eight grams, and there are seven-and-a-half and eight cartridges. Use an eight for the first target and a seven-and-a-half for the second, then you reduce the load to give yourself time.'

'Pull!' The two of them jumped as an ear-splitting crack racketed round the bluff and wood pigeons broke from the trees, clattering skyward.

Two hours later Billy-Ray and Isobel stood together at the first station, twenty-seven yards from the trap, as the others gathered by the shooting brake, tipping the remnants of hip flasks into glasses, finishing the last of the coffee, watching them. Isobel had scored four hundred and seventy from twenty-seven yards, Billy-Ray a perfect five hundred from sixteen. It was Isobel, sweating a little, sweating on her upper lip, who had suggested a sudden-death play-off.

'I knew you wouldn't be a beginner,' she said, wiping residue from her hands with a cloth, the broken shotgun resting comfortably on her arm. 'That was too easy for you.'

Billy-Ray, who'd enjoyed a few tipples from various hip flasks as his success was toasted, laughed. 'Fish in a barrel.'

'Would you accept a challenge?'

'Depends what it is.'

'You need a handicap – a twenty-seven-yard handicap.' Isobel wiped hard at a smudge on her thumb. 'I suggest that you and I have another round, shooting from the same stations.'

'What's in it for me?' Billy-Ray laughed again, full of air, whisky and Isobel's lips. 'You know us Americans – we bet on which fly moves first.'

'No bets, Billy-Ray.'

'Let's go. Twenty-seven yards.'

'I'll speak to the trap boys.'

Billy-Ray rubbed his thigh, looked at the sun, low as a spinning clay pigeon, sliding dime-size across the landscape. 'Mind if I ask you a question?'

'Of course not.' Yet Isobel Chalfont stiffened a little, seemed wary.

'How old are you?'

'Twenty-one.'

And now the two of them were standing at the first station, shotguns loaded, being watched by a ragtag crowd of landed gentry and passing hikers.

'Shall we toss a coin for the first?' asked Isobel.

'Ladies first,' said Billy-Ray.

'Pearls before swine,' replied Isobel, snapping the shotgun to, raising it, shouting 'Pull!', setting the stock on her shoulder and blasting both clay pigeons to smithereens.

'Shit,' muttered Billy-Ray, who wanted to win.

He didn't, of course. Isobel scored a near-perfect four hundred and ninety, missing one target out of fifty, and Billy-Ray scored four hundred and seventy. He didn't look at Isobel until the echoes of the last shot had died, not wanting to see a tall, blonde woman recoiling from gunshot, reminding him, once more, of his mother.

Once the shoot was over, once the back-slapping and toasts were done, blankets were rolled, glasses emptied and the ersatz hunters piled into the cars, Isobel touched Billy-Ray's elbow.

'Would you care to walk back? There's a bridle path across the fields. It can be a lovely walk, especially at this time of year.'

'I certainly would.'

Isobel walked quickly and Billy-Ray had to step out to keep up with her as she pointed out various berries and birds. Pheasants scooted across their path as Billy-Ray told Isobel about the wood-chucks, gophers and coyotes that appeared on the farm. Reaching the end of the bluff, as he told her about the raccoons waking him in the night rummaging through the barns and yard looking for food, Isobel stopped, pointed out Sherston Park below and asked for a cigarette.

'Sorry, didn't know you smoked.'

'I don't, not really. But occasionally I like to have one. I'd prefer it if Mummy and Daddy didn't know, so I don't smoke at home.'

Billy-Ray flicked his worn brass Zippo and Isobel wrapped her extraordinary hands around his, lowered her face towards his palms. He resisted the urge to stroke her cheek with his forefinger. 'I got another question for you.'

'You're very inquisitive.'

'Not really. I just wondered what this "honourable" tag means. You know, when you came last night you were called the Honourable Isobel Chalfont something.'

Isobel smiled. 'Chalfont-Webbe. Ridiculous name. I drop the "Webbe" most of the time. And I'm afraid the "honourable" has nothing to do with my character. It simply means I'm the daughter of a lord.'

'That sounds very grand. Very . . . very English.'

'Well, it would, wouldn't it? No other country has the same class system. I actually think it's insane. Daddy goes up to Town every now and then for a sitting in the House of Lords and votes on bills that have nothing to do with him. He votes on issues to do with housing and welfare, state education and hospitals, as if he has any idea about it. I mean, good Lord, we don't even have a constitution as such. We're all subjects and not citizens.'

'What d'you mean? You got no Bill of Rights?'

'No.'

Billy-Ray frowned. 'That don't seem right.'

'Well, of course it's not,' said Isobel with some spirit. 'But I have a feeling things are changing. And about time. You may think that England is all country homes and shoots, dinners and drinks parties, but it's not. Some people have very little. I do realize, though, that I'm hardly in a position to pass judgement.' She dropped the cigarette on the damp grass, ground it out and motioned for them to begin walking again. In the hollows they could see silver mist gathering as cows lumbered through the fields, following deep-worn tracks back to the milking sheds. 'America must be quite a country.'

'It is. Can't say I've seen much of it but what I have seen is different from here. I haven't been down south but I was in New York for a few days.'

'Have you been to Hollywood?'

A postcard sailed through Billy-Ray's mind. 'Nah. I'd like to see California though. I'd like to go to Yosemite.'

'What's that?'

Walking the last half-mile back to the house, Billy-Ray told Isobel about the waterfalls and ice-sculpted landscape. As they reached the gates of Sherston Park, Billy-Ray gesturing with his hands to show the three stages of Yosemite Falls – 'nearly two and a half thousand feet all in all' – he remembered that Jacqueline had been waiting for him to appear in her bedroom.

Jacqueline was glacial that evening, cold-shouldering Billy-Ray's attempts at apology. After supper, tables were set up in the library for bridge and two foursomes congregated, one including Jacqueline, who knew Billy-Ray didn't play, the other including Isobel. The remaining guests settled in the drawing room, drinking, reading papers and magazines, chatting quietly. Billy-Ray was bored, restless, prowled around the rooms, scanning book titles, magazine covers. He endured half an hour's conversation with Sir Sidney about the finer points of the internal combustion engine; it seemed, after all, to be the payment expected for enjoying the man's hospitality.

'Help yourself to anything you want, old chap,' Sir Sidney said, waving vaguely around the room.

Billy-Ray did. He took a bottle of vodka and an ice bucket into the conservatory at the back of the house and sat drinking, watching the night sky, lounging on the antique chaise longue he found in there. Which was how Isobel found him when her bridge was finished.

'Dreaming of Alaska?' she asked, sitting opposite him.

'I was just thinking the sky here is beautiful.'

'Don't you have eternal nights in Alaska?'

Billy-Ray sat up. 'Not down south. Up north above the Arctic Circle we do. It's to do with the curvature of the earth. In summer, around Kenai, the sun doesn't set till maybe two in the morning. Looks like it just dips down beneath the mountains and then rises again.'

'It sounds wonderful. I'd love to go there – you make it sound magical.'

Billy-Ray – who had been taught by his father to be wary of garter snakes, to be wary of the unexpected – turned suddenly, to see Jacqueline in the doorway. How long had she been there, watching them?

'I came to say goodnight, Isobel. Mr Rickman, will we see you in the morning?'

'Nah. I have to be back at work, so I'll be leaving early.'

'That's a shame. Still, it's been nice meeting you.' And Jacqueline was gone, leaving a golden, empty space in the doorway.

'Could I have one of those?' Isobel nodded at the vodka.

'Sure thing. I'll get you a glass.'

In the drawing room, a few diehard guests were still sitting near the fire, nursing brandies. Maggie, who was clearing ashtrays and tidying tables, wishing she could go to bed, glanced up and saw the tall blond American man who'd stared at her earlier.

'Can I help you?' she asked, straightening her aching back.

'I need a fresh glass.' Once again, Billy-Ray was arrested by Maggie's eyes, vivid as basswood leaves, sharp as glass splinters.

'Just a minute, sir. I'll fetch you one.' Maggie reappeared moments later with an etched lead-crystal tumbler.

Billy-Ray Rickman, who had mastered seven languages, wanted to speak and remain silent equally. Wanted both to talk to the green-eyed girl and to say nothing. Wanted to reach out and touch her lips with his fingertips. He took the tumbler and smiled. 'Thank you.'

Isobel, who had never drunk vodka before, didn't like it but nevertheless sipped and chipped away at it. The two of them sat in the conservatory until past midnight, Isobel telling Billy-Ray about the mountains she knew – in Switzerland, where she had been to finishing school – and asking him questions about America.

'Well, I must say goodnight. I shan't see you in the morning, I shouldn't think. Daddy's sending a car at eleven.'

Billy-Ray stood too, facing her, looking straight into those blue eyes. Isobel held out a hand and he took it, shook it and felt its weight, its size. 'It's been great meeting you.'

'I was wondering if you'd care to come up this way again and see the stately pile I call home. Perhaps you'd like to visit us for a week-end at some point.'

'I certainly would.'

Isobel wrote down her address and telephone number. 'You could ring me when you have a free weekend. Do you ride?'

'Yah.'

'And maybe we could have another go at the clay pigeons, see if you can beat me.'

'Sounds great.'

'Goodnight, then.'

Dawn the next morning, the sky flushed pink, the crunch of gravel like gunshot in the cold, brittle air as he walked to his car, and Billy-Ray Rickman turned back to look at Sherston Park for a last time. He caught a movement in a leaded window on the second floor. Jacqueline was watching him. Dressed in a beige housecoat, she no longer looked displaced but, rather, she blended, now, into the stonework framing her. Billy-Ray raised a hand but Jacqueline didn't move.

THE CHALFONT-WEBBES

The Chalfont-Webbes could trace their roots across centuries, through a vast, organic, dendritic mass of couplings and alliances. Originally French Huguenots, the Chalfonts never entirely shook off the blandishments, the seductions, of Catholicism. After all, pure faith was all well and good, but it wasn't as easy on the eye as a gilt-ridden church. Nor, to be honest, was it as easy on the soul. The Chalfonts had an intemperate, almost sybaritic streak running through them, as enduring as a vein of silica in sandstone, a streak that caused them many problems over the centuries. The marriage of the Chalfont name with that of the Yorkshire Webbes was an attempt to instil some backbone, some fixedness, some *restraint* in the blood line. Perhaps, for a while, it worked; after all, the clay from the Chalfont pits in Cornwall flowed north to the Webbe potteries in Staffordshire, ensuring pots of money were made. Titles were conferred, vast estates built, sons sent out to the colonies to spread their seed and influence. The Chalfont-Webbes prospered through the Industrial Revolution, through the Boer Wars, the Great War, the urbanization of Europe. So many shelves to be filled.

Any compromise, however, any negotiation, requires that a price is paid, either by one party or many. Newtonian physics do, after all, dictate that action and reaction are equal and opposite. The Webbe blood may well have been more stolid, slow flowing and reassuring, but the Chalfont blood, a quixotic sanguinary mix of the Roman and the Gallic, with a little Vandal thrown in for seasoning, was a heady brew. The result, as Newton would have noted, was a pendulum swinging between generations, as one generation became pastors and reformers and the next reprobates and adulterers. Dissolute sons were left to rot in Tasmania, and soon forgotten; fallen daughters walked the streets of Rome, never mentioned. Romance and rigour: a turbulent meeting, as turbulent as the waters in the Gulf of Alaska. By the time Isobel Alice Rowney Chalfont-Webbe arrived, the Chalfont-Webbe blood had been much diluted by mimsying Celts and dour Visigoths. Yet there was still a sufficient number of Chalfont-Webbe platelets to ensure she was both reformer and reprobate.

Isobel's first memory, which she thought must have been when she was three or four, was of standing at the nursery window, her hands (large even then) pressed against the glass, breath misting and clearing a heart-shaped cloud, watching her parents, two floors below. First she saw their shadows, long and thin, stretching across the tiled floor of the entrance to the house, black shadows moving on a golden rhomboid of light. Then her mother and father, dressed in finery, foxes and tuxes, walked gracefully across to the waiting car, their arms linked. The chauffeur was standing stiffly in the November cold, breath swirling, holding the door open. Just as her father was about to climb in, he stopped and looked up, scanned the blind face of the house until he saw Isobel, and he raised a hand and waved. Isobel lay awake all that night, convinced her father had been waving goodbye, that she would never see him again. She spent a fretful night, saying nothing to Nanny, for she was, already, a forbearing girl, used to solving problems for herself. Dawn found her pressed against the glass once more, her large palms freezing against the early morning frost. As the sun appeared, a slanting, dark pink shaft lighting the mist hanging over the dry-stone walls and ploughed fields, the car whispered up the drive, drew to a halt beneath her. Again the golden rhomboid slipped across the paving as the butler opened the huge double doors and her parents climbed out of the car. Her father looked up once more as her mother strode into the house, and this time he smiled at his daughter. Maybe this was Isobel's first lesson in life? That if you say nothing, make no complaint, then the situation will resolve itself.

There were other memories that Isobel could conjure up from her childhood, but they were mere fragments of a life – sitting in the back of the Bentley being taken to London for a fitting, arguing with

Nanny about eating the blackened skin of rice pudding, the first time she ate a formal supper with her parents in the dining room, how she had knocked over a glass in her nervousness. The succession of governesses she and her sister, Victoria, had to teach them (young, pale women dressed in ill-fitting dresses, soaked in cheap perfume) blurred into one. Isobel had a clearer picture of the head groom, Mr Tilbury, who had taught her to ride her first pony, Moppet. A novice stable hand had unwittingly grazed Moppet in a field scabbed with ragwort and Moppet had died slowly of poisoning. It was then Isobel realized that no matter how much she cried, no matter for how long, she could not change things with tears, could not undo things – particularly death – with tears.

By the time she went to Cheltenham Ladies College, at the age of eleven, she was already five feet eight inches tall. She had memories of playing hockey and tennis, of winning many trophies. She could recall learning the periodic table, burning bread, conjugating Latin verbs, studying the goddess Artemis, assimilating a mad kaleidoscope of facts, some of which proved useful in later life. Isobel sailed through Matric, and dreamed of going to university to study English literature; instead, after A-levels, she'd gone to finishing school at Frontin-sur-Mont rather than Cambridge, because that was what her mother had done.

When she arrived at the finishing school, Isobel was hard pushed to cook an ice cube, and not much better equipped as a cook when she left. Her attitude was that if she could read, she would be able to cook should the need arise. As for home management, well, that seemed like nothing so much as common sense, and etiquette was nothing but good manners. A year spent at Frontin-sur-Mont staring out of the windows at the pistes above the village, feeling annoyed and bored. In winter she skiied, in the summer she hiked in the mountains. Those afternoons she would remember all her life – walking alone along worn paths, through meadows, climbing gradually, up scree-covered slopes, to a peak, where she sat, at the top of the world, watching birds wheeling against a blue sky. Afternoons of silence, away from the prattle of empty-headed girls who talked of nothing but the Season and the men they would meet, brothers' friends and hem lengths. Afternoons occasionally shattered by the hollow boom of a hunter's rifle, which echoed around the arêtes and valleys, loosening ice-shattered rock, causing debris to skitter down the slopes.

Looking back at her younger self from the vantage point of adulthood (occasionally feeling waves of self-disgust wash over as she considered the paltry residue of such a privileged life), Isobel realized that her father had treated her as if she were a boy; had no doubt wished she had been one. Isobel could remember her father teaching her to drive, teaching her how to fish and shoot. If she concentrated, she could feel the weight of her father's huge hand on her shoulder, as the other guided her casting hand, looping the line into a graceful, parabolic arc, before launching the fly into swift-running waters; action and reaction. Lord Chalfont-Webbe took her to Scotland at the end of each summer, for the shoot, and for a week she and her father indulged a passion for blasting ptarmigan, pigeon, pheasant and grouse out of the sky; driven and rough shooting, wildfowling when the urge took them. Isobel could track a bird across the sky, keeping it in her sights, redrawing the bead, waiting until the moment the fowl was about to disappear behind cover before pulling on the trigger, absorbing the lash of the stock in her broad shoulders. On the driven shoots, Isobel excelled, the hours spent clay pigeon shooting sharpening her already sharp ice-blue eyes. In some ways she preferred the rough shooting, moving through the tangled undergrowth of woodland and forest, disturbing wildlife, causing deer to freeze and twitch as quarry flung itself skyward. Gun dogs stood stock still, foreleg delicately bent, quivering slightly, before pussy-footing their way through organic detritus to retrieve the blood-warm corpses, bringing them to Isobel's feet in mouths as soft as a baby's foot.

At eighteen Isobel had refused point blank to have anything to do with coming out, being presented, or doing the Season.

'It's a cattle market,' she repeated over and over. 'I refuse to be part of it.'

'Isobel, it's your birthright and your duty,' her mother replied icily. 'Everyone is doing it. You'll simply look stupid if you don't. All your friends are already making plans for their dresses and filling in their diaries.'

'I won't do it. The whole thing's an insult.'

'An insult to whom, Isobel? I don't understand you. The women of our family have been debutantes for generations. I remember my coming-out season as the highlight of my life – a summer of nothing but parties and dances. What more could you want? You'll meet people—'

'I'll meet men, you mean.'

'What on earth is wrong with that?'

'Because they're only there to find themselves a girl, marry her, and make sure they get an heir and a spare.'

'Isobel! Don't say that. And anyway, what's wrong with it? It's the way we've done it for years, for centuries.'

'Who's "we", Mother? Who do you mean by "we"?'

'You know perfectly well who I mean.'

'Sadly, yes, I do.'

Lady Chalfont-Webbe, standing in the drawing room, arms crossed over an elegant cashmere cardigan, looked at her daughter, dressed in muddied jodhpurs, smacking a whip against her thigh in fury. 'You don't have a choice.'

'Why do you want me to do something so insulting?'

Lady Chalfont-Webbe sighed. 'What do you mean, "insulting"? I don't understand.'

'Because all of it, all the parties and the weekends and the shoots and everything, has nothing to do with fun.'

'But of course it has.'

'It hasn't, Mother, and you know that. Don't make me say it.'

'What?' Lady Chalfont-Webbe was puzzled. 'Don't make you say what?'

Isobel stilled the beating whip, stood as tall as she could. 'Because it's all about parading us as eligible.'

'What's the problem with that? You *are* eligible.'

'Why?'

'Because you're charming and pretty and you have poise and you come from a fine family.'

'You know and I know it has nothing to do with that. What makes me eligible is that I'm a virgin. The blood lines can't be tainted, can they? That's why I'm to be paraded around.'

'Isobel! How dare you say that!' But Isobel was walking away, whip switching again. Lady Chalfont-Webbe stared at her daughter's long, retreating back and wondered at the source of Isobel's defiant nature.

Isobel was right, of course. The parading of England's rosy youth did all come down to blood and its purity. The sanguinary mix of the Webbes and the Chalfonts had birthed her – reprobate or reformer?

The matter was left, finally, in Lord Chalfont-Webbe's hands, hands Isobel had inherited. After weeks of argument, his wife gave up and asked him to talk to their daughter. Isobel was called to his study – a dark, brooding place, full of leather and stuffed dead bodies, reeking of stale cigar smoke – and Lord Chalfont-Webbe put it to her that she did indeed have a duty to be a debutante. Isobel, who admired her father, who loved him dearly, tried to argue. She railed against the costume, ridiculed the defunct custom of wearing three ostrich feathers and curtsying before a cake. In a moment of inspiration she drew parallels with the ritual sacrifices to Artemis of virgins dressed in white, and her father thought (not for the first time) of the pitfalls of educating girls. She pointed out that she was a better shot, a better horsewoman, a better sailor than those men she would be required to watch and admire at Cowes, Henley and Ascot. She explained once more why she found the process insulting – that six months of inane frivolity were all predicated on the existence or otherwise of her hymen.

It was at this point that Lord Chalfont-Webbe snapped, and the roars could be heard as far away as the stables. Lord Chalfont-Webbe was a wily operator – he had, after all, spent years in the House and followed events in the Other Place. He knew when to negotiate, when to appear to admit a degree of defeat. What he said to Isobel, once he had calmed himself, was that she would go to the ball . . . and the cocktail parties and the court and Cowes, Henley and Ascot, go to all the London parties and luncheons. For the next six months, from April to September, she would immerse herself in the Season. If, at the end of that time, she had not found a suitable fiancé, well, then she was free to do what she wished. Isobel accepted this and father and daughter clasped their huge hands over the desk and shook on it. What Lord Chalfont-Webbe did not allow for was the appearance, a couple of years later, of a vodka-soaked American oil man at the Coopers' dining table.

By the time the Hon. Isobel Chalfont-Webbe laid her remarkable hands on starched linen cloth, snagging the attention of Billy-Ray Rickman as Jacqueline Cooper looked on, she had learned many lessons. Amongst them, that if one kept one's own counsel and did not complain, problems would resolve themselves; that no amount of crying could bring back the dead; and that one should not exercise the option of turning and walking away, no matter how unattractive the alternative of staying might seem. Chalfont or Webbe? Reprobate or reformer?

THE REICHMANNS

Pigs don't read telegrams, they don't appreciate the fact that slips of paper can bring human beings, even one as robust and practical as Irochka Reichmann, to their knees. Pigs keep eating, respiring, excreting despite the arrival of telegrams. As Oliver opened the envelope, pausing before reading the contents, Wilhelm-Rajmund watched from the doorway, still trying to reverse time. A pain, which started in his sternum, spread through his ribs, down his spine, focused in the dent on his thigh. *Bitte, Gott, lass es Dieter sein.* The pain intensified. Oliver gave the telegram to Irochka, stared at the horizon, tears running down his cheeks. Irochka read the news, turned to Wilhelm-Rajmund.

'It's Deet,' she said, and Wilhelm-Rajmund began to howl.

In the fields the pigs kept eating, respiring, excreting.

Oliver barely spoke after that moment, moved liked a man in thick fog, slowly, considerately. The pens still needed to be mucked out, the feed spread in troughs, water tanks refilled, a fence still needed to be fixed. But he did these things so slowly. Irochka spent hours in church, on her knees, head bowed, fingering rosary beads, muttering one prayer after another for her son's soul. Wilhelm-Rajmund took to his bed, lay there staring at the postcards Deet had sent, hoping that his brother had had a good time in Biloxi, Memphis and Hollywood. Occasionally he thought he should get up, but each time he tried he began to cry. He felt tainted, corrupted. Felt damned. (*Bitte, Gott, lass es Dieter sein.*) He began to press the scar on his leg until the pain was unbearable; this was his penance.

On Sunday, after a mass during which prayers were said for Dieter, a trickle of visitors appeared at the Reichmann farm, the women bearing bowls of stew and soup, the men holding their hats in their hands, crushing the brims as they shuffled, uncertain of what to say. Irochka greeted them all quietly, wept a little when the women hugged her.

'Dieter was a good boy,' the men said as they shook Oliver's hand, perhaps wrapped an arm around his shoulders. 'A good boy. A *brave* boy.' And Oliver looked at them with a pale face emptied by shock. 'If we can do anything . . . If we can help, let us know. Maybe we could take over for a few days?'

'No,' said Oliver.

'Dieter was a good boy,' said the women as they rocked Irochka in their arms. 'A handsome boy. A *happy* boy.' Irochka would shake her head slightly, as if denying this. 'If we can do anything . . . If we can help, just call us. Maybe you'd like us to take Willie for a few days while you are sorting things?'

'No,' said Irochka.

And upstairs, Wilhelm-Rajmund lay on his bed, pressing his flesh.

Monday morning, and Wilhelm-Rajmund did not go to school. Neither his mother nor his father said anything about this. The three of them sat in the kitchen, the door closed, sat at the table saying nothing. Eventually Irochka – who had been to six o'clock mass, who was bone weary – stood up and began to cook the breakfast. But soon she ground to a halt and sat down again. Wilhelm-Rajmund wondered whether breakfast would always be different now; a daily reminder of hearing the news. Oliver stood (but so slowly), said he was going to work on the fence beyond the lake. Wilhelm-Rajmund considered going with his father, wondered whether it would be a good thing to labour at something, to dig and heft in an attempt to displace his misery. But he continued to sit at the table, inert. When Oliver had gone, Irochka began to cry. Wilhelm-Rajmund went back upstairs to his room, took off his clothes and climbed under the blankets. He fell asleep and woke to the sound of his own screams, to his mother shaking him awake.

'Willie, come on, get up. This is no good.' But Irochka sat on the bed, wrapped her arms around him and rocked him, eventually feeling him unfurl, much as Jacqueline Cooper was to do many years later. 'I've made some pancakes. I've made some *kaszka* and bread. You must eat.' His mother helped him to dress, touching his face and his hair, as if he were something precious, and the two of them went down to the kitchen and ate the beef-and-barley soup, tasting nothing.

'I've made sandwiches for your father. He must eat too. I've packed a bag with sandwiches and apples and some coffee. I want you to take it to him – stay with him and make sure he eats. And then this evening we'll have *czarina, kotlety z móżdżkami* and *chustciki*. You can tell him that.' Irochka essayed a smile and Wilhelm-Rajmund knew she was gathering herself together and he was relieved. His parents, the giants of his childhood who seemed invincible, had for a while appeared fragile and helpless. 'Take Roosevelt, the exercise will do you good.'

The exercise *was* good for Wilhelm-Rajmund. He spurred Roosevelt on, galloping across rolling hills, splashing through shallow rivers, ducking under the boughs of prairie oak, thinking of his mother's small smile. Both boy and horse were sweating as he spotted his father, his black shirt moving against pale barley. Wilhelm-Rajmund slowed to a canter as he called out. Oliver turned and waved (but so slowly).

Wilhelm-Rajmund and his father sat in the shade of a leafy basswood and he told Oliver about the evening's fare. 'It's your favourite, isn't it?'

Oliver nodded, kept chewing.

'How's the fence coming on?'

Oliver shook his head. 'Ground's hard.'

'You want me to stay and help?' Wilhelm-Rajmund wanted to see signs of recovery in his father, the man who could lift a six-hundred-pound corpse.

Again Oliver shook his head, carefully folded the paper the sandwiches had been wrapped in, put it back in the bag. 'Nah. I want you to be with your mother. She needs you.'

Not as much as you do, thought Wilhelm-Rajmund. 'She said I could do with some exercise.'

'Go home, Willie. Roosevelt needs a rub-down anyway. Make sure you do it straight away.'

'You sure? I could come back in the truck.' Wilhelm-Rajmund looked at the pick and shovel, the mound of pointed stakes, imagined working through the afternoon, shirt off, sweat pouring, hands busy, not thinking of Deet.

Oliver sighed, stood and brushed his jeans off. 'Go home, Willie.'

Wilhelm-Rajmund began by walking the horse home, his fury mounting. Why was his father pushing him away? Couldn't he understand what he needed? He passed Home Lake, remembered the day when Siggy had saved Deet after he went through the ice. And for what? What was the fucking point of that heroic gesture if a few years later an unknown man, a stranger who had never known Deet, had never even met him, killed him in a place called Salerno in Italy? What was the fucking *point*? Wilhelm-Rajmund was galloping again, even though Roosevelt was blowing, galloping through rough terrain, wanting danger. He crested the last rise and reined Roosevelt in, hoofs slipping and cracking on gravel. From his vantage point he could see a navy-blue jeep making its way along the hard-packed dirt road towards the farm. He could see his mother, the recovering, invincible Irochka, sweeping the porch, unaware of the jeep's approach.

Wilhelm-Rajmund Reichmann, Minnesotan farm boy, beloved fifteen-year-old son of an ever-diminishing family, slammed his heels into Roosevelt's flanks, bent low over the horse's labouring heart, and thundered across the fields, wanting to stop the jeep, to stop it and banish it for ever. But he was too far away, Roosevelt's legs were not long enough, not strong enough, to cover the half-mile in time. The jeep pulled up and its door swung open. Irochka stopped sweeping and turned to see a uniformed man walking heavily up the steps, his cap tucked under one arm. This time Wilhelm-Rajmund had no prayers left to offer. This time, he knew already, the pain would never go away. This time Wilhelm-Rajmund realized God was indifferent. He watched, unaware of his yells, his own ragged breathing, the horse stumbling, as Irochka fell, strangely graceful, on to the clean boards of the porch. Fell slowly, and as Wilhelm-Rajmund came close enough to call her name, close enough to see the concern on the captain's face, he imagined he saw the spirit leave his mother's body, like a wisp of smoke.

In the fields the pigs kept eating, respiring, excreting.

THE REGANS

Sean Regan missed his daughter. He missed her silent company in the cab of the truck as he drove around the country. Missed the strange stories she'd come out with about lovelorn dragons and fish that walked on water, her babble over breakfast and dinner about menhirs and cromlechs. The way she knew exactly what needed to be done when the two of them worked together on the Whyte estate. But what he missed most was seeing his beautiful daughter sitting on the wall outside the house, just sitting there on summer evenings, staring out at the island-littered bay as if she were searching for something. There were so many things he thought of that he wanted to tell her – he wanted her to know how much he missed her. That he thought it was wrong that she'd been sent away; that he was sorry he hadn't stopped it. He wanted to ask her to forgive him for letting her go.

One autumn day, as he watched the mountains disappearing in thickening mist, he conceived of sending Maggie a letter, and that night he walked up the hill to Eileen O'Riorda's, having told Annie he was stepping out to Macafferty's for a Guinness. Eileen O'Riorda opened the door of her mean stone cottage and squinted at Sean.

'I'd like you to write a letter for me,' said Sean, holding out a newspaper-wrapped parcel of grilse.

Eileen O'Riorda snatched the parcel and looked at the fish, examined them by the light of an oil lamp, sniffed closely and, satisfied her literary skills weren't being short-changed, let Sean in, motioned to the table in the kitchen. Sean sat down, fished in a pocket for the paper with the address in London.

'That's where it'll be going.'

'Hmm.' Eileen O'Riorda held the piece of paper close to, studied it. 'London,' she said disapprovingly.

'That's right. I'm wanting to send a letter to Maggie.'

Eileen O'Riorda looked at him with her hazy, myopic eyes. 'Maggie?'

'She's been gone a while now and I'd like to write her.'

'Well, we'll see what we can do.'

As Eileen O'Riorda gathered together paper, pen and ink bottle, arranging them with the solemnity of a priest at the altar, Sean said, 'I'd be appreciating it if you didn't mention this to Annie.'

Eileen O'Riorda raised a greying eyebrow. 'Is that so?'

'Yes, it is.'

It took a long time, with a deal of puffing, finger-stretching and rewriting on Eileen O'Riorda's part, to scribe the letter, but it was finally done.

Dear Maggie,

How are you? Are you enjoying your work in London? Things hear are the same. Noel has his teeth and Brigid is walking. The fish have not been good this year. I have had to work 2 mornings every week at the Estate to make up the money. Mammy is with child again. The van is getting bad and I have to take it up to Michael nearly every week for some thing. Well I think thats it.

Write if you can.

Your Da

Eileen O'Riorda read it back to Sean, slowly and with squinting eyes. 'Now I'm not saying the spelling is as good as might be, but she'll know what you're saying.' As she laboriously inscribed the address on an envelope, Sean sat watching her, seething with frustration. How could he say what he wanted to say? How could he sit in that kitchen and tell Eileen O'Riorda to write that he loved his daughter, that he often thought of her? That Danny Maconnell had not come back to the estate. That he understood why Maggie had done what she'd done – that a bit of loving was all right, that sometimes it was the only thing you had. That she had been punished too much. How could he tell Eileen O'Riorda to write that he thought Annie was wrong to send Maggie away? So he took the letter and left the fish and on the way home he cursed himself – for being weak, for being tongue-tied, for being who he was – and he tore the letter into pieces and let it flutter away on the wind.

The sea was emptying, Sean was sure of it. He'd cast for hours off Purteen Rocks, trying to lure huss and codling during long nights, ballan, cuckoo wrasse and mackerel during the damp days, and nothing would happen; sometimes he'd have the boys with him, straggled along the surf line, and between them they'd catch what he alone would have caught ten years before. The vegetables seemed to rot more often as the rains grew heavier, and his father's secret land potion no longer worked its magic.

Sean sometimes wondered whether it was just that he was getting older and crabbier, as his father had done before him. He'd look at his skate-wing face in the mirror above the sink and see his father staring back. Sean was forty-two and looked sixty. He felt his joints aching; on Sundays when he knelt to pray – for what? and to whom? – he could feel his knees grinding bone on bone, could hear them fire off like rifles. Most Sundays he folded his hands together and drifted away, into a land not unlike sleep, his eyes closed, his back aching. Sometimes, though, he did pray – he prayed that Maggie would never come back to Ballysod, that she'd find a man who would give her what she deserved and keep her away from the life that was lived there, in Mayo. That she would eat food that was not wilting and drink wine that was not blood. Occasionally he prayed that he would wake up one morning and not feel tired. But his prayers had never been answered before – why would they be now?

Still Sean carried the messages and the newly knitted baby shawls, cardigans and second-hand shoes from one house to another. Still he listened as the old farmers who were trying to eke out a living on the boggy, mountainous land fingered his goods, scratched their heads and complained about their lot. As Sean drove around the peninsula he'd pass fields of cattle which would look up in surprise, chewing as he passed, and he'd wind his window up against the ammoniac stench of the pigs as he locked his secrets away.

As the months passed after Maggie's leaving, Sean found himself becoming more irritable. He would think, as he passed the lonely thatched cottages stranded on mountainsides, about the unfairness of it all. About the randomness of it all. If he'd been born a hundred miles away he could be ploughing rich, thick soil, sowing barley and wheat. If he'd been born down Dingle way, he'd be pulling in bass and plaice, great hauls of mackerel. If only he could stop himself from climbing on Annie every Sunday afternoon maybe things would be easier. But what else did he have that he could enjoy? Not that he enjoyed it much anyway. Instead, all he had was a van rusting away beneath him, a cramped, dismal house and a family large enough to break a bank. Sean would think of Eamon de Valera and sigh – yet another one who promised miracles and then sat on his hands. Year after year he'd driven from Aasleagh to Doogort, Ballysod to Porturlin, seeing the same pinched faces, the same dilapidated houses, over and over. Bunnahowen and the road out to Constance Wycherley was another journey he made often, for Constance, with her new-found wealth, was always a good bet to be buying something and not minding too much about the cost.

One wet January day, more than a year after Maggie's leaving, he trudged up the path of the old farmhouse, to the freshly painted cherry-red front door. He knocked, found the door open and called in.

'Mrs Wycherley?'

'That you, Sean Regan? Come in, come in,' Constance shouted, from upstairs it seemed.

Sean had never been in the house before and he stood awkwardly in the front parlour, admiring the new carpet, the gas fire with its brass decorations, the polished walnut table, not wanting to sit down and dirty anything. There were flowers in a vase sitting next to a newfangled transistor radio. Sean had heard something about these but had never seen one. It looked very small.

'You may as well come upstairs, Sean Regan.'

Sean frowned, uncertain what to do with the box he was carrying. In the end he left it in the hallway, took off his cap and climbed the stairs to the attic. And there they were, six of them, in their cots – pink, mewling babies. The light up there was dim, a suggestion of yellow from a single bulb, and the babies seemed to glow a little as they waved their arms and stared about themselves with wavering eyes. Rain whispered on the thatch. Constance was leaning over a cot, picking up a baby who was coughing, near barking. 'Croup,' she said. 'Do you have a minute to spare, Sean Regan?'

Sean nodded.

'You can help me, then. I'll make it worth your while.'

Sean followed her back down the stairs and into the kitchen, where Constance closed the door behind them. Sean went to the sink and, without being asked, began to fill kettles and saucepans with water as Constance held the baby, jigging it gently, rubbing its back.

'I see you've done this before, then.'

'Too often,' said Sean, lifting the lids off the pans as the water bubbled. 'Poor little thing – the coughing always sounds so bad, deep down, like. Shall I make tea as there's all this ready?'

'Yes, why not?'

The kitchen, with its shiny gas hob and gleaming, scrubbed surfaces filled slowly with steam, clouding the windows as rain spattered. Sean, who was damp already from the weather, began to feel warm and sleepy as he sipped from the cup, leaning against the wall, black hair falling in his dark eyes. He watched the sweat beading on Constance's pale temples, her hair growing limp. Her raw-knuckled hands were gentle as she stroked the baby's cheek and her bony face softened as she murmured over the hacking.

'You're doing well, then?' Sean nodded at the cooker, at the new pans, nodded at all of it.

'I'm comfortable, yes.'

'I've brought you some fresh codling, drove up to Stonefield for it this morning.'

'That'll be nice.'

'Where do they come from? The babies?'

Constance raised a gingery eyebrow. 'I'd have thought of all men you'd know that by now.'

Sean blushed under his skate-leathery skin, looked down. 'I mean, well, you know what I'm getting at.'

Constance shifted the bundle on to her other shoulder, dabbed at her lip. 'Sean Regan, you know as well as I do what goes on. A

Saturday night dance, a pint over the odds, and the next thing you know you've got a girl of fourteen or fifteen with not much to be looking forward to. It's about the easiest thing in the world. Better to keep the girl at home, or send her away to Cork or Dublin saying she's gone to help the family, and then let her come back alone and send the mistake on to me.'

'How do they know where to find you?'

Constance smiled. 'Well, I don't advertise but the word goes round. If you need to know you'll find out is my motto.'

'Well, Annie knows nothing about what you're doing – and it's chewing her up, I can tell you.'

Now Constance laughed out loud, surprising the baby into a moment's silence. 'It must be a well-kept secret then, if Annie Regan hasn't heard. But then she doesn't need to know, does she? There's a few women do it. Not in the cities, of course, but out here in the country, it does a service.'

'It's illegal.'

'So's poaching, so's salvage without lien, so's sleeping with your daughter. I don't mean you, Sean Regan, I know you too well.' As a matter of fact she hardly knew him at all but she had always thought of him as being other-worldly in some way. 'That last is where a lot come from.'

'But where do they *go*?'

'People buy them.'

Sean frowned, put down his cup. Was there nothing left that people wouldn't buy? More – that people wouldn't *sell*? 'Who? Who buys them?'

'People who don't live here, in County Mayo, that's one thing I can tell you. I'm paid to take them and paid to give them. That's all I know. I look after them well.'

'But what about . . .' Sean paused, embarrassed. 'What about milk?'

'I have certain expenses and one of them is for wet nurses.'

'Wet nurses?'

'Wherever girls are giving birth there'll be milk. Put on more water, will you?'

Sean fussed with taps and pans and then said he had to be going.

Constance Wycherley watched him set his cap, knew their conversation was safely locked away wherever Sean put all the confessions he heard. 'I said I'd make it up to you, for your help.' She looked into his eyes, made a movement with her mouth that Sean didn't see but knew had happened.

'That's all right. It's good to be able to help the baby.'

'You're sure?'

'I'm sure.'

As he walked down the path, counting the coins she had given him for the codling and realizing she'd given him far too much, Sean thought about Constance. Her husband had been a long time dead, to be sure, but you'd think with all the evidence of what a bit of making up could do, right there up in the attic, it would be the last thing on her mind.

THE REICHMANNS

The women in the congregation of the Church of St Teresa no longer looked at Irochka, fingering their rosary beads and asking forgiveness for feeling envy. Now they watched her, fingered their beads and prayed for her, pitying her. The men no longer looked at her at all, unable to look into her eyes. Irochka sat alone, in the Reichmann pew at the front of the church, her desolation in full view. The women now gave thanks that their husbands – who did drink, who did beat them – were not as crazed as Oliver Reichmann. The whole of Blue Earth County knew what went on up at the farm and few people were brave enough to visit. Even Oliver's Uncle Siegfried had abandoned his nephew to his despair and his drinking after a month of trying to talk him round.

Oliver's grief was boundless, untethered – it flew around him. He began drinking vodka each evening, drinking more and more, until he passed out – the only respite he had from the tin-wing sound of grief in his ears. During the day he dragged himself around the fields and barns, pens and sties, seeing the pigs shitting and breathing, birthing and suckling, and he hated them. Machines were left uncleaned, began to rust, fencing sagged, trees were left unpollarded. A well lining collapsed and the head was left to grow over with weeds and grasses. Feed bags were stacked sloppily and rats gnawed their way through the sacking. Stagnant water sat in troughs for days, became still and mossy, breeding gnats. The fecundity of the land appalled Oliver, reminding him as it did of lost generations. His planning, his forethought, his earlier industry ensured the farm limped on, still breaking even as it rotted around him.

Soon, of course, Oliver began to drink in the mornings, and then through the day as the farm ground itself down. His grief, pickled in sixty per cent raw spirit, mutated into self-disgust and a loathing for the Church, which had swallowed his wife whole. Every morning, Irochka, dressed head to foot in black, looking like an emaciated *babushka*, like a scarecrow, like death itself with her hollow cheeks and fervently staring green eyes, would try to slip past him on her way to mass as he snored in the kitchen. Many mornings she managed it; he was too dead drunk to be woken. But other mornings he would wake with a start, stare at her with bloodshot eyes and begin to shout about Papists and blood, damnation and superstition. Oliver would follow Irochka out on to the porch, shouting and staggering, hurling abuse as she fumbled with the truck keys.

A trucker, unfortunate enough to have to visit the Reichmann farm, repeated the story of the morning he drove up to find Oliver wrestling with black-clad Irochka, dragging her off the porch, in all the bars in Bow Regard.

'I din' know what to do – he was so mad that morning and he's a big guy, pretty drunk too, I reckon. So I sounded the horn, thought maybe that'd stop him. Don't think he even heard it, he was hollering so much. Strange thing was, he dragged her to the edge of the yard, kinda picked up a handful of mud and rubbed it all over her face, jus' kept rubbin' it in. She din' say nothing, guess she couldn't case she was made to eat it. And all the time he jus' kept yellin' the same thing over. About the smell of blood, about how the earth smelled of blood. Weirdest thing I ever saw. And her not, y'know, fighting back, just hanging there with her face all muddy as he yelled. She looked like somethin' from another world. I got back in my truck and got the fuck outta there. Din' even drop off the machinery.'

Karl Munchssen, who was listening to the man as he sucked on a Coors, said, 'You're not from round these parts?'

'Nah. Live up Duluth way, but I'm making a five-day trip dropping off machine parts, specialist stuff. Pays good if you can string 'em together. Got my own rig and a heavy loan on it, so I need the work. This guy – Reichmann, was it? – he ordered a new winch and hook months ago but it only jus' came in. But I can do without crazies like that – rather not have the money.'

Karl Munchssen nodded, drank a little more beer, then he turned to the man. 'I think you should know a few things before you go round shooting your mouth off. The Reichmanns were about the kindest, happiest, most *decent* Christian family hereabouts. There were three sons – and all of them the kind of boy you'd want your daughter to date – nah, the kind of boy you'd want her to *marry*. Siggy and Deet, the older boys, volunteered and both of them were killed in Italy, on the same day, about a year ago. But the telegrams came two days apart. Two days. Deet was shot in a skirmish. Siggy drowned under friendly fire. A bomber made a mistake, down went the frigate and that was the end of Siggy.' Karl Munchssen, who was not a sentimental man, looked down at the Coors bottle. Stopped speaking.

'Shit,' muttered the trucker. 'That's tough. Shit.'

'So I don't want to hear about you running round telling anyone anything. OK?'

'OK.' The trucker finished his beer, slid a single on the bar, hitched his trousers and slipped out the door.

Karl Munchssen sat there, staring at the bottle, thinking of the day Siggy had brought Willie into town to give back the stolen candy bars. Remembering how Siggy had gently pushed Willie out of the truck and smiled. Karl thought of how Willie had looked when he apologized – his young, beautiful face looking stunned, looking hopeful, looking like it was waiting for absolution. And Karl Munchssen had not felt able to give it.

Hans, the barman, came over, took the note, wiped the bar down. 'Couldn't help hearing. Sounds pretty crazy up there.'

'Yah.' Karl sighed. 'But what can you do? You can't do anything. People got to lead their own lives. So he wants to drink – who's going to stop him? She wants to spend every day on her knees in church – who's going to stop her?' Karl waved the empty bottle and Hans opened another, put it on the mat. 'The one I mind about is Willie. What's he now? Shoot, must be sixteen, and he's up there with those two. We were talking about it the other night, Greta and me, saying someone should go up there and get him. But what can you do?'

Hans considered this. 'Don't think I'd try it.'

'Who would?'

*

Wilhelm-Rajmund often wished *someone* would try it. Wished that someone would come and collect him and take him somewhere else. The first weeks, after he'd seen his mother fall gracefully on the porch as his father gouged holes in packed earth, had a ghostly quality about them, as if, when he remembered those weeks, the figures moving in his mind were insubstantial, grey. It was the *sound* of that time which had a lifelike quality. The sound of his mother's shallow breathing as she lay motionless, the timbre of the captain's voice as he asked whether there was anything he could do, the grinding of the transmission as the jeep's engine fired, the man going to fetch Oliver. The click and roll of Roosevelt champing on his bit. Wilhelm-Rajmund kneeling by his mother, not looking at the piece of paper skittering quietly over the boards in a light breeze. The sounds of the time. His father's breaking cries when he returned. His father's shouts. Tables and chairs crashing in the kitchen. Wood splintering with greenstalk fractures.

That night, as Wilhelm-Rajmund lay in his bed, knees pulled up, rocking himself to stay awake, not wanting sleep and its nightmares, he heard the kitchen door slam. Crossing to his dormer window, he saw his mother, bare headed, shoeless, running across the yard, through the gate, carrying a rifle. Wilhelm-Rajmund whimpered, not wanting more of this. He struggled into his clothes, his hands shaking too much to button his shirt, and clattered down the stairs, saw his father drinking from a bottle.

'Ma's gone! She's got a gun.'

Oliver looked at him, shrugged. Drank. 'Let her go.'

Wilhelm-Rajmund ran out of the house, saw his mother, tall, rangy, still running ahead of him. He could see, now, that she was running towards the church, following the familiar, worn path from the farm across the fields. She'll slow down soon, he kept thinking, his breath rasping, she'll slow down soon. But she didn't. Irochka kept on sprinting, blonde hair flowing, an invincible giant indeed. The church gleamed in the night, the windows cobalt, emerald and ruby, lit from within by the ranks of candles burning for Siggy and Deet.

Irochka reached the gate, pushed through it and stopped, panting. She shouldered the rifle, sighted along the bead and fired. The stained glass from Warsaw imploded, shattered into a thousand gem-like pieces which scattered over the pews. Wilhelm-Rajmund, pressing a stitch in his side, slowed by the pain to a walk, saw his mother reload and sight again, the thick glass shattering with a boom, as Father Ambrose ran out of the main doors, covering his head with his hands. Irochka methodically shot out every window, leaving the church eyeless, the candles guttering, failing in the through-draught.

Yes, Wilhelm-Rajmund often wished someone would come and get him, as he watched his parents melt away and disappear, Oliver genie-like into the bottle, Irochka saint-like into the church. After Irochka's destruction of the windows, Father Ambrose became a daily visitor to the farm (appearing only when Oliver was absent). Father Ambrose wooed Irochka, seduced her with talk of her creator's love and forgiveness, absolution and the state of grace, the heaven where she would be reunited with Siggy and Deet. The priest spoke quietly, soothingly, as he comforted and Irochka repented. She wore black, she carried rosaries, she filled the farmhouse with crucifixes and brash, bright figures of the Virgin Mary. Irochka neglected her last son as she prayed for her first.

For three years Wilhelm-Rajmund stayed in Bow Regard, waiting to graduate high school. He arranged his own SATs tests and completed the application forms for college without help. He made his own breakfast, prepared sandwiches for his lunch pail, laundered his own clothes, took himself to the barber and the doctor. Every night he cooked his own dinner, ate it alone in his room, at his desk, reading, studying, preparing himself to run. The kids at the school and many of the teachers, too, who had known his brothers, did not know how to speak to him, making do with 'Hiya' and 'How's it going?' before moving on, as if they were needed urgently elsewhere. Wilhelm-Rajmund didn't speak often and his layers of language lay dormant in his chest, atrophying. For a while he accompanied his mother to Sunday mass, wanting to see whether she would come back, whether his mother would return. But the fervour in her eyes, the fixedness of those eyes as they stared at the crucifix above the altar, made him realize she was lost, and he began to stay in bed each Sunday until she had left for mass.

For three years Wilhelm-Rajmund walked the dusty track down to the road alone, hiked through the fields, fished the lake and lay in the tall grasses watching the gadwall skimming the flyway, doing those things he had done with Siggy and his father, but now always alone. Sometimes the pain of this loneliness was physical, gathered in his thigh, in his chest. Some nights, he believed he could see a darkness gathering at the edge of his world, believed it was encroaching into his life, changing him, and then he would pray; although he didn't believe, he would pray. Who did he pray for? What did he pray for? To be gone. To be gone and to be loved. To be forgiven. He didn't think he ever could be but sometimes he prayed to be forgiven. *Bitte, Gott, lass es Dieter sein.* Wilhelm-Rajmund lay in his bed in the attic above his brothers' empty room, aware of the earth spinning, aware of the continents floating, aware of his lack of faith, fighting nightmares, fighting metamorphosis.

The only person Wilhelm-Rajmund could talk to during that time, the only person he felt easy with, was Magde, the girl Siggy had left behind. The girl whose breast Siggy had touched at a barn dance, sending Deet into a fever of jealousy. Magde sought out Wilhelm-Rajmund, would turn up in her father's Buick on Saturday afternoons and persuade him to leave his books and his rocks, to go into Bow Regard or Mankato to a movie or a dance. Over the years, as Wilhelm-Rajmund changed from a withdrawn fifteen year old to a wary eighteen year old, the two of them spent a great deal of time together. It was Magde Wilhelm-Rajmund talked to about Oliver and Irochka, about the things they were doing to each other. They'd drive out to a lake and sit with a six-pack, throwing stones into the water, as Wilhelm-Rajmund described how the farm was rotting, how it was becoming an organic mass of decay. Magde talked about her secretarial job at a bank, how dull it was, how she wanted to go to Chicago or Minneapolis. Magde's family was from Dresden, and sometimes the two of them spoke in German about their many disappointments. Often they talked about Siggy, about things he had done, clothes he'd worn. What he said to the history teacher, how he could hit a can from a hundred and twenty feet with an airgun. His smile, his laugh. Over time the two of them canonized Siggy and he faded into the pantheon of saints, joining his mother. Wilhelm-Rajmund would not talk about Deet; if Magde mentioned the name, he tugged at the conversational reins and steered the talk away. Wilhelm-Rajmund told Magde many things but he never explained why he couldn't speak about Deet.

It was obvious why Magde sought out Wilhelm-Rajmund's company: she was spending time with a quieter version of Siggy, a compensation for having lost the original. It was also obvious why Wilhelm-Rajmund left his desk and went out with Magde whenever she called: she was still the prettiest girl in town.

The Saturday Wilhelm-Rajmund went down to the mail box at the end of the track leading to the farm and found in it a letter from Seattle University, Washington, accepting his application to study there starting September, it was Magde he told first. He called her up and asked her to come over – he had some news. As he waited for the Buick to crunch up the track, he stole a bottle of vodka from his father's stash, put it in a bag with a bottle of Dr Pepper's, two glasses, a pack of Lucky Strikes, a half-loaf of bread and a slab of Monterey Jack.

'Where we going?' asked Magde, looking alarmingly beautiful in an emerald dress which highlighted her copper hair.

'Let's go somewhere special – I got a surprise.'

Magde thought how like Siggy Willie looked when he smiled. 'H'okay – what about Moose Falls, out Cottonwood way? It's pretty there.'

'You don't mind using the gas?'

'Nah. Pa can always get it. What you got in the bag? That the surprise?'

'Part of it.'

The two of them sat in easy silence as Magde drove through the May afternoon. It was a day of fresh blue skies, glittering lakes, the air dry, the temperature not yet soaring as it did in summer. Moose Falls was deserted and Wilhelm-Rajmund spread a blanket by the pool, under an old oak. When they were settled, he took the bottle out of the bag, opened it and poured two shots.

'Where d'you get this, Willie? Didja steal it from your father?'

'Yah. He won't notice.' *I know it's wrong.*

'But what if he finds out?'

'He won't – he's so drunk most of the time he doesn't know his own name.' *And so do you.*

'You sure?'

Wilhelm-Rajmund downed the clear liquid, gasped as it stripped his tongue of its feeling. Shook his head. Anything to drown out Siggy's voice. 'Go on – drink yours. I'm not drinking on my own.'

Magde drank the spirit, coughed, her eyes watering. 'Shoot – that's like fire.'

Wilhelm-Rajmund poured them each another.

'So,' said Magde, topping hers up with Dr Pepper, 'what's the surprise?'

'I'm getting out of here.'

'What d'you mean?' Magde frowned.

'I'm going to Seattle.' He pulled the letter from his pocket, handed it to her.

'You're leaving?'

Wilhelm-Rajmund had often talked to her about his ambitions, about going to college, but somehow that was always some time in the future. How could Willie leave Blue Earth County? He didn't know anything else.

'Willie – how can you leave? You ain't got the money to go to college.' An image of the dilapidated farm spun through Magde's mind.

Wilhelm-Rajmund smiled. 'Remember Mr Svensson up at the school? He helped me apply for a scholarship – it's a Jesuit place and the Church gave me money. Plus he has a brother in Seattle who'll help me out.'

Magde pulled at the lush grass by the water's edge, squinted up at the water cascading into the pool. 'When you leaving?'

'Next week, I'm thinking. I'll hitch out there. Maybe I'll be able to get some work before the semester starts, get together some money.'

'Next week? What *will* I do?' Magde asked, wonderingly.

It was, perhaps, inevitable, given the sun, the blanket, the vodka, the thought of his imminent departure, that early that evening Wilhelm-Rajmund and Magde would make short, clumsy love by the water. Given that their conversations had forever been founded on disappointments and absence, it was hardly surprising that the occasion was not a happy one. Both of them cried a little after-wards – Magde because Willie was leaving and she knew he would never come back; Wilhelm-Rajmund because Siggy had asked him to look after Magde, not to take her virginity. In all those years Siggy had never taken from Magde what Willie stole. For years after this event, indeed, until he met Jacqueline Cooper, sex always reminded him of disappointment and absence. *Der Enttauschung und das Abwesenheit.*

1958

Maggie Regan had been working in Jarman House for a year and she was no longer overawed by the house or by its occupants. She was no longer scared to step out on the streets of London. Now she would visit the flea markets around Notting Hill, picking through the junk and flotsam, or walk along Regent Street and Piccadilly, window shopping. Sometimes as she walked she thought of her da and missed him, missed his company in the cab of the truck, or in the gardens around Whyte House. Her siblings, however, were a pale, dark-haired blur, as they had been in life – all of them, excepting poor Mary, who she wished she could save from her fate. As for her mother, well, what could Maggie think? Every time Annie's image swam into Maggie's mind, it was with a handkerchief pressed to her mouth, her other hand pressed to her heart, as she watched her daughter fornicating. Best forgotten. Her life in Ballysod, County Mayo, became a life that had been lived, surely, by someone else.

London in winter had little more to recommend it than Ballysod in winter, in Maggie's opinion. Still she stuck to her routine of visiting museums and near-drowsing in the stuffy, dusty air, at first imagining walking along the coast with Danny Maconnell, holding his hand, being pulled into a hidden granite corner and her skirts being lifted as he smiled in the way he had. But as the months passed she found herself thinking not of Danny but of other men, men she had seen at the dining table in Jarman House. She imagined their hands moving over her, sliding along her thigh. When she thought of this, perhaps among the Georgian costume jewellery displays of the Victoria and Albert, she would come to with a start, look about herself to see whether other visitors had guessed what was on her mind.

Even the glass-hard month of December has its soft spots, how-ever, and one Saturday Maggie woke to a brilliant blue sky to be told that Miss O'Toole – the gaoler – had gone back home to care for her dying sister and she would be gone for at least a week. Maggie might have celebrated had she known that Miss O'Toole's sister was Sister Immaculata – the barefoot, canting harridan who had made her childhood near unbearable.

As it happened, Maggie was given something to celebrate: Lady Cooper (made magnanimous by sex with Billy-Ray the night before) gave the servants a whole weekend to themselves. Maggie washed, dressed, checked her purse and walked out of Thurloe Square in search of adventure. Instead, after losing her bearings, she found Westminster Cathedral. Wrapping her coat tightly around her, Maggie sat on a bench and stared at the building. What on earth was it? All striped and looking like a badly wrapped present. She sat for a long time, becoming more and more irritable because she knew she'd eventually go inside. When the fourth man accosted her, laying a too-familiar hand on her arm, she shrugged him off and marched into the cathedral, fuming, forgetting even to cross herself. The marble, the Byzantine domes, the lavishness of the interior nearly undid her – where did they get the money? All the Catholics she knew didn't have a bean, didn't have two pennies to rub together, so what was this? She wandered through the nave, came to the stations of the cross and stopped. The Roman soldiers were flattened, Mary and Veronica were flattened, even Jesus Christ Himself was flattened, as if he'd been *ironed*. She stared at the mon-tage, frowning. Stopped at the exhortation to the women of Jerusalem. Thought of Mary, her sister, sinless, hopeless Mary, on her knees in a draughty, loveless convent, murmuring relentlessly, relentlessly asking to be absolved. And still Maggie couldn't imag-ine what Mary had *done*.

The cathedral was cold and Maggie shivered, sat in a pew to look around herself. A congregation was shuffling in, filling the benches around her, old women crossing themselves and thudding on to prayer mats, hands clasped, dressed in worn coats, crushed hats. Maggie watched as the nave filled with, she suspected, the sinless and the hopeless. Certainly the desperate. Stunned by the despondency around her, by the opulence of her surroundings, Maggie sat in a stupor.

The mass began. The liturgy of the Word. The liturgy of the Eucharist. The consecration, the transubstantiation. 'Do this in remembrance of me.' Maggie watched the wine become blood, remembered herself as a child wondering about the miracle of life when there seemed to be an abundance of it, far more than anyone could wish for. Certainly more than anyone needed and far more than the land could bear. The union of Christ with the faithful. Remembered her father's expression when he had said she should believe in God, how she had known that he didn't. 'This is my body.' Maggie thought of Danny Maconnell's hands, thought of his mouth saying 'Godolphin Barb'. Thought: This is *my* body; stood as the desperate filed for communion and walked out of the cathedral.

With Miss O'Toole gone, Jarman House was a much happier if less efficient place. Maggie was detailed for three days to clean shelves in the library, a task that appealed to her, since she liked to spend the days alone, surrounded by books and pictures. Climbing down the steps one morning, balancing an armload of books, Maggie was surprised to see Jacqueline come into the library, a cup of coffee in one hand, *The Times* in the other. Maggie dropped the books on to the long, polished table and wiped her dusty hands on her apron.

'I'm sorry, ma'am. I was told to clean the shelves in here. I didn't know that . . .'

Jacqueline waved a hand, sat at the table. 'Don't mind me, carry on. There are workmen in the drawing room fixing something to do with the lights. Just carry on.' Jacqueline sipped her coffee and turned to the headlines. America had test-launched Atlas, the first ICBM; Donald Campbell had travelled at 248.62 miles per hour in *Bluebird*, flashing across the albino salt flats of Colorado. Always moving farther, moving faster. Sometimes Jacqueline felt she was living in a time warp, idling her life away outside the loop of the world. She sat back, lit a cigarette and looked around the high-ceilinged, panelled room, its shelves serviced by a beautifully carved, moving stepladder, running the length of the wall. Maggie pushed the ladder to the next section of shelves and climbed up, to reach for the top shelf where hundreds of unread books were stacked. Jacqueline smoked and studied Maggie's long, pale legs, her broad shoulders, her blue-black hair, held back from her face by a band. Jacqueline studied Maggie in much the same way as Danny Maconnell had when he thought she was stealing a roof, and came to the same conclusion.

'It's Maggie, isn't it?'

Maggie turned in surprise and a first edition of *Where Angels Fear to Tread* slithered to the floor, its pages creasing on impact. 'Oh – I'm sorry.' Maggie climbed quickly down the ladder, picked up the book and smoothed the pages.

'Don't worry about it – no one ever comes in here to read anyway.'

Maggie laughed. Stopped herself.

'So – you're Maggie?'

'That's right, ma'am.'

'How long have you been with us?'

'More than a year, ma'am. I came last November the tenth.'

'And do you enjoying working here?'

Maggie pondered this and then shrugged. For a moment Jacqueline felt a flash of the fury experienced constantly by Miss O'Toole. But then, she said to herself, she'd asked the question. 'Where you from, Maggie?'

'Ballysod, ma'am. County Mayo.'

'And how old are you?'

'Sixteen. I'll be seventeen next June. Ma'am.'

'Hmm.' Jacqueline looked Maggie up and down. What was it about the girl? Made you want to just keep looking at her. Uneducated and delicious. Made you want to reach out and touch her. 'What are you going to do with your life, Maggie? Surely you won't stay here? You must have plans.'

Maggie looked through the long, arched window at the well-tended square. Thought of living in a Czechoslovakian castle. Watched a Dandie Dinmont, attached to a lead held by a blue-rinsed matron, squat and empty its bowels on the leafless lawn. 'I'd like to be a gardener. Or maybe a painter – you know, not an artist, more a decorator like. Painting houses.'

Jacqueline was nonplussed. 'A gardener?'

'Yes, ma'am. I worked with my da gardening and painting before I came over here.'

Jacqueline noticed Maggie's distracted expression, misunderstood. 'Do you miss your family?'

'No, ma'am.'

It was Jacqueline's turn to laugh and stop herself. She looked at Maggie again, studied her and, just as Billy-Ray had, she wanted to reach out and touch Maggie's lips with a fingertip. Maggie recognized the look; after all, she'd seen it often enough. She shifted, smiled slightly and Jacqueline realized she'd been rumbled. 'Do you have a boyfriend, Maggie?'

'No,' said Maggie, but you do, she thought. She'd noticed the handsome, blond American at cocktail parties and at Sherston Park when they had weekend house parties; noticed how Lady Cooper behaved when he was around. She'd also noticed how he behaved when she, Maggie, was around.

'Well, I guess there'll be time enough.'

But, of course, for Maggie Regan there wasn't.

1946

'It says Wilhelm-Rajmund Reichmann right here. *You* signed it.' The thin, blonde woman was troubled, a slight frown betraying her emotions as she pointed at the form.

'Yah, I know. But I'm called Billy-Ray Rickman. That's what everyone calls me.' In fact, very few people had ever called him Billy-Ray Rickman. The name had come to him as he hitched his way from Bow Regard to Seattle. When the third trucker picked him up, he asked Wilhelm-Rajmund his name and Billy-Ray said, 'Billy-Ray.' He'd stared through the windshield as they drove the rainy streets of Pukwana, spraying young mothers wrestling with prams in a sudden late-spring storm. Then he'd said, 'Billy-Ray *Rickman*,' and the trucker had stared at him as if he were nuts. And now here was this thin, blonde secretary, working in the admissions office of Seattle University, quizzing him about his new identity when he was still unsure of it himself.

'We-e-e-ll,' the blonde woman said, scratching her scalp with a pencil, not wanting to muss her hair, 'I don't know. I jus' don't know. Can't have two different names on the same form. I mean, if everyone did this where would we be?'

Not everyone *needs* to do this, thought Billy-Ray. How many people need two lives? How many people *want* two different lives?

'How 'bout you sign *this* form Wilhelm-Rajmund Reichmann and then when the semester starts you can sort it out with the vice-principal? Register whichever name you prefer?' The secretary smiled, obviously relieved to have found a solution. And she wanted to find a solution to this problem because she liked the young man from Bow Regard. He had an honest face, and, if she were being honest with herself, a handsome face; plus he was polite. The minute he'd walked in and she'd seen his shoulders and hands she'd known he was a farm boy.

Billy-Ray nodded. 'Yah – that sounds good. And it means my fees and tuition are still paid? The scholarship covers that?'

She smiled as she marked small crosses on the form where he should sign. "Course it does.' She pushed the form across the desk. 'Sign here.'

Billy-Ray leaned over the form, scanning it, and she looked at the thick, tousled hair, the flawless skin of his cheeks glittering with a young, blond beard.

'There's a few months to go before the semester starts. You got somewhere to stay?' she asked, as Billy-Ray pushed the form back across the desk.

He hitched his bag on to his shoulder. 'Yah – I'm staying with a family in Ballard.'

'You're Swedish?'

'Nah – I'm American.'

'And y'know,' she said that evening, sharing the day's events with her sister, 'I never know what to say when they come out with that. "I'm an American". I mean, what point's he makin'? Of *course* he's an American. We all are. I just meant, well, where was his family from. Y'know? But some of them – well, they jus' get so sensitive or something. Anyway, then he asks about any work going, so I told him to go down to the docks. Always work down there, I told him. Especially for a boy like that, what with his build. *Particularly* for a boy like that.'

Her sister, who was neither blonde nor pretty, said rather sharply, 'Think you'll be seeing him again?'

'Good Lord, no! He's jus' a farm boy, a sweet, eighteen-year-old farm boy. All brawn and no brains. You know what they're like. They last one semester, missing Mom and the hogs, dreaming of home cooking and big, wide skies, and then they leave, go home and marry the girl next door. No – I'm waiting for the GI Bill soldiers to start coming through – then I'll be seeing some real men.'

'Some *married* men, you mean,' and the two of them laughed.

The journey to the registrar's office at Seattle University had taken Billy-Ray eleven days – seven of them spent eating in truck stops and diners, sleeping in the cabs of Mack trucks, their axles grinding, roaring and belching smoke as they toiled west. Through the plains of South Dakota to the Missouri River and there the foothills of the Rockies began to rear up from the land. Billy-Ray tried not to sleep during the day then because he wanted to watch the land as it changed, folded in on itself, as the tree line showed stark against the mountainsides. On the third day he passed through Billings at dawn and as the sun broke through low cloud cover it lit up the Absaroka range, throwing long, shallow shadows over the peaks, burning mist away. Billy-Ray knew how the Rockies were formed, understood the orogeny of the event, the bullish arrangement of the strata – but he had never had an idea of how damn *big* they were. He was a farm boy from Minnesota – he'd never seen a hill more than four hundred feet.

'How high're these mountains?' he asked the trucker, who was delivering spools of telegraph wire to Butte.

'How high?' The man leaned forward over the wheel, scanned the horizon. 'Reckon about ten thousand, maybe less. The far ones'll be bigger.'

'Ten *thousand* feet?' Billy-Ray remembered a time he'd felt dizzy standing in the upper branches of a prairie oak. He saw a sign for Yellowstone National Park, watched it disappear in the mirror. Billy-Ray wanted to stop there as much as he wanted to keep moving west. He wound down the window, stuck out his tanned hand. The air was cold. The truck kept grinding through the gears, farting, nearly stalling as the incline rose and fell, the trucker's tattooed fist forcing the stick as he double-declutched. The truck seemed to be the only vehicle on the road. Hours passed without them seeing another car, Billy-Ray saying nothing, just watching the world go by. They arrived in Butte and the trucker, who was, beneath his tattoos and body odour, a kindly man, gave Billy-Ray a couple of dollars and told him to get something to eat whilst he delivered the cable, and then he'd drop him west of Butte, at the junction.

'See – I'm heading south, to Blackfoot. You need to catch something north, head for Spokane. You might even get something all the way 'f you're lucky. You sure *look* lucky.'

'You do this all the time?' asked Billy-Ray. 'You drive around like this? Through the mountains and all?'

'Yup. All the time. All the fuckin' time.' The trucker slowed, pulled into a side road, blocked by locked gates. A guard walked towards them, clipboard in hand, noting down the plate. The trucker looked over at the tall, blue-eyed, blond boy who looked strong as an ox. The blue eyes were misted, unfocused. 'Look – what's your name? Billy-Ray? You said you was goin' to college. You get to college and you *stay* there – y'hear? You *stay* there. This ain't no job for no one. Might seem like a nice ride now – but you see it in winter. Tyre blows in the middle of nowhere and it's twenty below. Black ice, snowstorms, roadblocks. Y'end up sitting in the cab waiting for the storms to pass and you're losing money ever' minute.' The guard reached up and rapped on the window. 'Wish I coulda gone to college. You fuckin' stay there. I'll meetcha across the road at Elsie's in ten minutes. You can order me the special, 'salways good.'

A couple of hours later Billy-Ray was sitting at the junction near Butte, waiting for a truck or car to pass heading north, sun shining, as snow began to fall. Billy-Ray laughed, held his hand out and watched the fragile crystals melt as they touched his skin. He sat on his backpack, looking about himself at the strange, new land, and he thought of the farm in Blue Earth County, thought of his parents and of his brothers' empty room, dusty and unchanged. The morning he'd left, a few days before, his father had turned his back on his son, his mother had ignored her son's farewells. Billy-Ray sat at the junction, surrounded by snow-tipped mountains, blacktop stretching and twisting away on either side of him, cresting hills, leading places he'd never been, and he heard the sound of the stove clicking in the farm's kitchen, the sound of a cork being pulled from a bottle's tight grip as darkness encroached. He'd never go back there.

Outside Spokane Billy-Ray was picked up by a lone woman. Lucca Barzini smoked, wore bright red lipstick; she talked too fast, she drove too fast. She often looked at Billy-Ray and not at the road.

'Where you headed?' she asked as they sped away from the town.

'Seattle.'

'Why?'

'I'm going to college.' Billy-Ray was uncomfortable under her scrutiny.

'Why?'

Why? 'Well, to study,' he said.

'What? What are you studying?' Lucca dextrously lit a cigarette with one hand using a book of matches, tossed the spent match out the window. 'Party trick,' she said.

'I'm majoring in geology.'

'Why?'

Billy-Ray frowned. He looked at Lucca. She was thin, probably quite short, although it was hard to tell. Her hair looked darker than it should have been. She was old – forty-two, maybe forty-three, around the same age as his mother. 'Because I like it.'

'What's your name?'

'Billy-Ray Rickman.'

'Lucca Barzini. Well, Billy-Ray' – the car swooped around a curve, threw up gravel, settled – 'how can you like geology? I mean, you can like martinis or pasta or cats or sex but you can't *like* geology. It's not in the same league.'

Billy-Ray had never heard a woman say 'sex' before but, then, neither had he heard a woman say 'pasta' before. He sat in the car, stunned, trying to work out why it was OK to like geology. 'I think, in a way, it's all there is. It's like a . . . a starting point. Before we can do anything else. It's a starting point. If we don't know what the world *is*, then how do we know what to do with it?'

Lucca Barzini, who was a journalist, who had been in Spain in '36 and had seen the futility of trying to know what the world is, let alone what to do with it, smiled. 'Where you from, Billy-Ray?'

'Bow Regard, Blue Earth County, Minnesota.' Billy-Ray was hugging his bag on his knees. He felt strangely vulnerable when Lucca looked at him.

'Ah – the flatlands. What are you – Swedish? Dutch?'

'I'm an American.'

Oh shit, thought Lucca. 'Well, of course you are. I just wondered where your people are from.'

'Germany and Poland.'

'Have you visited there?'

'Nah. Never been outside Minnesota before now.'

'I guess the Rockies must have been quite something when you saw them?'

Billy-Ray smiled and Lucca thought how charming he looked. 'Sure were. I never realized how big they'd be. I mean, I guess I never thought about how they just go on and on.'

Lucca lit another cigarette with her complicated routine of finger snapping. 'If you've never been out of Minnesota, you've never seen the ocean.'

'Can't say I have.' Billy-Ray knew he sounded like a hick, like he had a straw in his mouth, hog shit on his shoes, but Lucca made him uneasy. She looked like something from a movie, with her black clothes and red lipstick. She almost looked like a boy.

'When are you due in Seattle?'

'You sure ask a lot of questions,' said Billy-Ray.

'Of course I do. It's my job – I'm a reporter.'

Billy-Ray stared at her. 'A reporter? A *newspaper* reporter?'

'Yeah. That's right. A *newspaper* reporter.' Lucca smiled. 'I file copy for the *Post* and *Tribune* in New York, syndicate a couple of weekly columns.'

Billy-Ray considered the glamour of this. Everyone he knew was either a farmer, a storekeeper, a religious maniac or dead. 'That must be great,' he decided.

'Sometimes – sometimes not. I've been up around Kalispell for a few days, staying in a so-called motel. No hot water, dirt for a floor, rags hanging in the windows.' Lucca shuddered theatrically. 'Bears and snakes. Ugh.'

'Why were you there?'

'There's been a few murders up in the back of Kalispell, way up in the hills. You know, where the nearest neighbours are ten miles away and the nights can get too long. Turns out they're all related. Not just the murders – the victims too. It's all inter-breeding. Maybe there's more jealousy when it's just one big if not happy family.'

'What? You mean they all . . . y'know? Cousins and all that?'

'Fathers and daughters, mothers and uncles, brothers and sisters. Brothers and brothers too. All of them.'

Billy-Ray thought of what he'd done with Magde, imagined doing it with his mother. Thought of the fore-sail wrapping round him as Siggy held him and banished the Wave. *'Das ist widerlich,'* he muttered.

'What?'

'That's disgusting.'

Lucca watched him for a moment. 'I can't say it appeals much to me either, but they're a long way from anywhere. I guess they don't have too much choice.'

'Disgusting.'

'You didn't answer my question.'

'Huh?'

'When are you due in Seattle?'

'Any time. School doesn't start until September. I thought I'd come out early and make some money. Can I have one?' Billy-Ray took Lucca's cigarettes from the dash.

'Sure. Light me one while you're there. So you left home already? Don't you have a reason to stay the summer? A girlfriend or something?'

Billy-Ray fidgeted with the matches. 'Nah. Nothing like that.' Thought of Magde crying quietly, overflowing with disappointment.

A road sign told them they were leaving Everett, twenty miles from Seattle.

'Would you like to see the ocean?' asked Lucca.

'Yah – I'm going to. In Seattle.'

Lucca laughed. 'That's not the ocean – that's just a big river. I mean the Pacific Ocean in all its glory.'

'Yah. I'm hoping I will, one day.'

'OK – well, I have to go into town to file some copy, deliver some papers. Then I'm heading out to the coast, south of the city. A friend of mine's got a cabin out there, near the Columbia River, and she's loaned it me for the weekend. I'm driving back into Seattle on Monday afternoon – I could drop you off then.' Lucca drew smoke deep into her lungs. 'If you want to come, that is. If you want to stay the weekend.'

Billy-Ray Rickman might have been a hick from the flatlands but he knew what was going on. 'Can you see the ocean from the cabin?'

'I don't know. I think so. Maybe.'

'OK, yah, I'd like to come.'

Lucca dropped off the papers and then stopped at an A&P on the outskirts of Seattle. She and Billy-Ray walked the aisles, collecting together the ingredients for breakfast, some steaks, potatoes and salad.

'D'you like beer?' Lucca asked.

'Yah. And vodka.'

Lucca picked up a carton of Lucky Strikes, some beers, vodka and brandy, along with a few bottles of wine. Billy-Ray stood behind her, holding the groceries as she paid, trying not to register shock at how many bills she handed over. More money than his mother spent on food in a month. The woman working the cash box glanced at Billy-Ray and Lucca, smiled an odd smile, and Billy-Ray blushed.

'Do you want to go to the drugstore?' asked Lucca once the bags were in the trunk. She shaded her eyes against the glare of the midday sun. Standing in the street, dressed in creased clothes, she looked older than she had in the car. There were faint wrinkles on her neck and crow's feet by her eyes. Billy-Ray saw she was wearing trousers, black, tailored, high-waisted trousers, creased at the groin.

'Excuse me?'

'Look, all I'm asking is if you need to visit the drugstore. I'm a little too old to be a mother. Here.' She held out two dollar bills.

'Right.' Billy-Ray was sweating in his jacket. 'OK. Right.'

When he came back, two packs of rubbers rustling in his jacket pocket, Lucca was sitting in the passenger seat, smoking. 'You drive,' she said. 'I've been at the wheel since six this morning and I need some sleep. Here's the map.' She flapped a creased Rand McNally at him.

Billy-Ray slid on to the driver's seat, stared at the dash, not understanding it. 'Where's the gears?'

'It's automatic.'

'It's what?'

'The car deals with the gears. You just put your foot on the gas pedal or the brake. Simple. If you can drive a tractor you can drive this.'

'What kind of car is this anyway? Never seen one like it before.'

'You won't have done – it's a Cord Eight-twelve. They only made a thousand or round about.' Lucca folded a cardigan for a makeshift pillow. 'Then the damn war came along and you couldn't buy a new car or even parts for the goddam old one.'

Billy-Ray turned over the engine, slipped the stick a notch and grinned as the car slid forward. 'Where are we going anyway?'

'Out past Aberdeen. I've marked it on the map. Highway twelve, then south on the one-oh-five.' Lucca laughed. 'Can't miss it – it's called Cape Disappointment.'

And Billy-Ray's stomach lurched when he heard that name. *Der Enttauschung.*

But there were compensations – Billy-Ray loved driving the car, he loved the privacy, the luxury of the Cord 812. He'd only ever driven ancient John Deeres and battered Dodge pick-ups – and he'd never encountered the idea of driving for driving's sake, to arrive somewhere with the sole purpose of having fun, not to load bales of hay or move hogs or replace a rusted trough – simply to go somewhere because it was somewhere else. As Lucca slept he floored the gas pedal, taking the car up to sixty, the ragged verges flashing by. Then he slowed, lit a cigarette, cruised along the highway at forty, fantasizing about owning a car like this, simply driving in a car like this, maybe with some girl. Grinned as he thought of the people he'd left behind in Bow Regard – he'd only been gone three days and look what he was doing. At a junction he passed a hitcher, a tall, blond boy with a bag at his feet, a boy who looked hungry, who looked loose, who looked a long, long way from home. For a moment Billy-Ray burned with shame (Siggy would have stopped, reversed, picked up the boy), but then he thought, well . . . you make your own luck. At the very moment Billy-Ray was considering luck in all its guises, the Cord crested a rise outside Aberdeen and there it was: the biggest ocean on earth. Billy-Ray coasted the car on to the verge, climbed out and looked, breathed deep. He stood watching an uneventful sea break on the coast, line after fractured line of foam and spume rolling, snagging on sea floors, hidden rocks, weak sandstone cliffs, until the train of heaving water met the rising sandy bed. And there the waves crowded each other as the train ploughed into land. Billy-Ray knew that these waves had travelled thousands of miles to break at his feet but it still seemed inconceivable. He scanned the arc of horizon, which extended as far as he could see – unending ocean, flat, unbroken.

'So what d'you think, Billy-Ray?' Lucca had woken and now stood beside him.

He looked at the horizon, saw a tanker in the distance. 'Do you know what's across there? On the same latitude?'

Lucca lit a cigarette, with some difficulty given the stiff onshore breeze. 'Surprise me.'

'Japan.'

Surprised, Lucca Barzini, ex-war-reporter, stared across the waters. It was May 1946. 'Japan?'

'Yah,' said Billy-Ray.

'Jesus,' muttered Lucca.

'It's OK,' said Billy-Ray, putting an arm around her shoulders. 'It's thousands of miles away.'

The cabin on Cape Disappointment was a two-room, timbered shack, shingled and weathered but well built and sturdy, entirely functional. Functional apart from its location – inelegantly, unnecessarily but beautifully perched on a rise in the dunes, where the view from the small porch was of the waves rolling in from Asia. Inside, the wood-fired stove had been swept and cleaned, but there was a layer of fine pale sand on everything. Lucca found the linen and made up the bed as Billy-Ray lit the stove and sorted the groceries. Billy-Ray finished his chores before Lucca and he stood in the doorway of the bedroom, watching her thin, wiry form as she forced a pillow into its linen case.

'What's your problem, Billy-Ray?'

'Huh?'

'I have the feeling you're in a hurry to be doing something.'

'I'd like to walk along the beach, before it gets dark. I just . . . I just want to walk.'

Lucca straightened and looked at the young, handsome man, standing in a wooden doorway, his hands working, bunching and releasing. She knew he was too polite to press the point, and too fired up to sit out on the porch and wait for her. He looked hungry for something, loose almost. And a long, long way from home. 'Let's go.' Lucca dropped the pillow and walked past Billy-Ray, picked up a bottle of wine, a corkscrew and two glasses, put them in a bag which she slung over her shoulder. 'C'mon, let's go.'

The two of them walked silently along the spit, clambered down a rocky path and began to tramp the hard, damp-packed sand which crunched satisfyingly. Billy-Ray took off his boots and socks and walked barefoot, turning every now and then to watch his shallow prints fill with brine and then fade. After half an hour Lucca stopped, unhitched the bag from her shoulders and sat in the dunes, held the bottle and corkscrew out to Billy-Ray, who took them and stared at the corkscrew as if it were an unwanted weapon. He had never used one.

'Here, give it to me.' Lucca, a cigarette hanging loosely from her lips, her eyes screwed up against the smoke, wielded the corkscrew, drove it snug into the cork, handed the bottle back to Billy-Ray. 'Just pull on the damn thing.'

He pulled and heard the sound of stale air phutting.

'Here, fill 'em up.' Lucca held out the glasses.

Billy-Ray thought of the gnarled Portuguese corks his father yanked from his bottles of firewater. Thought of miraculous wafers, thought of a tall blonde woman firing into the air. He looked at the blood of Christ he held in his hands and he wondered. Billy-Ray had never drunk wine other than on his knees. He fell to his knees by Lucca and glugged the wine into the glasses. He turned and sat, looking out over the restless water, gunmetal grey, its surface skittering, catching sky-light. Next to him, Lucca buttoned her jacket and wrapped her arms round her tiny waist.

'So, Billy-Ray, I guess this is where you get to tell me about your family and why you left them.' Lucca groped for the ever-present packet of cigarettes and busied herself with her party trick.

Billy-Ray drank the wine, a poor Californian from a failing vineyard – swallowed it down in a draught, like a drunk, like a rabid man, like a vampire – and frowned. 'No.'

'OK. Then this is when you tell me about your childhood sweetheart and how much you miss her.'

'No.' Billy-Ray poured himself another glass.

'Right – so this must be where you tell me about how misunderstood you feel.'

Billy-Ray turned his cold eyes on Lucca. 'I don't.'

Lucca shrugged. 'OK.' Drew deeply on her cigarette and burning specks of paper flew in the breeze.

The two of them sat on the damp sand watching the light in the sky change, drinking, Lucca waiting for him to say something, to ask her something about her life. But Billy-Ray just drank the wine and stared at the horizon as Lucca remembered the selfishness of the young, their preoccupation with their lives and how they might be lived.

'Blue earth,' Billy-Ray said suddenly, and smiled.

'What?'

'Blue earth, that's what the sea is like – blue earth.'

Lucca frowned, held her hair back from her face with a hand. The breeze had picked up. 'Didn't you say you came from there? Blue Earth something?'

'Blue Earth County, Minnesota.'

'Look, can we go back? It's getting cold and I'm hungry as hell. You can come and stare at your blue earth all day tomorrow if that's what you want to do.' Lucca gathered together the empty glasses and bottle, stood and shouldered the bag.

Billy-Ray cooked the steaks over a small fire he built in a sand hollow beyond the porch as Lucca drank more wine and made potato salad. When the food was finished Billy-Ray banked up the fire and the two of them huddled by it as the damp rolled in across thousands of miles of blue earth, precipitating itself at their feet. Lucca drank brandy, chain-smoked, moved to lean against the bulk of the young man. Billy-Ray drank vodka, listened to the salt water dragging pebbles, grinding them down, heard brine percolating through sand.

Lucca downed the last of her drink, tossed the butt of her cigarette into the fire, watching it flare green before moving forward, kneeling in front of Billy-Ray, between him and the heat. She looked feral, her eyes narrowed, predatory. She took his face in her small hands, felt the beard against her palm, felt the bones beneath her own. As she pulled him towards her, Billy-Ray spilt his vodka, soaking his jeans, dropped the glass, and he reached for Lucca's bird waist, tugging at the blouse tucked there. Still Lucca held his face, kissed him, running her tongue around his lips, pushing at him as he tore cotton and his hands moved to her small, hot breasts, moving them against her ribs. Embers scattered around them as Billy-Ray kicked out, wanting to have more purchase, and a log tumbled. Something was gathering at the base of Billy-Ray's spine and he wanted to concentrate on that. As if a gyroscope were spinning there, growing hotter.

Lucca drew away, still holding his face, holding it tight. Leaning over him, her short, dark hair blowing across her face, a face that looked somehow heavier, vascular, expectant almost, she asked, 'Do you want to go to bed?'

Billy-Ray, breathing heavily, nodded.

Lucca Barzini had spent ten months in the Sierra de Malagon, the mountains north of Madrid, nine years before. Ten months of spine-tingling, exotic danger. Nine months of snatched sleep in bivouacs or caves, weeks spent eating only dried meat, raisins, salted cod and beans. Days spent scanning the horizon with binoculars, looking for troop movements; writing notes when she could in her tattered, wine-stained journal, notes that were fuel for the book she would write when it was all over. At night she was comforted by the acrid smell of cigarettes being smoked furtively outside the tent, by that and the scent of pine. Enrique – the reason she was there at all – stayed with her every night, lying next to her, taut as a lyre string, talking, as she jotted down the manifesto Enrique had for the world. He was short, dark, smelled of horse's sweat and tobacco and Lucca loved him. His energy was focused in his dark brown eyes, which seemed to follow everything. His body movements were considered, almost languid; only his eyes flickered, taking in information as he plotted. So, when Lucca saw him, early one March morning, as snow thawed, strung damply between the needles, when she saw Enrique running, scrambling up the mountainside, small boulders and scree tumbling behind him; when she saw him hauling himself up the slope, pulling at branches, trunks, anything, pulling himself towards her, she knew something had gone wrong. The morning patrol had left two hours before, six of them, and now there seemed only to be one, scrabbling, slipping down now, as the scree and dry needle cover deepened. Below Enrique, Lucca caught a glimpse of a beautiful bay horse between the trees, flanks quivering as it toiled up the gradient. A bay horse, an epaulette, a high leather boot. A rifle. More horses, shouts. A squadron of Franco's Falangists emerged from the thickly wooded lower slopes. Eight men, eight rifles. As Lucca was pulled away from her ledge, pulled out of sight, she saw Enrique stop, fall, roll himself into a ball among the pine needles, hands tucked beneath his chin. As she was pushed into the cave, as tarpaulin and webbing were pulled over the entrance, shots echoed through the hills and she began to shake.

When Lucca Barzini went back home, back to New York City, and saw for the first time Robert Capa's photograph of the soldier falling, his shirt improbably white, his arms akimbo as if hoping for his mother's embrace, she threw away her notes and journals. She knew then that nothing she could write about those months in the Spanish hills would ever match the simplicity, the pathos, the *potency* of that image. She moved out west, to be near mountains, away from the idle bitchery of New York. Once she had settled she began to develop a taste for young, tall, restless blond boys. Boys who would keep running; boys who would not roll into a submissive ball before dying.

That long weekend at Cape Disappointment was one Billy-Ray remembered often. Later, it seemed a hiatus before his new life began in earnest. He and Lucca spent the days walking, watching the blue earth move, drinking slowly but steadily. They also spent a great deal of time in the sawn-timbered bedroom. Lucca was entirely without inhibitions, had reached the age – she was forty-four, indeed the same age as Irochka Reichmann – when she knew that the always unequal battle against years of sun and smoke, liquor and excess, was lost. She was what she was. She allowed Billy-Ray (as she allowed all her blond boys) to look at her, touch her as he wanted, told him what worked and what didn't, taught him how to arouse her. Billy-Ray, for his part, came to find her near-androgyny strangely exciting. The thought of her pale, thin body, pliant as a whip, lying on the sheets, open, waiting for him whenever he asked, fired his spinal gyroscope, started his blood racing. Lucca found Billy-Ray one of the best-lovers? playthings? fucks? (just what *was* she supposed to call them all?) – she had had. He had a sure touch – which, of course, he would have: Billy-Ray knew how to fondle a horse's soft underlip, how to seduce a muskellunge into taking bait, how to cradle a dying hog. Turned out the lessons Oliver taught him were useful after all.

'So – what're you going to do with your geology, Billy-Ray?' Lucca asked as he drove the two of them back to Seattle on a wet Monday afternoon.

'I don't know yet. Reckon I could do a few things – mapping, maybe archaeology. Or exploration.'

Lucca lit a cigarette, shifted on the seat, feeling tender. 'Can't imagine there're that many places left to explore.'

Billy-Ray laughed. 'No way! There're places we never even heard of – well, we maybe heard of them but we don't know about them. The map of the world isn't finished. Like the sea? We don't know much about what's under there.' Billy-Ray thought of the shifting blue earth. 'Under there, there could be anything. Mountains and trenches, volcanoes. And on land there're rivers and deltas we've never seen. Like in Africa? The coastline's pretty clear but in the middle, well, there's jungles and craters and deserts which need mapping. There's lots of places we've never been.'

Lucca studied his Nordic profile. 'Who d'you mean by "we", Billy-Ray?'

Billy-Ray shrugged. 'Y'know, places we've never been.'

'Who d'you mean by "we"?'

Billy-Ray stretched his neck, put his hand out of the open window, felt the rain coming down. 'You know, us.'

'"Us?"'

'Ah, c'mon. Y'know, Americans. I guess. We haven't mapped everything. Haven't discovered things we need to know.'

As they crossed the river, Lucca watched a barge manoeuvring logs to the dock of a sawmill on the banks of Willapa Bay. 'I think,' she said, 'that you need to be careful, Billy-Ray. You're – what? Eighteen? You don't know anything. You don't know *anything*. What are you? Third-generation American? Maybe. Maybe second. You said your people are German and Polish. Think about it.'

'I'm an American.'

'Well, shit, Billy-Ray, so am I. But I'm also an Italian. My people are from a town near Pompeii. Do you know that nearly two thousand years ago the Romans had baths, theatres, spas and coliseums? When Pompeii got buried the Romans ruled the world. They had an army, they had a forum, they had roads and markets. They had all the maps they ever needed. And so did the Red Indians – they had everything they needed too. Until "we" came.'

'I don't understand what you're saying. I just want to find things out. I just want to find things and put them on a map. I don't see what your point is.'

Lucca shivered, threw her butt out of the window and closed it. 'Neither do I right now. All I'm saying is, don't think, don't imagine, that just because somewhere isn't mapped and named means that no one's been there, that no one lives there.' She lit another Lucky Strike, reopened the window a crack. 'Don't think that just because an American hasn't been somewhere it doesn't exist, that it isn't important.'

'I don't think that.'

'Good.' Lucca turned away from Billy-Ray's Brownshirt profile, watched the small, ugly coastal towns of Washington passing, single-storey, shingled, ravaged by rain, neon flickering. She remembered the towns of Catalonia, the dusty, red earth around Zaragoza, remembered the musty bodegas, the colonnades of Santo Domingo de Silos, where she had eaten grilled sardines as she listened to Gregorian chants, unchanged over centuries, floating from the cathedral across the square. Thought of fallen empires. Thought of the taste of cool Spanish mountain air on March mornings. Pictured a man curling into the smallest space possible before dying.

'Where in Italy are your folks from?' asked Billy-Ray.

'Salerno.'

Bitte, Gott, lass es Dieter sein.

When they arrived in downtown Seattle, Billy-Ray grabbed his bag from the trunk as Lucca shunted over to the driver's seat. He knew –

and he wasn't sure how – that he wouldn't see Lucca again. He bent down, looked through the window and watched her flick down the visor, looking in the mirror as she applied blood-red lipstick. In the harsh morning light, in profile, she looked old, older than Irochka.

'Uh, Lucca . . . thanks. Thanks for the weekend.'

'No problem.' She slid the column stick into drive, glanced at the traffic piling up at the junction of 3rd and Virginia. 'Hope you find your deserts and mountains and volcanoes, or whatever it is you're looking for.' Lucca turned to look at his young, blond face. Lit a cigarette and smiled at him. 'Be good, Billy-Ray, be good.' She winked and drove away.

1958

Jarman House was no castle, as Maggie Regan realized over time. The mansion shrank as it wrapped itself in familiarity – the creak of a floorboard, the stiffness of a handle, a scratch in a pane of glass. It became, first, as familiar as the dingy, cluttered house she had known in Ballysod, and then, as the months passed, Jarman House became Maggie's home, replacing the cramped, sour rooms of her childhood memory. She became used to space, used to walking from room to room, arms loaded with linen or towels, passing shuttered windows before climbing wide, sweeping stairs. The geometric patterns of the tiled floors, the swan-wing curve of fanlights, the blurred diamonds of sapphire on ivory walls, thrown like water by stained glass, all of these things became familiar. Hot water, food, laundered clothes, time – she enjoyed all these comforts, if not to excess, and eventually came to expect them. The fact of having her own room, albeit a small garret beneath the eaves, with low, sloping ceilings and ill-fitting window frames, never ceased to amaze her, however. Every night Maggie would close the rhomboid door, cut to accommodate the sloping, shifting floor, and savour the silence, the loneliness, of the hole beneath the attic. Over the months she'd bought a few things to decorate the room – a watercolour of a bay that reminded her of Achill, a small petrol-glass vase and – her prized possession – a snowstorm. She'd found it on a stall in Portobello, a small glass dome with a tiny turreted castle on a hill trapped inside; when she shook the dome a snowstorm blew across the miniature forest and craggy peak. It had cost her a guinea but she loved it and kept it on her bedside table. At night, once her door was closed behind her, she'd wash and shuck on a thin shift before climbing into her narrow bed, where she'd stretch her limbs, before tucking herself into a ball, hands clenched beneath her chin, feet crossed against the cold. Reaching out, she'd shake the snowstorm and, watching it, she'd begin to drift.

Maggie could join her father in the cab of his ancient van, redolent of fish and earth and freshly baked bread, could hear the rasp of a match as her father lit one of his thin cigarettes, feel the draught as he lowered the window to toss the spent match. Or she might find herself sitting on a hard, unforgiving slate floor, her bare feet cold, blue as ice, as she watched her sister, poor Mary, praying on numb knees, pale fingers laced, thin chest labouring against an unremitting, unrelenting infection. Maggie could also drift to the kitchen in Ballysod, where she found her mother, the worn, rotund Annie, sitting at the battered table, her hands wrapped around a mug of tea, her eyes vacant, as she stared unseeing at a wall covered with photographs and postcards sent by Maggie's siblings.

Sometimes Maggie found herself with Danny Maconnell, as he sat on the grass with a girl, his tanned, muscular forearms wrapped around his knees, talking, talking, his mouth wrapping itself around the words 'Godolphin' and 'Barb', and Maggie would watch as the girl's lips parted and her legs moved a little. Then Maggie would begin to dream of other things, would imagine the feel of Danny's hands stroking her breasts, squeezing her nipples, imagine the sensation of Danny pushing into her.

Maggie had her room with its own door. She had peace when that door was closed. She had money to buy knick-knacks. Maggie was almost happy.

1946

The family Billy-Ray stayed with in Seattle, during his first summer there, were relatives of Mr Svensson, the geography teacher in Bow Regard who had given him the biography of the planet. As it happened, Billy-Ray stayed only a week in the house on Pike Lane in Ballard. Mr Svensson's brother, Urban Svensson, owned a sixty-two-foot purse-seiner, *Viveka*, moored at Fishermen's Terminal, and when Urban first met Billy-Ray he knew his crewing problems for the summer were solved. Here was a good, steady, strong boy who wanted to earn money, who *needed* to earn money – he was a scholarship student – and who also spoke Swedish. So Urban asked whether Billy-Ray would join him and two of his sons for the summer season.

'But I've never been on a boat,' Billy-Ray pointed out. 'Well, only on Home Lake.'

Urban, a stocky man with short silvery hair and irises the colour of oxygen-starved ice chips, looked Billy-Ray up and down. 'You want to try it out? Only problem might be seasickness. You want to maybe go out and see how you feel?'

Billy-Ray laughed. 'Why not?'

The next morning Urban took Billy-Ray down to the moorings off the Ship Canal and borrowed a yacht from a friend. Standing on the dock, Billy-Ray thought for a moment of the Wave that haunted his sleep, pushed it into a dark recess of his mind and stepped gingerly into the frail, rocking craft, his world sliding left and right, over-balancing, underbalancing. Urban slipped the line and the two of them set out for the Puget Sound – a paddling pool to Urban, a naked, heaving swell to Billy-Ray. They sailed away from the city, into the Sound, the yacht rolling and yawing a little, Billy-Ray hanging on to the seat so hard his bones ached.

'Usually we're gone by now, second week of May.' Urban had to shout to make himself heard above the blustery wind, which was snapping the sails as rain pelted on the taut canvas. 'But I have to wait for a replacement camshaft, maybe a week. So we are preparing *Viveka* for the summer.' Urban smiled. 'She's a good boat, deep draught, built in Sweden – where else? It is important to do this – to prepare well. New ropes, shackles, turnbuckles and chain. Everything must be sound. How do you feel?'

Billy-Ray's equilibrium was returning, seemed to be located in a different place and he stood slowly, felt his legs as elastic, absorbing the movement, allowing him to adjust to the world moving. 'Yah – I'm fine. I'm OK.'

'Good. Let's take her farther out.' Urban tightened the halyard, and the wind blew flat against the sails, herding the boat into choppy water. Still Billy-Ray stood. 'Usually Teodor, Lars and Eskil are with me. But Lars has a broken shoulder – crashed his truck last week – and I need an extra hand. If you still want the work, you can help us fit out this week and then we leave Monday. We'll be gone maybe two, three months. You have one share – that's ten per cent of what we take.'

'How much will that be?'

Urban smiled thinly. 'How can we know? It may be nothing. It may be thousands of dollars. It depends on what the sea gives us.'

'But where do we *go*?' asked Billy-Ray, looking around at the expanse of water – gunmetal grey, blue, white, which seemed to go on for ever. Which, of course, did go on for ever.

'Alaska.'

That night, once Billy-Ray had been declared seaworthy, Urban laid out maps on the kitchen table, leaned over them and pointed out the different routes he had taken over the years. Billy-Ray, taller than Urban by six inches, stooped next to the fisherman and watched the man's diesel-grimed fingers trace patterns in the Gulf of Alaska, around the Aleutians.

'That trip, out to Togiak, must have been in thirty-eight. It was a bad year. We were gone three days short of four months. Weather was bad, fish were shy, had to keep running for shelter. But since forty it's been easier.'

'Why's that?'

Urban, who knew something of Billy-Ray's background from letters his brother, the geography teacher, had sent him, stood up and stretched his back. 'More fish, fewer boats. Fewer boats, more fish. Last year we were only out seven weeks.'

'Why fewer boats?'

Urban leaned back over the map, not looking at Billy-Ray. 'The war. Fewer men left to crew.'

Billy-Ray frowned and swallowed, sucked his lower lip.

Viveka, Urban's wife after whom the boat was named, who had been knitting yet another intricately cabled oiled-wool jumper, came up and touched Billy-Ray's shoulder. 'I made some babka this morning, Billy-Ray. Would you like some?' Billy-Ray nodded. 'I'll bring you some coffee too. He'll keep you here all night talking about lines and nets if you're not careful.'

When Billy-Ray looked at Urban again, it was to find the man staring at him.

'I thought your name was Wilhelm-Rajmund Reichmann. A German name.'

'Nah, everyone calls me Billy-Ray. Billy-Ray Rickman.'

Urban regarded him – it was a look Billy-Ray became used to: neutral and cool. Urban was calculating what it was, exactly, this young man was trying to do. He knew about Siggy and Deet, knew that Billy-Ray was running. But what *exactly* was it he was running from? His past? His culture? His *name*? This boy was prepared to shed his name, and Urban knew it was the one thing that anchored you. That it told others what you were, who you were, where you were from. Urban turned back to the map.

'What do you catch?' asked Billy-Ray.

'Chinook, herring, mainly salmon. Depends where you are and when you're there. And on the weather.'

Viveka brought a plate of sweet raisin bread for the men and retreated back to her chair. Urban ate in silence, then he dusted off his hands, folded his arms, leaned back against the table. 'Billy-Ray, Wilhelm-Rajmund, whatever you want to call yourself, I have to tell you a few things before you say yes or no to coming on board. You may make hundreds of dollars, maybe even thousands. But you may make nothing after I've taken money for food and gas. The work is hard. Not so bad if we stay on the east side of the gulf, but even there the storms are bad. You don't know storms at sea. If we have to go farther, west to the Aleutians, Bristol Bay, maybe even north of there, the spray turns to ice on everything. You don't sleep, you don't eat, you stay alive. You survive.' Urban glanced at Viveka's back. 'Or you don't. Every season boats go down, maybe they begin a roll and they keep rolling or they demast and hole themselves. There's nothing you can do. Boats go down. Waves fifty, sixty feet high. Eddies, whirlpools, where the sea turns brown and white, sucks you down. You don't last a minute out there. It's too cold. I haven't asked whether you can swim or not because it doesn't make any difference. Think about it. If you still want to join us be ready to come to the terminal at seven tomorrow morning. If not, you can always get work at the docks on dry land.'

The room Billy-Ray was given that night was small and sparsely furnished, with a wooden chair, table and bed, all of them stained or painted shades of blue, green and grey. He felt he was already all at sea, sinking into a watery place, living in a blue earth. He didn't bother undressing, just shucked off his boots and lay down on the bed, thinking. He calculated the height of the room and tried to picture a wall of water six or seven times that height and failed. Tried to imagine the ocean frozen. He thought of the few days he had spent with Lucca Barzini at Cape Disappointment, sitting on the warm, rocky beach there, watching the Pacific glinting in the late spring sun. How could that freeze? How could that water freeze as it moved lazily on the shingle? Billy-Ray dozed for an hour, only to be woken by the image of *Viveka* rolling, broadsides, down a mountain of water. Turning, reaching a point of stasis then rolling again, turning over into the water, as he fell from her deck along with nets and lines and winches and radios and other men. He woke with a yelp – it was the Wave, still chasing him. He pressed the scar on his thigh, rocked on the bed and eventually he slept again. At dawn he woke to the sound of Eskil and Teodor washing in the room next door, talking as they pulled on boots which he heard being stamped on the wooden floor. The sky was cloudless in the window and he thought of the landlocked farm he had left, thought of his parents, of Magde and what he had stolen from her. Billy-Ray came to a decision, sat up and pulled on his own boots.

During the first few days, as *Viveka* chugged through the scattered islands of the Puget Sound, weaving a path through the masses of purse-seiners, crabbers, gill netters, ferries and barges, heading out to the Juan de Fuca Straits, Billy-Ray thought often about his night-fright when he had imagined plunging from a vertical deck into fifty feet of frozen water, and he smiled. *Viveka* was threading her way through densely forested, craggy islands, dotted with clapboard houses. The sun shone each day and the wind kept him cool without kicking up the water.

For the past week he'd loaded crates and boxes of tinned food, jerky beef, flour and pulses on board, but no alcohol, which Urban prohibited on *Viveka*. He'd filled the fish hold with the first consignment of ice they'd use that summer. The rest of the time he'd stayed by Urban's side, listening to his terse instructions about securing lines, managing the line-feed drum, locking hatches, hosing down. He practised gutting fish (if fish was *fiska*, *fisch* and *fisk*, why was it also *ryba*?), slow at first and then more adept with the passing days – but that was on a flat, static surface. On the Thursday Billy-Ray sliced open his palm and didn't even notice until the blood ran off the slab, the blade edge was so keen. He thought then of what it might be like wielding the knife in a gale. He soon found out.

The first few weeks out were calm and cool, *Viveka* trawling up the west coast of Vancouver Island, Billy-Ray getting used to the rolling and yawing as the boat stood to and made a set, getting used to always being in motion. Getting used, too, to always feeling tired – much like pigs, fish also ignored the hands of the clock, swarmed in great shoals whenever they felt like it. Billy-Ray got used to hearing Urban, Eskil or Teodor hammering on the hatch, yelling, 'Coming on!' at all hours of day and night. Out he would roll, stunned by a moment's sleep, still wearing weatherproofs. And then there would be the roar of the line-feed drum and flying spray spattering his face as the haul was dragged up, vast nets bulging, herring arguing and fretting against the rope, against each other. Watching the winch come up, swing over the deck as the purse was opened. Then mad hours spent slicing and yanking out livers, fine pink tissues, shit and hearts, throwing the detritus of the butchered fish overboard as the gulls screamed and Billy-Ray's legs buckled, straightened, bent and loosened with the roll. The barrels filling with silver gold, beautiful even in death; the herring cascading into the hold, coming to rest on an icy bed. Then the regathering of the net, the checking of the floats and weights as Urban checked the coordinates, calculated the catch, made notes. Billy-Ray hosed down the deck and scrubbed the choppers, knives and boards as father and sons decided which route to take next, where to set the nets. Sometimes *Viveka* stayed in the same spot, Urban thinking more were coming through. Then Teodor and Eskil would again go out in the small net boat, taking the weights at the end of the net with them, dropping them, pulling the carefully coiled purse behind as Urban gestured and yelled instructions. Billy-Ray sat on an upended barrel, trying to smoke a damp cigarette, holding it pinched between deep-cracked, saltined, stinging thumb and finger, drawing piscine smoke into his lungs. Teodor and Eskil set the net, drawing it back to the mother boat, as Urban stood at the gunwales and scanned the water, watching for ripples, for currents, strange aquatic movements which Billy-Ray – greenhorn – didn't yet understand. Then the winches would begin to strain, the floats pull against the tide and Billy-Ray knew it was all about to start again. But sometimes Urban scanned the horizon and saw other boats nearby and *Viveka* would move on, chug northward, towards Alaska. Then Billy-Ray would fall asleep, still sitting on the barrel, his brain no longer registering the rolling motion, his body going with it, rocking as he slept.

Viveka ploughed on across the tidal surges of Queen Charlotte Sound, passing the southern tip of Morseby Island, hugging the coast closely, yet still hanging over waters two thousand feet deep.

'Coast just keeps going down, a mountain under the sea,' Urban told Billy-Ray. 'No shelf at all. Can get a bit rough.'

On past Cape Knox, Billy-Ray's hands toughening up, the cracks no longer bleeding, so he could hold ropes and knife handles, axes and cigarettes. His body had learned that it wouldn't often sleep and he watched the land change, watched the sea change. Across the Dixon Entrance and Billy-Ray was back in America, bobbing about in the Gulf of Alaska. Sometimes he wondered what he was doing there, when the fist hammered on the hatch at one in the morning and the sun was still lighting the ocean, and there was another giant, dripping teardrop of herring swinging over the side. Other times he couldn't remember what it was like to be on land – he was becoming a moving element of this blue earth.

The distant coastline changed one quiet night as *Viveka* – her holds full, weighted down with seventy thousand pounds of frozen herring, packed so solid a sardine couldn't weave its way aboard – ground her way towards Cape Pole, allowing Billy-Ray eight hours' sleep. He woke at false dawn, lay in his bunk, listening to Teodor and Eskil muttering and snoring; listened, too, to the sound of the ocean clawing at the wooden sides of the boat, scratching at it. Pans and utensils swung and tapped against the latched stow cupboards, in a rhythm almost syncopated. Billy-Ray scratched himself, raked his hair – a solid lump of matter, glued with dried salt – and examined his hands with interest. Red, chapped, scarred and abrasive – they surely should belong to someone else? He tumbled out of the bunk and headed up to the deck.

And there, to the east, were the mountains, the glaciers. The ranges just sitting there as they always had, making the foothills of the Rockies seem like hillocks, molehills. Billy-Ray could only glimpse the peaks – owing, of course, to the curvature of the earth – but even then the landscape made him stop his scratching and stare, slack jawed, unbelieving.

'Cat got your tongue?' asked Urban from the wheelhouse.

Billy-Ray said nothing, simply stood and stared at the vista of water, ice and granite, green-coloured by sitkas.

'Hey – look.' Urban pointed to starboard, where a barnacle-spotted, white-stained tail glistened as it flipped gallons of water skyward and the humpback dived, cutting the water dead, leaving no wake, merely a ripple.

Billy-Ray turned and turned again on the deck, arms akimbo, taking it all in, wanting to hug this wilderness close to his chest.

A bald-headed eagle, crossing the path of *Viveka*, cruising the thermals as the white tips of its wings ruffled, scanned the blue earth with its mad, golden eyes and fixed in its sights a tall, blond boy spinning below, loose and free. Swooped down to assess the damage that might be done, but there was no scent of blood. One last look at the turning man and the eagle swivelled its head, flexed its talons and headed for richer pickings, drifting over to the island of Heceta.

June, and the salmon were starting to run. *Viveka*'s hold was filled with fresh ice at Cape Pole and she headed north, weaving her way through the Alexander Archipelago, up to the southern tip of Baranof Island, where she turned west, out into the gulf, out over deep waters, in search of the gyre. Urban was, literally, in his element. The swell was slight, the wind light and the chinook, pink, coho, sockeye and, of course, chum were running in packs, in packs of hundreds of thousands, piling up, jamming the waterways of the Pacific. The ocean churned silver and gunmetal as the fish raced for home in a single-minded quest to find the river of their birth. A succession of crystal days, marked by the passing of orcas and humpbacks, ran one into another, and Billy-Ray found himself near-hypnotized by the sounds and colours and movement of his new life. The relentless unzipping of the purse and the hours spent gutting had ceased to register with him – he worked and he watched the world as the seiner traced an unlikely course towards Sitka. Ten days later he found himself throwing a line to Teodor as *Viveka* moored up near the Anderssen cannery near Sitka. In the hold they had thirty thousand pounds deadweight of chinook, and Urban couldn't stop smiling. Billy-Ray yanked the last line tight and stretched his back, looked round to see Urban and Eskil standing, arms crossed, leaning against the gunwale, watching him.

'What? Have I missed something?' Billy-Ray turned to check the mooring lines.

Urban shrugged, kept smiling. 'No – it's fine. You go on, we'll catch up with you.'

Billy-Ray went below, collected his pack, checked for razors and soap, fresh clothes, relishing the thought of a hot tub and a shave. It had been four weeks. He glanced in the tiny mirror hanging above the gimbal-swung stove and rubbed at his beard with the back of his damaged fingers. He clambered back on deck to find Urban and Eskil still standing there, talking desultorily, glancing at him.

'Go with Teodor – he knows where we wash up.'

'OK – see you later.'

Billy-Ray climbed the ladder to the pier, hauled himself on to solid land, took two steps on the planks and found himself rolling like a drunk. He staggered left as his brain swam in his head, trying to find an actual horizon. Billy-Ray grabbed a railing and shook his head. Took two more steps and he plunged involuntarily sideways, clutching at Teodor, who was laughing himself sick. Looking back with swimming eyes, Billy-Ray could just make out Urban and Eskil doubled over, roaring. He straightened, took a step and lurched again as the earth shifted beneath him.

'Shit!' he yelled, raking his free hand as far as he could through his matted thatch. 'Shit!'

Again he tried to walk, rolling about, lumbering left and right, shuffling whenever possible to make up some ground. Billy-Ray began to snicker, then giggle. He felt light headed, unhinged, as if he were not of this world, as if he had gills; as if he were the Little Mermaid, an axolotl. A hand slapped his back, sent him into a shambling circle trying to right himself.

'Come on, I'll give you a hand. It wears off. Just takes a while.' Teodor was still laughing.

'How long?'

'Couple of days. Then we go back out on the boat.'

'Shit.'

That night the four of them went out on the town, painted it yellow and blue, red and white. They drank first in the Smoked Sockeye, then ate imported steak and fries in Janssen's diner before getting down to some serious drinking at Ed's Bar. Sitka was pulsing with newly washed, freshly shaved drunks of all nations, many staggering as Billy-Ray did, legs buckling like spruce in a quake. Billy-Ray reached the point where he wasn't sure whether it was the beer or his sea legs which were making him reel. In a dingy, foul-smelling bar off Halibut Road, Urban proposed a shaky toast – they had already hauled enough to pay for the gas and food for the duration. Any fish from then on were clear profit.

Billy-Ray tried to focus on his beer. 'D'you mean,' he asked, 'that what we've done so far ain't made us *anything*?'

'No, not yet.'

'Well, that don't seem right.' Billy-Ray stretched the skin of his face, felt the sun, salt and wind in his pores.

'You're standing here, with a drink, having been four weeks at sea. You haven't paid a penny for rent, food or gas.' Urban downed a shot of vodka. 'That's the way it works.'

Billy-Ray thought about this, for a long time, then nodded. 'You're right. You're absholutely right. Let me buy y'all a drink.'

'You can't – you haven't any money.'

For some reason this struck all four of them as a great joke and they howled, beat the bar with their palms, bringing the barman over.

'Four doubles, on me,' yelled Billy-Ray, and the vodkas appeared as the laughter crept up a notch.

A Russian crew came through the doors, chafing their salt-damaged hands together, talking of cunts and money.

The sound of Irochka's voice, the words she had taught him as a boy, came tumbling back to Billy-Ray. He swivelled as best he was able and asked them to watch their language.

One of the crew, a man who had obviously been dipped into a genetic stew of Mongol, Tlingit and Slav, narrowed his eyes and focused on Billy-Ray. Urban shifted, downed his vodka, motioned for the others to do the same.

'What's your fucking problem, pretty boy?'

'I don't like the way you talk.'

'Well,' said the remote descendant of Genghis Khan, 'I don't fucking much fucking like the way you fucking look. What you gonna fucking do about it?'

Urban, who didn't understand a word of Russian, didn't need to to know what was happening. He grabbed Billy-Ray's arm, hauled him away from the bar, waving an apologetic hand at the Russians as Teodor and Eskil guarded the flanks of their little party.

Billy-Ray was shouting in Polish, Russian and German as they dragged him outside, on to the near-empty streets of Sitka, sea fret blowing over them. Down at the harbour below them the boats were chafing each other, looked as if they were anxious to be on their way again. Urban rubbed at his eyes as Teodor and Eskil held Billy-Ray.

'What should we do with him?'

Urban watched Billy-Ray crying in the feeble street light. Shrugged. 'He'll be OK in a few minutes. Let's go back to Ed's, it's on the way to the boat.'

Teodor and Eskil propped Billy-Ray up as he sat at the bar and slurped beer at Ed's and Urban swapped tales of desperation and ecstasy with other captains. There were no shades of grey there – either the catch or the weather was the best or worst they'd ever seen. Alashka – the Great Land of extremes.

The next day, which happened to be a Tuesday, Billy-Ray was apologetic. He was also hamstrung, dumb-struck, made mute almost by the excess of beer and vodka. He woke, fully dressed in his bunk on *Viveka*, and at first wondered what the strange noise was, thinking he was sheltering under Siggy's welcoming, sail-like sheet. Then he recalled that he was in a seiner jostling with hundreds of other wooden-built boats in the harbour of Sitka, sharing a life with a family that was not his own because his own had disappeared. The sound he could hear was the schuffing of water. Billy-Ray turned in his bunk, lay on his side so his back was turned to the Svensson brothers, and tried to piece together the night before – there had been sounds of Russian, German and Polish. His languages. Had he tried to converse? Had he sinned? Hail Mary full of grace. Something to do with his mother. His mother . . . Irochka falling, but so gracefully.

'So, Wilhelm-Rajmund, tell me what you think of the trip so far.' Urban was sitting up on deck, his back against the feed drum, a mug of coffee in his hand. The temperature was up in the high sixties and, like Billy-Ray, Urban was wearing shorts and a T-shirt. Teodor and Eskil had gone into town to chase down some clevis pins and shackles, leaving the captain and greenhorn to sun themselves.

Billy-Ray set his mug down on the deck, lit a Lucky Strike, one that didn't taste of chinook. His hangover had made him soft and slow. He thought before he spoke. 'It's not what I thought it would be. The work is harder than I thought it would be. More . . . what's the word . . .' Billy-Ray's Swedish was fairly fluent, but occasionally still rusty when he tried to turn the key in the lock of language. 'Physically demanding. Yah – it's very hard.'

Urban watched a shabby gill netter slide by – he knew the boat, *Skutvig*, and its captain: a Norwegian drunk who'd only stayed afloat because he didn't share his vodka with the crew. He slapped at his ankle, crushing a bug, smearing his blood. 'You know, Billy-Ray, people see us on the docks, maybe cleaning the boats, maybe sanding the decks, fixing engines. And then they see us sitting having coffee or beers and talking, comparing situations. Month after month. Just tinkering about is what it looks like. This is what they don't see. Well, not this' – he gestured at the sun, at his coffee – 'but what goes on out there. Someone in Phoenix, Arizona sits down in a restaurant, orders a salmon steak and they don't even know what the sea looks like.'

'I guess I never thought about it either. Y'know, before I came to Seattle.' Billy-Ray stubbed out the cigarette, grimacing. 'How long you been doing this?'

'Me? Since I was sixteen and old enough to go out with my father. Thirty-two years now. I don't know anything else.'

'When will you stop? You know, give it up?'

Urban's cool, neutral gaze settled on Billy-Ray. 'When I start to feel scared.'

'What d'you mean?' Billy-Ray couldn't imagine Urban ever feeling anything other than in control.

Urban shifted, gestured at the cigarette packet, which Billy-Ray threw to him across the deck. 'Thirty-two years is a long time. It's not a job for a man who can't react quickly, whose heart starts jumping around.'

'Have you ever been scared?'

'Yah – of course. The storms out there' – he waved his mug at the placid ocean – 'are like nothing you've seen.'

'In Minnesota we get winter storms,' said Billy-Ray defensively, as if protecting his home state from an accusation of clemency. 'Been cut off a couple of years – snow way deep.'

Urban smiled faintly. 'Maybe – but you're on land, in your home, with some beer and babka to keep you company. Out there, you're nowhere. Nothing's fixed. A storm comes in from the west, you better run for cover. I've known winds over a hundred and twenty miles an hour. Think about it. There's nothing between us and Russia – only water. That wind just keeps going, gets faster, because there's nothing to stop it. Nothing to break it down. So when it hits land mass – rain, hail, snow, ice. All moving at a hundred and twenty miles an hour. And the water. I told you – waves maybe seventy feet tall. Not like waves you see on the beach, little things with white hats, all in neat rows, coming in one after another. No – these waves, these seventy-footers, they're all over the place, not waiting in line. They're going against each other, running north, south, east, west. Sometimes they're going into each other and you better hope you're not at the point they meet.'

'D'you know when a storm's coming?'

'Usually. I've been in a couple when they blew up in a moment. Others, you can tell by the sky, by the way the water's moving. Or maybe you hear, on the radio. Then you drop everything and run for the coast and hope you find safe haven. A harbour, somewhere to shelter. But even that can be difficult – you've seen the coastline. You know now what it's like. Not many little cosy ports with a bar and hotel.'

Billy-Ray stared at the horizon – flat and uneventful, the sun throwing up blades of rippled light – and he considered this. 'Did your heart jump around?'

Urban smiled. 'It didn't jump around, it was dancing, going off like a gun. It's strange, the fear comes later, when it's all over and you've survived. When you realize you've got to stay out there and you got to go through it all again just to get home.'

'Why don't you stop?'

Urban shrugged. 'Like I said, it's all I know.'

Billy-Ray lit another cigarette, which tasted better than the last. 'So what will you do when you finish? When you retire?'

'Go back home.'

'Back to Seattle?'

'No.' Urban looked Billy-Ray right in the eyes. 'Back home, back to Sweden. I have some land there, near Vänersborg, on the lake.

Viveka and I will build a little house there, with a jetty. I shall buy a small dinghy and spend my days fishing.' The two of them laughed. 'I'll go walking, read the papers, eat too many crayfish and pancakes. I'll go to church at Jul and see my family.' Urban stood and stretched. 'Or maybe I'll go to Baja.'

'Baja?' said Billy-Ray, incredulously.

'Yah – why not? Maybe we can build a shack on the beach instead, Viveka and me. Sit in the sun and drink tequila. I always wanted to catch a black marlin. Heard someone say they caught one last year off Baja, was over sixteen hundred pounds. Think of that. Bringing *that* in on a long-line. Sixteen hundred pounds.'

Billy-Ray knew he was listening to a dream. Urban and Viveka would go back to the old country. Back home, back to Svenska.

"Course,' said Urban, smiling again, 'might just have been bullshit.'

'Maybe,' agreed Billy-Ray. He wanted a beer, knowing that it would cut away the cobwebs in his throat. But Urban didn't allow beer on board. Billy-Ray would have to go into town and go to a bar. 'When will they be coming back? Teodor and Eskil?'

Urban shrugged. 'Who knows?'

'I'd have thought they'd be back by now. Just a few shackles, after all.'

'Oh, they'll have done that already. They're finding themselves some girls.'

'Girls?'

'Yah – you know, the ones with breasts and everything else.'

'Oh,' said Billy-Ray.

'Don't you want some?'

'What I really want is a beer.'

'Seems to me you've got your priorities wrong.' Urban picked up a waterproof jacket and motioned to Billy-Ray. 'Come on, let's get you your beer. I think you've suffered enough hangover already this morning.'

Billy-Ray and Urban sat in companionable silence at the bar in the Smoked Sockeye, turning bottles of Schlitz in their hands, doing nothing for the first time in weeks. Billy-Ray tried to think of something to say, something that would interest Urban. He wanted Urban to like him. He wanted Urban to be his father.

'So, Billy-Ray, I asked you before and you didn't answer – why
have you changed your name? I know you were always Wilhelm-
Rajmund back in Bow Regard because my brother told me so in his
letters. Somewhere between Minnesota and Seattle you lost your
name. Maybe you threw it away by mistake.'

Billy-Ray thought back to the moment in the truck's cab when he
had jettisoned his heritage. Could think of nothing to say.

'You were upset last night, very upset, very angry. Can you
remember? When we left the bar with the Russians.'

Billy-Ray screwed up his eyes, raked through his memory banks.
Shadowy thoughts of shouting and . . . crying? . . . came back to him.
'I'm sorry. I just got drunk.'

Urban drank his beer, slapped the bar to ask for another. 'I don't
like anyone upset on my boat. I don't like unhappiness on my boat.'

'I'm sorry.'

'You were shouting in a language I couldn't understand.
Something like, er, shrowass Maria, lass . . . something.'

'I said that?'

'Yah.'

Billy-Ray stared at his beer.

'What does it mean?' asked Urban.

'It's Polish.'

'OK. But what does it mean?'

'*Zdrowas Maria, łaskis pełna*. Hail Mary, full of grace.'

Urban toyed with his bottle of beer. 'OK.' He looked at the young
man. 'Billy-Ray, I know about your brothers. And I'm very sorry. I'm
sorry it happened. It shouldn't have.'

Billy-Ray looked down at the wooden bartop, saw someone had
carved his name there: Sven 03/28. The month of Billy-Ray's birth.
Everything he had done, everything he had ever thought and said
and done, and this small act of vandalism had been there the whole
time.

'You want to talk about anything, now's the time. We're shipping
out tomorrow.'

And so Billy-Ray talked. The Smoked Sockeye gradually filled, its
scarred tables and dimly lit pool table surrounded by men desperate
for a good time, for a last drink, for a final fuck before leaving and

going back out to explore the blue earth. Men with wads, scads, *bundles* of notes, jostled at the bar, shouting for bourbon, whisky, vodka, giniver, schnapps, waving the rolls of dollar bills in the air. The bar was lit by a blaze of sunlight each time the door banged open and in poured Norwegians, Finns, Swedes, Greenlanders, Icelanders – the bar was awash with Vikings as Billy-Ray talked. Nordic languages rolled around the room, bounced off the walls, firing their collective ancestral memories of raids and theft, danger and spoils. As Billy-Ray described Siggy, men downed the contents of shot glasses and roared for more. As he told Urban about Oliver and Irochka and what happened to them, how they had been, how Oliver rubbed mud into his mother's face, the floor at their feet became slick with sixty-proof spirits. A glass flew across the bar and shattered against a timbered wall as he recalled seeing Father Ambrose bolting from the church, fleeing the cascade of false gems raining down on the candles lit for his brothers. Four men linked arms and began to sing a mournful Norwegian dirge about distant family, swaying with an excess of bourbon and emotion as Billy-Ray whispered, 'And as I stood there, I thought, *Bitte, Gott, lass es Dieter sein.*'

'What?' Urban cupped his ear, leaned closer.

'*Bitte, Gott, lass es Dieter sein.*'

'What does that mean?'

Billy-Ray swallowed. 'Please, God, let it be Dieter.'

Billy-Ray's beautiful, young face was turned to Urban, looking stunned, looking hopeful, looking as if it were waiting for absolution. Urban sat back, scratched his cheek, took a swig of beer, lit a cigarette. Thought of Teodor and Eskil, thought of Lars, back in Seattle with Viveka, nursing a broken collar bone. Thought of standing on a porch holding a fork and a telegram. Tried to imagine it, what he would feel, what he would think. What Teodor would feel, what *he* would think. Urban reached out and drew Billy-Ray's head roughly on to his shoulder and Billy-Ray cried for the second time in twenty-four hours, as the sound of four lachrymose Norwegians echoed around him.

After that day Urban watched out for Billy-Ray, as *Viveka* headed north-west, following the coast, scooping up the shifting bio-mass of salmon. He watched out for him because he knew that Billy-Ray wanted from him something he could not give; he could not absolve Billy-Ray for his sins; Urban could not give him absolution. But he took to sharing watches with the young man, knowing that Teodor and Eskil were loved enough, that they were as safe as they were going to be, with him at the helm. Urban and Billy-Ray sat through the hour-long nights in June, watching the magnificent coast slide by, tracking the moon and sun as they flirted with each other between the peaks of the Elias range. Sometimes they talked, other times they sat and watched as a world full of more shades of blue and grey than Billy-Ray could ever imagine existing slipped past.

Urban would sit in the cabin, those quiet nights, a foot up on the rail, an ashtray nearby, one eye on the compass, the other on the barograph, and talk about the future.

'Thing is, Billy-Ray,' he said one night, pushing a wad of Sköl tobacco against his gum, 'this really is the last frontier. After this, there isn't anywhere left to go.'

Viveka had already unloaded tons of salmon twice more, at processing plants in Yakutat and Katalla, and now she was labouring past Strawberry Hill, Prince of William Sound beyond. Billy-Ray was always astounded when he looked at the charts and maps and saw, after so many weeks, how much of the Alaskan coastline there was left.

'Out there,' and Urban nodded at the distant peaks, 'well, they haven't even begun to explore it. They don't even begin to know what's out there.'

'You ever been?' asked Billy-Ray, sitting on the deck, back against the cabin doorway, rocking gently, watching the landscape slide past. 'Off the boat, I mean? Into the interior?'

'Nah. It's too dangerous. I mean, I went into downtown Anchorage a few years ago – it was a joke. Like the Wild West or something. Now? They have the army there. They have soldiers all over the state building roads, airports. But it seems to me, no matter what they do, it will still be dangerous.'

'How can it be more dangerous than being out here?'

'Oh – many ways. Out there they're all men – no women. And women, as we know, have a civilizing influence.' Urban smiled.

'And then there is the land, the country. Glaciers, earthquakes, volcanoes, slides, falls. It's a wild place. You know that the Indians were scared of it? The people who were here first? They were so scared of the land they practically lived on water.' Urban glanced at the compass, adjusted the wheel a little. 'Like I said, I've been doing this thirty-two years, since 1914. Of course, I never came this far north then; my father's boat was small, only forty foot, and he didn't have the instruments.' Urban sighed. 'Never thought then I'd live through two wars.' He glanced at Billy-Ray. 'Sorry.'

'Don't be.' But Billy-Ray's eyes dropped.

'Like I said, thirty-two years is a long time. Heard lots of things in that time – bears standing twenty feet tall, diamonds the size of your fist, fingerless monsters that live on the seabed and swallow ships. Fire and ice running towards a man.'

'That could happen,' said Billy-Ray.

'I'm not saying it couldn't. Reckon all the above are true – bar maybe the diamonds.' Urban scratched his cheek. 'Maybe even those. Thing is, Billy-Ray, I reckon in a few years they'll be crawling all over this state, digging it up, blasting it open, cutting down the forests. And when they're done with that, they'll start to mess around out here, in the ocean. And for what?'

'Resources,' said the twelfth-grade A-student.

'Money. And because it's there. And when they've cut it all down, what then?' Urban checked the route, swivelled the wheel, and in the distance Billy-Ray could see the pinpricks of a settlement in the clear air as the purse seiner passed across the entrance to a sound.

'Where's that?' Billy-Ray pointed.

'Tatitlek. Behind that there's a place called Valdez, but you can't see it for Goose Island. It's pretty up there. Just a deep, empty fjord, a few Indian villages, lots of trees and silence. Spent a few days fooling round up there with Teo a couple of years ago, just camping for a few days. You know, building fires, cooking up salmon, pretending to be bushmen.' Urban smiled hugely, his weathered face breaking up like the Aleutian coast. 'Slept on the boat each night, though. Reckon those Indians know a few things.'

Billy-Ray smoked a cigarette, fiddled with the suspenders holding up his weatherproofs, picked at a new scab on his thumb. 'Urban?'

'Yah?'

'I don't see what's wrong with exploring. I mean, we need to know these things.'

'It's not the knowledge I don't like, Billy-Ray, it's what they do with it. They take things away to make money. I don't know what it will be – copper? gold? – if I did, I'd be a rich man and wouldn't be out here, three months away from my wife. Look at what happened out in the Midwest – they cut down all the trees and they planted crops and, sure, for a few years it was fine. But the rains didn't come and the winds did and people died and cattle died and they couldn't put it back like it was. And they won't be able to do that here. Look at the fish – we drop our nets and they come up full – OK, it's a good year. But I listen to the Indians, you know, when we're in port. We treat them like shit when we should be asking for their help – they're wise people who have lived here for thousands of years. I listen to them and I don't like what I hear. They say the fish are scarcer every year and I believe them. So, what are Teo, Lars and Eskil going to do? Dip their cup into an empty bowl?' Urban spat tobacco expertly over the side. Immediately the water boiled as salmon thrashed around it. 'Thing is, when these things happen, it's not one man, not a few men. It's many men, a company. And then each man doesn't feel responsible. You know what I mean? You understand what I'm saying? If each man looks at what he does – well, it's nothing. But together they can make a storm.'

'My father said that once.' Billy-Ray picked at the scab again. 'He said, "We cut things down and we don't replace them. We take things away and we will never find them again."' Billy-Ray didn't want to think about this, about Oliver being right.

'Your father's a wise man.'

'He's a drunk.'

'Maybe he's both – you ever thought of that?'

Twelve days later Teodor, Eskil and Billy-Ray were fooling round with the net, making out they were gladiators and lions, just horsing round on the deck, waiting for Urban to finish the logs. It was the second week of August, and after a stop at Cordova *Viveka* had turned south-west to trawl, harvest, pillage, loot the ocean, following the depths of the Aleutian Trench, which, at that longitude, ran deep. Ran rich, ran fertile. Urban had decided the time had come to turn for home, but reckoned that a little recreation, some long-lining for bottom-fish, might be in order. They'd baited four lines and rigged them from the corners, cast them off in the Shelikoff Strait, near Black Cape. Billy-Ray kept checking the lines, tugging at them, wanting his first taste of halibut.

Urban wrote the entries in the logbook for the day: 58°10'18"N,153°05'22"W. He checked the charts, reached for a slide rule, yelled at Eskil to fetch him coffee. Picked up his cigarettes, glanced at the barograph, looked away, looked back. Checked the barometer – it was falling faster than a weighted line. He swung out of the cabin, looked west to see a bank of towering cumulonimbus rolling in, tumbling along, frolicking in a gale. Then the cloud bank slid across the sun like an eyelid. Like a wink. The radio chattered and Urban retuned, listened to the forecast. The swell began to rock *Viveka*, rolling her side to side, pushing her broadsides. Eskil came out from the galley, holding the rails, steadying himself, staring at his father. Billy-Ray froze, watched the front roaring towards them, lurched suddenly as the deck tilted.

'Get your proofs on, check your buckles and straps. Teo – cut the lines. Billy-Ray and Eskil, lash and batten down. We got no choice here – we have to make for Port William.'

'How far's that?' Billy-Ray shouted over the rising wind, his clothes already saturated by the flying spray. Found he couldn't swallow.

'Just do what I said.' Urban's voice was calm, measured, somehow made itself heard above the escalating noise. But he felt his heart begin to dance and he wondered whether now was the time to give it all up. Too late – *Viveka* was bucking like a bronco. Urban slipped into his waterproofs, shackled himself to a rail, yelled instructions and then motioned for the boys to go down, batten the hatch.

Billy-Ray didn't want to leave Urban, his hero. Didn't want to leave him, yet wanted to get away from the bedlam. He turned, protecting his eyes from the stinging salt water, slipped as the deck slid away to port, fell, skidded across planks to crash into the line-feed drum, grabbed the cable and felt as if he were swimming as the waters of the strait thundered over him, rich and scummy. He gasped as the icy waters sluiced away and *Viveka* righted. A hand grabbed his arm and yanked at it. Billy-Ray looked up through the spume plastering itself to the rigging, to see Teodor. And beyond Teodor, beyond that prematurely weathered, fearful face, was the Wave. Billy-Ray whimpered, his breath jamming in his chest like a fish bone. He had forgotten it, but there it was – the Wave, rearing up, glorious and malevolent, a shimmering wall of light-hatched water which leaned back and then began to curve towards him. Billy-Ray scrabbled across the deck, fingers numb, following Teodor's yellow beacon of a jacket, crashing into padlocked boxes, grabbing at lashed barrels. He didn't want to be on deck when the Wave broke. He never wanted to see it again. It looked black, it looked infinite – it looked malicious. Billy-Ray thought, as he helped Teodor batten down the hatch with shaking hands, that the Wave looked as if it had scoured the oceans looking for him and had finally tracked him down.

Urban, being tossed about in the wheelhouse, was trying to save *Viveka* as best he knew how, which was to steer into the roll and hope to come out of it. Follow the wind, give in to it. Try to remember that you've survived this before. How do you steer when the rudder rises up out of the streaky white waters and the nose dips? You don't, you just cling on to the wheel as you watch the bow going down, see the ocean smash against the glass. Don't waste time praying, keep your eye on the compass, which is spinning like a dervish, flying back and forth, swinging to all points, and the world turns upside down. Reaches a point of inertia and – somehow – rights itself, only to swivel again as a gull, freewheeling, turning like a wind-blown piece of paper, smacks into the glass, breaks up and is whipped away. Ignore the smells of salt and blood and fury. Try not to think of the noise, which is not noise but more than that, a world of its own. Brown and purple tumult – radio hissing and sputtering, rain thundering, wind baying, grunting, growling. And it's impossible to tell what's cloud and what's ocean as the two darken and become one.

Urban felt *Viveka* twist beneath him, reaching the limit of her torque, looked through the now cracked glass to see a towering pile of water growing before him, growing by tens of feet, reaching skyward in an explosion of energy. He thought he heard a boom that echoed against the clouds and bounced back to earth. The boom that two sixty-foot waves make when they meet head on in winds of a hundred and eight miles an hour. 'Fuck,' muttered Urban, spreading his feet and squaring his shoulders. He wondered for a moment whether Billy-Ray was saying his Hail Marys, wondered whether it would help.

Billy-Ray was hanging on to the sides of his bunk, lying face down, whimpering in abject terror. He knew he was going to die, that he was going to sink into the raging waters. Drown out here, at the edge of the world. He threw up violently over the side of the bunk, which suddenly dived down, dived deep into the abyss, and Billy-Ray shouted. He didn't know what he shouted, it was meaningless, had no language. Then the bunk rode up, turned nearly vertical, and Billy-Ray was scrabbling to find a balance, any balance. His feet found the cabin wall and he snatched at the table to steady himself, before being thrown against Eskil. *Viveka* plunged, hung for a moment, reared up. He was going to die. His damaged fingers grasped anything they could find, as he wondered whether Siggy and Deet had been as scared as this, hoped that they hadn't, hoped that they hadn't known this maddened fear.

Seven hours it took for the storm to blow itself out. For seven hours Urban braced himself in the wheelhouse, not steering, not trying to find safe haven, not knowing where he was and not caring just so long as he took another breath. The cyclone moved on, having toyed with *Viveka*, and headed east. The wind dropped to seventy miles an hour, the rain thinned and the sea calmed itself. Curled up and licked itself, pleased as punch. Urban waited until the winds dropped again, down to fifty, then thirty, before unlashing himself, fumbling with the shackle. He stood at the wheel, his aching hands resting there, and he breathed deep, drew the salty air right down into the pit of his lungs. Held out his hands, saw the fingers trembling. Urban knew he had been scared, not now, as he told Billy-Ray happened – when it was over, when it was done. No, he'd been scared when he saw the front moving in. He'd been terrified the whole fucking time. He rubbed at his beard and sighed.

By the time Urban hammered on the hatch, the sun was weak, hung low beneath the clouds. The hatch was unscrewed from below and Urban heaved it up, looked down into chaos.

'How about some food out here? Huh? How about some chow for the captain? What have you all been doing down there? Sitting on your hands?'

The brothers were laughing, as Billy-Ray sat, shell-shocked, or, rather, storm-shocked, on his bunk, wondering whether he'd ever laugh again.

Once they'd cleared the debris – although the deck, of course, had already been swept very clean – the four sat down to tinned stew and Urban asked, 'Shall we go home now?'

'Yes,' said Billy-Ray, perhaps a little too loudly, a little too quickly, and Urban smiled one of his cool, private smiles.

The voyage home was relatively uneventful – a broken finger, a couple of flesh wounds, another sixty-eight thousand pounds of fish, and one endless day after another, the sun merely flirting with the horizon. Billy-Ray watched pods of orcas cruising, humpbacks breaching – forty tons of whale meat hurling itself into the air, careening back into the water with a thunderous wallop. He'd lean out over the rails to follow sea otters as they floated by, plump and surprised, boasting more whiskers than Billy-Ray could imagine they would ever need. Sometimes *Viveka* would surprise a small colony of otters snoozing, wrapped in kelp, bobbing on the waters, paws wrapped across their podgy stomachs. Puffins zoomed around the boat as it made its way, first, to Seward to refuel and unload and then along the coast, past the Bering glacier, past the Malaspina ice sheet – bigger than Luxembourg in Europe, Urban told him. Billy-Ray watched, as awed as he had been the first time Urban had pointed to the Coast Ranges, weeks before. But what Billy-Ray looked for most often, over his aching shoulders, was the Wave, which must still be searching for him.

The last week of August and the temperature was beginning to drop, as was the sun. The nights were longer – a few hours now – and Billy-Ray wore two sweaters under his waterproofs. *Viveka* turned east, through Cross Sound and past Glacier Bay, into the maze of islands, where small settlements and processing plants hud-dled on the coast, surrounded by dense forest. Teodor and Billy-Ray were put on log watch – hanging over the rails, scanning the churn-ing waters for vast trunks, some more than a hundred feet long, maybe eight feet in circumference, which could hole a boat without even changing course. The thing to look for, Billy-Ray was told, was the root system – the body of the tree could be under water. Urban slowed *Viveka* and crawled through the ever narrower channels, crowded with dinghies, sail craft, gill-netters, seiners, to moor up in Juneau. Billy-Ray looked around himself and realized he was back in civilization – there were people sailing for pleasure, fishing for the hell of it, walking the docks to see what the fishermen were bringing in, shopping for groceries, walking children to school. There were cars and trucks moving along the front. Bars, hotels and restaurants, and people were leaving them, dressed in jeans and jackets, carrying newspapers. Immediately, and with surprising force, he wanted to be back out on the ocean, watching the coast pass by.

'Weird, isn't it?' asked Urban, coming to stand by Billy-Ray. 'Just feels weird. People going to work, having lunch, going home to listen to the radio.'

'Is it over, then?'

Urban scanned Billy-Ray's face, knew what the boy meant. 'Yah. Until next year.'

1958

Highbury, the ancestral seat of the Chalfont-Webbes, made the Coopers' country home in Sherston look like a bungalow, a prefab, a caravan. The original Elizabethan pile had burned down in 1767, as Lady Chalfont-Webbe lost no time in telling Billy-Ray over high tea, and it was a conceit on the part of her husband's great-great-great grandfather to have a Georgian mansion built in its place, designed, of course, by Robert Adam.

'People always mention Osterley House when they talk of Georgian Palladian-style buildings.' Lady Chalfont-Webbe dabbed at the edges of her mouth with a linen napkin. 'But *really* – in Middlesex, after all. Some people say Highbury is inappropriate, but I think the red brick enlivens the ambience of the Cotswolds.'

Billy-Ray stared at Isobel's mother, having absolutely no idea what she was talking about. Middle sex? Was he supposed to speak now? 'I like the porch.'

Lady Chalfont-Webbe smiled absently. 'So, Mr Rickman, what is it that you do? More tea? Or perhaps you'd prefer coffee?'

'Ah, no, tea would be just fine.'

'Earl Grey, Assam or Darjeeling?'

'Excuse me?'

The door to the drawing room was flung open and there stood Isobel, dressed in jacket and muddied jodhpurs. She pointed her whip accusingly at Billy-Ray. 'You said you'd arrive on the six o'clock.'

'Managed to catch an earlier train, so I thought I'd come up.' Billy-Ray smiled broadly. He'd forgotten how *tall* Isobel was. How blonde she was. How really very, very lovely she was.

'Isobel, dear, Mr Rickman has just remarked on how impressed he is with our porch.'

'Well, how the hell was I supposed to know? We didn't cover Ionic capitals and – what was it? entabulatures? – at Bow Regard High. Not much call for them.'

'Modelled on the temple at Bassae. An absolute embarrassment, of course. Used to be a nightmare bringing school friends up for the weekend. They'd see Highbury and wither. I wish we lived some-where else, somewhere less ostentatious.' Isobel linked her arm with Billy-Ray's. 'What about a ride before lunch?'

'I don't think I made a good impression on your mother.'

'No one does.'

'I mean, I made the house sound like a trailer in Peoria.'

'Really, don't worry about it.'

When they were in the stables, Isobel watched Billy-Ray as he introduced himself to the horses, watched the way he held their gaze, touched them between the eyes as he stroked their soft under-lips.

'Isn't it the softest thing?' he asked Isobel, smiling, as his fingers brushed the velvet flesh.

'That's Sophocles – my favourite. All the horses have Greek names, don't know why. Family tradition, I suppose. I used to have a beautiful bay, Aristotle, but he broke a leg and had to be shot not long ago. Actually that was only a few weeks ago, when we met at Sherston. That's why I was late.'

'That's damn hard.'

'Yes. I miss him.'

'I had a fine quarter horse when I was a boy.' Billy-Ray stroked Sophocles' muzzle and thought of Roosevelt. 'We used to name ours after American presidents.'

'How very patriotic.'

'Maybe.'

Billy-Ray helped Isobel carry the saddles to the stables, watched as she slid the girth strap beneath Sophocles' taut belly and pulled it tight, watched her fingers roll the buckle.

'Hope you don't mind me saying, but you've got extraordinary hands.' Billy-Ray fought the desire to take one of them in his own.

Isobel laughed, looked at her palms, turned them over. 'I know, I know. They run on my father's side of the family. My mother has long, elegant piano player's fingers and I've got these shovels.' She waggled her fingers, bent her thumb. 'In England we call hands like these murderer's hands.'

'Murderer's hands?'

'Look.' Isobel flexed her thumbs once more and they curved back. 'Apparently they're perfect for wrapping around someone's neck. Hardly aristocratic.'

It had been a while since Billy-Ray had ridden. He fumbled with the tack, then felt the horse, Plato, mean and skittish beneath him.

'OK?' Isobel asked as she walked Sophocles in the yard, a mere touch on the reins, a shift of her thighs directing the horse.

'Fine.' Billy-Ray could feel the horse pulling, testing him.

'Come on then, let's go.' Sophocles trotted through the arched gateway out into the parkland and Billy-Ray followed, twitching the bit.

He'd been right, Billy-Ray decided as they galloped across the estate: Isobel was a far better horse-rider than he would ever be.

When the weekend – three days of walking and riding, shooting, eating, drinking, talking – was done, Billy-Ray returned to his London home. He closed the door behind him, dropped his case on the floor and sat at the foot of the stairs in darkness. He replayed every moment he had spent with Isobel, tried to conjure up every time he had looked over to see her staring right back at him. And each time he saw her blue-blue eyes he felt as if he had fallen in love again. He would do anything – wear a hair shirt, walk barefoot on burning embers, eat with snakes – to be near Isobel. Billy-Ray knew he had to go back to Highbury, knew even then that he couldn't leave Isobel alone. When he was in her company, he knew he changed. It was as if he became a boy again, as if he were picking up his childhood where he'd abandoned it – astride Roosevelt, listening to gravel crack. For the first time in many years, ever since he'd looked up to find Urban watching over him as he sat on the deck of *Viveka*, Billy-Ray felt wanted. Dared to feel wanted. He sat at the foot of the stairs, smoking, tapping ash into his palm, and thought of the boy he had been and the man he became as his parents fought each other with silences and words. Thought of Wilhelm-Rajmund praying – praying to be gone, praying to be loved. Praying to be forgiven. And finally, perhaps, he was?

'She won't allow it, you know. Lady Chalfont-Webbe.' Jacqueline shaped the tip of her cigarette in the ashtray, drank a deep mouthful of gin martini. 'I hear you've been to Highbury quite a few weekends now, sniffing around.'

'I am not sniffing around.' Billy-Ray, irritated, finished his drink and motioned for another. The two of them had met in the Savoy Grill – and why would they not? After all, Billy-Ray knew the Coopers well, dined at Thurloe Square often.

'Then what are you doing? Researching a book on debs?'

'No.' Billy-Ray watched the barman mix more martinis.

'Then what? Girls like Isobel don't give it away, Billy-Ray.'

Billy-Ray turned his worn brass Zippo over and over in his now office-soft fingers. 'That's not the point.'

'Oh dear,' said Jacqueline. She watched Billy-Ray adjust his cuffs, finger his collar. He was nervous, distracted – what? *What* was wrong with him? It was then that she realized that she was losing him by degrees. Wondered whether that had been the case months before, when she'd seen Billy-Ray and Isobel together in the conservatory in Sherston Park. 'Like I say, Viola won't have it. Don't forget, I've known them a long time. I've known this whole set-up a lot longer than you.' Jacqueline leaned back to allow the waiter to place a drink in front of her. Leaned forward, so close Billy-Ray caught the familiar scent of Chanel, tobacco and vanilla. 'The Chalfont-Webbes aren't me and Sidney, Billy-Ray. You're messing with one of the oldest families in England. You know what that means? They're not a bunch of upstarts like the Stuyvesants or Vanderbilts. Their name was around before the bloody Pilgrim Fathers even made out a shopping list.'

Billy-Ray laughed at this; remembered why he enjoyed Jacqueline's company. 'I'm only dating her.'

'They don't "date" here, Billy-Ray. They have chaperones and long engagements. You get to home plate in three years at the earliest.'

Again Billy-Ray laughed, drank some more. When he was with Jacqueline, when she was like this, he sometimes wondered why he needed anyone else; she was familiar in so many ways. But then he'd see Isobel and he fell in love over and over again.

'I'm just trying to save you from yourself. If you've got any grand plans you're in trouble. Girls like Isobel marry earls, lords, or at the very least a knight.' Jacqueline, who'd been at the gin even before she came out to the Savoy, had a sudden parallel vision of Lancelot and Guinevere. The rough saviour manqué, the outcast come to save his lady. 'Pig farmers' sons from Minnesota don't really make the cut.'

'I know.' And Billy-Ray looked so defeated, so lost – such a long, long way from home – that Jacqueline sighed, remembering why she liked him.

'I know you know. I'm just reminding you. Viola still hasn't forgiven us for 1773 and Sidney's always trying to get her onside. That's why he drinks toasts to the Boston bloody Tea Party. No Yank is going to take her Isobel away from her, no matter how young and handsome.' Jacqueline downed her drink. 'You want to fuck?'

Later, much later, when they'd rucked the sheets and messed up the bathroom, the two of them lay on their backs on the bed, not touching, losing each other by degrees.

'D'you remember,' Billy-Ray said suddenly, 'the advice you gave me on the boat on the way over?' He was thinking of old English money.

'I gave you lots of advice, like don't wear pink. It wouldn't do anything for your skin tone.' Jacqueline looked at his profile, at the way his hair fell across his face. Thought how much she'd miss him. 'You know, Billy-Ray, I've had lots of affairs. Been with lots of men.' Billy-Ray rolled back on to his side, propped his head on his hand, looked down on her as she confessed. 'You asked me once if I'd done this before. Well, yeah – I have, many, many times. Don't get me wrong, I love Sidney in some ways, and I love my life in many ways.' Jacqueline gestured to him for a refill. 'I have to be honest, you were one of the best.' She caught her own use of tense – giving herself away. 'Point is, Billy-Ray, I'd have given it all up for you, if you'd asked. But I always knew you wouldn't – ask, I mean. Plus,' Jacqueline fumbled with a cigarette, 'I sometimes wonder about you. I mean, it's like you could have been such a nice guy but there are things you do which I don't get. You're just not as nice a guy as you should be somehow. Sometimes you laugh, other times you look like you're gonna kill someone. It's like you're two different people, like a boy and a man. In the bar tonight? I knew you were all wound up but you laughed. Other nights you don't laugh.' Jacqueline frowned. 'I can't explain what I mean. It's like there are bits of you missing. Important bits. Like about your family. You never say anything about them.' The Gordon's was kicking in now, making it hard for Jacqueline to arrange her thoughts. 'It's when you drink vodka you change. You shouldn't drink it, Billy-Ray. Don't drink vodka.'

Billy-Ray lay in silence, thinking of the farmhouse as he had last seen it, dirty and unloved. Much like his father. His mother, Irochka, the invincible Irochka, swathed in black, her face pinched by perdition, her hair grey and unkempt. Kneeling, always kneeling, before a makeshift shrine to Siggy and Deet. The last morning he had been there, before he walked down the track to the local road and stuck out his thumb, to make his way to Seattle. Shouldering his pack and holding out his hand to Oliver, who looked at his son with eyes made mad by spirits. Then Oliver slowly turning his head away, shifting in his chair so his back was turned, crossing his arms, denying his son. In the corner, Irochka, also made mad but by rather different spirits, knelt before a statue of Our Lady, her hands clasped. Wilhelm-Rajmund had dropped his pack and walked over to his mother to say he was leaving. Irochka bowed her head and Wilhelm-Rajmund reached out and touched her greying crown, as if conferring benediction. Then he'd walked out, into the sun.

'You awake, Billy-Ray?'

'Yah.'

'I think we both know this is the last time, don't we?'

'I guess so.'

'You won't cheat on Isobel, will you?'

'What d'you mean?'

Jacqueline rolled on her side, pulled the sheets up to her chin. 'Now you're seeing her, you won't cheat on her. You won't want to see me.'

Billy-Ray thought about this. Considered the prospect of not having it all, for once. Considered not having it all – not because he was scared of being found out but, rather, because it was the right thing to do. It was what Siggy would have done. He nodded. 'It's not that I don't want to see you. I just don't think—'

'It's OK, you don't have to explain.' Jacqueline threw the sheets back, began to dress. 'Really, it's OK. I understand.' But she knew she didn't, not really. Jacqueline Olivetti, of Albany, New York, who, after all, had smarts to go with her looks, was smart enough to realize that she'd never felt for anyone the way Billy-Ray appeared to feel for Isobel. She'd come close with Billy-Ray himself but had never felt the need to deny herself what she wanted for someone else's sake. And if that was love, did she even want to feel it?

Billy-Ray watched Jacqueline, watched the way she slithered into her silk-lined skirt, the way she tucked in her silk blouse. The twist of the shoulders and torso as she closed the side zip, then the lifting of the skirt, revealing stockings and garters, to pull the blouse down. Lowering the skirt, smoothing it. A shuffle of the shoulders. Next, he knew, was the opening of the compact, the sitting on the side of the bed, brushing her skin with powder, the lipstick being applied, lips rubbing together, two dabs at the edge of her lips with the tip of her little finger. A tilting of the head first one way and then the other as she checked her eyeshadow. Then the snapping of the compact, eight strokes of a brush through her hair. Slipping on a shoe awkwardly, her leg bent, looking over her shoulder. Three little hops and then the other one. Another shuffle of the shoulders. He had never known a woman as intimately as he knew Jacqueline.

'I guess we'll meet again, probably at Jarman House, knowing how fond Sidney is of you. You might as well stay here – the room's paid up.' Jacqueline was smiling faintly as she held out her hand to the naked man on the bed. 'Hey – no hard feelings, OK?'

Billy-Ray took her hand and held it for a long time. Wanted to pull her back into the bed.

'If you're ever at a loose end, y'know, give me a call, OK?' Jacqueline gently pulled her hand away, checked her skirt a last time. She leaned over – Chanel, tobacco, vanilla and sex – and gently kissed his forehead. Crossed the room, opened the door and a shaft of light flew across the red carpet. 'See ya around.'

'Not if I see you first.'

Jacqueline smiled, raised a hand and closed the door. Cried a little as she waited for the elevator.

1946

As Billy-Ray began his studies at the university, living in rooms in a three-storey redbrick off East James and Broadway, he found he was haunted by the summer months just passed, haunted by Alaska itself. He'd lie in bed and remember the coastline passing, the thousands of islands, each wilder, more sublime than the last. The sitkas and spruce coming down to the boulders and crags separating water from land, golden-eyed eagles following the boat's passage from their eyries, unblinking, heads swivelling. The distant mountains that looked too silent, as if they were poised to fling off snow and ice sheets and speak with a roar. The bears roistering in swift-flowing rivers, flipping salmon on to the banks with a slap from a huge, hairy paw. The smell of salt-rain and chinook, fish guts and diesel, cigarette smoke and whales' foul breath-plumes. He'd lie there and grey and silver dreamscapes floated by, the pig farmer's son from the landlocked Midwest drifting on a remembered ocean. And buried in these dreamscapes were other remembered images: Teodor and Eskil talking together; sharing cigarettes, passing them back and forth, fingertip to fingertip; working like clockwork cogs in the small net-boat, blond heads almost touching as they dropped the weights. The blond heads were always there, in the foreground of Billy-Ray's silver-and-blue panorama. Two brothers. Billy-Ray would shake the dreamscapes loose, clamber out of bed and go to the bathroom. Look in the mirror hanging over the sink and see Siggy staring back. His doppelgänger. His absent, six-years-older twin.

Every weekend Billy-Ray visited the Svenssons' house in Ballard. Some Saturday nights he sat out on the stoop with the brothers, drinking beers, maybe not saying much, just happy to be there.

Other nights he was invited to family meals, Viveka fussing over him, piling mounds of food on his plate as she was convinced he never ate. Urban sat at the head of the table, talking about tackle, nets, machine parts he'd ordered, checking everyone had enough food, pouring them beer and vodka. Every Saturday night Billy-Ray slept in the watery silver, blue and grey bedroom, dreaming of Alaska. Sometimes dreaming of the Wave, waking himself with his own shouts and then Urban would come in and shake him, drag him out of the rearing waters.

The blonde woman who tapped Billy-Ray on the shoulder as he was cramming in the library for end-of-term papers was familiar but he couldn't place her. Then it came to him – the secretary who didn't like him having two names.

'Billy-Ray Rickman?' She was whispering so quietly he could barely hear her, yet still other students looked up from their books, frowning.

'Yah.'

The woman beckoned and led him out into the corridor. 'Um, a message has been left at the switchboard for you. An urgent telephone message, from some place – um, oh, I've written it down, I can't remember. Anyway, you better come to the office and call back. Come on.' She set off down the corridor, heels tapping.

Billy-Ray jogged to catch up with her. 'Was it from Mr Svensson, ma'am? The message, I mean?'

'Can't remember. But it wasn't that.' She smiled at Billy-Ray. 'But I do remember the day you first came, to register. Something to do with your name. How you doing? Enjoying it here in sunny Seattle?'

'Yes, ma'am.'

'Did you get work for the summer? I remember you asking about it.'

'Yah – I went fishing, up the Gulf.'

'Wow – that must be something. Hey, just remembered, not Svensson, another weird name – German or something. Oh, what was it? Never mind – here we are.' The woman unlocked a door leading to a small office, gestured at the phone. 'I'll get the note.' She rummaged on the untidy desk and whistled when she found it, handed it, smiling, to Billy-Ray. 'That's a relief, thought I might have lost it.'

Billy-Ray read the note and wished she had: Karl Munchssen, 785 0113 (Minn). He dialled. 'Could I speak to Karl Munchssen, please?'

'Is that you, Wilhelm?'

'Yah.'

'Can't hardly hear you, the line's so bad.'

'I can hear you just fine.'

'Listen, Willie, I thought I ought to tell you . . . ah, shit, look, there isn't a good way to say this. I'm very sorry but your mother's dead. I knew your pa wouldn't call, hasn't got a phone anyway. So I thought you ought to know.'

Billy-Ray stared at the blonde woman, who was rearranging pieces of paper, just moving them from one part of her desk to another. She looked up and smiled brightly.

'Willie? You there?'

'Yah.'

'Look, here's Greta – she wants to speak to you.'

Billy-Ray noticed a small, dusty frame hanging on the wall behind the secretary. An old clipping, 1891, about the Jesuits and the founding of the university. In the photograph, yellowed by time, the scholars looked confused and ill at ease.

'Willie? It's Greta. Oh, I'm so sorry.'

'What happened?'

'*What?*'

'What happened?' Maybe it was something in his voice which made the secretary glance at him, frowning slightly.

'We don't know. She was missing for a day or so and nobody could find her anywhere. Then Oliver saw the boat out on Home Lake, you know, untied, loose. She was there, Willie. She drowned. Oh my Lord, you poor boy. Look, if it makes it any easier, Dr Frank said in cases like that, a body dies so fast, just kind of drifts away. It was eleven below, that night. There's no pain, he says.'

'That's good.'

The secretary looked relieved, relaxed her shoulders a little.

'Look, Willie, the funeral's in three days' time. Think you can get here? You can always stay with Karl and me. We'd be happy to put you up, you know that. Better than being up on the farm, you know what I mean?'

'Yah.'

'So when will you be here?'

'I don't know.'

'Willie? You still there? I'm just so sorry.' Greta started to cry. 'You poor boy. You have friends out there?'

'Yah.'

'Good, good.'

'I'll call you and let you know when I'm coming. Thank you, Mrs Munchssen.' He put the phone down. 'Thank you for letting me use the phone.'

'I'm afraid we'll have to charge you for the call.'

'That's no problem.'

'Minnesota, wasn't it?'

'Yah.'

'Three and a half minutes – that'll be . . . a dollar twenty-eight cents. Make it a quarter, eh?'

Billy-Ray took a bill out of his pocket, searched through some coins.

'So everything OK at home? I remember you was from Minnesota.'

'No, not really. My mother's dead.'

If death was *död*, *døden* and *Tod*, why was it also *smrt* and *zgon*?

'And you know,' the secretary said to her sister that evening, 'the weird thing was he didn't really react. I mean, I felt just dreadful, y'know, asking for the money for the call. He just stood there messing about with all the coins like he couldn't make sense of them. So I told him it didn't matter. Forget it. And he just stood there, like he couldn't hear me.'

'Well, maybe he was in shock or something.'

'Yeah – I guess.'

'Reckon he'll go back home?'

'What?'

'Y'know, like you said – they last one term and miss home so much they leave.'

'No.' The secretary frowned. 'I don't reckon he will. Something about him, something kinda hard. I dunno.'

'Well,' said the sister, who had been made cynical by life's many disappointments, 'at least it means he won't be missing Mom's home cooking any more.'

'Honestly, Lindy! Have a little charity.'

That afternoon Viveka made Billy-Ray *babka* and brought him sweet, black coffee with a belt of brandy in it. 'Drink it down quickly, it will settle you. You must have sugar.'

'Urban,' said Billy-Ray, 'Mom never took the boat out, she never would come in the boat out on Home Lake. She didn't trust water. She couldn't swim, never wanted to learn. The only time she went on a boat was to come to America.'

Urban nodded.

'You know what I'm saying? Urban?'

'Yah, Billy-Ray, I know.'

Billy-Ray pushed the cake around the plate. 'Perhaps she didn't think it counted. Perhaps she thought it didn't count, just falling asleep in water.'

'When will you go back?'

'I don't want to go back.'

Urban sat up, stretched. 'You must go. You should leave tonight – the bus takes a couple of days, I think. I don't know. We can find out.'

'But I have exams beginning next week. I need to study.'

'You must go.'

And because it was Urban who said Billy-Ray should go, he went. He caught the seven o'clock Greyhound to Chicago, planning to change buses at Des Moines. At the bus station, cavernous and stinking, Urban asked him whether he had written to his parents and Billy-Ray lied and said he had. 'Good,' said Urban. The driver called the passengers on board and Viveka hugged Billy-Ray, told him to visit when he got back. Billy-Ray sat in a rear window seat on the bus, his small case on his knees, a dark suit borrowed from Teodor folded inside it. Urban and Viveka waved as the bus reversed, made its way out of the station.

Billy-Ray didn't make it to Des Moines. He didn't even make it as far as Helena, instead getting off the bus in Missoula. For eight hours he sat looking through the glass at rain and sleet lit by the head-lamps of passing cars, as the bus passed through settlements and towns, street lamps fizzing on the wet blacktop. Then the winding journey following the passes through the Bitterroot range, the night black as soot. And all the time Billy-Ray imagining arriving at Bow Regard, being driven out to the farm, stepping onto the porch where Oliver had stood before him, holding a fork and a telegram, where Irochka had lain, breathing deep and slow. Imagined seeing Oliver in his tattered, manure-stained bib and torn jacket, his muffler shroud-ing his gaunt, crazy face. Imagined seeing Magde by the grave. Tried to picture the coffin being lowered into the frozen ground by the Church of St Teresa, with its new, clear glass windows. They were going to put Irochka in the ground there. Billy-Ray sat on the lum-bering Greyhound and thought of all the letters he had never written to his mother, of all the things he had never said, thought of all the mornings he lay in bed feigning sleep when she came in to ask whether he wanted to go to mass. He could feel the rough skin of her thumbs smudging his tears away, could imagine the smell of the skin of her neck when she hugged him. Imagined the sound of Father Ambrose's voice, as he stood, vulture-like, at the head of the grave, addressing a God Billy-Ray no longer believed in. They were going to bury her, bury his mother, whose bread was miraculous, whose laugh made Billy-Ray think of water falling, whose legs were long and strong enough to run with a rifle and the weight of all her grief. It was this last thought which made Billy-Ray put his case down and walk up the bus to the driver, to ask to be let out at the next stop.

It was snowing when the bus stopped at a small, cinder-block building by a parking lot. Billy-Ray clambered down and trudged over to the shelter, which was locked. Looking at the timetable pasted on the door, he saw he had seven hours until the return bus arrived. He sat on a bench and peered through the blizzard, wishing more than anything that Lucca Barzini would pull up in her Cord 812, fingers flipping, cigarette burning, and offer to take him some place. Any place. But Lucca never came.

*

Billy-Ray never told Urban and Viveka what happened; he went back to his rooms in Seattle and stayed in his room for days, venturing out only to buy milk and bread. When the following weekend came round, he went over to Ballard and he lied about the funeral as the brothers shook their heads, said how sorry they were, and Viveka stroked his hand, murmuring about how awful it must have been. Urban watched Billy-Ray as he told them about how his father had cried over the coffin. Urban watched and said nothing and Billy-Ray remembered sitting in the Smoked Sockeye, telling Urban about Oliver and Irochka, about their madness, about Siggy and Deet. And Billy-Ray began to cry again then, began to cry for all of them – Deet, Siggy and Irochka. As his eyes emptied, he found he was crying even for Oliver and what he had become. Lars, Teo and Eskil looked down at their plates, not knowing what else to do. Viveka pushed her chair back and went to Billy-Ray, hugged him awkwardly as Urban sat and watched and said nothing.

Four summers Billy-Ray went out in *Viveka*; for four summers he helped to haul in the silver gold with his adopted family. He learned to love the shabby towns where they stopped to refuel and unload. Learned to love the foul smell and cacophonous din of the canneries, the loud, dingy bars where they'd drink until they fell over. He saw the towns growing, saw tarmac spreading, neon spattering hillsides. Float- and ski-planes buzzed overhead in ever greater numbers, darting between islands and crags to dump supplies and people on the docks or on ice fields – losers, wild men, criminals, dreamers – all racing for the last frontier, hoping to disappear or make their fortunes. More ferries churned up the Inner Passage, carrying cars and engines, prefab houses, refrigerators, tomatoes, rubber boots, cans of tuna, oilskins, netting, matches, pastrami – whatever was needed had to be brought in. There was nothing in Alaska – nothing except sitkas and rocks, water and ice. (And the black gold, bubbling below the waves, but no one knew it then.) Billy-Ray saw garbage piling up outside the towns and canneries: plastic and rope, tyres and rusting chain, cardboard and shards of broken bottles. Shards of broken *boats*. Oilskins floated on the water, sometimes with bloated corpses trapped inside, spinning slowly in the currents. The sound of gunfire rolled around the shacks in the muddy, rutted streets of Platinum, False Pass and Yakataga. Lars was shot at one night by an irate boyfriend, whose aim had been compromised by nearly a bottle of Jim Beam. (The bullet missed Lars, winged the barman and careened into the beers behind the bar.) Baseball bats smashed cars, smashed engines and wheelhouses. Fists crushed noses, knives slashed skin, boots thudded into stomachs. The crew of the *Viveka* drank and watched out for each other, watched out for the boat, took to keeping watch in it whenever they moored up. So much watching. And every day the floatplanes and ferries rolled in, bringing the desperate and the crazy.

'Getting pretty wild up here,' Urban remarked, thinking of his wife sitting by the radio in the house in Ballard.

Billy-Ray loved it.

Out on the ocean, in the Gulf, far from the coast, nothing changed. The work was still hard, the wind and rain still came down, and still Billy-Ray kept an eye out for the Wave. With each year that passed he studied and he learned more about the earth and how it worked, about why the winds blew and the sea ran as it did. He'd sit with Urban and explain to him about Pangaea, Wegener's theories of convergent and divergent plates, transform boundaries, orogeny. Urban would sit and listen, frowning, grappling with the idea of the continents wandering over the planet. He was a good listener, sitting there on the deck, thick, sinewy arms folded, focusing on Billy-Ray. Asking questions, always asking questions.

'So nothing's fixed? Nothing's stuck down?'

'Stuck down?'

'You know,' and Urban gestured with his meaty, scarred hands, 'stuck down. Fixed.'

'Oh, I get you. Nah – nothing's fixed.'

Again Urban frowned. Looked around himself at the blue earth. Picked up the logbook. 'But look, here, I can write this and know where I am.' He pointed to the neat columns of coordinates, his numerals surprisingly small and delicate considering the hands that wrote them.

'Yah, OK. But when you think – the earth itself is moving, the whole solar system is moving. We're sitting on this boat and moving round the sun at maybe sixty-five thousand miles an hour, and spinning round the axis at about a thousand miles an hour.'

Urban put a hand on the gunwale as if to steady himself during this dizzying gallop through space. 'And America is moving as well?'

Billy-Ray laughed, loving the fact that he could dazzle Urban – who was, after all, his hero – with his new-found knowledge. 'Yah – it's moving.' He scrabbled around in the cabin, found paper and pencil, drew the west coast, from Baja (where black marlin sported) to Attu Island. He drew a line across land and sea, pointed to it. 'That's where the break is. *That's* why there are earthquakes.'

'That's why I don't live there,' said Urban.

'You think floating around here is any better?' Billy-Ray drew an arc along the Gulf, out past Attu Island towards Siberia. 'That's the Aleutian Trench. It's about two thousand miles long and maybe twenty, twenty-five thousand feet deep.'

'And what does it do?'

'It makes volcanoes and earthquakes. It turns waves into monsters.'

Billy-Ray first went out into the Gulf with the Svenssons in 1946, when the Wave came hunting him as radioactive dust from Hiroshima and Nagasaki still circled the globe a year after the bombs fell. The second summer: 1947, when the gunshots began to ring out in Platinum as the cold war settled over the northern hemisphere like an occluded front. The third summer: 1948, when Germany was carved up as smoothly as a pat of butter and Berlin was blockaded. And, finally, the summer of 1949, when the fish were harder to find, when boats began to ram each other as the silver gold began to disappear, when they had to stay out for weeks and made it all the way to the shallow Bering Sea, where, it seemed to Billy-Ray, all the crazies and the desperate had settled. That last summer was the hardest, the longest and the least remunerative. The summer when even Urban began to curse as the nets came up near empty over and over again. One more summer, Urban said repeatedly, and he was going home, back to the old country.

One warm evening in May 1950 Billy-Ray took himself to Ballard to tell Urban that he wouldn't be fishing with the Svenssons that summer. He knew, then, that he wasn't going to be an archaeologist, an explorer or a cartographer.

'Why not? Why aren't you coming with us?' Urban was standing on the stoop in bright, late sun, his icy blue eyes squinting in the light, arms folded, looking down at Billy-Ray.

'I'm going to do some fieldwork.'

'What do you mean?'

Billy-Ray stood on the steps, looking up at Urban, and told him about the man from Atlantic Refining who had come to the university to give a talk to the faculty about the job prospects opening up in the oil industry. About the training they'd be given, the burgeoning of opportunities for geologists, geophysicists, engineers; opportunities for all of them. But mostly he'd talked about money and how they could all get a piece of it.

'So, we get to go to their camp in the Kenai and work for the summer, learn about what they're doing. Work with the geologists there.'

'What for? Doing what work?'

Billy-Ray shrugged. 'Looking for oil.'

'That's not work. That's speculation. What are they paying you?'

'Nothing. We get rooms and food.'

'You're *giving* yourself away? You should come with us – it'll be better than last year. That was just a freak summer. This one will be better. Maybe we'll spend a week in Juneau, maybe we'll make a million dollars.'

'Sir, Urban, I'm going to the Kenai. I want to go to Alaska.'

'You can see it from the boat.'

'Let it go, Pa.' Teo, who'd been sitting on the steps, smoking, spoke up. 'Let *him* go. It's what he's spent four years studying for. Let him go.'

'That's right, sir. Four years and I want to use it.'

'Use it to do what? Billy-Ray? Use it to do *what*? Dig it all up? Dig Alaska up? Blow up mountains and cut down forests? Or maybe look under the sea? You going to blow up the sea now? You going to look in your precious trench?'

'I'm going to the Kenai.'

Urban looked down at Billy-Ray for a long, long time, then turned and went into the house, closing the door quietly.

'Hey – I think it's a great idea. When you going?' Teo looked up at Billy-Ray, shading his eyes.

'Beginning of June we get flown there, to Anchorage, and then go overland.'

'Wow. That'll be something.'

'Mmm.' Billy-Ray glanced at the closed door.

'Hey – don't worry about him. About Pa. He'll be OK.'

'I hope so.'

Teo stubbed out his cigarette on the worn step boards, tossed the butt into the yard. 'So, you ain't coming with us? Well, we'll miss you. I'll drink a beer for you in Platinum.'

'Don't forget to duck.'

Three months Billy-Ray spent on the Kenai, learning how to take core samples and analyse them, how to decipher, how to interpret, how to draw maps of this new land. He was taught how to operate the new sonar equipment, how to measure and analyse density vari-ation in rock mass on land and under sea, and the principles of laying transverse lines. He travelled up and down the Cook Inlet in dinghies powered by small outboards, spending time on drilling ships around the Middle Shoals, and often he thought how different the prospect was, how different the water was, from being on the *Viveka*. Billy-Ray loved the land, the size of it, its wilderness, he loved the company of the other workers; more, he loved the game of hide-and-seek he played with the blue earth.

The letter looked like any other – a plain white envelope, crumpled by its long journey from Seattle. Billy-Ray took it from the mailman who drove out to the camp at Nikisiki every week, along with two other letters. He walked over to the canteen, a large tent by the water's edge, where he piled a tray with eggs, bacon, toast and jam, grabbed a quart of milk. The cook joked about the weather, which was unseasonably warm and clear, and Billy-Ray laughed. He sat at a trestle table with a couple of other students, said hi, and stuffed a piece of toast in his mouth as he ripped open the envelopes. The first two he discarded: a demand for payment of fines for overdue library books and an invoice for thirty-five dollars for the storage of his effects whilst he was in Alaska. He stabbed a sausage and began to chew as he read the third letter. Read it twice. Read it again.

A minute later Billy-Ray was standing outside the canteen tent, staring at the still, calm inlet waters, diamonds and lozenges of light skittering across his face. He'd been wrong. It hadn't been him the Wave was looking for; it hadn't been for him that the Wave criss-crossed the globe, hunting. It had been Urban it was looking for all along. And the Wave had finally found Urban, Teodor, Lars and Eskil off Chernabura Island, on the lip of the Aleutian Trench. Urban wasn't going back to the old country after all; Urban Svensson wasn't going anywhere at all.

Billy-Ray Rickman stood there, at the edge of the world, holding a fork in one hand, a piece of paper in the other, looking out at the ocean, wondering whether it was *finished* yet, whether it was sated. The blue earth had taken them all – had taken Irochka and Siggy, Urban and Lars, Teo and Eskil. Deet, however, had been slaughtered in a butcher's shop in Salerno, the familiar scent of blood all around him. Billy-Ray scanned the waters and wondered whether he was going to be punished all his life for that one misbegotten thought?

Bitte, Gott, lass es Dieter sein.

That September, 1950, Billy-Ray Rickman was offered the opportunity to work as a geophysical prospector for Karbo Inc., and he snatched at it. Then he began to contemplate revenge.

1959

Maggie Regan had ceased merely to dream of the sensation of flesh on flesh, she no longer relished the feel of a warm palm on her thigh as she served at the table, forced to take that memory to her bed as a plaything. For she was now stepping out with Michael, the gardener. Twice a week they went to the cinema and then to the Lyon's Coffee Shop in Piccadilly, where they sat at a table saying very little. Michael was content to be seen with Maggie, staring challengingly at every man who eyed her up and down. Maggie, for her part, sipped her tea and examined the fashions of the passing women. Lady Cooper had taken to giving her her cast-off clothes and Maggie had bought a little make-up, powder and lipstick, and had her hair styled in a short bob. She knew her clothes were dated, out of season, but she also knew she looked arresting, delectable. She knew this because of the way men looked at her: the same way they had always looked, all her life. She and Michael would sit in near-silence until the time came to catch the bus to South Kensington. This was the part of the evening Maggie most enjoyed – when they stepped on to the pavement and made their slow, extremely circuitous way to Thurloe Square, along streets lined with elms, the thin orange light of street lamps puddling between the trees, the houses occasionally raked by the headlights of passing cars. The route was littered with bomb sites, cleared plots of land, patchworked with dark corners and recesses. Michael would steer her into a pool of darkness, push her against a rough, damaged wall, and begin to move his hands over her body. His mouth was not as soft as Danny Maconnell's, his hands not as sure, but then Michael didn't deal with animals, didn't coax animals into giving in to his wishes. Yet Maggie was happy to allow him to fondle her, to slide his unsure hand up her skirt to touch the pale, powder-fine skin there, happy for him to fumble with the lattice-work of elastic and nylon that he found. Eventually Maggie realized that Michael could perform magic of a sort, if she allowed him, if she wrapped her arms around his neck and relaxed, if she waited long enough for his uncertain fingertips to touch her there, then magic happened. Michael, breathing hard, a rattle in his chest, would sometimes take her hand and try to move it, force it down, but Maggie, who knew exactly what she would find there, pulled her hand away, whispering, 'Not yet,' and smiling. In fact, Maggie *wanted* to slide her hand inside Michael's trousers, wanted to exercise the power she knew that holding him would give her. So why not let Michael do what he wanted? Because Maggie realized that by not doing it, by not feeling him, not letting him lift her skirt in the darkened corner to probe his way into her, she was exercising power of a different sort. Maggie made Michael want her and then withheld herself, because always in the darkness she could see a pair of teddy-bear eyes. Michael could have taken her, could have put Maggie on her back and taken her. Indeed, he dreamed of doing just that every evening, but he knew that Maggie had Lady Cooper's ear, that she was Lady Cooper's pet thing. Michael had decided that even Maggie wasn't worth losing his job for, but he couldn't stop seeing her, couldn't stop touching her. When Maggie was done, Michael always escorted her to the back door of Jarman House, making sure she was back by ten, and as he walked away, seething, feeling he had more blood in his body than he needed, he often noticed Lady Cooper standing in a bay window, smoking, watching him until he turned out of the driveway.

Miss O'Toole had changed; she had returned from her trip to Ireland, where she had buried her sister, the martinet known as Sister Immaculata, a different woman. A broken woman. She no longer terrorized the staff, preferring to sit in the kitchen, a cup of tea at her elbow, and dab ineffectually at the tears leaking from her eyes. Maggie, who may not have believed in God but nevertheless considered the Old Testament a work of common sense, thought the old bitch had got her just deserts. Jacqueline, aware of the housekeeper's collapse, tried to persuade her husband to fire her but he refused.

Miss O'Toole had been employed by his first wife and he felt obliged to retain her, despite her deficiencies. Sir Sidney, it transpired, would not discuss the matter, so Miss O'Toole sat in the kitchen, lamenting and banking her pay.

Jacqueline realized that she needed to get a grip on the domestic situation in Jarman House. Given that she could no longer tap O'Toole for a supply of needy Irish girls, she contemplated her options and decided that Maggie might provide a solution. Ever since their conversation in the library, when Jacqueline had felt that Maggie was reading her, that she was following her thoughts, she'd revised her opinion of the girl. Maggie might be uneducated but she was far from stupid. Jacqueline called her into the library one evening and asked whether she'd be willing to accept more responsibility in return for more money.

Maggie crossed her arms, put her weight on one leg and leaned on her hip – precisely the pose that had infuriated Sister Immaculata – and considered this. Eventually raised her finely drawn eyebrows. 'I think I'd like that.'

'You'd still be expected to go to Sherston at weekends when we're there. And also to help me with my wardrobe. Plus I'd expect you to make sure the others are doing their work. Can you read and write?'

Maggie was stung by this. 'Of course I can.'

'Good – you can help me keep account of the stores.'

'And I'd still be having Saturday afternoons and all day Sunday to myself?'

Jacqueline chewed her lip. 'I'll see what I can do.'

'Thank you, ma'am.'

Unthinking, Jacqueline dipped a finger in the brandy she was drinking, rubbed at her lower lip as Maggie looked on. 'You might not have as much time to see Michael.'

Maggie shrugged. 'As long as I have my free time, I don't mind.'

'What do you *do* at the weekends, Maggie?' Jacqueline had never thought of this before – what the help did when they weren't helping.

'I go around the shops and markets, ma'am, just looking. Or I go to the museums.'

'The museums?' Jacqueline had never even considered doing this.

'Yes, ma'am. They're quiet. I can think when I'm there.'

Jacqueline wanted to ask Maggie what it was she thought. 'Well, that's settled then. I'll make sure you get your extra money.'

'Thank you, ma'am.' Maggie smiled and left the library, left Jacqueline to wonder what it was that the delicious Maggie thought when she was alone.

After that conversation Jacqueline began to rely on Maggie, asking her to help with the staff rota, to oversee the delivery of goods and to look after her suite as well as her wardrobe. Yet still she insisted that Maggie serve at table when they had guests.

Maggie, for her part, preferred this new arrangement because it helped her to believe that everything would be all right, that her punishment for watching Danny's mouth saying 'Godolphin' was beginning to come to an end. She had been gone from Ballysod for nearly a year and a half and she began to believe that she would have a life, even a good life. Maggie knew, by then, that she would never live in a castle in Czechoslovakia, but she began to dream again. Not, this time, about talking dogs and walking fish, but about marrying and having a house of her own. Perhaps even a garden of her own. She knew Michael wasn't the one, wasn't the one she would marry, but as Lady Cooper had once said, there was plenty of time for that.

Maggie also began to realize something Sir Sidney did not: that Jacqueline was unhappy. Maggie would have found it difficult to say when she first noticed this unhappiness. Perhaps it was not a moment in time? Perhaps it was? Perhaps the moment when Maggie was serving wine at a supper party and she glanced up to see Jacqueline staring at the blond American man? The American man Maggie had noticed months before at Sherston Park, who she had noticed looking at her in a way that was all too familiar. The American man who had arrived earlier that evening with a very tall, beautiful blonde woman. Maggie expertly turned the bottle, preventing a drip falling on the linen tablecloth, and, thinking about it, realized that Lady Cooper had not been out much lately, indeed, for months; that she moped about at home, smoking, leafing through the newspaper, playing with her food, not eating. Maggie stepped back from the table and watched from the shadows, saw that the American man was unaware of Lady Cooper's gaze. He was looking at the tall blonde, seated down the table, looking at her as if she was something precious that he didn't want to lose. How could he do that in front of everyone? Maggie stood stock still, knowing that then the guests would forget her, stood stock still and watched the tall blonde woman. The Honourable Something. She was, Maggie decided, a cold fish, no better than she should be. Snooty tart, she looked like, cold as ice, cold as her pale blue outfit.

Jacqueline was quiet that night, smiling absently when spoken to, smoking too much, drinking frosted glass after glass of Sancerre, merely turning her food with a fork. She had thought that seeing Billy-Ray and Isobel together would mean nothing, that they would simply be another couple making up the numbers. Instead, she found she had a marble of resentment and something else she couldn't identify – longing, maybe? – lodged in her throat, making it impossible to swallow anything but wine and smoke. The room was stuffy, seemed time-locked. Jacqueline looked at the heavy, brocaded curtains, the massive, low-slung chandelier, the dark Queen Anne furniture, and felt oppressed – by a lack of air, a lack of purpose. Once again she felt she was moving outside the loop of life, wondered what she was doing. Jacqueline drank the last of her wine and Maggie stepped forward.

Maggie stood at Jacqueline's shoulder, refilling her glass, and she could feel Jacqueline's panic – like a thin green mist. Without thinking, she touched Jacqueline's arm, squeezed it very gently, and stepped back into the shadows. Maggie stood on aching feet, thinking that she felt sorry for Lady Cooper and wondering what she might be able to do about her sadness.

1959

For a year Billy-Ray Rickman courted Isobel Chalfont-Webbe, offering her the best of himself. After two months he gave up Jacqueline Cooper, after three he gave up vodka. He still travelled around the unfashionable outposts of Europe, buying up parcels of the earth and oceans for Karbo Inc., but he itched to be back in England, to be with Isobel. She'd meet him off the boat train at Waterloo, and Billy-Ray could walk down the platform and see her in the crowds, a head taller than most, blonde hair flashing. Just as his father had seen Irochka years before on Ellis Island, but Billy-Ray didn't know this – he imagined he was the first man to feel such desire, such a sense of submission. Billy-Ray – who strode along the echoing catwalks of drilling rigs, who sat in board meetings with empty eyes watching others talk, who could imagine the feel of crude rubbed between finger and thumb – saw Isobel in the crowd and wanted nothing more than to lay offerings at her feet. Each time he saw her, he fell in love and wondered what he could give her. Alaska – he could give her Alaska.

The accident, when it happened, was shocking, as all accidents are, the difference between accident and incident being but a hair's breadth. Billy-Ray and Isobel were riding Sophocles and Plato across a ridge bordered by woods. Isobel slowed to a canter, looked over her shoulder, saw Billy-Ray approaching at a clip and spurred Sophocles again. The gunshot, when it rang out, echoed across the shallow valleys, followed by another retort even before the first had faded. Sophocles, despite his name, was no tragedian. He didn't want to be involved in violence, disaster and resolution, and so he shied away from the sound of the poacher's bullets, then reared up, nearly tipping Isobel. Coming down to all fours as the third shot rang out, the horse bolted. Horse and rider careened across the valley. Isobel tried to rein him in, tried every trick she knew, but Sophocles stood eighteen and a half hands and had a mind of his own. He might have burned himself out, burned up his panic, if he'd stuck to the valley contour, but instead he tried to clear a too-narrow gap over a hedge. All Billy-Ray could see, as he galloped in pursuit, was a jumble of legs and hoofs as a low-slung branch thudded into Sophocles' broad chest and the horse went down, his rear legs clipping fencing hidden by hedgerow. The impact made a crunching sound, like bone splintering, like wood splitting with greenstalk fractures, like red-stained glass shattering. Sophocles screamed and squirmed on his back, his hoofs narrowly missing Isobel's body, which was lying dead flat, one arm over her stomach.

Three days later, in a private room in a London hospital, Isobel opened her eyes and whispered, 'Hello,' her voice sounding as if it had been scraped bone dry.

'Well, hi there. Nice to have you back with us.' Billy-Ray felt like crying, as Isobel's parents crowded around the bed and her sister ran to fetch a nurse.

Billy-Ray went to the hospital every evening after work, arriving as other visitors began to drift away. At first Isobel slept most of the time, Billy-Ray holding her hand and watching over her in the dim light, ignoring the strange sounds of trolleys and footfalls echoing in the corridors beyond the door. He watched her because he didn't want to lose her; he believed that if he stayed with her, if he stayed awake as she slept, Isobel would be all right. Billy-Ray touched the hard white plaster on Isobel's leg and wished the bones would heal. He stared at her abdomen, where the internal injuries had been worst, tried to imagine the mess of tissue closing, folding over itself.

One evening Billy-Ray arrived to find Isobel sitting up in bed, her hair washed and brushed, looking alert, looking alive, turning the pages of a paper. She glanced up, saw him and smiled.

'Marry me,' Billy-Ray said. 'Marry me.'

'BR, how can I?' Isobel smiled again, pointed to her leg. 'I won't be doing anything for a while.'

'Marry me.'

Isobel stopped smiling. 'How can I? I hardly know you.'

The dam Billy-Ray had been building since the Wave engulfed *Viveka* burst, and out roared a river of words. Billy-Ray stood in the doorway of Isobel's hospital room and described the hog farm in Minnesota, described his childhood and what it had been like. Told her about Siggy and Deet and what happened to them; told her about Irochka and Oliver. About what he took from Magde. He told her how he had run as far away as he could; told her what it had been like to see the ocean for the first time, about the summers fishing with the Svenssons. Told her what happened to Urban, Teo, Lars and Eskil. His voice was by then so soft Isobel strained to hear him, as he described the Wave, how he still had nightmares that it was hunting him. And finally, staring at the floor, not wanting to look at her, Billy-Ray told Isobel about his prayer. *Bitte, Gott, lass es Dieter sein.*

Isobel looked down at her murderer's hands, lying on the white, creased sheet. 'You didn't have to tell me that.'

'I wanted to. See, it's been nearly ten years since Urban died. No one else knew but him.'

Isobel sighed. Looked up, only to see what had undone Urban Svensson all those years before in the Smoked Sockeye bar: Billy-Ray looking stunned, looking hopeful, looking as if he was waiting for absolution. 'It's not a crime, Billy-Ray; it's not a sin. It just means that you loved Siggy so much.'

'I loved Deet too.'

'I know. I know that.'

'Marry me.'

And at that moment the soft tissues in Isobel's abdomen ruptured and she began to haemorrhage, petals of blood blooming on the sheet like a pox.

THE REGANS

Sean Regan had never heard the word *chernozem*, nor the words podzol, lessivage or calcifuges, an absence of knowledge that was understandable but nevertheless regrettable. Sean would squat on his haunches at the end of his garden, chewing on a grass stalk, hands hanging between his bony knees, and stare at the soil, wondering what was happening to it. Fact was, he knew what was happening: the soil, the ground, the earth itself, appeared to be wearing out; what he didn't know was why this was happening. He squatted and he stared and he willed the potatoes, onions and cabbages to grow, to burgeon through the long, misty summer evenings. He strained to recall what his father had told him about how to treat the land, how to seduce it into giving itself, but nothing worked any more. The soil was increasingly grey with each passing year, minerals flashing on its surface when the sun shone just so, water puddling and frazzling into salts. To be sure, the vegetables did eventually grow, but now they were etiolated, blue-green and near inedible.

Unknown to Sean, the area around Ballysod was a geological anomaly: the Dalradian rock on which he lived had once been part of the Laurentian shield, which extended from Baffin Island all the way down to Blue Earth County, Minnesota. The Iapetus Ocean had once lapped where Sean squatted, and when it dried up, a section of the shield had docked in County Mayo. Ballysod sat uneasily on the lip of an eroded anticline where granite had been corrupted by an excess of ferrous materials, a rare example of the contamination of regolith, a contamination so extreme it would register wildly on a Geiger counter. (It was this invisible radon gas which was taking the pigs; all over the area swine were growing thin, fading away as cancer cells multiplied in their bones.) Not only did this degrading mass of igneous bedrock release radon gas into the atmosphere, it also produced a poor, acidic soil, thinly veiled by mor humus. That anything grew at all was a miracle, a miracle assisted by the barrow-loads of manure emptied and spread over the land for generations. What Sean also didn't realize was that, as with anything, soil constantly lost and gained materials and energy and this cycle of loss and gain was closely linked to the process of primary succession (much like the Hon. Isobel Chalfont-Webbe). The soils of Great Britain had taken fourteen thousand years to form, after the ice sheets of the Pleistocene had retreated, fourteen thousand years of the regolith breaking down under the assaults of rain, sun, ice and wind, as water, gases and humus infiltrated and fungi, bacteria and insects fermented the litter. Millions of days had passed while the transformation from granite to soil took place and yet this transformation (perhaps even more miraculous than the shift from water to wine?) was undone in a few years. Farmers forgot to plough in the clover, forgot to allow the land to rest, forgot the agrarian principles so hard learned by their forebears. Instead they began to saturate the land with phosphates because they could not see the phosphates leaching into the water table, could not feel the compounds being absorbed in their skin. The farmers, the fellahin, the peasants all forgot the various uses of guano, shit and bones and turned to the agri-chemical industry for answers to the problem of rejuvenating the earth.

Sean Regan, driven by honour, by hunger, by need, began to buy the sacks of miracle cure, bags filled with phosphates, calcium, potassium, copper and nitrogen. He slit the sacks with a knife worn slight and razor fine by his father's whet-stone, tipped the contents on the earth and raked it over, turned it in with a spade. The Regans used the sacks for many other purposes, and Sean's children were often puzzled by the words stamped on the canvas: Iraq, Sind, Trinidad. These words would be mouthed, sometimes spoken, as the children frowned. (How was Sean to know that the oil being sucked up from beneath the oceans' crusts was broken down to produce elements of fertilizer?) Sean kept buying the miracle sacks, emptying them on the land, convinced the meanwhile that if his favoured daughter were there, this would not be happening. As Sean had always suspected, there were other places where he would have more luck, where the soil gave up its bounties without such a struggle. Russia, for example, where the world's largest reserves of *chernozem* were found. *Chernozem* – black earth.

Sean Regan, who knew the earth was wearing out, also knew *he* was wearing out. When he squatted on his haunches in his garden, when he knelt to pray to a God in whose beneficence he did not entirely believe, his knees protested. They cracked, they ached, they became swollen. Sean Regan – priest or shaman? – was himself wearing out. He sat in Macafferty's staring at his hands, which were beginning to twist like hawthorn twigs. His father and mother had suffered this, this gnarling of bones which was always worse in the damp of winter. He watched his knuckles change, as the cartilage wore away and bone spurs gathered. He watched as his fingers grew lumps and began to freeze. More than this, he knew that the quality of his fatigue had changed; he knew that it could be cured not by sleep but only by oblivion. Sean knew Annie was beginning to wear out too – her sunfish face was beginning to fracture, fall apart. And the monthly spilling of blood was diminishing, becoming erratic. Sean Regan stroked his rasping, skate-wing cheeks with increasingly distorted fingers, and he measured the length of his days, the length of his life, savouring the memory of the feel of a black-haired, blue-eyed baby's foot snug in his palm.

Sean and Annie Regan birthed twelve children, testament to an alarming degree of fecundity. The older children, being Irish, sharing their ancestral memories of famine and overcrowding, soon began to disperse. Some stayed in the Republic, a couple went to England, where they found menial but well-paid work. Others went farther, to the cities of Boston, Toronto and New York, where they prospered. Padraig ended up in jail somewhere in Colorado, convicted of larceny, but most prospered. This diaspora, displaced by economics and indifference, carried its heritage with it. The emigrants married steady men and sturdy women from their own peasant stock, and they began to spread their seed. The double helix of DNA, bearing the imprint of generations, began to spread across the continents of America. One twist of chromosomes even made it all the way to Aotearoa, to New Zealand. Occasionally a postcard, or a flimsy, battered airmail envelope, made fat with photographs, would arrive at Ballysod, and then Sean would sit at the kitchen table as Annie haltingly read aloud the messages from various parts of the world, before passing him the photographs so he could examine the familiar faces set against alien landscapes. Over time, they sat at the worn table and read about what all their offspring were doing; they even received a prison-issue letter from Padraig. This last made Annie weep and berate herself for her failings as a mother, as Sean sat, smoke roiling from the hand-rolled cigarette between his fingers, and watched her. There was one notable caesura in the ever-growing mosaic of photographs, which were taped to the walls of the parlour: Maggie Regan, who had walked on to a ferry in Dublin and disappeared. Sean sat at the table, drawing smoke into his failing lungs, fighting tiredness, and hoped that his daughter had made good her escape.

1959

Jacqueline had been wrong about Lady Chalfont-Webbe's dislike of upstart colonials. For the first time, she misjudged the mood of the moment. She realized this on New Year's Eve, 1959, at the party she threw in Thurloe Square. It was a wild night – the drink flowed, the food was replenished over and over, music blared from the new hi-fi, drowning out the string quartet playing in the marbled entrance hall. In the drawing room the carpets had been turned back and the younger set were dancing to the new American music, R and B – Elvis, Buddy Holly, Fats Domino, anything they could buy from the States. The older set, who thought, like Oliver Reichmann, that they could feel the future pushing back, shoving them aside, drank too much, too fast, spilling food, braying at each other, trying to make the best of this, their last night before they were washed away by a tide of youth. Jacqueline felt stranded – between ages, between continents. The announcement made at two minutes to midnight by Lord Chalfont-Webbe, to an unruly, raucous, red-faced crowd, that Mr Billy-Ray Rickman and his daughter, the Honourable Isobel Chalfont-Webbe, were engaged to be married, was met with wild enthusiasm. The roars of approval drove Jacqueline to her room, her lonely ascent of the stairs watched by Maggie.

As Billy-Ray fought his way to the bathroom, he was met by slaps on the back, kisses on the cheek, hugs from strangers. He closed the door behind him and locked it, breathed deep, urinated, washed his hands. He looked in the mirror – and what did he see? Not Siegfried, his absent doppelgänger; nor Dieter, his incubus. What he saw was a head of tousled blond hair setting off a face of Nordic symmetry. The face of a man who had been absolved.

It just means you loved Siggy so much.

Billy-Ray splashed water on his face, ran fingers through his hair and towelled himself dry. He could feel heat rising through him – he'd not drunk vodka for more than a year but that evening he'd been throwing it down, made nervous by the thought of Isobel's father's announcement, made hollow chested by the thought that Jacqueline was the hostess. It was Isobel who had insisted that they celebrate the New Year at Jarman House, and how could he have refused? On what grounds? As it was, he'd hardly seen Jacqueline. Billy-Ray looked once more at his reflection. He looked honest. He looked innocent. He looked drunk. Billy-Ray splashed his face again. He didn't want to leave the sanctuary of the bathroom because he was scared. Scared of being found out. He was a hick, son of a hog farmer – what was he *doing*? Billy-Ray sat on the toilet seat and leaned his forehead against the cold, ornate tiles. He was scared of being found out and he was scared of Isobel, who was cool and composed, who was educated and accomplished, who was very beautiful and very rich. 'Marry old English money.' Which was precisely what he was doing and it made him scared. The door handle rattled and a fist hammered on the panels. Billy-Ray stood, staggered a little, then straightened his tie and opened the door, smiling at the man who pushed past him.

In the hallway stood the green-eyed girl he'd often noticed, at dinner parties, at Sherston Park. Billy-Ray had the fleeting sense that she had been standing there for an age, waiting for him. In her hands she held a silver salver, on which there was a single tumbler, brimful of ice and vodka.

'I thought you might be wanting another of these, sir.'

'Wouldn't say no. What's your name?'

'Maggie, sir. Maggie Regan.'

'Thank you, Maggie. And Happy New Year.'

'Thank you. You too, sir.'

Billy-Ray watched Maggie walk away, blue-black hair tied up in a knot, long legs encased in black stockings, and he swallowed mouthfuls of firewater.

THE RICKMANS

The Brooks Range, a rumpling of the earth like the snagging of a linen cloth on a long, long dining table, ran the width of Alaska, dividing south from north, effectively marking the line of the Arctic Circle. North of these mountains was two hundred miles of coastal plain where nothing grew but tundra, sprawling sloth-like on permafrost. The tundra was a dull orange-green, the sediments that had been folded into mountains were slate-grey; the light snows, when they came, coated the peaks white. Sometimes, when the sun hit the Brooks Range in the height of summer, when it was restless, when for weeks on end it never sank below the flat horizon, sometimes, then, it lit the sediments in such a way that the slate was transformed and the ranges appeared to be sand dunes. Endless, rippling sand dunes running east to west for hundreds of miles, like those in the Sahara. In fact, at the western end of the range, there *were* polar dunes, the desert a reminder of the long beaches that had stretched across Alaska millions of years before. The plains ran north until they reached the Arctic Ocean, a junction hard to distinguish, where permafrost met ice floes and snow-slow seas. Here the landscape was leached of colour, appeared albino. Yet the Inuit could name a hundred colours, point to ice, snow, sleet and frost and discern within these different forms of water a rainbow. There were no trees, there were no plants. Caribou, wolves and bears were the only inhabitants, other than migrating birds and spawning fish. Which were joined, first, by the Inuit and, later, by the white man.

Billy-Ray Rickman saw the mirage-like phenomenon of the apparent sandy desert on his first flight north of the Brooks Range, in June 1961, when he joined a small geological field party which was flown by Karbo Inc. to an airstrip at Umiat, in the foothills of the Brooks

Range. The awful barrenness of the place, the tenuous links the party had to the rest of mankind, unsettled him, unsettled all of them, and so they worked like men possessed, wanting to be away from there, wanting to see colours, hear sounds made by others than themselves. Billy-Ray found himself glancing over his shoulder, as if something were there – a wave, an inarticulate angriness, a mad-eyed wolverine. For six weeks the team took core samples and aerial photos, flying north as far as the plane would allow. Branching out, flying in a spider's-web pattern, eyes trained on the soggy, unbroken land below. Eventually Billy-Ray grew accustomed to the absolute silence, grew used to the unchanging plains, where every morning he was greeted by the same view, the morning a mere mark on his wristwatch as night had never come. On the last day of the survey, the team packed their kit and equipment, folded tents and flew away, leaving a patch of scuffed land, a few sheaves of paper which shifted in the breeze and a couple of empty tin cans, which would take years to rust away in the dry air. The team hopped south through the ranges, stopping at the outposts of Wiseman, Stevens and Livengood, where caches of fuel were kept, arriving at Fairbanks many hours later, battered and bruised by turbulence. Billy-Ray had always thought Fairbanks the ugliest place in the world, thought it made Anchorage look like Paris, France, or somewhere. But that night the neon, the powder pink cars, the roar of Harleys and blaring car radios were manna to his sensation-starved soul.

For two years Karbo concentrated on sucking up the gas and oil from the Middle Shoals in the Cook Inlet, and sent Billy-Ray out and about around the Kenai peninsula and Bristol Bay, where he squatted and stared at the curvature of the earth, trying to imagine what was happening fifteen thousand feet below his feet. In June 1963 Karbo Inc. called up a couple of geologists from Los Angeles, chartered a Bell G2 helicopter and a Cessna 180, and then phoned Billy-Ray Rickman. He flew with the team back to Umiat, dreading the three months of silence and absence that lay ahead. Why did he go? Because he'd looked at the maps, sat in on the meetings, discussed findings with colleagues and he was convinced that there were oil seeps which indicated a good prospective basin. Billy-Ray had never forgotten the day he'd spent drinking in the Savoy in London, when the telegram from Karbo had come through, announcing that oil had been found in the Cook Inlet. This time, he was going to be there.

The Cessna approached the airstrip, and even from two hundred feet Billy-Ray could see the damage the last trip had done, years before, to the gravel banks and the tundra, that damage now another unchanging aspect of the landscape. For three months the field team explored the area south of Umiat and flew into the Alaska National Wildlife Refuge. The two-passenger helicopter took them to the outcrops where the geologist assessed the rocks as the geophysicist took plane readings. When this was done, the Bell G2 lumbered along the outcrops at sixty miles an hour, as photographs were taken, its open lattice tail boom creating mournful music to accompany the shattering racket of the rotor blades, which scattered distant herds of caribou. As the party began to name places, began to pin a mental sheet on this blank section of the globe, the Cessna chuntered back and forth from Umiat, setting up camps and caches, at first using skis, swishing off from frozen lakes. When the permafrost thinned and the lakes broke up, floats replaced skis and the lakes were rocked and rippled as the Cessna belched and roared. At first this worried Billy-Ray, as he watched gravel shifting, footprints sinking into tundra, the smudge of smoke rising from their fires into a vast, seemingly uncaring, unaffected air dome. Billy-Ray lay on his back in thin, rustling tents and tried to ignore the memories of his father telling him you could never put anything back, tried to forget the look on Lucca Barzini's face when she had turned to stare at him in the Cord 812 as he talked about mapping the earth. But then, in August, they surveyed a section of the wildlife refuge and found good oil sand; this happened again on the river banks at Sagwon, where they unearthed a petroliferous expanse, and Billy-Ray forgot about the wolverine, about the rocking and rippling of the lakes, the scattering of caribou. The briny scent of an aeons-old, quiet, Shelleyesque sea basin was in his nostrils and all else was forgotten.

The Rickmans lived in a large, ugly A-frame house off Diamond Boulevard in Anchorage, overlooking Campbell Lake. It was set in more than five acres of land, with large concrete-block garages set apart. The house was in some ways a remarkable structure: the pre-fabricated frame, constructed in Reedport, Washington, had been driven over the Alaskan Highway on a wide flat-bed, a journey of twelve days; the clapboard had been logged on Vancouver Island, cut and seasoned in the lumber yards of Nanaimo and transported through the maze of the Alexander Archipelago, a journey of four years; the icebox, the stove, the sofas, beds and tables had been factored in the mad, filthy northern cities below the 48th parallel, wrapped, labelled and flown, sailed or driven through hailstorms and heatwaves. A lot of effort had been made by many people - indeed, some of them had risked their lives making this effort - so that the house could perch edgily, warily on the outskirts of the city. Nothing in the house was Alaskan; no piece of furniture, no scrap of material. As ever, in Alaska, what was remarkable about the house was that it was there at all.

Billy-Ray had flown to Anchorage on his own two years before and spent three months renting an apartment while he looked for a house for his family. Because every realtor knew he was an oil man, a rich man, a man going places, he was shown only the top-of-the-range housing – which was still mighty unattractive. When he saw the A-frame Billy-Ray knew he'd found what he wanted. The house was newly built, airy, and nearly five thousand square feet. More than that, it had its own dock for a boat or floatplane. He made an offer and signed the papers that afternoon. Then he went back to his rental, called Isobel and announced it was time she and Tufty came out to join him. That was in January 1961.

By October 1963, with Billy-Ray working a stint up on the North Slope, Isobel was looking her third Alaskan winter in the face. Six months of ever-diminishing sun, days eventually reduced to just over five hours of light – a grey, murky light at that. After a couple of years the house was a little battered, the edge and shine of it a little dulled. In the evenings, when Billy-Ray wasn't there, Isobel padded around in a pair of thick slippers and she'd stand, long arms crossed at her chest, staring at a chair, a plate, a pair of gumboots, and wonder at the astounding ugliness of it all. It was not that she objected to being surrounded by these objects – rather she was puzzled that anyone would willingly buy them. Isobel spent the long winter nights sitting in an armchair, long legs tucked beneath her, reading, or sitting at the English oak table she'd imported, writing letters home. Sometimes she lay on one of the sofas in the living room, by the fire, listening to the radio. She'd listen to music fading in and out on the ether, listen to the static chatter of ships' pilots and fishermen, occasionally tuning into the weather channels to discover when the next ice storm or bout of freezing fog was due. On those evenings she'd try to remember what it had been like to live in a Georgian neo-Palladian-style mansion in the Cotswolds, taking tea, riding to hounds, sitting at a table which comfortably sat thirty, to eat a six-course banquet. It seemed like a different world (which, of course, it was).

On winter nights when she couldn't sleep, which were many, Isobel wrapped herself in fur-lined parka, gloves and mukluks and strolled around the garden, which was prettier in winter, under the mask of snow. The birch and aspen looked fragile and other-worldly, the bare dirt and dust of the yard covered in a powder-white snow, unbroken and whole. Sometimes she'd open the garage doors and look at the ever-increasing pile of objects Billy-Ray spent his life accumulating: tools, bait boxes, coolers, boots, lines, hooks, welding equipment, mallets, tents, hard hats, canvas sheets, tin containers, oil drums, crates, tape measures, theodolites, engineer's levels, reels of electric wire, car batteries, beacons, two-way radio sets – more and more disparate items heaped untidily. Against the side wall stood a chest freezer, smeared with oil and decorated with perfect, bloody fingerprints. Next to the freezer was a padlocked cabinet mounted on the wall where Billy-Ray kept his hunting rifles. Outside the garage, to the left side of the house, was a Piper Super Cub on blocks. Billy-Ray had a pilot's licence like just about everyone else who could afford it; he'd managed to get his SES in two months when he first came back. Isobel was fascinated by the improbability of the delicate web of struts that held it together. She felt that the plane was a construct of everything she found in the garage – a Heath Robinson of a machine but beautiful none the less. The shiny leather seats, shallow and worn smooth, the dents in its hollow wings, the implausibility of it severing its ties to the water or land.

Isobel sometimes walked around the garden for hours, trying to walk herself to sleep, stopping to stare over the lake at the mountains behind, stopping to light endless cigarettes, exhaling freezing smoke as she willed the sun to rise. She walked in her yard on winter nights, with the temperature sometimes twenty below, because she felt near-maddened by claustrophobia.

When Billy-Ray was away on a shift, which could be anything from five days to two months, Isobel was left to her own devices. She had a daily routine which varied little and which revolved nearly exclusively around Tufty. Billy-Ray's absence meant that Isobel could devote herself to her daughter's needs – love, food and stimulation, in that order of importance. In the mornings there was the bathing and breakfasting, followed by the laundry. Then came the bundling on of clothes, layer over layer, and the drive downtown to buy produce from the market. Isobel had a pram she kept in the back of the Chevy and she'd push Tufty through the frozen sludge lining the sidewalks of Hyder and Gambell around 7th and 8th, wrestling with the pram as it caught in ruts and snow-filled potholes. As Tufty grew the pram was mothballed, and the two of them would slither around town, flailing on black ice and falling into small drifts. What they found in the shops depended on whether the freight planes had come in and what they were carrying. Isobel often visited the mail office on 4th and E Street, which she hated to do. It took a while for the Hon. Isobel to realize the nature of the neighbourhood, whores and alcoholics not having played a great part in her upbringing. She pushed the pram, with some difficulty, around the bodies of sleeping Native drunks, lying sprawled, drool frozen to the sidewalk, to their lips. She manhandled, sometimes even picked up and carried the pram, in order to skirt the women in tatty furs and short dresses, with vivid red lips and tousled, dyed hair. Native men stood in clusters outside the twenty-four-hour bars, most swaying with beery befuddlement, and watched her walk by with dulled, unfocused eyes. But then, everyone watched her as she walked past. At six foot, Isobel, with her pale blonde hair and ice eyes, was, after all, worth watching.

One grim, dark morning, as sleet fell and hardened, Isobel turned on to 4th Street, to find three whores kicking a Native as he lay on the freezing pavement, the pointed toes of their stilettos sinking into his cheeks and ribs with stabbing motions. Isobel stopped, held Tufty close. Other pedestrians stepped off the sidewalk to avoid the ruckus, ignoring the man's quiet grunts.

'Stop that,' Isobel said loudly.

The women did stop their kicking, looked at Isobel with smudged eyes, as they wiped smudged lips. 'Why don't you jus' fuck off?' asked one of them, almost conversationally.

'Yeah, ain't your fuckin' business.'

'Stop that, or I'll call the police.'

Tufty began to whimper.

'Ooooh – listen to her. "I'll call the police".' The whore's attempt at an English accent made her companions laugh.

But the women moved away as Isobel walked towards them, Tufty by now bawling.

'Here, hold her please.' Isobel gave Tufty to the raven-haired loud-mouth with the bitten nails. Then she knelt down, her knee freezing in the sludge, and helped the man to his feet, dabbed at a cut on his nose with a damp tissue. 'Are you OK?' she asked him.

The Native looked up at Isobel with bleary eyes and nodded. Shuffled away.

'Thank you,' Isobel said as she took Tufty from the woman.

'Hey, look – we din' mean anything. He was hasslin' us for hours, askin' for a blowjob, y'know, like we'd do that? They're always hasslin' us, drunk as skunks and no fuckin' money. You gotta understand.'

Isobel tucked in Tufty's scarf, slipped on her gloves and walked off, the women watching her as she turned down a side street, heart hammering.

In the afternoons Isobel tried to cook, wishing she'd paid more attention in cookery at Frontin-sur-Mont, before reading aloud to Tufty, or playing games with her. Love, food and stimulation. The afternoon was the time she found tolerable – when the heat from the stove and the warmth generated by the spinning tumble dryer made the echoing A-frame seem snug. She liked working in the kitchen as Tufty chewed on a rusk or, later, a homemade cookie in the high chair, always watching her mother. As she tried to cook, frowning, rereading recipes over and over, Isobel talked to Tufty, in a companionable, adult way. 'Now I've measured out the flour – see? – so I'm going to cut some butter up into it. Not all at once. We can add a bit at a time. Apparently.'

'Time,' Tufty would say. 'Buttle.'

'Butter.'

'Buttle. Tufty cut buttle.'

'Tufty cut *butter*.' And Isobel would lift her daughter on to the table and help her cut.

'Floor and buttle,' said Tufty, slapping her hands in the pile and throwing up a cloud.

'As you say, floor and buttle.'

In the short summer life was easier. The two of them could drive out to Chester Creek Park or Russian Jack Spring and have a walk, taking a picnic. In the summer the days were long, the temperatures in the seventies, fireweed and poppies splashing against south-facing walls. In the summer the Chugach range was green and snow free. In the summer they could walk from the house down to the lake and play at the water's edge or drive out to the zoo. In the summer, the A-frame house was delightful – it did, after all, have views over the lake and mountains. Sometimes, during summer nights when daylight never entirely faded and the moon rode between the peaks, Isobel would go out into her unloved garden, smoke a cigarette and watch starlight flicker on water, breathing deep, aware of the immense dome of darkness hanging over her, aware of the endless space around her, relishing it.

In winter Isobel sometimes thought she might be losing her mind. And then she would close her eyes and try to imagine what Billy-Ray was doing.

Billy-Ray was earning his money. Come winter or summer, Billy-Ray was earning his money. He had renegotiated his contract with Karbo Inc. and he was sent back to the North Slope with seismic crews, to shoot long, north–south seismic lines in winter, and mapping crews and geologists in summer to decipher the land. This frantic activity did not pass unnoticed and Humble, Richfield, BP and others began to airlift men and supplies to the tundra, which by now was becoming very scuffed indeed. The Karbo lines were extended over a smooth, bulging anticline that had been named Lucy, which the geologists were sure would eventually pay off. This last was important, this hope of being paid off, because the companies were spending money like water, like oil itself. Millions of dollars were thrown at the North Slope, for fuel, planes, cargo barges, food, equipment, expertise, pilots. The companies began to merge again, like blobs of mercury melding into each other. Even Richfield began to feel the squeeze and sold half its interest in the Slope to Humble (which would later be subsumed by Exxon). The state of Alaska meanwhile was consolidating its acquisition of the lands along the Arctic coast, where possession had been a thorny issue during its time as a territory, before statehood was granted in 1959. Eventually Alaska began to sell itself, began to sell the leases to the wilderness north of the Brooks Range.

Billy-Ray was a gem, a diamond in the firmament of the oil business: he was a geophysicist, he was a surveyor, he was trained in management, he could speak seven languages (increasingly badly). He was wildcat, roustabout and executive. Billy-Ray Rickman was flying – the farm boy from Minnesota made good. The flatlands boy who had swapped the hogs and the crucifix and Magde for a life spent searching for black gold beneath the blue earth. And he found it. Billy-Ray had a nose for it. He spent hours poring over the maps the surveyors threw on the table, spent days out in the field collecting samples, Zodiacs having dropped him off on barren coastlines with only Dall sheep and bears for company. Unlike most engineers and geophysicists he spent a great deal of time hunkered down on the water's edge, looking, watching its movement. Remembering everything Urban Svensson had told him about the mystery of the motion of fluids. Plane surveys were one of his specialities, his calculations of the bearings of traverse lines were flawless. The length of a north–south traverse course multiplied by the cosine of its bearing gave its distance; the length of a west–east traverse course multiplied by the sine of its bearing gave its distance. Billy-Ray could calculate this in his sleep. This specialism meant that Billy-Ray was also a mean geodetic surveyor. He could look at an expanse of land or water (watching always for the Wave) and compensate for the geoidal contortion, because in his mind was locked the true north–south meridian. Perhaps as a result of the gyroscope buried deep in his spine, which Lucca Barzini had set spinning all those years before on Cape Disappointment? Perhaps because of his first foray into the Puget Sound with Urban in a small dinghy? Who knows? A boy from the flatlands standing at the edge of the world and reading it.

Billy-Ray spent his days away from Isobel flying in lumbering C-47 aircraft or fragile Cessnas and Grummans, or bouncing out on glacial waters in flimsy dinghies powered by 50cc outboards. He was bounced about on the thermals and turbulence over the Brooks Range in six-seater de Havillands, sometimes not believing he would arrive at his destination. He slept in air-conditioned bunk rooms in the summer, in winter oil-fired heating kept him warm. He ate like a king, slept when he could. The exploration went on twenty-four hours every day of the year – out in the Cook Inlet, up on the North Slope – and Billy-Ray was there. In his shirtsleeves, or in his Arctic parka, yelling instructions in Norwegian, German and Russian. When bits broke, when they needed replacing and it was sixty-eight degrees below and the bit team wanted to knock off, Billy-Ray was the one who was sent out to offer cigarettes, sympathy and a two-hundred-dollar bonus for every man out there if they'd haul up the pipes and change the bit. More, he stayed with them as they did it, hauling up the pipe load over and over, dragging the sleeves of metal across the icy platform, changing the bit and then resetting the sleeves. And when it was done, when the men had earned more in a day than most Outsiders earned in two weeks, there would be a lot of back-slapping, puffing and swaggering. After all, these men were living at the edge, living at the extremes of the earth, living where men did not belong, their backs turned to the shimmering, polar display of lights in the sky as they shattered permafrost and hammered the land to pieces. The ocean exploded in gouts and spouts as depth charges blew and leaks of oil sashayed in slicks on the waves.

As the bit team fell to eating lobster and steak, fries and dough-nuts, Billy-Ray would be called to a meeting of the suits from Dallas. What about the unions? they would ask. What about the fucking Teamsters? What about the supply line to the oil camps? What about

the problem with the fucking Natives and homesteaders? Billy-Ray
Rickman was paid a huge amount of money for what he did, but
perhaps rightly so. Having been on the drilling site for thirteen
hours, to change a single bit piece, Billy-Ray had to pour oil (if only
he could have done) on troubled waters. He calmed people, he
soothed nerves – there were, after all, billions of dollars invested in
the hope there might be oil on the North Slope and under the Bering
Sea – he slapped backs and he smiled, when all he wanted to do was
sleep. When all he wanted to do was sleep with Isobel. Isobel – his
haven. *Der Hort. Bezpieczny Zakatek.*

There were times when the Rickmans had fun. There were the
summer weeks in Halibut Cove, the weekends camping in the
Chugach, spent fishing and walking. There was the 4th Avenue
Theater, when Billy-Ray was home and they'd arrange a babysitter
for Tufty, have a burger out and then catch a movie. A favourite pas-
time was to drive out to Peggy's Airport Café on East 5th, near
Merrill Field, and watch aircraft taking off into the sun – Cessnas,
Super Cubs, de Havilland Beavers, Piper Aztecs. Sometimes it
seemed all Alaska was disappearing into a solar ball. Sometimes,
Isobel thought, sitting at the greasy Formica table, watching what
seemed to be a mass exodus, it was as though she, Billy-Ray and
Tufty were the only ones left in the territory.
    There were the lavish receptions and cocktail parties, thrown by
the oil companies in the Westward Hotel. Isobel and Billy-Ray were
always invited – such a handsome couple, such a happy couple,
such a *rich* couple. Isobel found these evenings baffling at first.
Executives and their wives up from Texas would waft in, trailing
sequins and diamonds, nails varnished, hair teased into stiff bee-
hives, and they'd talk to the locals as if they were *idiots savants*. The
Anchorage wives looked defeated by all the razzmatazz, stood awkwardly in their mail catalogue dresses, looking at the floor. Isobel, all
seventy-two inches of her swathed in a classic Schiaparelli or Dior,
was the exception. Some of the Dallas wives had heard she was a
someone, royalty or something. Billy-Ray and Isobel would always
make a bet, as they dressed for these evenings, about how many
primped and crimped women would curtsy before asking Isobel

whether she was enjoying living in Anchorage. They'd also bet about how many women would notice Isobel's huge hands and be struck dumb in mid-sentence.

Men Billy-Ray worked with asked them over to barbecues, pot-luck dinners, parties. Billy-Ray loved these events, standing in the garden or the kitchen, a cold tin of Amber in one hand, a cigarette in the other, yakking to burly men about floatplanes, the best ammo when encountering a bear, comparing snow chains, discussing how to rebore an engine for maximum performance, which snowmobiles were best. Meanwhile, Isobel sat in the living room with the wives and girlfriends, trying hard, but always failing, to keep a grip on what was being said. Indeed, trying hard to get a grip at all.

'So Isobel, darlin', you coming next Wednesday afternoon? Sure be fun to have you there.'

'Next Wednesday?'

'Sure – it's Lorraine's baby shower.'

Baby shower? Baby shower? Isobel stared at the pregnant Lorraine, wondering what on earth was going on. Images of falling, tumbling, naked babies. 'Good Lord,' said Isobel.

And, of course, the wives and girlfriends all laughed and asked her to say it again.

'Oh, Isobel – say it again? Doncha jus' love that accent?'

And the conversation moved on to recipes, the new teacher up at the McKinley Elementary School, where to get your hair done, the new rotisserie section opening in Carr's supermarket, how to clean floors so you could get rid of the crankcase oil people walked in from the street. The beers and bourbon, highballs and martinis would keep flowing through the day. The girlfriends and wives loos-ened up as the day wore on, taking it in turns to fetch the bottle and check on the children. The talk would move on to the general unac-ceptability of men – their filthy clothes, the fact they didn't do things round the house, the mess they made, the food they ate, the beer they drank. Isobel couldn't disagree with these assertions, certainly with reference to the men. They must indeed eat and drink a great deal because they were all as fat as houses, but then, so, too, were the women.

'Isobel, honey, how much do you weigh?' (This was another thing

Billy-Ray and she always bet on – whether she'd be asked how much she weighed.)

'Ten stone ten pounds.'

'Come again, honey?'

'Oh, sorry – a hundred and fifty pounds.'

'Shit, honey, you need some flesh on those bones else how you gonna make it through winter?'

Then the women, who by now were sprawling on the sofas, on the carpets and rugs, would light into the subject of winter. Getting the home fuel tanks filled, fitting the triple glazing, getting in the coal and logs, fixing the snow chains, winterizing the car, getting the engine heater out and running cables to the garage. The cold. The freezing fog. The darkness. Getting the kids to school; getting them up at all in what seemed like the middle of the night. The utter dreariness of it all. Still one of them was fetching the bottle and checking on the kids. Then someone would put a record on the turntable and the women, or at least those who could still walk, went out to the kitchen or the garden and tugged at their partners, tried to pull them away from the comforting embrace of testosterone.

When it was Isobel's turn to fetch the bottle, she went out into the yard to check on Tufty, and found her making mud pies among the fireweed with Sam, Lorraine's son.

'Well, that's impressive,' Isobel said, kneeling down by her daughter and examining the stacks of goo.

'What's impressive mean?' asked Sam.

'Means good,' said Tufty.

'That's right.' Isobel stroked Tufty's short, spiky blue-black hair – the reason for her nickname – as Sam frowned.

'Mrs Rickman, Tufty talks strange, talks like you.'

'That's right, Sam,' said Isobel, standing and thinking, Well, thank God for that.

'Impersive,' muttered Tufty, slapping down another mud pie.

Isobel took the bourbon bottle into the living room, along with a bucket of ice, and found a hard core of women still sitting there, eyes glazed. Isobel, a moderate drinker, poured them another shot and poured herself a glass of soda. Lorraine, who was indeed showered with babies, leaned forward conspiratorially and, over the sound of Skeeter Davis singing about the end of the world, asked, 'You take precautions, Isobel?'

Precautions? Against what? Bears? Hypothermia? Loneliness? Alcoholism? There was so much to be wary of here, how could one take *enough* precautions? 'Against what?'

'Y'know, against gittin' pregnant.'

'Oh, I see. No, I don't.'

'Ah want to take this new pill thing. Y'know? You jus' take a little pill ever' day and you never git pregnant. But Casey don't want me to do it, he says it's unnat'rel.' Lorraine's eyes filled.

Isobel looked coolly over at Casey. A moose of a man, a lout with a solid mass of gut, a dung belly, hanging over his belt, tattoos on his forearms. Beer dribbled over his beard as he finished a tin while reaching for another. He caught Isobel looking at him and blushed. There was something about Mrs Rickman which unsettled him. Something that unsettled all the men. They watched her and imagined taking her up against a wall, on a dirt floor, in a bed. (As ever, the men did not think of this as rape but, rather, an approximation of love.) But if she was ever near them, or if she ever spoke to them, they stopped their belching and swearing and, eyes lowered, shuffled their feet, uncomfortable. They watched Billy-Ray, handsome, successful, rich, *lean* Billy-Ray, and they admired him. The Rickmans – the envy of the Anchorage municipality.

'I believe,' said Isobel, turning back to the now weeping Lorraine, whose mascara was beginning to run, 'that you can arrange to see a doctor and have the pill prescribed without your husband's permission. And if that's not the case it certainly should be.'

'I couldn' do that. I couldn' do that to Casey.'

'Well, in that case your only other course of action is to abstain.'

Lorraine stopped sniffing. 'What's that? Like another drug or somethin'?'

'No, no. I mean that your only course of action is to stop having sex.'

Lorraine blinked, swigged from her glass. 'Oh, I couldn' do that.'

'You must enjoy it then.'

'To be honest, honey, I don'. But Casey sure does an' so I don' have much choice, do I?'

'So it would seem. Would you excuse me?'

'It's My Party' was blaring as Isobel went to look for Billy-Ray, avoiding the gyrations of a few couples who were dancing as best they were able, trying to frug and twist. Isobel found Billy-Ray standing out by the smoking barbecue, turning moose burgers with a pair of tongs, a beer in the other hand, surrounded by other Karbo workers. This always happened – the men would split into groups according to whether they worked for Standard Oil, Shell, BP or Karbo. Splitting into tribes. Isobel kissed Billy-Ray's cheek, slipped her arm through his. The Karbo men were talking about the Natives. Brad Honker (whose name always made Isobel smile even if the man himself did not) had been at the Jim Beam all day and was voluble on the subject.

'I'm telling you, man, if just one of those fuckers . . . oh, sorry, Isobel . . . if one of those . . . one of those freakin' Red Injuns could do a week's work, y'know? Jus' one of them do one fucking week's work . . . sorry, Isobel . . . I mean, shit, they take the fucking welfare and spend it in the bars. You can't walk down Fourth without falling over them. Cut the fucking welfare and see what they do.'

'Perhaps,' said Bent Prick (whose name had completely *undone* Isobel when they'd been introduced), a visiting Swedish geologist who had a rather different world view, 'they don't have the education or the training?'

'Oh, right,' sneered Brad Honker. 'Like how much intelligence does it take to pick up a fucking hammer?'

'Yeah, right,' chimed in Dave 'The Caribou' Peltzer. 'Government gives 'em houses, cars, sends 'em food parcels and fuel and fuck knows what. And you know what? Now they want all the fucking land too. Sorry, Isobel.'

Brad Honker laughed nastily. 'I mean, this ain't finders keepers – this is goddam Alaska. This is goddamn *America*.'

'What do you think, Billy-Ray?' asked Bent.

The men stopped laughing and drinking, looked at Billy-Ray, who kept turning the burgers, holding Isobel's arm tight. 'I think,' he said, 'that it's a difficult situation.'

Isobel, who was also looking at him closely, asked, 'Why?'

'Because they were here first. Before we were. Sometimes . . .'

Billy-Ray thought of the night Urban had told him that he talked to the Natives, listened to what they had to say because they knew more than him. Remembered Urban saying the Natives understood the land and how to use it. Thought of fire and ice chasing a man; thought of the Wave hunting a man.

'Sometimes what? BR?'

'Sometimes I think we should ask them more. Like when the fires start, or houses and roads sink, sometimes I think we should ask them what to do, get them involved. Sometimes I think we're wrong. They know things we don't. Sometimes I don't think we treat them so good.' Billy-Ray shrugged. 'On the other hand, yeah, a lot of them are drunks, and yeah, they don't like work.'

'Halle-fucking-lujah,' said Brad Honker. 'Sorry, Isobel.'

'I'm going to check on Tufty.'

'You want a burger?' asked her husband.

'Not at the moment, thank you.'

Later, when the children were asleep upstairs, before the party got too wild, Isobel danced with Billy-Ray. Danced to long, slow numbers, holding him loosely around the waist, feeling the muscles in his back moving, breathing the scent of Old Spice (which she insisted he wear), her head resting on his shoulder. She held him too close because she loved him too much. The Rickmans danced gracefully, seemed hardly to move, and gradually the other couples sat down, lost in a warm, alcoholic haze, and watched two blond giants moving each other gently around the room

There *were* good times, but only when Billy-Ray was home. When he was away, confusion came back to haunt Isobel. Why was she there? Why did Anchorage bear no resemblance to the land Billy-Ray had talked about, the weekend they had met? As she and Tufty walked the streets and parks of the city, Isobel sometimes thought about leaving, thought about going home, back to Highbury. She hadn't really considered what this would mean, this moving to Alaska, with a young baby and no nanny. Isobel felt isolated because she didn't know how to talk to anyone – except Billy-Ray and he was absent much of the time. But she was too proud to admit defeat, too proud to admit that what so many people had said – her friends in

London, her sister, her old school friends – was true: that she was making a mistake marrying out of her class, out of her heritage. It was the Chalfont genes which kept her there in Anchorage. The sanguinary fingerprint memory of the explorers and mercenaries, the reprobates and reformers they had been which kept her there. Besides, she knew the consequences of turning and walking away from a problem. So Isobel stayed in the house on Campbell Lake, loving Tufty and counting the days until Billy-Ray walked back in the door, mulish, bullish and bearish. She played out the rituals and waited for the real Billy-Ray to emerge and then she made love to him.

Isobel wrote many letters home during those early years of her exile, to friends and family, describing the Halibut Cove weeks, the fishing, barbecues and parties, the trails they hiked, the beauty of the mountains and rivers. She wrote witty asides about moose burgers and caribou sausages, baby showers and hookers. She sent interesting clippings from the *Anchorage Times*, clippings about avalanches, temperatures, the Iditarod. There was one newspaper article that snagged her attention which she decided not to send, however. A woman, Cheryl, had recently married a backwoodsman, and been dropped off at her husband's place by floatplane, his cabin was so remote. Cheryl, according to the pilot, had been excited by the prospect of her new life with her new love. Six weeks later the pilot flew back to check on how the newlyweds were doing. As he neared the cabin he saw a message written large in the snow, a message formed by the laying down of birch branches in the snowfields: Cheryl Had Enough – Can You Collect? Sometimes on her nighttime walks in the yard Isobel thought of this. Thought of laying out the message: Isobel Had Enough – Can Someone, Anyone, Collect? But pride and love made her stay, bound her to the ugly city.

1960

Lady Cooper's observation that pig farmers' sons didn't quite make the cut when it came to marrying the daughters of English lords was, in essence, right. After her lonely ascent of the stairs on the night of New Year's Eve 1959, an ascent watched and mourned by Maggie Regan, Jacqueline lay on her bed and stared at the ceiling as the raucous singing of 'Auld Lang Syne' rang out. So Billy-Ray Rickman and Isobel Chalfont-Webbe were to be married? How could that be? What about the blood lines? What about the titled, eligible males who required an heir and a spare? The primary succession of the English upper classes? Jacqueline lay on her bed and worried at the conundrum. It made no sense. As she had told Billy-Ray, she had known the Chalfont-Webbes for a long time. She knew Viola was a stickler for tradition, for the right way of doing things, the *old* way of doing things. Jacqueline had a word for all this, for this insane attention to details – the seating at the dining table, the wording of invitations, the laying out of ranks of cutlery, the order in which wine was served – these things she labelled jackassery. But she knew the attention to detail was the price paid for privilege, and it seemed to her a small price. But whilst it might be possible to overlook the incorrect laying down of a dessert spoon, it was quite another to allow your eldest daughter to marry out of her class, out of her world.

In the hallway below, a tray was dropped and the echoing sounds of shattering glass and shouts, followed by laughter, caused Jacqueline to roll over on to her side, her legs drawn up, her hands crossed beneath her chin. Why? Why should this worry her so? After all, she didn't care about Isobel – she liked her well enough but she knew she would survive, cushioned as she was by wealth and ancestry. But she did worry for Billy-Ray because she knew he loved

Isobel. A man like Billy-Ray Rickman shouldn't love. In the drawing room beneath her suite someone turned up the volume and the bed vibrated to a bass thump. Jacqueline didn't have to be down there among the dancers to know how they would look, how they would behave. The men would be red faced, collars digging into the soft skin of their necks, as they brayed and shouted, cigars burning between doughy fingers. Their women would be standing in gaggles, elbows sharp and naked, long satin gloves rucked around wrists, whispering about nothing, eyeing the cut of each other's dresses, bitching, jawing and unconcerned. These days, Jacqueline often found herself remembering times in Albany, New York, when she and her brothers might drive out to a roadhouse after a day in the orchards, dressed in jeans and high boots, plaid shirts and neckerchiefs, the rich smell of apple juice and soft fruit bruises impregnated in their skin and clothes. They'd slot dimes in the jukebox and dance through the evening, Jacqueline waltzing with her brothers in turn, knowing she was safe, knowing what she had to do, knowing how to live the next day and the day after. Why hadn't she stayed there? But she knew if she went back, after all these years, she would no longer know how to live the next day there, back in Albany. She would be a trespasser, a stray.

There was a gentle knock on the door and Sidney looked in, squinting across the room with his weak eyes.

'Came to see if you were all right.' He smiled vaguely.

'I'm fine. I have a headache, so I thought I'd lie down a while.'

'Shall I ask someone to bring you some powders?'

'If you could. Find Maggie and ask her.'

'Will do. Well, well . . .' Sidney trailed off, stared at the floor. 'Damn good evening,' he said and closed the door.

As the volume of the music rose, Jacqueline rolled on to her back and stared at the rose on the ceiling. Maybe Billy-Ray had fooled them all? Maybe they believed he was what he pretended he was? Maybe he believed it himself? If Viola could feel his hands, feel the roughness of his skin, feel the thickness of his muscled neck and thighs, then she would know the truth. Jacqueline had only ever told one person about her thoughts on jackassery, and Billy-Ray had known exactly what she meant.

Again, there was a knock at the door and Maggie came into the room, with powders and a glass of water. Wordlessly, she motioned for Jacqueline to get up and Jacqueline did. Maggie undressed her employer, pulled back the heavy counterpane on the bed, prepared the pillows and helped Jacqueline to lie down. She mixed the powders and watched as Jacqueline drank them, and then she moved around the room, folding clothes, closing the curtains and fetching a carafe of water to put at Jacqueline's bedside. She looked at Jacqueline's face and noticed that her skin was pale, that she looked wiped out, as her mammy would have said. Looked broken.

Maggie switched off the overhead light and Jacqueline said, 'Thank you,' before pulling the blankets over her head and burrowing into the bed. Maggie stood in the darkness, chewing her cheek, wondering what was to be done.

THE RICKMANS

'So how was your shift?' Isobel asked Billy-Ray as he lay in the tub, smoking a cigar, a bourbon on the shelf. Isobel was sitting on the floor of the bathroom, back resting against the wall, long legs stretched out on cork tiles. Billy-Ray had returned that afternoon from four weeks out in the Cook Inlet, four weeks of sleeping in bunk rooms, being on call twenty-four hours. Four weeks of cursing and back-slapping, growing a beard and turning into an asshole. Isobel knew the symptoms now. Knew that when Billy-Ray came back from a stint out in the field he'd burst into the house overflowing with testosterone and bullishness. He'd throw his stuff around, disrupt the house, criticize the way things had been run in his absence and then he'd jump on her bones. This jumping had nothing to do with love (was barely an approximation of it). Much as Jacqueline had years before, Isobel would wonder whether her back was about to be broken. After an hour or so in bed, after a drink and some attention, the layers of days spent in the company of men were peeled away and Billy-Ray was back again. But today he seemed worse than usual, more truculent, angrier.

'Fucking nightmare. You got no idea the amount of crap I put up with day after fucking day.'

'I don't suppose I do.'

'Wash my back.' Billy-Ray held out the soap and leaned forward. Another ritual of his homecoming.

Isobel took the bar and began to rub her husband's shoulders, massaging them with her huge thumbs, working the spaces between his bones. She bent him forward and worked up the line of his neck, into his shaggy blond hair, down again, all the way down his spine, soaking the cuffs of her shirt. Then back up to his shoulders, slipping her hands over them, thumbs locked into his back, pulling his shoulders back until they were stretched to breaking point, making him yelp at the intersection between pleasure and pain. Billy-Ray sat up suddenly, grabbed Isobel's wrist and pulled her towards him, and she laughed. Kissed the back of his neck.

'Supper in fifteen minutes.'

'Ah c'mon.' Billy-Ray doused his cigar in the water, tossed it in the bin, reached for her again.

Isobel slipped away. 'Fifteen minutes.'

At supper, Tufty sat in a high chair between them and hurled mashed potato around at will, gurgling whenever she hit her target, which appeared to be Billy-Ray's beard. As Isobel cleared the table, washed the plates and tidied Billy-Ray's mess away, he played with his daughter. He lay on the rug in the living room and tossed her in the air above him, played peek-a-boo, let her tug his beard. Then he sat in an armchair, Tufty on his lap, and asked her questions.

'Did you annoy the Honourable Isobel while Daddy's been gone?'

'Have you learned to cook yet?'

'Have you fixed the boiler?'

'Did you clean up the yard?'

'Did you argue with any bears?'

Tufty jumped up and down on her daddy's knees, slapping at his beard and yelling 'No! No! No!' Giggling and collapsing every now and then, as Billy-Ray tickled her plump little ribs. Another ritual.

Isobel put Tufty to bed, which involved waving stuffed animals and speaking in silly voices, playing out a pantomime involving various teddy bears and a raddled old donkey which had belonged to Isobel when she was a girl. Tufty gurgled and clutched at her favourite bear. When she was tucked up under the sheet and blanket, a light left on, Isobel crept out of the room and downstairs to the living room, steeling herself for what she might find there.

Billy-Ray was cracking open a fresh bottle of bourbon and he poured two slugs, gave his wife a glass and they sat at either end of the long Naugahyde sofa, looking at each other.

'So how you been, Mrs Rickman?'

'Fine, thank you, Mr Rickman.'

'Anything happened? Anything I should know about?'

'No, I don't think so.' Isobel stretched out her leg, rubbed Billy-Ray's damaged thigh with her foot. 'How about you?'

Billy-Ray poured himself another slug, lay back against the sofa. 'So much going on. Y'know? Out there.' Billy-Ray nodded at the drawn drapes. 'So much going on. The gas is coming in full flow. And this week, Thursday, we finally got the third semi-sub operating. It's the fucking tides, you know? It's a bitch getting the sleeves down and steady. Always shifting and snapping. Fucking thirty foot tides.'

Isobel kept stroking his leg with her foot, ignoring the language Billy-Ray was speaking – this man who could say 'I love you' and mean it in seven languages stretching across the northern hemisphere was talking like a bar-fly, like a convict, like a rapist of language. Another ritual.

Billy-Ray downed his bourbon. 'And it won't get any better. They got people coming up from Texas, Oklafuckinghoma, anywhere, and these people don't understand the fucking tides. They work in goddam deserts – what do they know about the ocean? You take them out to the rig and they're puking all over the boat. Only thing is, I don't think I'll be going out there much longer.'

'What do you mean?'

'Looks like Karbo and all the others are headed for the Slope. Port Nikiski's bringing it in now – thirty thousand barrels a day. That'll be enough to keep the planes flying to find more. We're all headed north.'

Isobel kept rubbing his leg, sipping at her bourbon, thinking. North? North of Anchorage? God in heaven – what was up there? What could be colder, darker, more ugly than Anchorage? Whatever it was, she was sure Karbo Inc. would be able to find it.

'Will you have to do longer shifts?' she asked.

'I don't know. I've renegotiated my package – seems to me if they want me to work with the unions, deal with all the foreigners, find the oil and then help set up the rigs, seems to me I'm worth quite a lot to them.'

'And to me, BR. Don't forget that. You're worth a lot to me too.'

Billy-Ray opened his eyes and stared at his wife.

'Let's go to bed,' she said, standing in one movement and walking towards their bedroom at the back of the house.

This time their love-making was slow and careful, careful of each

other. When it was done, when Isobel had finally peeled away the
last layer of Billy-Ray having spent four weeks with oil animals, she
filled his glass one last time and snuggled into his side.

'Want to head for Homer for a while?' Billy-Ray asked. 'Spend a few
days in the cabin?' It was his way of apologizing for his demeanour,
his language, his absence. Billy-Ray Rickman, apologizing.

'I'd love to. Let's go tomorrow.' Isobel ran a huge hand down to
the scar on Billy-Ray's thigh, let it rest there.

Billy-Ray downed the rest of his bourbon. 'Today would've been
Deet's birthday.'

So that was what had soured him. 'Happy birthday, Deet,' said
Isobel.

Billy-Ray turned off the bedside light, held his wife tightly. '*Alles
Gute zum Geburtstag*, Deet,' he said into the darkness.

The Rickmans' cabin on Kachemak Bay, near Halibut Cove, was the
element of Isobel's life that kept her sane, or at least, a little less confused. It took them a whole day to get there, what with the packing
and the journey, but she thought it was worth it. The morning after
Deet's birthday, she rose early and began to pack bags and boxes,
while Billy-Ray checked the cabin cruiser and hitched it to the Chevy
4×4. While he went to the gas station to fill containers with gallons
of diesel, Isobel took Tufty to the market to buy cans of vegetables,
flour, coffee, juice and milk, a few staples.

They left Anchorage at ten, hauling the forty-foot cabin cruiser
down the Seward Highway before turning on to the Sterling
Highway at Portage, at the head of Turnagain Arm. Tufty rode in the
back, her blue eyes wide, watching, always watching. She watched
the waters of Turnagain Arm, the mountains of the Coast Range
growing nearer, she pointed at other cars on the road and murmured
their colours to herself. She watched her parents when they talked,
occasionally reaching out for them and then Isobel would turn
around and talk to her, explain where they were going and why, rub
her tiny hands, smoothing the backs of them. As usual they pulled off
the highway at Snug Harbour Road and drove down to Cooper Lake.
There, Isobel prepared sandwiches and coffee, as Billy-Ray hauled
out his line and fished for Dolly Varden, their evening meal. He stood

at the water's edge, dressed in jeans and a T-shirt, laughing with other fishermen and Isobel watched him, thought how even a day away from the fields changed him. When he laughed in a certain way, he reminded her of the man, the popinjay, he had been when he blasted his first clay pigeon in the fields behind the Coopers' house.

Lunch over, they headed west again on the Sterling Highway, and at Sterling Billy-Ray turned north, up the road to the Swanson River, eventually dropping down towards marshland.

'What are you doing?' asked Isobel, who'd been thinking of how she'd need to pee when they reached Soldotna.

'Want to show you something.' Billy-Ray struggled with the cabin cruiser bouncing behind as he took the road to Nikiska, pulling up on the beach road and turning off the engine. 'There – that's where I've been the past few weeks.' He pointed to a slab of metal resting on vast pontoons, way out in the inlet, as he handed her binoculars. Isobel focused the binoculars, scanned the horizon, found the rig and refocused. Saw the girders and struts supporting the monster, watched as a boat belching fumes pulled up at the pontoon to collect workers. Two columns of smoke poured from outlet valves, orange flames licking inside them. A helicopter clattered above the car and Tufty began to cry. Isobel watched the helicopter closely as it made its way out to the landing platform, hovering there, kicking up the water. She lowered the glasses. 'That's obscene.'

'Huh?'

'It's obscene. In the midst of all this. It's so ugly and . . . dirty.'

'It's money,' said Billy-Ray, restarting the engine, moving off towards Miller Loop. They drove in silence through the area of gas processing plants and petrochemical tanks, piles of pipes rusting by the roadside, as bulldozers and Cats creaked past them, heading for the site, ready to level or fill another acre of land.

'Look, Isobel,' said Billy-Ray, putting his hand on her thigh, 'we have to have oil. America needs oil – what can we do without it?'

'What if something goes wrong?'

'Like what?'

'I don't know. An accident perhaps? Perhaps the pipe splits? Where does all the oil go?'

Billy-Ray laughed. 'Hey – d'you think Karbo didn't think of that?

There's more safety margins built into that than the Hoover Dam. It's not going anywhere – nothing can happen that hasn't been thought of. Know how long we spent planning this? Four years. I know it's not pretty, but it's there, which is some kind of miracle in itself.'

'You said last night that all the workers from Texas and wherever didn't know how to work in water.'

'They'll learn.'

They drove on in silence, Isobel feeling fury for a reason she couldn't articulate to herself. They took the beach road as they always did, Billy-Ray pointing out the peaks of the Chigmits and calling them out to Tufty, who looked dutifully west, frowning slightly.

'Keep a look out for bears, honey,' Billy-Ray said to her, catching her eye in the mirror. 'Lots of bears here. Might even be one on the road, waiting to eat a little girl.' Tufty squealed and Billy-Ray smiled as Isobel smouldered.

She was still smouldering, much like the open coal seams that ran along the sea cliffs near Homer, when they arrived at the ramp of the town. Isobel, who never smoked during the day, lit a Winston and leaned against the sea wall, eyes shut, breathing deeply, her face turned to the sun.

'Hey – you going to help here?' Billy-Ray was piling bags and boxes into the cruiser.

Isobel opened her eyes and was blinded momentarily by the light. She stubbed out the cigarette and began to help. When the pick-up was empty, Billy-Ray reversed the trailer down to the water's edge, until the stern of the cruiser was deep in water, and as it settled Isobel watched a beautiful, iridescent semicircle of rainbow-oil burst on to the surface of the ocean. Then Billy-Ray fired the engine, which plumed blue exhaust into the bay, and manoeuvred the cruiser up to the dock. Isobel climbed aboard, settled Tufty and waited for her husband, who, when he reappeared some time later, was cursing.

'Fucking tourists – couldn't hardly find a place. Had to park way up back. Shit – there must be two hundred vehicles in there.'

'Well, we're hardly residents ourselves,' Isobel remarked mildly.

'I own a fucking house here.'

'Don't you mean *we* own a house here?'

Billy-Ray breathed deeply. 'I'm sorry.' Billy-Ray – apologizing, always apologizing. 'But y'know what I mean.'

Isobel was thinking how, in fact, it had been her money which had bought the cabin as Billy-Ray began to steer the cruiser across seven miles of (nearly) pristine water.

The timbered cabin, built by a fisherman for his family from trees he had cut and seasoned himself forty years before, had two bedrooms, a bathroom and one large, open room with a fireplace, stove and sink. The walls were caulked and the windows, double-glazed now, were snug. In front was a long gallery overlooking the boardwalk. Isobel unpacked the food boxes as Billy-Ray sorted out his fishing gear, coolers and gasoline cans before lashing down the cover on the boat, trying not to think of how much the cabin reminded him of his weekend with Lucca Barzini in Cape Disappointment all those years before.

It was seven o'clock before the Rickmans sat out on the gallery, looking over Kachemak Bay. Isobel had never known there could be so many shades of green, grey and blue – and wondered whether she was unaware of shades of red. Had simply never seen them. For an hour they sat there in silence – Tufty asleep in Billy-Ray's arms – and watched the boats come and go, watched eagles cruising for prey, watched the tourists walking the boardwalk, rubbernecking the locals and their cabins.

'You're right,' said Isobel eventually, 'there are more people here.'

'Look at the *Danny J*.'

Isobel looked over to Ismailof Island and saw the long queue of tourists boarding the ferry that would take them back to Homer.

After supper, once Tufty was in bed and the oil lamps were lit, the two of them sat out on the gallery again. Isobel had a book open on her lap, although she barely read a word, too busy watching the sun set behind the Kenai, as she wondered about her anger. Billy-Ray picked patiently at a tangled line, a fine nylon thread that had knotted itself into a ball, occasionally breaking off to sip at a can of beer. Twilight was long, pink-shot lines of grey and white shifting on the horizon as the moon rose above distant peaks. They couldn't see the waters clearly now but could hear wavelets slapping at the pilings, shifting the timbers and boats, breaking gently on the rocks beneath them. They said nothing to each other for hours, as Isobel watched the dome of the sky darken. As time passed her anger faded, to be replaced by lazy contentment. She glanced at Billy-Ray and saw that he had dozed off. Isobel looked at her husband as he slept, his face cleared of tiredness and petulance, his scarred hands, his thick, muscled thighs, the old scar like a shadow, and she wished he did something else, that he was at home more. Waking him gently, she led the bumbling, sleepy Billy-Ray to the bedroom.

The Rickmans spent nine days in Halibut Cove, fishing for halibut in the afternoons, sometimes surf-fishing for salmon along the gravel beach at Glacier Spit in the early evenings, and cooking their catch in spiky, orange flames set amongst rounded stones. They walked the stairs and boardwalks of Seldovia, browsing in the artisans' shops, they hiked a couple of trails looking for bears, Billy-Ray carrying Tufty on his shoulders when she was tired. They drank beers in the early evening sun on Homer Spit, they lay in the sun and they talked. They talked as much as they could because, when this was over, Billy-Ray would be getting on a plane and flying north to the Slope for a month.

Isobel hated to leave, to repack their gear and leave, but at the beginning of September that was what she had to do. As they approached Anchorage, driving through Potter, a low cloud belt came over and light snow fell, thin and insubstantial, melting on contact with the earth. Billy-Ray laughed, turned on the wipers, turned up the heating in the car.

'Can you believe it?'

Isobel felt like crying. Snow in September?

THE REGANS

By the time Matthew, Maggie's brother, was old enough to leave the Regan house in Ballysod, his father was spending more time in Macafferty's, a spare, unadorned pub, with a couple of tables, a long bar and racks of pint glasses stacked next to shot glasses. Macafferty sold Guinness and whiskey: Jameson's, Paddy's and Black Bush, the bottles never on the shelves long enough to become dusty. Sean Regan made a hollow for himself there, sat on a stool that wore down to fit his thin buttocks, a rung that matched the curve of his boot heel. He sat at the end of the bar, leaning against the dun-coloured wall, eyes squinting against cigarette smoke, touching the pint of Guinness, forefinger occasionally stroking the glass, and he listened. The men drinking there did not expect Sean Regan to speak but they were comforted by his presence in the same way their wives were. Sean did not speak because he could not imagine what he might say. During the long, damp days he heard what the women said about the men he drank with; during the evenings he listened to the men and learned of their indifference to the women they lived with. Sean's tongue was cemented to his palate by so many different things – honour, love, pain. The men and women of the dying peninsula need not have worried that Sean would undo them with a word.

The evenings in Macafferty's passed easily, in wavering fields of tobacco smoke, the lilt of known voices, the comfort of beer. Sean sat there, long, thin legs crossed, fingers playing with matches, with glass, with silence, and he thought of many things, things he could not think of at home with the prate of Annie droning in the background. He was aware of the bluster of the men around him, how they bullied each other into submission but also into hope. Sean listened to their plans, listened to their hopes, and he remained silent.

He said nothing because he knew the seas were still emptying; there were fewer fish, fewer wrecks. There was little salvage left. More than that, there was no romance any more. It seemed that Maggie had taken romance with her when she had left. How could that be? How could a young girl wrap the romance of a land in a parcel and take it away with her? But she had. Maggie had managed to do that.

Sean sat on his bar stool and mourned the loss of romance, mourned the loss of his June-born daughter. He sat and he smoked and thought how tired he was, thought that he wasn't yet forty-six but he felt his life was over, that it was finished and done with. Perhaps that was the scheme of things? As the fish grew sparser and the pickings of the land ever thinner, he had fewer mouths to feed as his children grew older and moved away. Sean felt increasingly redundant. He knew the world was changing, moving on so quickly it was like a fast-flowing river on the banks of which he stood, watching. Sean sat silently on his stool and sometimes he wondered about his father, whether he had felt the same way. Now his father was dead and he'd never asked him. Somehow he didn't think so, didn't think Patrick Regan had worried about his place in the world, had not worried about dying without having done something.

In the mornings Sean now prepared his own breakfast, which involved nothing more than the making of tea and slicing of bread. Sometimes, if he felt reckless and hollow, he'd fry up bacon, eat it piping hot, hot enough to scorch his gums, burn his fingertips and then wipe the pan with a crust before setting out for work. In summer, during the warm, balmy days, when daylight strung itself out for hours, playing with dusk, Sean was fine, he was unafraid. But as autumn drew in, shunting the sun aside, he began to feel uneasy. He'd fetch a barrow, spade and hoe from the workshop (always wondering where it was, exactly, that Maggie had committed her sin, for he was never told), and as he tried to wrap his hand around the shaft of the spade, wind his fingers through the handle, the bones protested. His knuckles grew as the precipitation increased and the temperature dropped. Sean stood in ornamental gardens, by beds of roses, a sculpted topiary of birds, and tried to flex his fingers, but they were as stiff and curved as elephant tusks. This made Sean uneasy because he didn't know what else he

could do to put food on the table, drinks on the bar. So he forced his
fingers as best he could to hold the familiar tools which he had used
all his life. Because his own land was exhausted, because the seas
were empty, because he no longer scavenged for salvage. He'd drive
home after a day of digging and bending, trying to flex his ossifying
body, and see lush green fields, mobs of contented cows, gaggles of
plump, bad-tempered geese swarming around farmhouses. The
Cogleens owned a herd of pigs, and Sean would see them each day,
snuffling around the trough, ears flapping, butting each other as
piglets screamed and scuffed between legs.

Some afternoons, when the hills and outcrops were draped in a
gauze of fine, pure rain, when it was impossible to distinguish between
land and sea and thin braids of water ran across roads and verges, Sean
grew melancholy as he bumped and slithered across tracks in his
ageing van. Then he would turn north and head for Bunnahowen and
Constance Wycherley's spotless, polished home. He and Constance
would sit over tea and plates of biscuits, perhaps in companionable
silence, or sometimes they would talk of how things were changing in
Mayo, in the Republic, all over the world. Sean often spent time in the
attic, overseeing the babies, allowing Constance the opportunity to go
into town, collect her post and buy groceries. He sat in an old hard-
backed chair in the corner, watching over the cots, watching small,
plump, stellate hands working in the air. Occasionally he stood up
and meandered around the cots, touching a lock of hair, gently squeezing a soft, unblemished foot, tucking in blankets and murmuring to his
charges. Sometimes there would be a girl with a down of black hair or
wide blue-blue eyes, and then Sean would kneel on his crocked knees
and stare at the baby, thinking of Maggie. He would remember her
stories of talking dogs and fish that walked, cows wearing suits, and he
wondered where they had all gone, those mythical animals.

In the evenings, when the day's work was done and dinner was
eaten, Sean smoked a cigarette out in the porch and then washed, his
braces hanging around his thighs. He soaped his armpits, scrubbed
at his neck, greased his hair – still thick and heavy, streaked badger-
like with grey and silver. When he was finished he stood and stared
at his hands, at his face, repelled by what time had done to the Sean
Regan he still hoped to see in the glass. His legs were knotted with

small bunches of blue grapes, his toenails as thick as mussel shells, as yellow as hard cheese. His face, his skate-wing face, seemed longer, crack-glazed with arterioles, his blue eyes dulled. He knew the back of his neck was cross-hatched with wrinkles, coarse grey hair sprouting. How did he know this? Because his father had looked the same. He buttoned the shirt, snapped his braces back in place and fetched his jacket from the kitchen, always bidding a farewell to Annie before he left for Macafferty's.

Men dream of many things – travelling west, finding gold, walking on the moon, leaving the earth and flying, wrapping themselves in soft furs and women. Some manage to do these things. Others make do with recasting themselves, reproducing themselves, their expectations decreasing by small increments over years. Oliver Reichmann dreamed of a dynasty and was denied, was eventually crushed. Sean Regan had dreamed of something similar, although he could not have said what that thing was. Perhaps to not replicate his father? To aspire to a better life? To a life that did not leave him exhausted, unable to love, living on contaminated land in a tumbledown house, which he did not own? It seemed to Sean, as he sat ruminating on the buttock-smoothed stool in the corner of the bar, that nothing had improved during his life in Ballysod. Indeed, there was less of everything; his world had shrunk. No one confessed to him any more, no tales of loss and troubles were told him as he stood holding bags of fish and bread. It seemed that even his deep-buried confessions were redundant, too old to be of interest; perhaps, even, too innocent to snag the attention. So Sean drank and kept his own counsel, as he always had, yet a seed of outrage, a speck of emerald-green, rock-hard bile, lodged in the fertile mess that was his guts. To have laboured so long, to have lived among slate and rain, catching myriad glimpses of a land of plenty on the horizon, and yet to look at empty hands turned to the sky, hands that never filled . . . When Sean one night overheard in the babble of talk in Macafferty's, as he pulled a thread of conversation from the skein of yabber, that Constance Wycherley was thinking of packing up and moving to Dublin, and he realized that he might never again hold a minute foot, soft as warm butter, in his corrupted palm, he despaired, for then there would be no consolation.

1964

The winter of 1963 was unexceptional for Anchorage – temperatures rarely dropped below ten degrees Fahrenheit, the snow lay two feet deep, freezing ice fog blanketed the city only for a few days, when the pollution was bad. The electricity supply functioned with relative efficiency, there were few outages. The sun forced its way through cloud on a number of occasions. Thanksgiving and Christmas came and went for Isobel in a welter of silver paper, steaming fowl, tinsel, pumpkin and Billy-Ray. So Isobel made it, she made it through the dark months, the cold times; she made it to the other side. Tufty, who was three by then and talking up a storm, made Isobel laugh. Billy-Ray bought Isobel a malamute at Christmas, a beautiful puppy, with pale grey and white downy fur, teeth like needles and glaring, mismatched eyes. Isobel walked the streets of Anchorage with a husky in one hand and Tufty in the other, and between them they decided to call the puppy Husky, but Tufty couldn't say Husky and soon the puppy was known as Hukky. Isobel read, she listened to the radio, she played with her daughter. She survived. Still she skirted the drunk Natives on 4th and 5th, still she sighed at the news on the radio. And she still walked in her yard late at night, patting the Super Cub, thinking of the message she might leave in the snow, written in birch branches.

One night, Isobel lay on the sofa next to Billy-Ray and she told him how lonely she was when he was away.

'Hey, Isobel, most guys do eight-week shifts and then have two off. We're lucky I get to see you as often as I do.'

'But that's not the point. All I'm saying is I'm lonely sometimes.'

'Well, why don't you invite someone over? You know – have a

pot-luck with Lorraine and Anne? They'd sure like to come, I know. I mean, there's plenty of women in this town with time on their hands.'

Isobel frowned, thought of the women Billy-Ray was talking about. 'I don't know. We don't have much in common.'

'Why don't you ask them over and see?'

Isobel stretched out her arms, examined her massive hands, waggled her fingers and turned her wedding ring. 'Maybe – I'll see. Do you ever think of England, BR? I mean, do you ever think of the time you spent in Europe?'

Billy-Ray frowned, rubbed his beard. 'Yah. Sometimes.'

'And what do you think about?'

'Uh – nothing much. I mean, I'm glad I went – otherwise I'd never have met you. But it was, y'know, just so small, so crowded. I think back to working in London and I just remember lots of noise and people all the time. There was no space. And anyway, it wasn't . . . it wasn't me. Getting up and dressing in a suit every day and going to meetings and sitting in offices and writing reports. Know what I mean? But yah, I enjoyed it. I mean, I liked London, don't get me wrong. But I'm glad to be back home.'

'But this isn't really your home, is it? You're not from here.'

'Maybe not, but it feels like it now. Feels like home. I lived here ten years before I went to London and I worked out of Anchorage all that time. So, yah, it feels like home.'

'Do you remember that weekend we met at the Coopers'?'

'Sure I do.'

'And you talked about America for hours, about how wonderful it was?' Isobel twisted to look into his eyes. 'I'd like to see more of it, BR. I'd like to see the places you talked about. I'd like to go to Minnesota, to visit your father. I'd like to go to Hollywood. I was reading about the old Spanish missions in California, on the Camino Real. I'd like to see them. We have the money to do whatever we want, BR. I'd like to feel the sun. See something different. It would be good for us all to get away.'

'OK, I'll see what I can do.' Billy-Ray refilled their glasses. Bow Regard, Blue Earth County, Minnesota. Hollywood, California. Oliver and Dieter Reichmann. Billy-Ray swallowed vodka.

Isobel, who was lonely, who knew that crying did no good, who could not turn and walk away, touched her husband's beard, laid her hand on his cheek. 'Don't leave me,' she said. 'Don't leave me alone here for too long.'

By the end of January Isobel was desperate enough to call Lorraine and ask her over for lunch. Isobel spent hours preparing then cooking mulligatawny soup and apple crumble. She even splashed out on a couple of bottles of imported French red wine, which cost more than a meal for two at the Ritz Grill.

Lorraine, when she arrived, was bundled up in down jacket, Pendleton wool shirt, gloves, hat and scarf. 'Twelve below out there,' she said, kicking off Snowpack boots. She dropped a paper parcel in the kitchen sink. 'There you go, honey. Present from Casey. He shot a moose last Sunday, a big one. Thirteen hundred pounds or more. He thought you might be likin' to make up some moose burgers. Took three days to butcher it out in the yard – shoulda seen the place. Bones and blood ever'where.'

'Why, thank you,' said Isobel. 'Would you like a drink?'

'Sure would – set 'em up. Hope you're gonna show me round, though.' Lorraine had never before been invited to the vast frame house on the lake.

Isobel poured them each a glass of wine and then showed Lorraine around the house. Lorraine, who lived out Raspberry Road way, whose living space was in the basement as she and Casey tried to save money to build upward, who lived next to a trailer full of Natives, whose yard was covered in rusting wrecks and broken-down snowmobiles, was entranced. She admired the fitted wardrobes, the walk-in dressing room, the bathrooms with their shower stalls and tubs. She eyed up the bidet that Isobel had imported, asked what it was. As Isobel explained, Lorraine thought there must be better ways of spending money.

'The French all have them, and of course I went to finishing school in Switzerland,' said Isobel, as if this cleared the matter up.

Lorraine, dazzled by this piece of information, remarked that if she hadn't been told what it was for, she'd have washed her feet in it.

The television, the gramophone, the thick carpets, the double-size Kelvinator, the new Maytag washing machine. Lorraine marvelled as she was eaten away by jealousy. All this and Billy-Ray too?

'Ready for lunch?' asked Isobel.

'Honey, I could eat a hog.'

Lorraine sat at the table as Isobel fetched Tufty's high chair and sat the little girl in it.

'Hi there, Tufty – how's it goin'?'

'Very well, tank you. How is you?'

'Hey – ain't that cute? Isobel?' Lorraine called out to Isobel, who was in the kitchen. 'Isobel, honey, Tufty here has some manners!'

Isobel reappeared with the lunch and said as she laid it out on the table, 'Well, I should hope so.'

'Shoot, honey, you should hear my crew – I whup 'em up but don't make no difference. Cussing and runnin' round. Not like the little princess here.' Lorraine reached out and stroked Tufty's hand. Tufty stared back at her with her blue eyes.

'Please help yourself.'

Lorraine looked at the food on offer. 'Well, this sure is different.'

'I beg your pardon?'

'What's this, honey?' Lorraine pointed to the soup.

'It's a traditional Scottish dish. I thought you might like to try it.'

Lorraine tentatively spooned some into her bowl. 'You got any bread, honey?'

'Of course.'

Lorraine tasted the soup, chewed a while. 'Mmm. Now at home, I like to cook up steaks, potatoes, maybe fry some chops or chicken. I do make a mean fried chicken, though I say so myself. If I've had a particular bad day, then it's TV dinners, I'm afraid. Out of the freezer into the stove, no wastin' time. You know the new Carrs? Well, the doughnuts there are something, I tell you. Whole range of 'em – and great chocolate cake too. Better'n Sara Lee any time.'

As they drank the first bottle of wine, the light began to fade. By the time they opened the second and Isobel was clearing the table and washing up, Lorraine was talking about Casey and the kids, about the schools and where Tufty would likely attend. By the time they were finishing the second bottle, sitting now in the living area, Lorraine was saying how much she missed her family back in New Orleans, how she missed just hanging out, walking warm streets, sunning herself in Memorial Park and listening to the jazz floating on the air.

'Always seemed like summer – know what I mean? Casey and me, we'd walk down to the old French quarter of a Friday night 'n' have catfish pie and gumbo, maybe a couple of margaritas. Then we'd dance. Lots of places to dance there. Then ever'one'd start dancin' in the streets. Just dancin' to music out in the streets with people standin' on their balconies, just watchin'.' Isobel looked over at Lorraine, who was smiling as she remembered sultry, jazz-filled evenings, and thought how pretty she could be if she had a haircut, lost a few pounds and changed her wardrobe. Lorraine sighed and her face pinched. 'But I guess it jus' feels like it was always summer. There were the floods and bugs too – but ya never remember those. Jus' the music and the jambalaya and the smell of bourbon and coffee. This is sure nice, hon. What is it?'

'It's red wine.'

'Never had wine before. It's good.'

'It's also gone. Would you like something else?'

'Bourbon'll do me. Hell of a lunch – usually git given a can of soda and a sandwich.'

'Lorraine – do you ever get lonely?'

Lorraine looked at Isobel. 'Sure I do. Ever'one does up here. Maybe that ain't so. Know what I think? I think the women git lonely and the men jus' lap it up. Take Casey, f'r instance. He came up here and now he thinks he's Daniel fuckin' Boone. Sorry, Isobel. Yeah – goes out in his furry hat and boat and thinks he's like some kinda hunter or frontiersman. Spends the weekend shootin' up all these animals and then brings 'em back and butchers them in the yard. Then, you know what he wants? A TV dinner and a roll in the hay. I got three freezers full o' wildlife and he wants a TV dinner. That's what I reckin happens. The men git what they want and the women stay at home freezin' and trying to deal with crap around the house.' Lorraine swigged down her bourbon. Looked over at the elegant and Honourable Isobel. 'Why d'ja ask, honey? You lonely?'

'Sometimes. I find the lack of sunlight difficult. There either seems to be too much or not enough.'

"Course, lotsa women leave. Number of divorces here – whooee. Which is fine if you got somewhere else to go. Either that or they find something a little nearer home.'

'What do you mean?'

Lorraine laughed, helped herself to another shot. 'They find some-one who ain't away for eight weeks at a time, someone who's here.'

'Good Lord – you mean they have affairs?'

Lorraine laughed again. 'Isobel, honey, the way you talk! Yeah, they have affairs if you want to put it like that.'

'People we know?'

'Sure.'

Isobel stared at the dark evening through the window. How little she knew.

'And if you're wonderin', and I guess y'are, yup, I've done it.' Lorraine shrugged. 'Ever'one has.'

'I haven't.'

'Well – you wouldn't, wouldja? I mean, anyone can tell that. Jus' lookin' at you.'

'Am I that dull?'

Again, Lorraine laughed. 'No, honey – you ain't dull. But I can tell, one, that you're honest – y'know, decent and all that. And two, I can tell ya love your husband. Well, shit, ever'one loves Billy-Ray. But what's more, ever'one can tell he loves you.'

'What about the men? Do they have affairs too?'

'Yeah, sure they do. Lots pay to go with the hookers. Seems like you can't walk downtown no more for fallin' over whores. Or Injuns. Ain't like it used to be. And the hookers don't make it out to the platforms or rigs – no, not allowed. So a lot of men make do with their wives and then go out huntin' and shootin' to make 'emselves feel big.' Lorraine sighed. 'I been up here six years now and even in that time things have changed. It's money and the military, honey. Where those two meet, you git hookers.'

'I suppose you're right,' said Isobel, who had never considered this before.

'Place has changed. It's changing all the time. When we all came up, musta been '57, we used to go camping jus' outside Anchorage. Maybe half an hour and we'd be in the middle o' nowhere. Now if we go, it's a trip, I tell ya. Gitting all the kids' stuff together, hitching up all the machines and that. And then having to drive for hours, and when ya git wherever you're goin' there's a hundred other RVs and trailers there. Seems like now we cain't be bothered. Casey goes off with his buddies on his own and I watch TV, look after the kids. Don't git me wrong, honey,' Lorraine lit a cigarette and sat back on the sofa, 'we came up here for the money – Casey gits three times what he was making in Louisiana. And I sure didn't come up here to hug trees or hunt bear.' She sighed. 'But it did use to be nicer. Cleaner or emptier or something.'

1960

The conundrum of Isobel's and Billy-Ray's marriage, which was to take place that autumn, nagged at Jacqueline for months, as the festive season passed and Jarman House returned to its normal rhythm of cocktails and supper parties. Miss O'Toole was finally let go by Sir Sidney, with a handsome pension and a ticket to Dublin, and Maggie, despite the fact she was not yet eighteen, began to assume more responsibilty around the house. Jacqueline was glad Maggie had taken O'Toole's place, not only because she was rather more attractive to look at but because she had about her an air of self-assurance, knowingness almost. As well as these, Maggie rarely spoke unless spoken to, seemed to relish fields of silence.

Still Jacqueline moped, sitting around the house, smoking, doodling with crosswords, reading about lives being lived elsewhere. She tried to reimmerse herself in her social life but was only irritated by her own distraction as she sat in restaurants or took tea with other idle, rich women. Thoughts of the orchards of Albany, trips to Niagara with her brothers, nights spent out on the porch watching fireflies – all these now disturbed her London life. Jacqueline found herself another lover, thinking this might dispel the novel sensation of self-doubt, but even this did not help. She seduced a diffident man who was as smooth as ground marble, as insubstantial as fine powder, who had no jagged corners on which she could bark her emotional shins. He was incapable even of speaking the language of sex, let alone in a myriad of tongues, and Jacqueline soon dropped him, given that the risk was hardly worth the reward. Occasionally, Sidney would appear in her bedroom at night, shuffling in sheepishly, his white, paunchy body covered in a striped silk dressing gown. Jacqueline dreaded these nights which, fortunately, became increasingly infrequent. Sidney would switch off the lights and slip awkwardly between the sheets, saying nothing. Jacqueline was thankful for the darkness, for in the darkness she felt guiltless as she imagined being taken in a shower, having icy Krug dribbled over her flat belly, being pinned by Billy-Ray to a floor, a mattress, a wall. When it was finished, once Sidney had sighed, wheezed and then broken into a hacking fit, Jacqueline would cross the dim room to the bathroom, leaving Sidney to tidy himself up and return to his own suite. She'd stand by the sink, naked, soaping her hands for minutes on end, avoiding the mirror, not needing to know whether she looked like the whore she felt herself to be.

Jacqueline began to seek out Maggie's company, electing to sit in the room where she was working, enjoying the silence, which was as soft as moss, in much the same way Sean Regan had when his daughter was a passenger in the cab of his van. Occasionally Jacqueline talked to Maggie, asking her about her childhood, wanting to move away from memories of her own, and over time she pieced together the fractured images Maggie described, of a squalid home set on a dangerous, craggy land. She'd watch Maggie polishing silver or filling out the ledger of stores in and out, and fight the resentment she felt for the promise of her youth. Uneducated and delicious.

A morning in April and Jacqueline and Maggie were in the garden room, discussing how best to lay out the furniture for a garden party that weekend, when Jacqueline saw Maggie lean against a table in a certain way, saw her put a hand to her back and frown. Jacqueline looked closely at her, looked at the line of her uniform, the fullness of her face, and she knew.

'Maggie,' Jacqueline said. 'Oh my God, Maggie.'

Maggie was stunned, felt as if she had fallen off the push-penny shelf once again, that she was falling so far, so fast it took her breath away. She'd been with the Coopers for nearly two and a half years, where she had her own room, her own space, as much food as she wanted, time to herself, when she could dream. But now she was being turned around and sent away, back to the Convent of the Immaculate Virgin. How had this happened? Maggie had always thought she couldn't fall pregnant – why, think of what she and Danny had done! And so many times – they had done it hundreds of times. She couldn't fall with child. But how was Maggie to know that when Danny Maconnell had said he'd been ill, that he'd been away from work for a few weeks, that he had been suffering from mumps, was now infertile?

Jacqueline, who liked Maggie, who feared for her, arranged everything, from the initial phone call to Miss O'Toole in Dublin, to payment for the train and ferry ride. She talked to the girl, explained that she, Maggie, could have the baby in seclusion, in the hospital at the convent. Her family need not know; the decision as to whether to tell them or not was up to Maggie. And when it was over, if Maggie wanted to, she could come back to Jarman House and pick up where she left off.

'I can come back?' Maggie asked incredulously.

'Sure you can.'

'But . . . ' Maggie frowned. 'I'll have a babby.'

'It's up to you, Maggie. It's your body, it's your life. You can leave the baby in the orphanage and come back here. Or, if you want, I guess you could bring the baby here. Or maybe you'll want to stay there, maybe you'll want to start doing your gardening and decorating.' Jacqueline smiled, trying to reassure Maggie, who looked suddenly so young, too young to be doing this. 'Or – and you might want to think about this – you needn't have the baby at all.'

'What d'you mean, ma'am?'

Jacqueline looked away, looked at a pile of glinting, highly polished knives piled on the white damask cloth, waiting to be laid out. 'There are ways of getting rid of it. But it can be dangerous.'

Maggie frowned, her hand rubbing the mound. She'd heard of this, heard of girls dying in pools of blood. Annie Regan had talked about a farm girl out Aasleagh way who'd tried it, talked to Sean about it when she didn't think Maggie could hear. 'No, ma'am. I won't be doing that.'

'It's up to you. Like I say, you can always come back here.'

'I . . . Thank you, ma'am.' Maggie chewed on the notion of having choices – another luxury.

'Is Michael the father?'

Maggie folded her arms and stared at Jacqueline.

'You don't have to tell me.'

'No, ma'am. I don't have to tell you.'

1964

March finally arrived and the grip of ice began to weaken in Anchorage. Mercury rose and water fell, from eaves, from gutters, cascading down mountains to trickle, then thunder along gravel beds. The sound of running water was everywhere as melt water loosened itself, as people loosened snow chains, as they began to loosen themselves. The hemlock, spruce and birch in the city looked at least expectant of spring if not overly chirpy. Isobel, however, *was* chirpy – they had plans, the Rickmans: they were headed for the sun. Every time Isobel slithered along a black patch, every time that spring of 1964 she stepped in a pothole of salt-thickened melt water, or couldn't start the car, or felt her chapped lips, she smiled, because something was going to happen. Something that would break the run of her days. The three of them were flying to Los Angeles on Easter Saturday for a fortnight's holiday, or two-week vacation, depending how you looked at it. Los Angeles. Hollywood. Sunset Boulevard. Seventy degrees. Shrimp salads. Fresh fruit. Sand. Sun. Roads. Marvellous. Isobel ignored the privations of Lent that year – she felt she'd already given up quite enough. But come Good Friday, God's Friday, she felt a tug in her emotional belly and she attended morning mass. There was some comfort in the familiarity of the service – the reading of the Passion, the veneration of the Cross, the communion. Isobel wasn't sure that she believed as such any more, but hearing the words that rang across the years since her childhood, she thought that God would know whether she was worthy or not when the time came.

As Isobel began to pack suitcases with new clothes – shorts and T-shirts, linen trousers and sleeveless cotton dresses – Billy-Ray was arguing with the pilot of the Grumman Goose that had been chartered to take Karbo workers from Seward back to Anchorage. The pilot was unhappy with one of the engines on the Goose, said it was running rough and he thought it had a bad mag. He wasn't prepared to fly anywhere. Billy-Ray offered him an extra fifty bucks to make the flight, explained he was catching a plane to LA the next morning with his family, but still the pilot refused. Furious, Billy-Ray humped his hold-all up and down the docks and late that afternoon he found a spare seat on a Beech 18 leased by Shell – which cost him sixty bucks cash. But there was no room for Bent Prick and Brad Honker. Well, the way he looked at it, you make your own luck, like he'd always said. Billy-Ray sat in a dockside bar for a couple of hours, nursing a beer and rubbing at his beard as he listened to Brad Honker. Brad was drinking hard, downing two beers and bourbon chasers to Bent's single beer. Brad's voice, which grated like an awl grinding in granite, rang out across the tables, calling for more bourbon, cursing the Natives, and all the while Brad was watching the barwoman, watching her move, watching the way she tidied her hair. Brad's hands, wrapped around his glass, were raw knuckled, red and scarred; oil had seeped deep into the whorls of his thumb and palm, seeped so deep it seemed he was absorbing it. Billy-Ray watched Brad getting drunker through the afternoon, listened to him taking the piss out of Bent, cultured, dandified, *European* Bent, who was wearing a pristine suit beneath a spotless, dazzling daffodil waterproof.

'Fucking yeller jacket, ya look like a fuckin' lemon. Watcha wear that for? You a fuckin' fruit or somethin'? That why you want to look like a fuckin' lemon?' Brad howled and slapped the bar.

Billy-Ray looked at Bent and shook his head slightly, thought how much he disliked Brad Honker. Unable to look at Brad's coarse, veined face any more, he walked to the window facing out over the docks, watched a tanker filling with crude at the terminal. As he stood there he imagined hugging Tufty, imagined getting much closer than that to Isobel. Billy-Ray wondered why he behaved as he did when he got home – knew he was surly and rude, when all he wanted to say was how much he'd missed them, how much he loved them. Maybe this time he could do it? Billy-Ray crossed his arms, rocked on his heels. He reckoned he needed the time away in California. He was drained, he was tired, he felt wrung out, as if Karbo were drilling in him, extracting his life force. So much money, so much to do for it, so much still to be done. Brad Honker's bruising laughter rang out and Billy-Ray turned in time to see him grab the barwoman around the hips, in time to see him lay his head on her belly, as if he wanted her to ruffle his hair. In time to see Brad's face as it nestled there, the woman's hand hovering above it, unwilling to touch him. In time to see loneliness settle in Brad's eyes.

At a quarter to five the Beech pilot came in and waved his passengers out of the bar. Billy-Ray crammed his tall, lean frame into the co-pilot's seat, the only space available for him. He fixed his belt and held his bag on his lap. There had been a time when a flight – a flight anywhere – had filled him with joy. When he would look out of the window and try to name every geological feature, every anomaly. But now he sat on planes and fell asleep.

The pilot of the Beech 18 greeted them all with a howdy, sat in his seat and tuned the radio. The faint chatter of instructions lulled Billy-Ray into a doze. He hugged his bag close and let his head rock on the glass of the window as the plane taxied out into the choppy waters, turned and manoeuvred itself, ready for take-off. Billy-Ray loved floatplanes, loved the way they thudded over currents and wavelets, rocking, waiting to reach the step and then suddenly free themselves from the sucking ocean, gliding into air as if released. These take-offs seemed more natural, more honest, somehow, than banging down along tarmac, being bounced into the air; floatplanes exchanged one element for another. At 5.21 p.m. the pontoons of the Beech 18 reached the step and parted company with the waters of Seward. Billy-Ray began to drift, imagining Isobel massaging his back, running her thumbs down his spine. The plane headed south for Cape Resurrection, where the pilot would make his turn and then head north along the pass west of the Chugach. An hour, give or take a few minutes, until they landed on Lake Hood. Billy-Ray dozed, thought he heard Tufty saying 'kayak' – her version of the word 'carry' – holding her hands up to her daddy. Billy-Ray smiled in his near-sleep, imagined playing with his daughter in the warm waters of the Pacific around Santa Monica, maybe teaching her to swim . . .

'Fuck!' the pilot yelled, and the Beech 18 twisted in the air. *'Fuck!* Look at that!'

Billy-Ray shook his handsome blond head awake (heart jumping) and looked down at the Prince William Sound, the Chugach mountains, the Kenai peninsula, and what did he see? Billy-Ray saw the earth moving – the fucking *earth* was moving. The mountains lurched and lurched again. Whole fucking mountain ranges were shuddering as glaciers heaved and tossed ice blocks down turquoise slopes. Avalanches and scree tore down trees as they raced for the sea.

The pilot reached for his radio as Billy-Ray watched, mesmerized. 'What the fuck is that?' the pilot shouted above the whining roar of the engine.

'It's a quake,' Billy-Ray yelled. 'It's a fucking earthquake.' The pilot – who couldn't have been much more than twenty, who didn't look old enough to be out on his own, whose hands had begun to shake, cupped a hand around an ear. Billy-Ray looked at his watch: 5.37 – and it had already been running for at least thirty seconds. He reached for the co-pilot's headset, watching the land below rumble the meanwhile. 'It's an earthquake,' he said into the mouthpiece, and the pilot's eyes locked on his for a moment. Then he reached for the radio, tried to raise his base in Anchorage, tried to retune, and Billy-Ray heard a snippet of a broadcast from Honolulu Observatory – 'unusual seismic activity' – 'move to open water' – 'This is Hinchinbrook. The whole island is shaking. We'll be back when it stops.' Billy-Ray looked at his watch again: 5.38 and the land was still shimmying, trembling and breaking apart. Two minutes? No quake lasted two minutes.

The Beech 18 banked steeply and headed back for Seward, as Billy-Ray remembered the tanker. The pilot was still shaking hard, having trouble tuning his radio, picking up static, shouts, nothing. The headset muted the roar of the plane and Billy-Ray could make out the tumult of a continental shelf shearing apart as the ocean bubbled.

Below the Beech, in the confines of the fjord, the tanker was wrenched away from the pipeline and Billy-Ray, breathing hard now, watched it bob like a cork on raging waters, watched a spark fly, saw a sheet of fire spread on the glacial waters.

'Oh, fuck! Oh, sweet Jesus!' the pilot muttered in Billy-Ray's ear. The flames spread just like the wildfire they were, as the tanker broke away from the dock, incapable of manoeuvring as it had powered down for loading.

The pilot was still trying to raise his base, trying to contact other planes in the air. Managed to locate a Grumman Goose flying over Valdez. 'There's a boat down there at dock, looks like a ferry or something,' the Valdez pilot yelled. 'Can't see what's happening – but it doesn't look good. What the fuck's happening here?'

'A quake that's off the fucking Richter scale,' Billy-Ray told him. He looked at his watch: 5.39 and still the earth reared up on its hind legs and roared like a grizzly. And now he could distinguish sounds above the engine – the twisting and shattering of granite, quartz, centuries-old ice, moraine and river beds. Seabeds were being lifted into the air along the coast, white expanses covered with dying calcinacious creatures. Railtracks were twisting, snapping, as span bridges teetered and fell.

The tanker below in Seward was dragged away from the dock, but it was moving strangely, as if holed. Billy-Ray could see people down at the dockside, pointing to the ocean on fire. An oil storage tank exploded, taking out the one next to it, and so on in a domino game of flames.

The pilot was finally talking to base in Anchorage. 'What should I do? Where do I head for?'

'Stay up as long as you can. Best place to be. Lake's filling with debris.'

'How bad is it over there?'

'What the fuck d'you think? We'll get—' Unknown to Billy-Ray and the youthful pilot, an antenna crumpled, snapped, pulled in two directions as the earth tussled with itself.

Billy-Ray knew it was only a hundred or so miles to Anchorage. In a quake like this, that distance was nothing, was an afterthought. What the fuck was happening to Tufty and Isobel? He, after all, was in the only safe place – the sky. But they were down there on the tortured earth.

What was happening to Isobel was that she was getting more confused by the moment. At a quarter past five she'd been in the kitchen, preparing Tufty's tea, listening to her daughter read from her book.

'Spot can run. Spot can sit. Spot can smile.'

Not only did the book lack narrative, thought Isobel, it was also fallacious.

'Spot walks. Spot takes.'

'Spot talks,' corrected her mother.

Hukky, who was six months old by then, stood and walked tentatively to the screen door, head cocked as if listening to something. His tail dropped, his ears flattened and he sat staring out at the early evening light.

'Spot runs to the shop.'

'OK, Hukky?' asked Isobel, frowning.

'Hukky OK,' said Tufty.

Hukky was far from OK. Hukky threw back his head and began to howl, an unearthly sound. Then he scrabbled at the door, scratching at it with his tiny claws.

'What's the matter, Hukky?'

Hukky howled again and Isobel wondered whether he was rabid. A rumble rolled across the city, rolled like a wave. Pans fell off a shelf in the kitchen, followed by two cans of beans. Isobel felt the floor tremble, stared at the glasses shifting on the table, watched an apple roll off the drainer. Another tremble and Tufty's chair rocked. Tufty frowned as Hukky howled, slunk away and lay down under the table. It was as Isobel ran across the trembling, fragmenting kitchen to grab Tufty from her high chair that it happened.

At thirty-six minutes and fourteen seconds past five on the afternoon of Good Friday, 1964, the coast of Alaska gave up its unequal struggle with the subducting Pacific plate and, after years of compressing itself, contorting itself into awkward shapes, the coast snapped and threw a tantrum. The beginning of this commotion was a sudden wrenching in the earth's crust at a depth of twenty-five kilometres, ten kilometres east of College Fjord, a mere ninety kilometres from Valdez, and only one hundred and twenty kilometres east of Anchorage, just over the Chugach range. The effect of this sudden rupture was to render the earth a large bell, thumped by an iron mallet. The shock waves, the reverberations, the ringing went round and round the globe. Waters fell in the bayous of Louisiana, well water in South Africa dropped. But the place where this ringing was loudest, most deafening, was in the Kenai peninsula and Prince William Sound. Billy-Ray was flying above it, his wife and daughter trying to find a foothold on it. For four minutes the two vast plates wrestled with each other, trying to get comfortable, trying to find a way of snuggling up without getting cramped.

Isobel grabbed Tufty and watched a wave three feet high pass along the wooden floor, rippling beneath her, taking her down. She landed on her back, quickly turned to shield Tufty as every plate, pan, glass and knife showered down on them and the floor bucked again. Looking up, Isobel saw the far wooden wall bulge, warp and then settle. Another wave, the cupboards coming loose, the Kelvinator bucking like a boat, the washing machine skittering towards them. She knew she should shelter in a doorway but all she wanted was to get outside. Holding Tufty, who was bawling, under her arm, Isobel made it across the living room to the door, rolling with the waves, narrowly avoiding decapitation as a glass-fronted bookcase slammed down beside them. Isobel realized she was crying. The glass in the windows on the kitchen side blew as the door frame tilted twelve degrees, sprang its hinges and Hukky shot out through the opening, yowling. Isobel crawled out into the garden and heard a crack like gunfire. Turning, she saw a large hemlock at the southern end of the garden split vertically into two slender trees, straddling a crack that was snaking towards her and Tufty. Isobel stood and ran for the street. Still the waves kept coming. She tried to keep her footing, but the pitching and rolling made her fall time and again. She couldn't think of where to go to be safe – where could she go to be safe? There was a little light snow but Isobel didn't notice. She had one arm around Tufty, squeezing her tight, her other hand on Tufty's head, to protect it. She could hear distant crashes, hear the grinding of metal as cars tilted on their sides and toppled over the fault line. Trees groaned as their roots were torn in different directions. There was the sound of demolition as the concrete garage in the yard snapped in two and caved in, crushing the Super Cub. Isobel saw her neighbours, falling, rolling on the tarmac, watching out for snakes rippling towards them, just as she was. Isobel was living through the second-largest earthquake ever recorded and she felt maddened as the earth fluxed.

Suddenly, there was silence. It was over. Or, rather, the spectacular tantrum was over – there were still a few minor spats to be had as the tectonic plates tried to get up close and personal, nine thousand after-shocks in all. Isobel didn't know it then – as she huddled on the verge, hugging her daughter, dressed only in a thin cotton shirt and trousers as a light snow drifted, covered with cuts and bruises, her left wrist fractured – but the effects of the earthquake were widespread. The Latouche Island area had been shunted fifty-five feet south-east. Meanwhile, the areas around Montague Island had risen up twenty-eight feet and Portage, just down the road on the way to Halibut Cove, had dropped ten feet. This vertical realignment of the earth's crust had affected more than a hundred thousand square miles of Alaska. There was more – the shaking and quaking were felt over an area of more than five hundred thousand square miles. Yukon Territory, Canada and Washington State reeled as well. Unknown to Isobel as she sat there, crying quietly and wondering what to do next, the Pacific plate had, in those four minutes, slipped roughly thirty feet under Alaska. What was surprising was that only nine people died during this cataclysm. Eventually, one hundred and thirty-one died, but not as a direct result of the quake; it was the blue earth that took them.

In the Beech 18, Billy-Ray was getting frantic. The pilot was circling Seward, unable to make up his mind what to do. He felt he needed more information. He retuned the radio – 'Move to open water' – 'CGSS Bittersweet and CGSS Sedge, give your positions please' – 'All except three thousand feet of Anchorage International Airport reported out'. Billy-Ray had calculated the quake at about four minutes – an eternity. He wanted out, he wanted to get to Anchorage. He wanted to get to Isobel. Ten minutes they'd been circling here.

'Hey,' he said to the pilot, 'what's going on?'

'Just waiting for more instructions from base.'

'Well,' said Billy-Ray, 'there's no point hanging out here – we can't land down there. Might as well go on. Seems to me like base has gone down.'

'Let me try to get them up again.' The pilot frowned, rubbed his forehead. He'd never had to call one like this before.

Billy-Ray looked down at the town of Seward. Noticed the flaming waters were receding, just as loud chatter came on the radio. 'We are aground in the Kodiak channel' – 'Water falling abnormally in Juneau and Ketchican' – 'Whole village of Kaiugnak has been wiped out' – 'The town of Valdez just burst into flames. The whole deck is afire and the tanks at Union have started to burn.'

'That's fucking weird, ain't it?' said the pilot as he peered down at the emptying fjord.

'It's the tsunami,' said Billy-Ray. 'Water's being sucked out but it'll come back big time.' He wanted to open the window and yell at the people on the docks to run, get moving, get up on to higher land. Get away from the shore.

'This is Honolulu Observatory. A seismic tidal wave has been generated and is spreading over the Pacific. Intensity cannot be predicted.' The radio voice flat, unemotional.

'Shit,' said Billy-Ray. He realized his fists were clenched, his legs rigid. He could make out Bent's daffodil jacket on the dockside, Brad Honker staggering next to him. Remembered loneliness appearing in Brad's eyes. Shouted, 'Run, for fuck's sake get *out* of there.' The fucking *helplessness* of it.

It took nineteen minutes from the moment Isobel's floor rippled for the tsunami to arrive in Seward. The ocean withdrew from the coast, as if sucking in its breath, inhaling as deeply as it could, and then it blew itself out as a wall of water. Billy-Ray Rickman – who had kept an eye out for the Wave all his life – saw it again that evening. Saw the waters racing up the fjord, cramming into an ever-narrowing space, rising all the time, spitting foam and boats as they raced for Seaward, at the drowned valley's head. But of course, there was the lake of raging fire still there, still eating at the docks. The tsunami picked up the docks, the fire, the oil tanks, the buildings and flung them at the people who were, at last, beginning to run. Ice and fire chasing a man.

'I'm getting the fuck out of here,' announced the pilot.

Bent's jacket – the same wild yellow as Teodor's waterproofs – disappeared. Billy-Ray watched the burning oil he had helped to suck up from below the ocean chasing the people of the town and he lowered his head, closed his eyes.

The pilot, sweating now, hands still shaking, headed north, over

Woodrow, Divide, Moose Pass and Silvertip, then out over the waters of Turnagain Arm. No one spoke, no one moved. The passengers stared out of the windows at the Chugach and the Kenai, looking for movement. Another quake, six on the Richter scale, shook the ranges, but lasted only seconds.

Billy-Ray and the pilot listened to the radio splutter, heard that in Valdez a vast block of land had slid into the sea at the head of the Arm, and the sea was boiling. There was nowhere for the sea to go in its fury. It was locked into a narrow channel and so it did the only thing it knew how – it rocked. Water smashed up one side of the fjord and then slid back and rocked up the other side, and it did this to a height of two hundred and twenty-nine feet. The sea racketed around the confines of the channel, taking out the pier, the waterfront and thirty-five people who had been greeting a ferry at the docks. Fifty mental patients who had broken out of the asylum there ran around like headless chickens, yelling about the end of the world. And for once they might have been right, thought those who heard them. Fifteen minutes after the town of Seward had been first purged by flame, and then cleansed by sea water, Kodiak village was flattened by the Wave, as was Chenaga.

An hour and forty-six minutes after take-off, the Beech 18 approached Lake Hood, talked in by a controller with access to a hand-held battery radio.

'Lake Hood – Beech 7895H at Twin Island Lakes. Inbound for the water with no fucking information.'

'Beech 7895H, Lake Hood Tower. Report the ball park.'

'Hood Tower – 95H – and what the fuck then?'

'95H – just get there.'

The Beech 18 flew on through the beginnings of dusk, dropping, losing height, and the passengers stared at a city that looked as if it had been bombed.

'Lake Hood, 95H at the ball park. Still no information.'

'95H – lot of damage to the main wall, but the debris is contained by the booms. Head in from the west, maybe two-fifty, stay as close as possible to south. Try landing west on east/west water lane. Come by the wall. Most of the slips are out, pilings snapped. But there are some spaces. And good luck.'

The tiny plane dropped, the pilot rigid in his seat, staring unblinking at the battery-operated beacon lights on the water. There was debris but not as much as Billy-Ray had expected. After the violence he'd witnessed, he'd expected blood and bones, shards of wood, whale carcasses, the keels of overturned boats. But instead the Beech 18 made an uneventful landing and surfed to a stop. The pilot gingerly nosed his way to the nearest undamaged dock. When he bumped the side, the pilot began to cry. The passengers grabbed their bags, pushed open the door. One of the men jumped on to the dock, another threw the mooring ropes, and they were gone. Billy-Ray noticed the pilot's shaking shoulders, patted them as he passed.

'Hey – thanks. You did a great job.'

The pilot looked up at Billy-Ray. 'My sister – she lives in Valdez.'

There was nothing Billy-Ray could think to say. He touched the man's arm again and stepped out on to the still-vibrating land. He felt there should be howling winds, a raging tempest to accompany the destruction, but found the wind was light, playful even, as the sun slipped away and the sky darkened. It was as if the sun and sky, the stratosphere itself, had taken no note of the quake. The electricity was down and as Billy-Ray jogged along Airport Road he stumbled on debris, falling once, grazing his hands. That was when he began to shake, his hands trembling as his heart danced. As the light faded he could make out headlamps headed for Minnesota Drive and he hitched a ride in a Dodge van driven by an airport worker. The headlamps picked out boulders on the blacktop, toppled telegraph poles, crashed cars that had been shaken off course. The van filled with hitchers desperate to reach Anchorage, as the driver crawled along, his hands tight on the steering wheel, eyes straining to see cracks in the road. No one spoke; all the passengers followed the path the light made through the damage all around them. The driver slowed.

'Fuck's that?'

Billy-Ray peered into the gloom. 'Want me to go see?'

The driver nodded.

'You got a light?'

Wordlessly, the driver reached under his seat and handed Billy-Ray a heavy-duty flashlight. Billy-Ray opened the door and spread the beam of light on the ground before stepping out, making his way cautiously to what seemed like a black hole, a mass of darkness. He played the light over it but the light beams flew off into the Alaskan evening and disappeared. Billy-Ray realized that the reason he'd thought of black holes was because he was staring into one. He dropped the light and there, twelve feet below, was the highway, the exhaust pipe of an overturned car smiling up at him.

'Road's gone,' he said as he got back in the van.

'Shit.'

'You could try going round Jewel Lake way,' said a woman in the back. 'Ain't heard anything about that.'

''Kay.' The driver reversed and hung a right. The sun had moved farther west, way down behind the Chigmit mountains, sliding towards Japan and the start of a new day. The van tilted and rocked through a night as dark as any Billy-Ray had experienced in the wilderness, the headlamps swinging over people hitching by the side of the road, their eyes white and wild. A tremor rippled across the peninsula and Billy-Ray felt the van shift.

'Shit,' the driver muttered.

They crossed a shallow creek bed in silence, and a state trooper stepped out, waved them down.

'Where you headed?' he asked the driver.

'Whitney Road.'

'Have to head up Karluk and round Reeve. City's down.'

'How bad is it?'

The trooper shrugged. 'Bad. Four Seasons has gone, so's Penney's. Looks like the school's taken a hit. Downtown's a mess, cars turned over, buildings down. You go easy.'

Billy-Ray was dropped on Raspberry Road and he wanted to run, wanted to drop his bag and sprint to his house, but the ground beneath his feet couldn't be trusted. He stepped carefully, followed others who had flashlights, watched the path ahead as well as he was able. It was a mile and a quarter from his drop-off to his house on the lake and it took him two and a half hours to get there. Billy-Ray never forgot that walk, through a city slashed by sirens, lit only by lamps and fires. Stairways stood leading to nowhere, wooden houses were slewed on their axes, and everywhere there were trees down, cutting off the roads, which had dropped and then heaved up more than ten feet. On the night air there was the tang of escaping gas and distant wood smoke. And all the time he was aware that the waves were still coming, pounding the coast, aware that the land could snap again.

By the time Billy-Ray turned into his street his hands were trembling so violently he couldn't light a cigarette. He picked his way across deep, twisting cracks in the road, turned into his drive, straining his eyes to see the house. By the light of a half-moon he could see the mound of concrete blocks that had been the garage, could see the crumpled body of the Super Cub beneath them. There was a faint light downstairs, flashlights illuminating unglazed window frames. Billy-Ray forced open the contorted front door and saw Isobel and Tufty, swaddled in coats and scarves, sitting on the floor of the living room, and he finally stopped shaking.

'Want Hukky,' said Tufty, and began to whimper.

'Hukky's gone,' Isobel told her husband.

Billy-Ray looked at them in the strange, muted light, sitting in the midst of catastrophe; tried to conjure up consolation but yet again words failed him. He thought of the mountain ranges jumping and lurching, boulders slamming down to the ocean, land sliding into the sea, creating seiches. Thought of the Wave, running through the earth. Rocks and language collided, came back to haunt Billy-Ray Rickman as the radio on the floor by Isobel began to belt out 'Whole Lotta Shakin' Goin' On'.

Two days later, on Easter Sunday, when Isobel should have been sunning herself in Los Angeles, City of the Angels, perhaps even celebrating resurrection, she found herself instead in a city of the dead and permanently damaged. Isobel – whose idea of how the world was ordered had been undermined when the Pacific slid under Alaska, whose confusion now knew no bounds – did the only thing she could. She took Tufty and ran as far and as fast as she could. They flew to Fairbanks, and on through Seattle, Denver, New York and Gander to London. The journey took three and a half days, three and a half days of Tufty asking where her daddy and Hukky were. Isobel had wired her arrival time to Highbury and when she walked out into the arrivals area, Lord and Lady Chalfont-Webbe were waiting for her. Isobel saw her parents and finally let go of Tufty, whom she had hugged tightly for days, since the first wave had rippled through the kitchen in Anchorage. She lowered Tufty gently to the floor and lit a Winston.

'I believe ladies don't smoke in public,' remarked her mother as she fussed with Tufty.

'And I suppose you believe the bloody earth doesn't move either,' snapped her sleep-deprived daughter.

1960

In the week before Maggie's return to Louisburgh, Jacqueline took her shopping, ensured that she had enough clothes – dresses, skirts and shirts large enough to accommodate her growing belly, fashioned from cotton and linen thin enough to keep her cool in the coming summer months. Maggie, still stunned, made almost mute by misfortune, said nothing as Jacqueline sorted out her finances, bought travel tickets and even arranged for Kendrick, the Coopers' chauffeur, to drive her all the way to Liverpool, where she would catch the ferry to Dublin.

The evening before Maggie left Jarman House, Jacqueline, who had been drinking her way through the afternoon, went in search of the girl, finding her in the garden, sitting on a little-used bench. The air was chilly and Jacqueline gave Maggie her cardigan to drape over her shoulders.

'Thank you, ma'am.'

'Do you have everything you need already packed?'

'Yes.' Jacqueline had offered Maggie a smart leather case, but Maggie insisted on taking the cardboard one she had brought with her from Ballysod. It seemed right. In it were the clothes Jacqueline had bought her, a few toiletries and the snowstorm.

Jacqueline lit a cigarette, sat back and looked at Maggie's profile. 'Do you think you'll come back here, Maggie? Reckon you'll come back here to work?'

'I don't know, ma'am. I'd like to, I think.'

'You're always welcome.' Jacqueline exhaled, followed the winking lights of a plane crossing the orange-hued sky. 'You'll be OK, Maggie. Everything'll work out. How d'you feel?'

'I feel tired a lot, ma'am.'

'Well, you look after yourself. And remember, you got money so you can buy anything you need.'

Maggie didn't know how to tell Jacqueline about the convent, that there was nothing there that money could buy; that there was nothing very much there at all. She didn't want to disappoint, so she said nothing, just sat on the bench and listened to London growling.

Jacqueline, made melancholy by gin, by loneliness, said suddenly, 'Guess you're wondering why I'm doing all this?'

'Doing all what?'

'Y'know, helping you like this.'

Maggie was trying to ignore the dragging at the top of her thighs, trying to ignore the clamping sensation as if she were wearing a girdle.

'Thing is . . .' said Jacqueline, 'I never told anyone this. I got pregnant. When I was sixteen, in my home town, many miles away and many years ago.' Jacqueline fell silent and Maggie waited. 'I can remember being so scared. Those days it meant damnation, hellfire and damnation.' Jacqueline snorted. 'Happened all the time but everyone pretended it didn't. I spent two months being scared, planning on where I was going to run, how far I was going. All the way to New York City.'

'What happened?' asked Maggie eventually, puzzled by Jacqueline's silence. How was Maggie to know that Jacqueline was thinking of a small-boned, dark-haired girl who lay in her bed, pounding her stomach in the early hours of every morning?

'I woke up one night and I lost it. I was lucky – I woke up because of cramps and I lost it. Made it to the bathroom, so no one knew.' A small-boned, dark-haired girl, knuckles crammed in her mouth, convulsing as she emptied. 'So I know how scary it can be.'

'I wish I could do that. Wish I could do that and stay here and not have to be going back there.'

'No point wishing, Maggie, no point wishing. We'd all do things differently if we could. You'll be fine.' Jacqueline stood, lurched a little and steadied herself. 'You're leaving early, so get to bed soon. I won't see you before you go. And remember – you can always come back here.'

Maggie slipped the cashmere cardigan from her shoulders, held it out.

'No – you keep it. It suits you.' Jacqueline bent down, carefully, gingerly, and Maggie caught the scent of vanilla, Chanel and tobacco as her lips kissed her forehead. 'Goodbye.'

1964

For the first week after Isobel left Anchorage, Billy-Ray stayed
drunk. He took the vacation time he was owed but he didn't fly to
Los Angeles. Instead he picked up a case of vodka and locked himself away in his damaged, sway-backed house, taking the telephone
off the hook (even though the lines were down anyway). He knew
Karbo would want him out in the inlet, overseeing repairs to the rigs
and platforms in the Middle Shoals, assessing the damage to
pipelines, containing leaks, but all he wanted to do was lie on the
sofa in front of an unlit fire and drink, drinking interrupted only by
the arrival of the utility companies as they relaid cables and restrung
wires. Contractors came knocking at the door, offering their serv-
ices – glaziers, carpenters, joiners, builders, painters. Each contractor
found Billy-Ray drunk, still standing but drunk. In the kitchen were
piles of ketchup-smeared plates, empty cartons of juice, a pile of spilt
coffee grounds on the floor. On the floor by the sofa was a collection
of overflowing ashtrays and glasses smeared with fingerprints.

Billy-Ray lay on the sofa and drank because he thought Isobel
had left him. He thought she had run away and that she was never
coming back. She'd left him because he couldn't tell her how much
he loved her. The only woman who had ever absolved him and she
had gone. He lay there during long days of light, a bottle by his
side, the sounds of sawing, drilling and demolition echoing around
him, and he thought of his wife. How she fitted him when they lay
in bed, how she danced, almost, around the kitchen as she cooked,
moving in a way she never did at any other time. Thought of the
evenings when he sat at the breakfast bar, sipping a beer, as she tried
to cook and they talked through their days. How she'd sit in the old
armchair and read, legs folded beneath her, fingers playing with a

lock of blonde hair, flipping it back and forth. When had he stopped telling her he loved her? Seemed like he came home and his treasure chest of languages slammed and locked itself tight shut. All he could do was cuss and swear and pick at the holes opening up in their lives.

Billy-Ray Rickman lay in his damaged house, drinking and thinking his days away. He thought of how Brad Honker had looked when loneliness washed over him as he laid his head on an unknown woman's belly; how the considerate, self-effacing Bent had smiled gently when Brad taunted him. Thought of the tsunami of fire, oil and ocean washing them away, how terrified they must have been, how much it must have hurt to die like that.

As the weak sun slid away each evening, peppered by snow, and the room shaded to grey and silver, Billy-Ray would pour yet another vodka and Siggy would walk in, barefoot and pale, Adriatic water dripping from his sodden uniform. *Dränka. Hukkua. Vebertoenend.* Siggy stood in the gloom, blue-white arms crossed, watching Billy-Ray cry. A *tupilaq* sent to unsettle. The stink of pigs, the rich scent of hay, the smell of Magde's skin drifted over Billy-Ray as he watched Siggy. Then Siggy's arm lifted slowly, as if inviting a dance, a kiss, shelter beneath a sheet, shelter beneath a sail, as he looked at his brother. Then and only then could Billy-Ray sleep. But one night as he slept, breath foul with stale tobacco, dill pickles and vodka, the scent of blood drifted over him and he opened his eyes to find Deet in the room with him. Standing in night light softened by snowfall, chest shattered, uniform drenched black, seemingly not with blood but oil. A butchers' school, a school for butchers. Maccelaria Scolaria.

'Bitte, Gott, lass es Dieter sein,' Deet said. Said again, 'Bitte, Gott, lass es Dieter sein.' His voice sounded wet, sounded abyssal.

Billy-Ray covered his eyes, curled into himself, tumbled into a nightmare – the Wave, thundering towards *Viveka* as two blond heads touched; the Wave, roaring along a fjord, waters burning, and he couldn't stop it. Billy-Ray couldn't stop the Wave.

He woke at ten o'clock that evening, woke to silent dead-night, shivering, still drunk. He stood and crossed the empty room, empty now of his brothers, and went to the phone, dialled.

'Is Isobel . . .' He stopped and coughed. 'Can I speak to Isobel, please?'

'I'm afraid she's still asleep, sir.'

'Then wake her up.' Billy-Ray squinted at the clock.

'It's six o'clock in the morning, sir.'

'I want to speak to her.'

'Perhaps you could call again later?'

'I'm her goddam husband and I want to talk to her right now.'

'Very well, sir.'

Billy-Ray stood, holding the phone, swaying slightly, his back to the room, not wanting to look, not wanting to see Siggy and Deet drenched in salt water and blood. Above the hissing of the trans-atlantic cable he could hear footsteps on marble. He imagined Isobel waking, the way she pushed her hair behind her ears. Willed her to move quickly, willed her to run. Heard footsteps approaching.

'BR? Are you OK?'

'Isobel?'

'Are you OK?'

And Billy-Ray began to cry, slumped down the wall in the darkness, coming to rest in a crouch, crying.

'What's the matter? BR, what's the matter? Are you OK?'

'I love you,' he said, voice like glue, like slurry. 'Don't leave me.'

'I'm not leaving you.'

'Please don't leave me.'

'BR, have you been drinking?'

He nodded. Wiped his mouth with the back of his hand.

'BR, have you been drinking?'

'Yes.'

'Why?'

'Because you left me.'

He heard the creak of a chair as Isobel sat down four thousand miles away. 'I didn't leave you, BR. It was just too dangerous for us to stay. I explained all that. Remember? Remember? I explained why I needed to leave.'

A tremor, a faint after-shock, caused the floor to shift and Billy-Ray looked around the room with bloodshot eyes, waited for another which never came.

'BR, are you still there?'

'Shocks are still coming.'

'Exactly. That's why I brought Tufty here.'

'I love you.'

'I know you do.'

Billy-Ray stared at the floor, touched it with his fingers. 'I keep seeing Siggy. He comes into the room. He comes here every night.'

Isobel considered this. 'What does he do?'

'He stands in the room, watching me. He's all wet. Isobel? He's all wet.'

'I think, BR, that you—'

'And then he moves his arm. Like he used to. When I had nightmares, like he used to.'

'Honey, that's what's—'

'But tonight Deet came too.'

Isobel listened, said nothing.

'Deet came. He was covered in blood. He stood in the room, covered in blood.' Billy-Ray started to cry once more, wiped his face with his T-shirt. 'He spoke to me. He stood there, with his chest all blown away, and he spoke to me. He said—'

'Billy-Ray, it was a nightmare, that's all. You have nightmares. You've always had them. I want you to go—' Isobel really didn't want to hear what Deet said.

'He knew, Isobel. He said—'

'Billy-Ray.' Isobel's voice had a razor edge as she tried to slice through her husband's drunk-speak. 'I want you to go to the kitchen—'

But Billy-Ray wasn't listening. 'Deet knew. He said, "*Bitte, Gott, lass es Dieter sein*." He said it, Isobel. He knew.'

'Billy-Ray, I want you to go to the kitchen and make some coffee, make yourself a sandwich, eat something. And then I want you to go to bed and get some sleep.'

'He knew.'

Husband and wife sat in silence, four thousand miles apart, both staring unseeing at the walls that boxed them in. Billy-Ray caught the sound of a match scrape, heard Isobel exhale quietly as she smoked.

'Go to bed, BR. Eat something, have a shower and go to bed.'

'Don't leave me.'

Isobel, who was sitting in the marbled entrance hall of Highbury, found her tongue hamstrung. She wanted to say so much but feared being overheard. 'I'm not. I'll be back soon.'

'When? Come home, Isobel. I miss you. I want you here.'

'I'll be back soon.'

'I love you.'

'I know.' A maid placed an ashtray at Isobel's elbow. 'I know. Goodnight, BR. I'll try to call tomorrow.'

'I love you.'

'Go to bed, Billy-Ray.' Isobel replaced the receiver gently. Smoked, staring at the rolling, rich brown fields on the horizon, and wondered at her inability to speak.

Picking up a *New York Times* from a kiosk outside the terminal in Tacoma, Billy-Ray made his way to the coffee shop and ordered a juice and a bagel. Still he felt hollow with hangover despite the fact that he had not drunk now for two days, had not seen Siggy or Deet for two nights, yet still he could feel them at his shoulder. He opened the paper and began to scan it, would have done anything to move away from the memory of Siggy lifting an arm. Already the earthquake had fallen off the front page, relegated to the business section, where journalists speculated about the amount of money the regeneration of Alaska would make for the construction industry, how it would affect defence spending. How, Billy-Ray wondered, would they defend themselves against nine point three on the Richter scale? And what would the military bring? Nothing but money and violence. Billy-Ray lit a cigarette and noticed a tremble in his fingers. Inhaling, turning the page, he found a long-forgotten face staring at him through swathes of frozen smoke, eyebrows slightly arched: Lucca Barzini, who smoked too much, talked too much and drove too fast. Lucca Barzini, who had remarked that whilst it was possible to love martinis, cats or sex, it wasn't possible to love geology. Who had held his hands in Cape Disappointment and showed him what to do with them as he kicked over fire.

Lucca Barzini, it seemed, had abandoned the memory of her

Spanish lover lying on a deathbed of pine needles. She had, too, abandoned the search for stories of bloodlust and incest in the foothills of the Rockies. Instead she now championed the cause of the Native American, had written a polemic on the massacre of the Sioux at Wounded Knee, a polemic inspired by moral outrage at the continuing injustices suffered by Indians, so flawless in execution that the book had finally won her a Pulitzer. No wonder Lucca smiled wryly through the wreaths of smoke clouding her face. It would also seem that she still drank and smoked too much, still cruised the highways in search of young, blond men. Billy-Ray smiled as he read the interviewer's conclusion, left the paper on the table as his flight was called.

The flight took three hours, three hours during which Billy-Ray chose not to sleep, during which he sat and watched the land pass miles below him. The Rockies, first rising, gouged by deep valleys, then falling away, rippling down to desolate badlands, before the plane crossed the Missouri River. Flew over the rich loam and till of Minnesota before descending to land in Minneapolis. Three hours to cover the journey it had taken his eighteen-year-old self eleven days to complete, young and hopeful, beautiful face turned to both sun and snow.

Billy-Ray hired a jeep from the Hertz office in the airport and headed south on the US35, driving slowly, just easing himself through the too-familiar land. The US35 followed the lazy bends of the Minnesota River, and Billy-Ray was riveted by the colours of the land as he drove, by the stands of trees, the blue waters, the blue, copper-stained earth itself, which seemed garish after the winter-leached landscapes of Anchorage and the North Slope. He began to recognize the road signs: Jordan, Assumption, Cambria, Norseland. (Norseland – the Smoked Sockeye. Glass falling at his feet.) These were places he had visited with Siggy and Magde, towns he had driven to when his father was whole and his mother was a blonde, invincible, smiling giant. Billy-Ray reached the outskirts of Mankato and was puzzled. The town had spread like warm oil over the land, engulfing Lehillier, Lime and Skyline. The roads and inter-sections he remembered were gone, had disappeared under acres of blacktop, and soon he was lost. He crawled along Riverfront and

Front Streets, took himself down backstreets, searching for the familiar. Bretts and Clement's Chevrolet were still there, along with Mocol's Supermarket and the Rany Seed Company, where his father had bought fertilizer. The Norwest Bank and Jakob's Lumber were still open for business. But there were so many new bars and shops, so many more people on the sidewalk, and he didn't recognize any of them. He was looking at a well-known face in a mirror, the familiar distorted and reversed. He crossed the river and there was the industrial sprawl, engineering plants, Mico, the Mankato Paper Box Company still spewing steam and ash. He saw the dereliction of Union Depot, the desperate state of the Saulpaugh Hotel, and he drove on. Headed south and saw the first sign for Bow Regard.

Billy-Ray left the Reichmann farm when he was eighteen. Eighteen years later he returned. Skirted the town of Bow Regard on US7, and now the familiar, the well known, flooded over him, threatened to fill his lungs and drown him. Lakes, flatland, creeks and glacial deposits. Passing the Bergmans' farm, two miles and the track on the right. Eighteen years. Only to find a chain stretching across the gateway to the farm, a rusting metal sign swinging from it. Atwood Realty, Mankato. The padlock on the chain already severed, lying on thin gravel. Billy-Ray unwound the chain, left it lying in the dirt. Climbed back in the car, slipped the stick into drive, and drove. Half a mile over a low crest and there was the farmhouse. Half a mile. Doesn't take long for a jeep to cover half a mile. Takes a horse longer than a jeep, no matter how deep the horse's chest, no matter how long the horse's legs. Billy-Ray parked by the porch, opened the car door, closed his eyes and heard the squeal of hoofs on gravel.

Eventually he moved. Eventually Billy-Ray moved, got out of the car, slammed the door and stood staring at the porch. Stepped up on to it, looked for a slip of thin paper skittering across the boards. The torn screen door was skewed on its hinges and the kitchen door was unlocked, three of four glass panes broken. In the corners of the porch piles of dead, dried leaves and unravelling birds' nests stirred in the stiff breeze. Billy-Ray pushed open the door and looked around the kitchen. The copper coffee pot was on the stove, etched with verdigris. A plate, stained with ancient, blackened ketchup, looked as if it had been pushed aside, and in its place was a glass, toppled on its side, cloudy with grease and dust. In the corner of the room, where his mother had kept her brooms, was a large cardboard box, stamped with the Rany's Feed Store logo, bulging, distorted by the weight of empty vodka bottles. A filthy, much-worn baseball cap sat askew the head of the Virgin Mary as she looked dolefully at the prodigal son. From the crucifix by the door hung a worn belt, dangling from the crown of thorns.

Billy-Ray climbed the stairs, stood in the doorway of his parents' bedroom and scanned the scene of a disaster. Dirty clothes, empty bottles, scorch marks on the grey blankets, stains on the ticking, bloodied hand marks on the walls. Tattered sheets hanging in the window. Towels, stiff with mould, crusted with sputum and diesel. A smashed mirror. On the back of the door a leather strop, ivory-handled cut-throat razor on the floor. Blood on the floorboards. And there was the smell. The smell of a lone drunk living for years in a catastrophe. The smell of trapped air, stale water. Water scooped from the benthic zone, old as the earth. Of metal and blood, a smell like jagged glass. The stench of someone living without hope. Or compassion. The smell of someone who had once held a fork in one hand and a telegram in the other as he chewed *placki kartoflane*.

Billy-Ray stepped back, stepped away from the picture of what his father had become. He walked past Deet's and Siggy's room, climbed again, up to the room under the eaves. Pushed open the door and saw sky. A section of the roof had collapsed, showering his childhood bed with shingles and rotting battens. Coon scat and bird droppings drew unlikely patterns across the floor. He opened the wardrobe and found that nothing had changed – his jeans were folded on the shelves, shirts and letter jacket hanging next to them. Billy-Ray touched the jacket and smelled his fingers. Must, it smelled of must and time. And next to the wardrobe was the pin board. Billy-Ray stared at it, stared at the leached cards, rain-spotted and dusty. Reached out and touched the card from Memphis. Billy-Ray searched for the picture of Sunset Boulevard but in its place was pale cork. He looked down and there it was, rusted pin still stuck in a corner. He bent and picked it up, took it over to the window. Turned it. The ink had faded to silver grey, near disappeared.

'Howdy y'all!! Well, LA is quite something. Sun always shines. Big cars and pretty women. So I'm happy! Hope you're all OK. Tell Willie – I reckon I saw Barbara Stanwyck in a Buick the other day! Your loving son, Deet.'

Billy-Ray stayed at the window, ignoring the cold wind blowing through the broken pane, looking at the words written more than twenty years before, the writing untidy. Untidy and thoughtless. As if Deet had been in a bar or a train station and remembered suddenly that he should write to his family. Dressed in his uniform, about to head back to his base after leave. Billy-Ray imagined his brother standing in a post office, frowning, checking his watch, dredging up these words. Jigging in the queue, running late. Running late, anxious to get going. Anxious to get posted. Anxious to get to Italy. Billy-Ray looked up, looked out of the smashed dormer window, saw Home Lake glinting under a paling sky. Wondered, as he always had, at the amount of faith needed to survive on the thin, brittle crust of this life.

He was ready. He walked down the stairs and pushed open the door to Deet's and Siggy's room. But Billy-Ray wasn't ready for what he found there. On the beds were sleeping bags, rumpled, used. On the chair between the beds, where the brothers had kept their candle and matches, was an ashtray and a dusty, half-empty bottle of Bud, a fly floating in the foul liquid. Long, slim trails of ash scarred the desktop. A carton of grey, soured milk stood on the window sill. His brothers' clothes and boots were gone. The silver football trophies and plated frames were gone. Billy-Ray searched the shelves for the photographs he knew should be there but they, too, had gone – Siggy, mud-crusted, helmet under his arm, smiling hugely for the camera as he was carried on the shoulders of his teammates; Deet holding up a five-pound trout he'd caught in Crystal Creek; the three of them standing in the boat on Home Lake, Deet with his hands around Willie's neck, pretending to strangle him as Willie rolled his eyes, giggling. The studio portraits of Siggy and Deet in uniform, standing tall, standing handsome, unsmiling, eyes locked on the lens, knowing that something important would soon happen to them.

Billy-Ray found himself driving too fast, smoking too much,

trying not to see tall, handsome blond boys on the road into Bow Regard. The town was prospering – a mall was being built out Victory Drive way, a new brick-built building had replaced the timbered school where Billy-Ray had learned about mirages, tectonics and language. He wanted to drink, needed to, and he headed for Mettler's Grill on Main and Second, but Kurt Mettler had sold up and moved on a long time before. In place of the bar was an Amoco station. Oil spreading. But across the street Munchssen's neon light flickered in the twilight. Billy-Ray pulled in and looked over at the milk bar, which was now a diner.

As Billy-Ray walked into Munchssen's, heads turned towards him. Three men sitting on stools at the bar, all eating the blue plate special, chewing untidily as they eyed him up and down, Artie Shaw's swing band playing on the radio. The older man, felt hat squashed into the belt of his jeans, face seamed by sun and wind, shattering (as Urban's had) when he frowned, stared at Billy-Ray for a long, long time, then turned back to his meatloaf, still frowning. Billy-Ray slipped on to a stool, watched the man behind the bar moving slowly, moving almost delicately, as if webbed by years. Karl Munchssen looked up from the coffee machine and saw Siegfried Reichmann leaning on his elbows at the bar, tapping a cigarette from a pack of Lucky Strikes, lighting it, tossing the spent match into an ashtray.

'Siggy?' Karl whispered, putting down the coffee jug.

'It's Willie, Karl. It's just Willie. Nothing to worry about.' The man sitting at the bar swallowed the last of the meatloaf and threw down his fork, wiped his scored lips. 'Just Willie come home.'

Billy-Ray looked at the man. 'Do I know you?'

'Probably not. Name's Wojciek Jancker. Well, yah, you know me but I guess you've forgotten. Been a while.' Wojciek Jancker threw two dollar bills on the bar, took a toothpick from the napkin stand and set his hat. 'See you round, Karl.' Walked out, closing the diner door quietly behind him.

'Willie?' Karl's beefy hands were working strangely, opening and closing by his sides. 'Willie? That you?' Karl looked at the man sitting at the bar, wearing a beard, blond hair long over his collar, his neck thick, eyes troubled. Older than Siggy would ever be. Then

Billy-Ray smiled, Karl noticed the twisted eye tooth and, taking off his apron, walked out round the bar to hug Billy-Ray. Felt the bulk of the man, the muscles of his back. 'Well, shoot! Willie Reichmann – how long you been gone?'

Billy-Ray smiled again. 'Eighteen years, thereabouts.'

'Time you came for a visit. Hey! Greta!' Karl shouted towards the hatch. 'Come see who's here.'

A grey-haired woman stuck her head through the hatch, looked at Billy-Ray and the ready smile was wiped off her face.

'It's OK, Greta. It's Willie – remember Willie Reichmann?'

Greta came through the swing-doors, wiping her hands on a towel, limping slightly, favouring her right leg. 'Willie – let me look at you.' Greta hugged Billy-Ray, took his hands in hers and rubbed them. Scanned his face. 'Jus' for a moment there, I thought I was seeing a ghost.'

Seeing a ghost. *Der Geist. Tupilaq.*

'Hey, you and me, we should go have a beer. Let's go to Hank's and I'm buying.' Karl slapped Billy-Ray on a broad, hard shoulder. 'That OK, Greta?'

'Yah – you go with Willie. It's quiet today. I can manage. But,' and she touched Billy-Ray's cheek with chapped, detergent-scoured fingers, 'only if you promise to come to see me before you go.'

'Yah – of course I will.'

Hank's bar was long and thin, dimly lit. Lamps hung low over tables and out back was a pool room with a jukebox loud enough to hear from the street. Around the table a group of tall, blond, blue-eyed boys wielded cues, lounged against the wall, sucking on beer bottles. Lucca Barzini would have loved it, Billy-Ray thought as he waited for Karl to come back from the bathroom.

'Way different from how I remember Mettler's,' he said as Karl sat down with a grunt.

'Yah, well, times have changed round here. Changed everywhere. Notice they're building a mall out Mapleton way?' Karl shrugged his shoulders, rolled his neck, stuck out his jaw. 'What do we need a mall for?'

'Drove through Mankato on the way here – hardly knew where I was.'

The two men talked for a while, Karl shrugging and sipping his beer as he talked of how things were, how they might have been. Billy-Ray watched Karl's face, lined now, grey stubble blurring his jaw line, listened to Karl's voice, a voice unchanged by decades spent in Blue Earth County.

'So, Willie,' Karl wiped the neck of his bottle, 'I always wondered why you didn't come back for your mother's funeral? All day we were expecting you but you never came. I said to Greta you must have had a good reason.'

Billy-Ray thought of the hours he had waited, freezing in the cinderblock bus station. 'I just couldn't, Karl. I can't explain it. I got on the bus and I had to get off.'

'So, why are you here? What has made you come back?'

'Wanted to see the farm. What's going on, Karl? What happened to my father?' Blood on the floorboards, faded to pale brown beneath the blade of a cut-throat.

'What happened to your father?' Karl rubbed at the bristle on his neck so hard Billy-Ray could hear the rasp. 'Greta says his heart broke. That he never got over what happened that weekend. She says his heart gave up. Not with beating exactly, but that he couldn't feel any more. I don't think that. I think he felt too *much*. That was the problem. He felt too much. Wasn't his heart that broke – it was his liver. But it was maybe too late. Now he doesn't drink but still he's dying.'

Billy-Ray lowered the cigarette he was about to light. 'He's still alive?'

'Yah. Sure he is, out at St Peter's in Mankato.'

'What's going on? The farm's up for sale, he's in hospital, there's blood everywhere and people been sleeping in . . . in the farm.'

Karl looked at Billy-Ray in the red-tinged light, could see the pool players moving around behind him, moving as Willie would have done if he hadn't been a farm boy, if he hadn't been a good boy. 'Ach, OK. What happened? Well, first your mother died and it was like the lights went out up there. In the farm. He still loved her, you know. You do know that, Willie? Your father still loved your mother. But he felt like the Church took all her attention, took all her love. Do you see? He was jealous of the Church.' Karl sighed. 'Then he had nothing. Siggy and Deet, then Irochka. And you had left. He had nothing but the pigs and the vodka.' Karl drew patterns in the melt water on the table with his forefinger. 'He tried. He did try. Sometimes he straightened out for a while – you know? Maybe was on the wagon for a few weeks and then he'd come into town and we'd talk. But mainly he drank. He managed to hold it together for a long time. Just enough. Fed the pigs just enough, kept things going but only just enough. Then,' Karl raised his eyebrows in surprise, 'he just got too old, I guess, too old to do it all on his own. You never wrote, Willie. That hurt him. You never wrote him.'

Billy-Ray had nothing to say. Breathed deep.

Karl began to crack monkey nuts, splitting them, spilling the kernels on the table. 'Why didn't you write? Wouldn't have hurt.'

Still Billy-Ray breathed deep.

'Well, I guess you must have had your reasons. I miss him, you know. Your father. Strange. Used to drive me crazy when he was around. But every now and then, when he was sober he was fine company. He had a lot to say. Your father was a wise man, Willie.'

'My father was a drunk.'

(Maybe he was both.)

'Gotta go to the bathroom again – gets that way, y'know? Get another beer in.'

Billy-Ray motioned for two more drinks and as the barman cracked the caps he suddenly remembered who the older man in the diner was – Wojciek Jancker, who was bringing feed pellets that Saturday morning. Wojciek Jancker, who never came. Instead, in his place, a telegram arrived.

Karl eased himself back into his chair. 'Cheers. Willie – I . . . this is very difficult for me. Look, when your father got sick I arranged for him to go to St Peter's, but they wanted money because he had no insurance. Well, who would insure him anyway? So I been paying the bills. We tried to find you – put adverts in the papers, you know, out Seattle way, but never got no response. So, that's why the farm is up for sale. There are a few creditors – Rany's, the oil company, the liquor store. But nothing much. Thing is, your father isn't going back there. He's not going anywhere. So we needed to sell the farm to pay the creditors. I wouldn't have done this if we could have found you. I'm sorry.'

'Don't apologize, Karl. Don't apologize. You did the right thing. The right thing. I should be saying sorry to you. How much have you spent?'

'Greta keeps the accounts. The diner does well but sometimes it's been hard. Oliver's been there a few months now. It all adds up, y'know? Bit by bit. But it's OK. When the farm is sold it will be fine. No problem, the lawyer says.'

'I'll get you the money tomorrow.'

'Willie,' Karl smiled, 'it's thousands of dollars.'

'I'll get it for you tomorrow. There's a First Federal in Mankato. I'll drive up there.'

Karl frowned, looked at the blond man. 'What d'you do, Willie? What do you do? For a living, I'm saying?'

'I live in Anchorage, Alaska, with my wife and daughter. I'm an oil man. I work for Karbo Inc. up on the North Slope. When I went up to the farm it looked like some people had been camping out there. You know anything about that?'

Karl grimaced. 'Yah. Some hippies stayed there a while. Broke in and stayed for a few weeks. But no one knew anything about it for weeks. Then when the sheriff went up, they'd already gone. Must have been a couple of months ago. Thing is, farm's way out of town. No one knows what goes on up there. Reckon kids get up there sometimes. I sometimes go check if I have time. Thing is, what you have to remember, Willie, it didn't look so different when Oliver was there. It got very bad.'

'What happened to the hogs?'

Karl shrugged. 'They went a couple of years ago. He was a good hog man, your father. Even when he was drunk he managed. But in the end he had to sell them. The day he took them to market – well, it wasn't good. Drunkest I ever saw him. Came into town that night and near drank Mettler's dry. Got thrown out and then smashed the street window with a trash can. Glass everywhere.'

The two men sat and stared at the bottles on the table, the fibrous debris of nuts.

'Will you buy the farm, Willie?'

'Nah. Nah, I won't. Will anyone else?'

'There's an offer been made – a development company out St Paul's

way. Want to build some kind of club there. A golf club, I think. The
lawyer has the plans. The land's worth a lot of money, Willie.'

'Anyone else interested?'

'Some farmer out Norseland way. But he can't afford it.'

Billy-Ray smiled. 'I'll deal with it, Karl. You've done enough.
Leave it to me now. Excuse me.'

Billy-Ray urinated in the bathroom, which had mirrored tiles on
three walls. He looked over his shoulder at an infinite number of
images of Siggy looking older than he would ever be, standing in
Hank's bar in Bow Regard, Blue Earth County, as Karl Munchssen
played with monkey-nut shells, listening to the velvet crack of pool
balls and remembering Willie Reichmann coming into the drugstore,
holding a handful of candy, his face looking young and beautiful
(looking as if it were hoping for absolution).

That night Billy-Ray stayed in the farmhouse, despite Karl's offer of
a room above the diner. He borrowed blankets and an oil stove,
picked up some groceries at the new mall and headed back out of
Bow Regard. The old dirt road was now metalled and paved but still
as dark as ever. He tuned the car radio and picked up a blues station
from Minneapolis, half listening to tales of despair and loss as he
watched the road and noticed lights flaring from houses that had not
been there before. Turning into the farm gate, the tyres bumped over
the chain in the dirt, and headlights bounced over the long grasses
and thick weeds that were threatening to overrun the track. He sat
out on the porch that night, shivering in sharp, cold night air, watching the stars wheel overhead, listening to the rustling of animals
and leaves – the new occupants of the Reichmann farm. Billy-Ray sat
and smoked, looking at the blurred outlines of the outhouses and
buildings in the light of a half-moon. The barn, listing now, the water
butts, emptied by a thousand rusted, serrated holes. In the distance,
the stables and paddock, where Roosevelt, Jefferson, Jackson and
Washington had spent their equine lives, pawing and snorting,
dreaming of fillies and hay and open skies. For a moment Billy-Ray
wondered what had happened to them – they'd all be long dead by
now. And dotted over the overgrown fields, the humps of sties and
lines of pens, shrouded by undergrowth.

At midnight Billy-Ray made his way up the stairs, carrying a flashlight, moving it over the grimy surfaces, the uneven stair boards. He stopped outside his father's bedroom, played the light over the bed and floor, the bloodstains, grey in the gloom, before crossing the landing to the other room. Throwing the musty sleeping bags in the corner, Billy-Ray took off his boots and lay down, fully dressed, on Siggy's old bed, the borrowed blankets wrapped around him. He turned off the light and the world disappeared. He felt safe, imagined an arm, a strong, muscled arm, wrapping around him, felt he was cocooned in a comforting white sailcloth.

The sun slammed into the curtainless room at dawn and Billy-Ray woke to freezing feet and sweat running from his neck and armpits. In the kitchen he half expected to find the smell of pancakes and salt bacon, the smell of miraculous corn bread, just baked, being lifted from the stove. But, of course, there was none of these, just the miasma of near-empty bottles and vegetables left to rot in the pantry. After a thin, weak coffee heated on the oil stove, he walked out into a cold, cloudless day, a day like a thousand he remembered from his childhood. He buttoned his jacket and retrieved his gloves from the jeep and set out to walk to Home Lake, barely able to make out the trodden pathways across the farmland. The mud of the sties had gone, dried up and grown over; many of the fences had collapsed. He could make out, even months later, the paths his father must have taken, deeper and more scuffed than the others. It would seem he had walked only between the farmhouse and the outhouse, from the porch to the nearest pens, and occasionally to the barn and troughs. Oliver's world had shrunk to a square quarter-mile; he had turned the rest of the farm over to the Minnesotan seasons, and nature was reclaiming it. Time and ice, time and heat, thawing and expanding, seeds bedding down in rich loam. The signs of the Reichmanns ever having been there were being eroded and drowned under the waves of seasonal change. Even Home Lake had changed. Of course, it seemed smaller; in his Alaskan mind he had remembered it as a vast expanse of ruffled, bright blue water, disturbed only by the flip of fins or the webbed feet of gadwall. That early April morning, the waters looked muddy, shallow, uninspiring even. Certainly not glittering or sharp enough to take a life. Standing on the shattered ancient rock of the land, he looked at the brown, churned lake and realized that it had indeed changed – the well heads nearby had collapsed, sealed over, and the waters had seeped through the earth, bringing with them silt and loam. The lake was silting up, might eventually disappear entirely; would certainly change beyond recognition. He looked for the old wooden rowing boat, could not see it. How was Billy-Ray to know that Oliver had holed it the night Irochka was found? Had holed it with a pickaxe, and watched it sink.

Billy-Ray crested a low ridge and looked down at the Church of St Teresa. The original rough, timber-built building had disappeared, replaced by a brick-and-concrete structure, box-like and low, a brutal building, a toad of a building that squatted on the ground, that did not reach for the skies. The pasturelands around had been paved over to provide a car park, the picket fencing replaced by an ugly brick wall. The cemetery was larger, much larger, than when he had last seen it. Billy-Ray pushed open the gate and walked among the rows of graves until he reached what he was looking for – the monument marking his brothers' lives, marking their deaths, an angel standing with hands and wings folded, head bowed. Lichen covered the stone, long, untended grasses waved around it. Billy-Ray stood for a long time, staring at the angel, wanting to wipe away the signs of time and not wanting to touch the words equally. Siggy and Deet lay near each other, thousands of miles away, Siggy's lungs awash with foreign sea waters, eyes brimming with the Adriatic, Deet's ribs shattered. Had been lying there for twenty-one years, as Billy-Ray sailed the Gulf of Alaska, hauling herring and chinook, as he laughed with Jacqueline Cooper, as he measured the curvature of the earth's planes, as he lay with Isobel in the sun arcing over Halibut Cove, as he sat and read to Tufty. All those things he had done since he last saw his brothers – and they had been lying near each other in a distant country. Just as when he was a boy and the three of them had walked the track to catch the school bus, Billy-Ray felt excluded, felt unneeded, even in death.

Next to Siggy's and Deet's grave was another – Irochka's. Billy-Ray had never seen it, never seen the plain, unadorned headstone, decorated only with the dates of her life, as if Oliver could think of nothing else to say about her. Or perhaps, as Karl would have suggested, Oliver had been tongue tied, had felt too much to be able to say anything at all? Billy-Ray didn't know, just as he didn't know what he was doing there, standing in the churchyard of St Teresa outside Bow Regard, on a beautiful spring morning, as geese flew overhead and leopard frogs and tiger salamanders thrashed through the reeds lining Home Lake. What was he *doing* there? Why had he come back? Because he needed peace, he needed to make peace with his brothers because they had come back to haunt him.

1964

It was true that, at first light, Lady Cooper appeared well preserved, elegant and composed, did not look as old as her thirty-four years. But anyone who took the time to look closely would notice the thin lines carved by pensiveness between her plucked eyebrows, the damaged nails, bitten until the skin oozed blood. She began to nibble at a tiny pig's foot by her thumbnail as the Daimler inched along Brompton Road that late spring day, heading for Piccadilly, where she was due for a fitting. Jacqueline frowned, winced a little as she tore the skin further. Sir Sidney was ill. Sir Sidney, she was sure, was dying. What should she do? Jacqueline dabbed at her sweat-beaded upper lip, realized the car had been stationary for a long time, rocking slightly as it purred. She opened a window and immediately closed it again, the noise of the diesel engine of a bus deafening her, as the smoggy air thickened in the car.

'What's the problem, Kendrick? Can you see what's causing this?'

The chauffeur turned his head slightly. 'No, ma'am. Just a jam, I fink.'

'Oh, God.' Jacqueline slumped back on the deep leather seat, rooted in her handbag for a handkerchief, wiped her neck. She stared at the crowds, which seemed thicker than usual, younger than usual. She was beginning to feel old, beginning to think she was wearing out. She had noticed her neck no longer hugged her throat snugly, that the skin under her upper arms was becoming papery. It had started. What to do? An orange-and-white poster, trapped beneath diamonds of wire, caught her eye. 'Beatles premiere – 10,000 fans stream into Leicester Square.' 'Oh, God,' she repeated.

The malaise that afflicted Jacqueline had settled around her a few days before; indeed, she could recall the very moment when she began

to feel melancholic: while being fitted at Dior she had heard a familiar
voice, a voice she couldn't at first place. As the seamstress wrapped a
tape measure around her (papery) arm, Jacqueline had suddenly realized who was speaking. She'd excused herself and, dressed only in a
silk shift, had pulled aside the curtain and stepped out.

'Isobel?'

Isobel turned from the rack of blouses she was riffling through,
and smiled. 'Jacqueline! Well, hey!'

Well, hey? Jacqueline and Isobel hugged, bussed each other's
cheeks before standing back and looking each other over. 'You're
looking well, Isobel. Very well. What d'you do to your arm?'

'It's nothing really.' Isobel waved the plaster. 'Fractured my wrist
in a fall. It's taking a little longer to heal than it should have done.
How are you?'

'Fine, I'm just fine.' Jacqueline became aware of her state of
undress. 'Look, why don't I get changed and then we can have lunch
somewhere, catch up.'

'That sounds delightful.' Isobel lurched as a small child cannoned
into her knees. 'Well, look who's here. Say hello to Jacqueline, honey.
Hope you don't mind Tufty coming along for lunch too.'

Jacqueline looked down at the black-haired, blue-eyed girl, who
seemed too tall for her age, whose eyes were unnervingly steady. She
looked at Tufty for a long time, but she said nothing. There was a
great deal she could have said but she elected to say nothing.

The three of them rode in the Daimler to Harvey Nichols, where
they had a long lunch punctuated by the serving of Tufty's needs –
the toilet, milk, attention – and between these interruptions
Jacqueline learned what had happened to Billy-Ray Rickman. Nearly
seven years had passed since Billy-Ray had pinned her violently
against the wall of a stateroom in the *Queen Mary*. Jacqueline would-
n't say that she had thought about him every day, nor had she cried
over him since she had waited for the lift in the Savoy, but she still
missed him.

'So you've been living in Anchorage?' Jacqueline lit a cigarette as
coffee arrived. 'That must be a strange place.'

'It is. I have to confess I don't like it much. I'd really like to move.
Tufty, honey, sit still. We won't be long.'

Jacqueline stared again at the child, who stared right back, as if she knew something, as if she had a hold on a fold of Jacqueline's life and was squeezing it tightly. As if she had known Jacqueline since she was born. Discomfited, Jacqueline looked away but still she said nothing. Tufty reached out and stroked Jacqueline's hand, touched her wedding band.

'Tufty – don't do that. Apologize to Jacqueline.'

'It's OK, Isobel. No problem.' But Jacqueline slid her hand off the table.

'Well, I think we'd better make a move.' Isobel folded her napkin and stood, smoothing down her shirt, shifting the belt of her trousers.

'I have to say, you look the part, Isobel. You know, like a frontierswoman or something.'

Isobel laughed. 'Yes, I know. We've been sent down to Town by my mother with strict instructions for me to buy a new wardrobe. She says I look like a Land Girl. She is, frankly, horrified.'

'Funny, now I've seen you, I can't imagine you in anything else.' Jacqueline gathered together her handbag, lighter and cigarettes, told the waitress to add the lunch to her account, waved away Isobel's protests, and offered to drop her wherever she liked.

'Thank you, but Mummy still has the house off Sloane Street. It's only a short walk.'

As the trio stood by the Daimler, Tufty hanging off her mother's massive hand, twisting on her heels, Jacqueline asked when they could meet again.

'I doubt we'll be able to. We're flying back in a couple of weeks and there's so much to do. Billy-Ray managed to telephone and the house will, apparently, soon be all fixed up as he would say. The after-shocks have just about stopped, so the coast is clear.'

'It's a real shame we didn't bump into each other earlier.'

'Yes, it is. I should have called or something, but Tufty hasn't been to England before so we've been doing a lot of sightseeing with Mummy and Daddy. But it is a shame. Next time we visit I shall make sure we arrange to get together.'

'Well, it's been great seeing you.' The women kissed as Tufty looked on; Jacqueline touched the child's cheek, pressed a finger to

Tufty's lips. 'Be good, little one.' The chauffeur closed the car door, and Jacqueline wound down the window. 'Hey, Isobel, give my love to Billy-Ray, won't you?'

'Sure I will.'

As the Daimler edged its way into the traffic, Jacqueline waved, and Isobel, tall and willowy, bent to pick up Tufty, and the child waved, her palm high above the crowds, turning, catching the late afternoon sun, like an eye winking over and over.

Fanning herself with a leaflet she had found in her handbag, Jacqueline remembered that moment, watching Tufty's hand waving like a semaphore, and knew that was when she began to feel melancholic. Isobel would be leaving in a few days now, would be packing her bags, preparing to fly back to Billy-Ray. The scratched, dented sides of the bus shuddered and throbbed a couple of feet away.

'Kendrick? Isn't there another route we can take?'

'Nah, ma'am. World and 'is bruvver'll be trying that.'

Jacqueline huffed, shifted again on the leather seat. What should she do? When it was over. When Sir Sidney had slipped away, leaving a legacy of nuts and bolts and a string of petrol stations and garages. Again, Jacqueline tugged at the bright pink triangle of flesh by the nail of her thumb. Perhaps it was time to go home? Perhaps she should go back to the States? The winds of change she had felt years before, howling through Jarman House on the eve of 1960, had since blown away just about everything, and Jacqueline Cooper, née Olivetti, no longer knew where she belonged.

1964

St Peter's Hospice in Mankato was a two-storey block building out on the east side of town, towards Skyline. Billy-Ray Rickman parked the rental jeep in the lot and walked the grounds for a while, smoking, before going in to ask whether he could visit Oliver Reichmann. The nun behind the desk looked up at him, her sharp, unadorned face unreadable.

'Well, that would be fine. Mr Reichmann doesn't have many visitors.' Billy-Ray couldn't place her accent at first, soft and lilting, as if she were whispering loudly. 'Are you related to Mr Reichmann?'

'I'm his son.'

She watched his mouth work, nodded slightly, and motioned for Billy-Ray to follow her, leading him down glazed corridors that glittered in harsh, Minnesotan spring sun, chrome flashing. Stopped by a door on which a piece of card was tacked, his father's name written in sloping letters. The nun put her hand on Billy-Ray's arm.

'Your father . . . you haven't visited before?'

'No, I haven't.'

'Has his condition been explained to you?'

'No.'

'He was brought in by a friend a while ago, with a very high fever. He's suffering from leptospirosis, which you may have heard described as Weil's disease.' She arched her eyebrows as Billy-Ray shook his head. 'It's a disease passed on to humans by rats. They think that we catch it by contact with water infected with rat's urine. It affects the heart, brain and liver. But in your father's case it would seem that his liver was badly damaged before the onset of the disease, heavily scarred and cirrhotic. I'm afraid that a side effect of the infection is a tendency to haemorrhage.' Billy-Ray looked at the white door, noticed fingerprints misting its sheen. 'How long is it since you saw your father?'

Billy-Ray looked into the nun's pale blue eyes. Remembered Oliver turning away from him, turning his back on him as Willie tried to say goodbye, his mother praying on her knees before a makeshift shrine in the kitchen. 'Eighteen years.'

'I see.' The nun's pale face registered nothing. 'Well, in that case prepare yourself for a shock.' She opened the door and stood back to allow Billy-Ray to step into the room, and there was Oliver Reichmann. A bloodied skeleton lying in white sheets. Blood bloomed, like the pox, on the linen; just as it had bloomed when Isobel absolved her future husband and the soft tissues of her abdomen had begun to bleed.

'It's the bruising, the haemorrhaging. We can't stop it.' The nun stood next to Billy-Ray, her habit spotless, hands folded. 'We pray for him every day.'

Billy-Ray stared at the remains of a life. His father's cheeks were covered with a fuzzy, grey beard, his hair was lank and greasy. Under grey skin his ribs rippled as he laboured to breathe; his hands, rich purple and deep blue, moved in spasms, nails scratching at the top sheet. This was all that was left of Oliver Reichmann, who had looked over the crowds on Ellis Island and seen sharp cheekbones. Who had laughed in summer sunshine as piglets squealed around his ankles, who had sat with his son during long Fall evenings and told him that you had to put back what you took from the earth. Oliver Reichmann, who had built his own farm, who had dreamed of a dynasty, who had spent his time planning, always planning. Had he planned *this*? To spend the past eighteen years alone, battling with bottles and razors? To spend the end of his life being tended by the brides of a Christ he despised? Billy-Ray closed his eyes and scrubbed at his cheeks with the heels of his hands.

'I'll leave you to spend some time with him. I have to warn you he doesn't respond to any questions. As I said, the infection affects the heart and liver, but it also infects the brain. Also, please don't touch him – it might trigger more bleeding.'

'Can he hear me?'

'We're not sure, but we think so. There's no reason why not. Stay as long as you want.' And the nun was gone, long white habit disappearing through the door as it closed.

Billy-Ray looked for a chair but there was none, for Oliver rarely had visitors. He moved towards the bed and knelt on the floor, resting his elbows on the edge of the mattress, careful not to touch his father's bruise of a body. He stared at the ravaged face, looking yet again for the familiar, but still he couldn't find it. The bowl of skull that held the infected brain seemed to have collapsed.

'Pa,' said Billy-Ray, 'it's Willie. Your son, Willie. Came to see how you're doing.' Billy-Ray scrubbed his face again. 'Sorry I been away so long. I've been in Alaska.' And as his knees started to flatten, started to ache, Billy-Ray told his father all about his life. Everything he could remember of it since he had hitched to Seattle. He slipped into German and told his life. Told Oliver Reichmann that he had a granddaughter. How was Billy-Ray to know that Oliver had planned to have thirty grandchildren, grandchildren who should be running around the Reichmann estate, in and out of each other's houses?

Billy-Ray stopped talking once he'd described Tufty and what she did, how she looked. He could think of nothing more to say. The son knelt in silence, still searching for the familiar. He became aware of his father's livid hand turning slowly, turning over, palm facing up, a bloodied spot like a stigmata dead centre. The fingers moved, in small jerks and Billy-Ray realized his father wanted him to hold his hand.

'I can't, Pa. I'm not allowed to touch you.'

Again the fingers moved and Billy-Ray reached out, wrapped his hand – warm and strong – around the shiny, wrinkled skin. Oliver, who had heard some of what Billy-Ray had said, scrambled and whipped in the old tongue, knew someone was there. He squeezed the flesh that felt so good on his skin, that felt like river water, like warm oil, like love, and his blood began to ooze.

Billy-Ray never knew from where the impulse came which made him look away from the stop light to catch sight of a Titian blur. He signalled a right and followed the battered sky-blue Pontiac as it speeded up and headed out of Bow Regard towards Mapleton. Pulling level with the car, riding the wrong side of the road, he hit his horn and waved. The driver looked worried, stepped on the gas, and Billy-Ray accelerated to match her. He wound down the window and waved again. The woman smiled, slowed, came to a halt on the damp, loamy verge, Billy-Ray stopping behind her. The two drivers climbed out of their cars, met and hugged each other tightly. The woman reached up, stroked Billy-Ray's hair out of his eyes.

'Willie,' said Magde, 'you came home.'

'Yah, I came home.'

They hugged again and Billy-Ray was surprised by just how familiar Magde felt, how even beneath her thick woollen jacket her ribs slid away, the way they had all those years before.

They sat in a booth in the Snowgoose roadside diner, hands wrapped around bottomless cups of coffee, and exchanged life stories. A conversation that swilled about the bowls of their different experiences, lives shrunk to nuggets of information. Billy-Ray did talk about Urban, did talk about Lars, Eskil and Teo; he did not mention how he had stood at the edge of the world and promised them revenge; did not mention how he had cried alone in his tent for weeks without end; did not mention how he often thought of Viveka and wondered whether she had returned to the old country to sit alone in the lakeside cottage. He told Magde about Isobel and Tufty, about their lives in Anchorage, showed her some photos he carried in his wallet; he did not mention Jacqueline Cooper or Lucca Barzini.

Magde watched him closely as he spoke and Billy-Ray noticed the scattering of lines above her upper lip, the tough grey hairs at her temple. Her hands had the sheen of dry-skinned auburn women, and between her eyebrows there was a single, deep crevasse where her doubts gathered. When the waitress brought the list of daily specials, Magde lifted a pair of glasses from the chain around her neck and held the card at a distance. She lived in Mapleton, worked in Bow Regard on the checkout in Tylko's hardware store.

'Remember a guy called Roman at high school? Couple of grades above us? Played goal for the hockey team?'

'Yah – big guy with busted teeth.'

'I married him.'

Billy-Ray thought of the short, stocky boy, wide as a truck, strong as a steer, and jealousy spurted through him. 'Roman Bialkowski?'

'That's right. Got us three kids. Three boys.' Magde looked away, played with her wedding ring.

The picture of three boys standing in a boat on Home Lake drifted through Billy-Ray's mind. 'Three boys?' he said, eventually. 'Well, that's great. So what does Roman do these days?'

'He drives trucks.'

'Right.'

'So – London, Europe, Alaska.' Magde sat back, looked at Wilhelm-Rajmund Reichmann. Recalled the last time she had seen him. 'Alaska.' She laughed. 'I often wondered where you ended up, Willie. Often thought about you and wondered what you did.'

'That's what I did.'

The crevasse between Magde's eyes deepened. 'You did it – you got out just like you said you would.'

'Guess I did.' And Billy-Ray knew he could not mention the city dream Magde had had, of working in a bank in Minneapolis or Detroit, of walking boulevards and tree-lined avenues, dressed in stockings and smart suits, carrying a handbag, laughing with friends, visiting the theatre, catching movies and eating in fancy restaurants. He looked at her woollen jacket, cuffs frayed, lining torn, looked at the limp, over-washed collar of her shirt, noticed her ragged cuticles, and said nothing.

'How long you staying, Willie?'

'I don't know. I want to stay and see my Pa. Until he, y'know, until then. Maybe a week, the doctor said. Then I have to get back.'

'Sure be nice to have you over.' And Magde looks up from her coffee, looks directly at him, and Billy-Ray can taste Monterey Jack, Dr Pepper and vodka. For the first time in a long, long time Billy-Ray considers the possibility of having it all.

This time Magde did not cry, did not turn her face away from him and curl into a ball. This time she kept her eyes open and watched his familiar face as he slid into her, watched his face, smiling faintly, until he came, and then she held him.

'You were my first, Willie. You know that?'

'Yah.'

'Siggy and me, we didn't do that.' Magde moved away from Billy-

Ray, lit a cigarette, balanced the ashtray on her stomach. 'Funny, I still think about him, y'know? After all this time. Still think about him now and then. Must be near twenty years.'

'Twenty-two.'

'Shoot, that long? Guess you must think about him too?'

Billy-Ray told her he thought of his brothers every day, told her about the desecration of their room at the farm; but he did not tell her about their ghosts, waterlogged and bloody, which had drawn him back to the farm; did not tell her about his June morning prayer. Nuggets of lives, sanded down and burnished.

Roman Bialkowski was hauling a load of steel over to Seattle, following the same route via Butte and Spokane as the young Billy-Ray had. He was due to be gone for eight days, coming home via Salt Lake City with generators as freight, to light the lives of the polygamous men in the mountains. For six days Billy-Ray drove out to the single-storey block house, with its rotting window frames, bikes lying discarded in the yard, rusted basketball hoop dangling from the garage wall. For six days he knocked and then stepped into the clean but shabby kitchen, the smell of meatloaf and milk hanging in every corner, and Magde would be waiting for him. Six mornings he visited his father, who each day grew bloodier, his skin molecule-thin, weeping sanguine tears, and Billy-Ray knelt next to him, speaking occasionally, holding his father's hand as it wept, until a nun came to end the visit. Then Billy-Ray drove to Magde's and spent the afternoons in her bed, erasing the image of his father the best way he knew how. On the sixth day Magde arched her back, whimpered and came, turned away from him and rolled into a ball, crying.

'Never done that before,' she said eventually, turning into him, throwing an arm over his ribs. 'Read about it once somewhere. Thought it was lies, y'know? Like made up?' Magde watched Billy-Ray's eyes roaming over the polystyrene tiles pasted to the ceiling in an attempt to keep Minnesotan winters at bay. Thought of the tall blonde woman, Billy-Ray's wife, laughing against the backdrop of a mountain. Thought how even in a photograph you could tell the woman had class, that she'd speak properly and know how to eat in fancy places. Magde bit at a ragged nail. 'Willie, you think your wife – what's her name? Isobel? – you think Isobel's coming back?'

Billy-Ray nodded.

Magde touched his beard with her roughened fingertips. 'Sometimes I used to wonder what woulda happened if, y'know, if you'd never left. If you'd stayed here in Blue Earth County. Sometimes wondered if maybe you and me woulda got it together. I missed you when you went, you know that? I waited for you to write or something but you never did. You just left and it was like you rubbed us all out.' Magde moved away, rolled on to her back. 'Eighteen years. You could stay away for eighteen years and I ain't been out of Minnesota more'n a week in all that time. Went out to Seattle for a funeral, maybe six years ago. Y'know, I spent that week looking for you? Went to the funeral and then spent the time looking for you. Not like a detective or anything, just looking at everyone on the streets. Holding hands with Roman and looking for you. Eighteen years.' Magde pulled again at the tearing nail. 'I loved you, Willie. You know that? I always loved you. Thought of you every day for eighteen years. I loved Siggy and then I loved you and then you left. And I married Roman.' Magde fell silent and the sound of the bedside clock ticking marked time. She looked at the man lying beside her. 'You're going to go away again, aren't you? You're going to wait for Mr Reichmann to die and then you'll go away and it might be another eighteen years before you come back. I'll be think-ing about you, Willie. When you go, when you leave, when you're gone, I'll still be thinking about you.'

Billy-Ray wasn't listening; he heard Magde but he wasn't listen-ing. He didn't want this, this burden of love. A barn, a harness, the smell of wax. *I don't think it's that. I think it's maybe that I got all I want anyway. And I know it's wrong.* The fear of being found out.

'It don't matter, Willie.' Magde's hand slipped down Billy-Ray's stomach. 'Don't worry, this don't matter. Want to know why? Because you were my first. Because I know I was your first. I was there before Isobel, so it don't matter. It's not like it's something new or anything. And it's not like I'll be telling anyone. Who'm I gonna tell? Roman? Guess things will just go back to how they were.' Magde imagined the run of her days, the run of another eighteen years sitting opposite Roman Bialkowski, watching him as he ate in his undershirt, bulbous forearms flexing as he wielded his fork. Her hand slid down Billy-Ray's body, came to rest on the scar on his thigh. 'I remember when you got that, Willie. Something to do with a hog. I remember Siggy was so upset. Poor Siggy. Poor, poor Siggy.' And Magde began to cry again as Billy-Ray slipped from the bed and dressed.

Billy-Ray shucked on his jacket, which he had left in the kitchen, and looked around the room. He considered leaving Magde some money, some money to plant out the yard, buy some new drapes, get a new icebox. Anything. But he knew he shouldn't; it might be misunderstood. Before he walked out the screen door for the last time he paused in front of a picture hanging on the wall by the window. Three boys, standing awkwardly, russet hair lit by Fall sun, half smiling for the camera, unaware of how much faith they might eventually need.

On the seventh day, Oliver Reichmann died. It was 5.36 in the morning and a sister was praying at his bedside, asking God to forgive yet another sinner. What might Oliver's sins have been? To have worked too hard? To have planned too much? To have loved too much? But how was the sister to know about these saving graces? So she prayed until the blood stopped flowing and Oliver's ribs, standing proud of his skin, shuddered to a halt. She closed the damaged tissues of his eyelids as best she could, stood up, knees creaking, and wiped the blood from her hands. And then she called Karl Munchssen because there was no phone out on the farm.

Oliver Reichmann's funeral took place in late April 1964, in the graveyard of the church he had helped to build. He was sixty-four years old, yet looked eighty-four. The years of exile, hog-rearing and despair had taken their toll on his tall frame. Forty-five years before, he had arrived at Ellis Island, searching for the American dream, and, for a while, for a few stunning, iridescent years, he had held it in his hands. His life had been lived in three acts – as brooding, fearful adolescent, as proud husband and father, and as lonely, vodka-bitten drunk. Billy-Ray stood by the grave, well wrapped and gloved against the serrated edge of a wind howling uninterrupted from the Yukon; Karl and Greta were the only other people there, the only people Billy-Ray had asked. Three people, one mourner for each life-act. Greta, her nose crimson against black crêpe, snivelled endlessly as Billy-Ray ignored Father Ambrose intoning at the graveside.

Overhead a bald eagle hovered, cruising the thermals rising from the land of a thousand lakes, and Billy-Ray watched the raptor, his hands bunched in his pockets, head thrown back. The eagle cruised over the glaciated land, the faux ailerons of its wingtips twitching, almost spinning, the wedge tail tipping to keep it on course. The bird spiralled slowly, losing height, until Billy-Ray could clearly see the unblinking, metalled eyes watching him. He saw himself spinning, laughing, on the deck of *Viveka*, arms akimbo, laughing because he loved the blue earth all around him, as Urban looked on. Urban – the father he had come to wish for. The eagle dropped suddenly behind a stand of poplars and Billy-Ray looked back to the gash in the ground. He tried to concentrate, tried to think of his father, to remember Oliver as he had been when Willie was a boy. But Billy-Ray couldn't concentrate. All he could remember was a long-lost afternoon when he was young and he and Oliver had been out in the sties, both ankle deep in muck on a broiling August day. Oliver had been bent over a trough, emptying a swill bucket.

'Know something, Willie? People think hogs are dirty, dull beasts.'

Willie, who was shovelling muck into a barrow, stopped and leaned on the spade.

Oliver wiped his forehead, leaving a green smear of rotted beans. 'But pigs are smart. You look at 'em and you can see that. Plus they're quick, they can move faster than you or me. And they can eat damn near anything. They give us leather and bristles so we can make things, and they give us meat and lard so we can eat. Always seemed to me we should be grateful to 'em. Must be hundreds of millions of them all over the earth.' Oliver stood, stretched, rubbed his back. 'Ever wondered how they got here? Got to America?'

Willie shrugged and shook his head.

'Well, one thing they can't do is swim – or maybe they could learn if they wanted to. Anyway, they came by boat, all the way from Europe. A man called Columbus brought them. Ever heard of Columbus? In history class?'

Again Willie shook his head.

'You will, Willie. He brought the pig over here.' Oliver picked up the next bucket, brimming with rot. 'There's one other thing they can't do. Any idea what that might be?' Oliver's blue-eyed, tanned face turned to his son.

'Nah. Play hockey maybe?'

Oliver smiled. 'Reckon they could even learn to do that. The only thing pigs can't do is look at the sky. They can live for years, but they never see the sky. How 'bout that?'

Willie looked away from his father and up at the wisps of mares' tails and the faint full moon, almost invisible against a bright sky.

Years later, Billy-Ray looked down at his father's coffin being lowered into the earth Oliver had once loved. He bent down and threw a handful of the rich till soil into the pit as Greta began to weep noisily. Within minutes, evidence of Oliver Reichmann having existed was covered as the wind sawed at living flesh. Karl touched Billy-Ray on the arm.

'It's too cold for Greta. I'm taking her back.'

Billy-Ray nodded. 'I'll see you there.'

Father Ambrose walked over, laid his hand on Billy-Ray's shoulder. 'I'm sorry, Willie. I shall pray for your father. We're having mass for him tomorrow, perhaps you'd like to come?'

'I don't think so.'

'That's a shame, Willie. That's a shame. I know it's difficult to believe at times like this but you will find the Church is a great comfort.'

Billy-Ray looked at the priest, remembered him running from the church as Irochka shot away the stained glass. Remembered how the priest crept into the farmhouse whenever Oliver was working the fields to work his pietistic magic on the bereft woman who had been his mother. Remembered what Karl had said – that when his mother had gone the lights went out for Oliver; that the Church had sucked the love from her, so deeply that she had none left for her husband. Billy-Ray brushed the priest's white, soft hand away, fought the desire to punch the pale, smooth face.

Father Ambrose compressed his full lips. 'Come and see me, Willie. We ought to talk.' And he walked away, black cape swirling in the wind.

For half an hour Billy-Ray stood shivering by the graves of his family, trying to concentrate and failing. Inconsequential snatches of conversation, unremarkable afternoons spent playing dodge ball, trivial arguments over breakfast, the memory of a torn sweater, a lost hockey stick – these were all that came into his mind. He strained to think dignified, noble thoughts but they eluded him. Billy-Ray didn't realize then, that afternoon, that these memories of bickering and borrowing, searching for lost balls in prairie grass, were the woof and weft of life. That the picture of his father looking sad because his pigs would never see the sky was, perhaps, the way that Oliver would have wanted to be remembered. Billy-Ray did eventually realize this but on that icy, cloudless day he didn't.

As he walked past the ugly building that was now the Church of St Teresa, Billy-Ray glanced up and saw the eagle, empty clawed, maddened eyes scanning, rise on yet another thermal. A swivel of the head, a lurch of the body and the predator tipped away behind the trees, preying.

There were many people at Karl's diner Billy-Ray recognized: farmers and their wives who had driven in from outlying farms, storekeepers from Mankato, Skyline, Lehillier. Greta and Karl had cooked up a feast, had taken the time to ask their Polish friends for recipes that Oliver might have eaten. And so when Billy-Ray pushed open the diner's door it was to encounter a crowd of seamed faces and the long-forgotten smells of *barszcz, galareta z nozek, wieprzowina z grochami lub fasolami* and *placki kartoflane,* as well as the heavy yeast of wheat beer and the metallic scent of vodka. After all, it was a private party, a wake, for Oliver Reichmann. Silence fell as Billy-Ray closed the door, which jangled, and then the crowd eddied around him, swallowing him. He was given a glass of beer as men's arms wrapped around his shoulders and women hugged him. Lined faces, wrecked by sun and cold, wind and time – much like Blue Earth County itself – acquired names and histories as Billy-Ray drank. Kurt Mettler was there, lamenting the sale of his bar; Leif Matthiessen boasted of his yields, reminding Billy-Ray how he had advised Oliver over the years; Rutger Kahn told stories of the times he and Oliver had held drinking competitions at the beer festivals in Mankato. Their wives sat at tables, sipping at the vodka, remembering the building of the old church and the weddings and funerals that the old wooden building had seen. As evening approached, some women began to cry, rocking slightly over the wet tables, pulling their hand-embroidered shawls closer. Their men, flushed and garrulous, began to shout a little, arguing over baseball teams, the next ice race, the finest feed mixes for Landrace.

Billy-Ray leaned on the bar, vodka heating his blood, listening to the sounds of the old countries, the strangled, slurred vowels of languages he had nearly forgotten he knew, the words now like hurdles to be cleared. As night deepened on the street and neon flared, the door jangled once more and he looked up to see Roman and Magde. The former hockey player's shoulders were snug in a dark blue suit and Magde, dressed in a cheap, shiny polyester skirt and black sweater, followed two steps behind her husband as he pushed across the room to Billy-Ray. Billy-Ray stiffened, stood as tall as he could, wishing he had drunk less. But Roman, whose wife Billy-Ray had relieved of her virginity, whose wife Billy-Ray had spent the past week balling, held out one hand, put the other on Billy-Ray's shoulder.

'Willie, maybe you don't remember me – Roman Bialkowski. I was in the hockey team in high school with Deet. Wanted to come and pay my last respects to your father. I remember him quite well. He sometimes gave me a lift after a game.' Roman turned to Magde, pulled her forward by her elbow. 'But, really, it was Magde who wanted to come. Remember Magde? She dated Siggy. You must remember her?'

Billy-Ray and Magde looked at each other, looked away, before engaging in a pantomime of having met again for the first time in eighteen years. Over Magde's shoulder Billy-Ray could see the long, sour face of Wojciek Jancker watching them. Roman propelled Magde towards the food and Wojciek Jancker drifted over to Billy-Ray, propped himself at the bar on pointed, callused elbows.

'So, Willie, how you doing?'

'Fine, Mr Jancker. Just fine.'

'So you do remember me. Think you'll stay round here?'

'Nah – I'm headed back home.'

Wojciek glanced at Magde, back at Billy-Ray. 'Reckon that's a good idea, Willie. Not much for you here. Or maybe too much.' He took a swig of cloudy beer. 'Hear you're doing good.'

'Not bad.'

'Ever think you might have sent some of that good fortune to your father?' Wojciek's eyes, set like slate in an origami arrangement of skin, slid sideways to challenge Billy-Ray.

'No.'

Wojciek turned his hand in a bowl of beer nuts, cradled them as he threw one after another into his thin-cheeked mouth. 'Ain't my business, I guess. But I just wanted you to know before you go back to the Yukon or Siberia, or wherever it is you're fucking up, that you'll hear a lot of shit from guys like Leif about how much help they had to give your pa.' Wojciek smiled a smile like a paper cut. 'S all bullshit. Oliver was the best hog man in Minnesota. Could really have done things if he'd had some backing.'

Billy-Ray drank his vodka, poured another.

'Reckon you think he was a drunk, a piece of shit. Well, he weren't. He was a good man. A man can't help what happens. Sometimes too much happens. That's all. Too much happens.' Wojciek Jancker, who had intended to deliver feed pellets to the Reichmann farm one day at noon more than two decades before, worked his mouth like putty. 'That morning, when the telegram came, I was driving out to your place. I left early because I wanted to get back and fix some joists and I weren't but quarter of a mile away. Saw dust kicking up from a car in the opposite direction and when I got close I saw the jeep turning up your track. I knew what was happening. What was gonna happen. I drove on, like I had somewhere to go. I drove on, jus' kept goin' like I had to be somewhere else. 'Bout five minutes later I stopped – musta been somewhere out on the Assumption Road. I stopped the truck and I jus' sat there. Know what, Willie?'

'What?'

'I sat there trying to work out which one it was. Never thought it'd be both.' Wojciek unscrewed a tin of Sköl, delicately picked out a peck of tobacco and jammed it by his gum, distorting his lips. 'Still owe you three bags of pellets.'

'Forget it.'

'I have.' Wojciek closed the tin, slipped it back in his vest pocket. 'Go home, Willie. Take your new ideas about how folks treat each other back to wherever you came from.'

Wojciek Jancker walked away, felt hat flapping at his hips.

Billy-Ray left Bow Regard two days later, having arranged for the farmer from Norseland to buy the farm at eighty per cent of the asking price. He gave Karl and Greta Munchssen a cheque for three thousand dollars, delivered a cheque for the same amount to St Peter's Hospice and mailed Magde Bialkowska a cheque for a thousand. He drove the rental back to Minneapolis and boarded a plane for Anchorage, the only mementoes of his return to Bow Regard five ageing, rain-spotted postcards in his jacket pocket. Those and the thought that his father's pigs never saw the sky.

The moment Billy-Ray Rickman flew out of Minnesota marked the end of Oliver and Irochka Reichmann's dreams of a dynasty. Billy-Ray never went back to Blue Earth County and neither did any of his family. No Reichmann ever set foot in the state again. All those genes, carried from the foothills of the Silesian mountains, from the fertile valleys of the Bobr and the Nysa, carried so carefully in the bodies of two emigrés, unique dual spirochetes spiralling in their blood – and for what? To fade away, to die out. The robust helix of a woman who could shoulder a rifle and take on the papal bull; the imagination of a man who believed he could flip a six-hundred-pound corpse and did, a man who believed the world could not eat oil and who was right – both of them gone. Four unremarkable graves standing by a small cinder-block church were all that was left of the Reichmanns of Minnesota as Billy-Ray cruised at twenty-five thousand feet, genetic memories of Siggy and Deet travelling with him, travelling in him.

THE RICKMANS

Isobel Rickman always thought Juneau was a strangely thin town, hemmed in by mountains and glaciers on the east side, squeezed by the blue waters of Gastineau Channel on the west. It was as if the town had sucked in its stomach and stretched out along a narrow north–south shelf. The houses and streets clambered up the foothills on the eastern side, clinging on to scree and moraine, two, three, four storeys high, as if straining towards light. Some streets were nothing more than wooden stairways, leading up steep inclines to more houses, lined with Victorian mansions ageing, shifting and resting their shoulders against flimsy salt frame houses, slithering towards the ocean despite themselves. Outlandish, ponderous buildings rising up in acknowledgement of the town's status as Alaskan capital. A lunatic settlement, teetering on the edge of a watery abyss, shaken by cataclysms, pounded by storms, digging its imported heels into the frozen slush so as not to slip into Gastineau Channel. A madhouse birthed by a mother lode. But when the sun arced high over the mountains, lighting the glaciers, the choppy waters of the Channel below and the dark green stands of spruce and sitkas rising to the treeline as the pastel-painted clapboard houses glowed, zigzagging along contours, it reminded Isobel a little of Dartmouth in Devon. She thought the town was beautiful.

When Isobel arrived at their new house, on Sitka Street, built in 1877 and practically Neolithic by Alaskan standards, she found a truck full of furniture parked precariously, precipitously in the street below, a group of Native Americans sitting nearby, smoking, staring into space. Isobel stepped out of the cab and the Natives looked over at her with interest flaring in their eyes. They'd never seen a woman so tall, so blonde, so *Aryan*. A man dressed in a three-piece

suit and garish tie stepped out of the house as Isobel climbed the
steps to the front door.

'Hey there. How you doing, Mrs Rickman? Been expecting you.
Just came along to see that everything is OK.'

'Good morning, Mr Haines.' Isobel's hand swallowed his.

'Good flight?'

'A little bumpy over the mountains.'

'Still – you're seeing the place at its best – seventy degrees today,
they say.'

Isobel smiled and stepped past the realtor, spent half an hour
looking around the house, bare now, floorboards varnished and
swept, walls blank. Alan Haines followed her, a little awed, as
always, by her silence, her composure. Isobel stopped by the dormer
window under the eaves, looked out over the islands, down at the
town below, aware all the time of the mass of rock and ice hundreds
of feet thick punching against the back of the house, aware of the
tongue of liquid ice moving behind her, and she smiled.

Isobel walked back down the stairs and began to direct the
Natives, taking the gang leader around and showing him where she
wanted the furniture placed. The Native man, whose name was
Charlie Red-Wing, said little, merely nodding as she spoke and yet
she knew that he was taking it all in. Once the truck began to empty,
Mr Haines shook her hand and invited her to step into the office
later, 'to sign a few papers so everything can be wrapped up'.

Thekla Willoughby, neighbour to the house in Sitka Street, looked
out of her window, saw the commotion next door, saw the woman
directing the flow of crates and chairs and practically fell in love.
Thekla admired any woman who weighed less than two hundred
and fifty pounds; she simply didn't see how it was possible. Given
that Isobel weighed a mere hundred and fifty at six feet tall (one
hundred and fifty-four in winter) Thekla admired Isobel hugely. But
then she did everything hugely – how could she do otherwise? For
no matter what Thekla did (or so she claimed), she could *not* break
through the two-hundred-and-fifty-two pound barrier. As Isobel
took possession of the house on Sitka Street, Thekla waddled over,
eyeing up the crates being humped up the steps by the Native
Americans.

'Well, hi there!' Thekla exclaimed, holding out a pale, plump hand. 'Thekla Willoughby's the name. Live right next door and I am *so* pleased to meet y'all.'

Isobel shielded her eyes against the sun, which was still so high in the sky it seemed to be spinning away from the earth. She also shielded her eyes against the glare of the pink housecoat straining against Thekla's girth. 'Good afternoon. Isobel Rickman,' said Isobel, shaking the proffered hand.

'Why!' Thekla near-screamed. 'I do believe you're Scottish!'

'No, actually I'm English,' said Isobel.

'We-ell, not so far out, was I? Now, can I getcha a cup o' coffee? Why don't you come in and sit a while and let these folks get on with whatever they're doing?' Thekla was nearly quivering with hospitality and Isobel took a step back.

'Um, I . . . I have to stay here to keep an eye on Tufty. She's asleep in the taxi.'

'Tufty? Tufty? Is that your dawg, honey? You can bring him too. We can always chain him up outside – got a spike in the yard just for it.'

Isobel smiled. 'Tufty is my daughter.'

'Tufty?' Thekla's quivering died down and she frowned. 'Tufty? How d'you spell that, honey?'

'T . . . U . . . F . . . Look, her name's not really Tufty. She's called Frances but everyone calls her Tufty.' Isobel looked around, searching for respite. She could barely understand this woman – Thekla Willoughby had an accent so thick you could carve it up with a spoon and still it wouldn't make any sense.

Thekla folded her vast arms, bunching nodules of fat under her hands, stood back and eyed Isobel up and down. 'How much d'you weigh, honey?'

It was Isobel's ingrained good manners (and her desire for a hot drink) which drove her into Thekla's house, where she found herself perched on the edge of a none-too-clean sofa, the still-sleeping Tufty shifting next to her.

Thekla lowered herself into an armchair opposite, sighing heavily as she settled, then smiling brightly. 'Mind if I smoke, honey?'

'Good Lord, no, of course not. I occasionally smoke myself.'

Thekla laughed and slapped the arm of the chair, which sent up a puff of dust. 'Never thought I'd hear anyone say that! "Good Lord" – ain't that something!'

Isobel smiled weakly, sipped the coffee and paled, imagining the soft tissue of her throat being stripped.

'So,' Thekla heaved herself forward a little, 'I heard that an American had bought the house. Someone from . . . shoot, now where was it? New England somewhere, I think.'

'Well, my husband is originally from Minnesota. So yes, he's American.'

'And you're from England?'

'Yes.'

Thekla raised her eyebrows, waiting for further information that would surely follow. Isobel sat silently, rocking Tufty.

'I'm from Virginia myself, but I been here near seven years now. Can't imagine I'll ever go back.' Thekla lit the cigarette she'd been holding between finger and thumb. 'Say – you OK with that coffee? Maybe you'd prefer something else? Some bourbon maybe? Or a beer? I got a few six-packs cooling.'

'Not for me, thank you. But please, you go ahead.'

'Maybe later. Hey, your husband must be pulling it down to buy up next door – it's been waiting for a while they was asking so much for it.'

'He's in the oil business.'

Thekla suddenly gawped like a goldfish and expelled a perfect smoke ring. 'Who ain't in the oil business here, honey? What's he do?'

'He's with Karbo Inc. He's a geophysicist but he also has executive responsibilities.'

Thekla's eyes – which were surprisingly large and luminous, if set in pudgy cheeks – narrowed. 'Executive? What, like travelling around and stuff?'

'Yes, he does travel a great deal. Sometimes he can be gone for months.'

'That can't be easy, what with Tufty and all.'

Isobel smiled as she looked at Tufty sleeping, reached out and brushed the black hair out of Tufty's eyes. 'Tufty's nearly four now. I like looking after her, we have fun together.'

Thekla turned awkwardly in the chair and stubbed out her cigarette, thinking 'looking after her'? Strange way of putting it, but Isobel was English so maybe that was it. 'My husband works in the business too – on the fields. He's a BOP man – y'know, blow-out prevention. One of the reasons we came up here, well, the only reason really. Used to live out Texas way – near Houston – but he makes four times what he was making there. Land of plenty, honey. Land of plenty. They reckon there's lots more oil out there, so much it'll keep us all happy for the rest of our lives. They reckon we'll all have new trucks and trailers and floatplanes and houses in Florida . . . and . . . and . . .' Thekla's imagination failed her. She could think of no more delights that she might need to be happy. 'Yup – we can all have whatever we want, whenever we want it. When they find the rest of the oil. Maybe we'll even get a road outta here. Then perhaps the Injuns will leave here, go back to where they belong, 'stead of hanging round the streets, drinking all day.'

Isobel eyed Thekla, rocked Tufty. 'Might I have a cigarette?' she asked.

'Why, sure, honey. You help yourself.'

Isobel stood gracefully and crossed the room to the table next to Thekla, withdrew a cigarette and lit it. Thekla stared at Isobel's hands – they were enormous! Raw-knuckled and nearly as large as Fin's!

'My husband's name is Fin,' Thekla blurted out as a result of this realization.

'Fin?' asked Isobel as she sat back down, back ramrod straight.

'Yeah – his daddy was mad for fishing.'

'Oh, I see,' said Isobel, who didn't.

'You were saying, your husband travels a lot?' Getting any information from this English woman was sure proving difficult.

'Well, he has been working out on North Slope a great deal, during the summer months. And out on the Middle Shoals when he's not up there. He also travels down the West Coast a lot. He's in San Diego at the moment.'

Thekla silently admired Isobel's slim waist. 'So where did y'all live?'

'We had a house in Anchorage. In fact we're keeping it, so that my husband has somewhere to stay when he's working up there.'

Thekla grimaced. 'Now I hope you don't mind me saying, honey, but that is one place I do *not* like. Flat and ugly, I always think. Sometimes fly up there for shopping – you know, Christmas maybe. I mean, it's OK for that, but I couldn't live there. It's getting to be like a real city, y'know? Like Outside?'

'It's not very attractive, certainly.' Isobel stubbed out the cigarette, put down her mug of barely tasted coffee.

'Well, you're in Juneau now, honey, and I can tell you it's beautiful round here and there's a whole lot of stuff going on – oh yeah, you won't get bored in Juneau. No sir. There's salmon drives, a beer festival, parades, tub racing, bake-outs – we got it all here. We got it all. We even got a game of bare-skin football on Founding Day, in November. That is, the men play and we watch. Mind you, it's so damn cold there ain't that much to see, 'f you get my meaning.'

Isobel was glassy eyed as she looked at the bulk of Thekla Willoughby, lounging in a puce housecoat, rubbing at the ash garlanding her breasts. Isobel thought of the gymkhana, the dog shows and summer fêtes of Stow-on-the-Wold – organized and patronized by the fully dressed.

'Here I am, talking away and I haven't even asked your husband's name. I do apologize.' Thekla raised her thin, over-plucked eyebrows.

'Wilhelm-Rajmund.'

'Well, ain't that just so *European*? Wilhelm-Rajmund.' Thekla rolled the name around her mouth like a walnut, breaking it into fragments. 'Wil-helm Raj-mund.'

'Actually, no one calls him that. Everyone calls him Billy-Ray. I usually call him BR.'

Did everyone in England do this? Thekla wondered, as Tufty twisted and began to stretch and yawn. Did everyone give a person a name and then go right ahead and call them something else? Nuts. That's what it was – nuts. Made you wonder what Isobel called herself.

What Isobel called herself was confused most of the time.

Tufty's bedroom in the house on Sitka Street in Juneau was on the top floor, reached by climbing sixty-four uneven, sloping steps, up through six turns of the palm-smoothed banister rail to the fourth floor. Her dormer window, set beneath a steep-pitched gable, was high enough to clear the houses around, and if Tufty pulled over a chair and stood on it, her hands pressed to the glass, nose flattened, straining on tiptoe, she could watch the ferries and cruise ships easing through Gastineau Channel. This view was framed at the apex by gables carved with curving fish and swoop-winged birds. Billy-Ray had spent a weekend painting the room before Tufty moved in, and he had chosen to decorate the first (but certainly not the last) room his daughter could call her own in washed shades of pale blue and green; the wardrobe, desk, chair and bed he stripped of varnish and painted in shades of grey, silver and pale ivory. Billy-Ray was, of course, recreating the room he had been given years before in the Svenssons' house in Ballard, where he had slept dreaming of the Wave. Isobel bought a native-woven quilt for the bed and this length of fabric, made vibrant by cross-hatched diamonds of red and ochre, always annoyed Billy-Ray; it disturbed the sense of being under water. At the first hint that it was warm enough, when summer began to threaten, Billy-Ray would climb the stairs and pull the quilt off the bed, fold it and jam it in the cupboard on the landing, before carefully rearranging Tufty's teddies on the pillows. Tufty would come home from school, step into her room and feel she was swimming, feel she was floating. But she loved her room because it also gave her the sense of flying, she was so high above town. Mounting the endless stairs, she began to feel weightless, awash with possibilities, dreams and fantasies. When she lay on her bed and read, the only thing she could see through the dormer was sky and clouds. When it rained – which was often – she'd watch the glass as it wavered against low cloud. She also loved her room because it was private, it was hers. The only other room on the same floor, jammed beneath the gables, was empty, a bed that folded in three tipped on its side in the corner. Her parents rarely came all the way up the stairs to call her, standing instead on the landing two floors below, yelling, and so she thought of the top floor, with its sloping ceilings, watery walls, sky and clouds, fish, bears and birds, as her own private realm.

Franklin Elementary School was two blocks from Glacier Avenue, out towards Auk Bay, an ugly, square, single-storey building, seemingly unaware of the grandeur of the land on which it was set. The first time she saw it, Tufty was reminded of Anchorage. She didn't often think of Anchorage, partly because she'd been so young when they left but mainly because her last memories of it were terrifying. Trees cracking, her mother crying as she stumbled about, holding Tufty too tight, falling over and over again, the garage splitting in half and falling in with a roar, crushing the plane. Glass flying everywhere as her mother's bones snapped. So Tufty pushed all of that to the back of her mind and thought of Juneau as her first real home.

The first day Tufty went to Franklin Elementary, when she was five, dressed in a new, scratchy dark blue sweater and jeans, brand-new school bag hanging on her shoulder, her mother dropped her at the school gate and dragged huge fingers through Tufty's hair before kissing her and gently pushing her inside.

'I'll pick you up this afternoon, honey. Enjoy yourself, OK?'

Tufty might have enjoyed it, might have joined in the play at lunchtime, enjoyed the sensation of eating a lunch she had chosen herself at recess, might have made a friend that very afternoon. As it was, when Isobel fetched her, she found her daughter standing alone as gaggles of other kids screamed at each other and waved to their parents. Tufty clambered into the car and sat staring ahead, made mute by embarrassment. Isobel said nothing, knew that Tufty would tell her story when she wanted to, when she needed to. It wasn't until the two of them were settled in the den – a sloppy room, warmed by afternoon sun which shone in through a bay window in the afternoons for a few months, before it dropped too low to clear the mountains – drinking chocolate milk shakes and eating blueberry muffins, that Tufty set down her glass and announced that she no longer wanted to be called Tufty. As it turned out, her humiliation had started early in the day, at circle time, when the new kids were asked to say their name and tell the class a little about themselves. She had managed no more than 'My name is Tufty Rickman' when a couple of boys had snickered, setting off the rest. Tufty had battled on, splashing about in the puddle of giggles and laughter spreading at her conversational feet.

'But, Mom, there were other kids with weirder names. There's one called Petal and . . . and . . . one called Rainbow. There's even one called Minto.'

'Hmm,' said Isobel, 'they *are* strange names. But I don't see what's wrong with Tufty.'

'I don't want to be called that any more,' said Tufty after a moment's silence. 'It's a silly name.'

Isobel looked at her daughter, noticed the set of her jaw. 'So what would you like to be called?'

'I've been thinking – I don't like Frances.'

'Well, that is your name, sweetheart.'

'I want to be called Frankie.'

Isobel pursed her lips, then nodded. 'OK, whatever you want. Can *I* still call you Tufty?'

'No!'

'OK – but don't blame me if I make a mistake every now and then. And don't think, just because you change your name, that you don't have to tidy up Tufty's room.'

'Who's Tufty?' Frankie giggled and grabbed another muffin.

Thekla Willoughby was even larger than she had been when the Rickmans had first moved to the house on Sitka Street. She had given up any pretence of dieting and now wolfed down doughnuts, Twinkies, Charleston Chews, peanut butter and jelly sandwiches, bowls of Buc Wheat and milk, whenever the mood took her. Thekla rarely bothered to get dressed, preferring to lounge around in house-coat and mules, the sides of which she had cut, to accommodate her corn-bulging feet. She sat in the Lazee Boy when Fin was out on the rigs, reading the *Enquirer* or the *Reader's Digest*, a cigarette dangling from her lips, economy-size bag of Frito's chips on the table beside her. Isobel thought it sad that Thekla did so little, that she wafted through her days, consuming, smoking and gossiping on the telephone, but she thought her heart – which must be labouring mightily – was in the right place. Occasionally Thekla slipped out of her housecoat and put on a vast pair of Levi's and a T-shirt of Fin's, with a faded logo of the Crimson Bears wildly distorted by the breasts beneath, and she'd drive to the mall to get the groceries. Returning from a shopping trip one day, Thekla saw the neighbour's girl shooting hoops on her own, making most of them too.

'Hey there, Frankie! How you doin'?' Thekla hefted a crate of

Boston Beans out of the car and headed for the garage, sweat trickling down her spine.

Frankie abandoned her game, wandered over to stand by the fence between the houses. 'I'm very well, thank you. How are you?'

'Well, Frankie, barrin' the fact my back's in a twist from all this, I'm jus' fine.'

'Mrs Willoughby, can I ask you something?'

''Course you can, darlin'.' Thekla crammed two cartons of Winstons into a paper bag already packed with Wonderloaf. Set the bag on the drive and wiped her forehead.

Frankie pushed her long, black bangs out of her eyes. 'When's Charlie coming next, Mrs Willoughby?'

Thekla straightened her back. 'Coming here Thursday, or should be. I called him out to fix some bad pipes out back before the rain sets in. But you jus' don' know with the Injuns. Maybe he comes, maybe he doesn't.'

'If he does come, is it OK if I come round and talk to him?'

'Sure you can – jus' don' put him off working. Don't take much at the best of times. I'll make sure to let y'all know if he's here.'

'Thank you, Mrs Willoughby. Goodbye.'

Thekla watched Frankie walk away, jeans low on her hips, sneakers scuffing the grass as she bounced the basketball, moving it around her feet. She was an odd one, no doubt about it. Stood out in the crowds of kids around town, mainly because of her height – why, she must be more than five feet tall and only seven years old. But it weren't just that. The way she spoke, the way she held herself, was different from other kids, like she was older or something. Thekla sighed and reached for the paper bag of bread and tobacco which would get her through the next week.

Frankie pulled open the screen door, pushed the kitchen door open with her foot, and went to find her mother. Isobel was typing in the study on an old Remington her father had given her when she left Cheltenham Ladies College, a machine as inefficient as it was beautiful.

'Bugger,' Isobel muttered as she noticed the word 'outrageous' had printed in red because the two-tone tape had snagged.

'You ain't allowed to say that,' said Frankie, slumping into a chair beside her mother.

'And you ain't allowed to say ain't.'

'Everybody else does.'

'That's no excuse, as you well know. There are people out there who spit in the street, people who scratch themselves where they shouldn't and swear and kill bears. That doesn't make it right.' There are even ladies who smoke in public, thought Isobel, and smiled.

'Minto picks his nose in class.'

'There we are, exactly the sort of thing I mean. Just because he does that doesn't make it right.'

'But Minto picking his nose doesn't make you saying "bugger" right either.'

Isobel looked at her daughter, who was grinning. 'Right, young lady, let's make an agreement that neither of us say "ain't" or "bugger".' She held out her hand and the two of them shook.

'What you doing, anyway?' asked Frankie, flicking the edge of a stash of papers, making the corner whirr and blur.

'I'm writing a letter.'

'You're always writing letters.'

'That's because I have a lot of letters to write.' Isobel managed to straighten the tape and pull it taut. She banged the return key and the platen jumped and jammed. She hit the key again and the platen lurched right. Looking at the letter, she decided that it was right for the single word to be red, to leap out and scratch at the reader's eyes.

'Charlie's coming over to Mrs Willoughby's Thursday. She says I can go talk with him.'

'Talk *to* him.' Isobel looked at the notes she had at her elbow, frowned and turned back to the keyboard.

Frankie's heels were banging on a strut of the chair, rubber making irregular smacking sounds. 'When's Dad home?'

'Next Tuesday.'

'Does that mean we can have waffles for breakfast?'

'You can have waffles whenever you like.'

'With syrup and bacon?'

'No.'

Isobel began to type, pecking uncertainly at the round keypads, wishing she had paid more attention during the commerce classes at Frontin-sur-Mont.

'Minto said yesterday you had big hands.'

'Well, at least he's observant.' Hands? She was all thumbs, all thick, bulbous thumbs, murderous digits fumbling over the keys.

Frankie pulled an odd-looking book towards her, printed on rough paper, a poorly drawn picture of a totem pole on its cover. Opening it, she found a dull list of the titles of other books, dates and endless numbers.

'I don't see how you can read these, they don't make sense.'

'They do make sense. They're not stories, they're facts.'

'Charlie tells good stories. What're these all about, anyway?' Frankie flicked through the pages.

Isobel glanced at the book. 'That's a list of land claims and the laws about them.'

'*Bor*-ing.'

'Maybe.'

'Who d'you write your letters to?'

'The government in Washington.'

'Do they write back?'

'Sometimes.'

'What do they say?'

'Not enough.'

'Is that why you go to all your meetings?'

'Yes.'

'I don't get why you do it. Why you write letters and all.'

'Because I mind about what's happening to the Native Americans. Because I think things should change.'

'But why do you write letters? Especially if the government don't write back. Seems to me you—'

'Frankie – I'm trying to type. I can't type and talk. I can barely type and breathe.'

Frankie lobbed the book back on the table, causing a pile of papers to shift and slide in an untidy heap.

'Tufty—'

'*Mom!*'

'I apologize. Frankie, are you bored?'

'Yes.'

'What happens to wasted time?'

'It goes to jail.'

'Quite.'

'Can I watch TV? *Rawhide*'ll be on soon.'

'No, you may not. Not until six o'clock. I suggest you either go out and play or read your set books.'

'Oh, Mom, it's still Dick, Jane and Sally. The books are boring.'

Isobel silently agreed with this assessment. 'Well, go and play then.'

'Can I go get Minto? Bring him over here?'

'If you must.'

Frankie tried to push the papers back into a pile before snatching up the basketball and running out of the room.

Isobel had trouble typing a number of words and 'understand' was one of them. Looking at the letter she saw 'udnrestnad'. 'Bugger!' she roared, tearing the sheet out of the typewriter, tearing it in half.

1960

Maggie's trek back to the convent in Louisburgh was uneventful, yet she felt that she was unravelling with every passing mile. The car journey took her through a landscape made beautiful by sun, through small, tidy hamlets, verdant hills providing a backdrop. England, she decided, was beautiful, and she wished she weren't leaving it. The ferry sailed a calm, blue sea, the train that took her from Dublin to Castlebar ran on time; at the station she took a taxi, the fare supplied by Jacqueline. As she neared the convent, Maggie saw the wild outcrops that broke the heaving waters of Clew Bay, and she felt panic rising. Nothing had changed – there, in County Mayo, nothing had changed. The pinched faces of the people she passed, their shabby clothes, the meanness of the land itself; she had been gone from there for more than two and half years and the sight of the peat fields, the creeping moss, sparked the taste of bacon in her mouth, the stench of cabbage in her nostrils. When the taxi turned a corner and the crowns of the old oaks surrounding the convent broke the horizon, Maggie's gorge rose, and she asked the driver to stop. Standing at the roadside, bent double, her empty stomach heaving, Maggie nearly decided to run; as bile burned her throat, she considered the idea of taking her cardboard case from the back seat of the taxi and running. But where could she go? The house at Ballysod was not an option because Annie would take one look at her bulge, with her tiny, black eyes, and slam the door. Besides, it was only a few months and then she could go back, back to the empty, echoing spaces of Jarman House, back to her attic room. Maggie wiped a dab of acid drool from her mouth, smoothed her coat and climbed back into the car. As she waited by the tall wrought-iron gates, she stared at the serrated finials, wondering

whether anyone had ever managed to scale them, wondering if
anyone had ever managed to escape.

Being only five months pregnant when she arrived, Maggie was
reminded of the rules of obedience and silence (chastity no longer
being an option), told her duties and then put in a dormitory with
other girls. The room was long and narrow, furnished with twelve
hardback chairs and twelve iron beds, ten of which were occupied.
There was little unpacking for her to do: she pushed the case under
her bed, having taken out a towel and the snowstorm, which she put
on the chair by the bed. She had to attend mass each day, she ate two
meals, of soup and vegetables. Between these daily events she
mopped floors, dusted ancient wood, rubbed her back, and wished
the walls had windows. Over time, Maggie grew large, grew heavy,
not with guilt but with blood and life. She lay in her hard bed at night
and rubbed the hard mound of her belly, felt the navel bump, traced
the strange dark line, which reminded her of a tail, of the Devil's tail.
Maggie lay there listening to the whispers of the other girls, some of
whom did not know which of many boys might be the father, some of
whom did nothing but cry and pray. Maggie said nothing.

During the days, as Maggie trod the worn slate floors in her bare
feet, she caught glimpses of the vegetable garden, the unkempt
grounds, and she wished she could heft and bend, wished she could
be outside in the sun, cutting and pruning, clearing and setting fires.
These thoughts reminded her of her father. Maggie found it difficult
to think of Sean because when she did she felt shame. She had never
once written to him in all the time she was gone, and she had never
sent any money. About her pregnancy she felt no shame but these
omissions made her burn. Why hadn't she written? Because Sean
couldn't read and she didn't want Annie to know anything about her
life. And she certainly didn't want Annie to have any of the money
she'd earned. Maggie had never forgiven her judgemental mother for
sending her away. At night, when the others whispered and muttered, Maggie drifted away to her father's van, to the gardens of the
Whyte House, the kitchen table, where he would be sitting in his
shirtsleeves, spooning stew before rolling one of his tiny cigarettes.

*

That summer, as Maggie gestated, growing slower, sinking into a strange state of contentment, was hot and cloudless. Sometimes, when the long evenings were too close, when even the Mother Superior found it hard to breathe the stale, hot air, the Fallen were allowed to sit out on chairs in the shade of the oak trees. Then Maggie would lower herself with a sigh, hitch up her billowing cotton dress and stretch out her long legs in a fading sun patch. She'd sit and look at the railings with their harsh spikes and wish herself gone from there, dream of the time when her confinement would be over. Rubbing clove oil over her sore gums and rolling her swollen ankles, Maggie imagined the Bay of Blacksod, the cliffs of Achill Island, birds wheeling around it, peat bogs, clear rivers and the springy softness of sphagnum moss scattered across granite out-crops. As the temperature rose during the month of August and the nuns allowed the girls to sit out every evening, Maggie was sur-prised by a filament of understanding that eased its way into her thoughts and wound itself around her: she was home – *this* was her land, not the filthy streets of London, crowded with cars and people. No, this was home. She had come back and she would stay. Maggie sat every evening until the sun set, when she wrapped Jacqueline's cashmere cardigan, worn thin now, around her, and looked into the future, which no longer scared her, which did not push back. She would rent herself a small cottage and live there with her babby, growing vegetables, tending other people's gardens. Maybe it wouldn't be the same as living in a castle in Czechoslovakia but it would be hers. She reckoned her father would like that, would like to know that she came home and it was all right, it felt good. Maybe she'd have her own business? Maybe she'd get rich? Maybe, once it was over, when she was settled, she'd visit her father? Or invite him over to the cottage for a visit? Ah, well, there was plenty of time for that.

Maggie Regan, dreaming. Always dreaming.

1968

Billy-Ray made sure he was on board the Lockheed C-130 Hercules that flew from Fairbanks to an exploration camp near the Sagwon River in January 1966; Karbo Inc. was finally going to sink a well and he wanted to be there when the gusher blew. The Hercules made more than eighty flights over three weeks to transport the construction equipment, the rig and the men to erect it. The plane landed on a compacted gravel strip, the gravel gouged from the river bed of the Sagwon by huge Cats that lumbered across the frozen tundra, crushing it. From there the mess of metal and men was taken overland to Lucy, where they put together a strip of ice and snow for the fat-wheeled Hercules carrying the rig components to land on. For weeks the crews laboured to build the rig, in temperatures of fifty below. Each man, made sharp, made nearly mad by cold, focused on his task, bent to it, never looking around himself at the frozen, fog-bound land, never aware of the bedlam, the electric-light scatter of arc welding, sound waves rolling along the plains, echoing against the distant foothills. The drill bit was dropped in March, began to turn and draw up the tundra, ice and regolith, spewing it out in mounds. Deeper than thirteen thousand feet the bit travelled, but when it was withdrawn it revealed mere traces of oil. In December the rig was dismantled and the well abandoned, the Hercules returned and the camp melted away. But of course, it didn't melt away, not everything melted away. There, on Lucy's slopes, were scars that would never heal, wounds that would never fill.

A year passed before caribou once again heard the sound of Lockheed engines and screaming Cat tracks. This time Karbo moved the rig sixty miles north by Cat train to a place called Prudhoe Bay, a desolation, a place that God had indeed forsaken. The Arctic Sea, frozen in mid-lap, framed this vista where there was no solace to be found. Again Billy-Ray bent to his work, turning his back on the picture of an unmoving, white-blue earth, on the startling sheets of other-worldly lights of the aurora borealis, and this time he was rewarded when the drill started to turn and the tundra screamed. The team of well-site geologists he was working with analysed the rock samples and smiled. At eight thousand feet the bit tore through sandstone and conglomerates (mementoes of a distant time when a long, unbroken beach had lined a warm sea) and the mud-logging readings went off the scale. Again the scientists smiled and bent once more over their desks. After Christmas, a well-stem test was run, to show whether, when the mud pressure was released, gas and oil would flow into the well bore. Billy-Ray had watched this happen a hundred times – usually there was a puff of gas which was diverted to a flow pipe and burned off in moments. But this time when the gas blew, the flame roared like a fighter jet's after-burn, like an incandescence at Cape Canaveral. There, at the edge of the world, in a snow-filled wasteland which had hunkered down against the winter gales, a flame hundreds of feet high burned for fifteen hours, even when the pressure cap was reset. Again the scientists smiled as the orange light bathed their battered, bearded faces, and they indicated that the drilling should continue, through an oil column, through a mixture of oil and gas, to the reservoir they now knew was there.

On Billy-Ray's fortieth birthday, 12 March 1968, the oil began to flow, at a rate of more than a thousand barrels a day, accompanied by an alarming, horizontal oil flare. Later the same day America was told that it had been saved – there might be more than ten billion barrels underneath Prudhoe Bay on the North Slope in Alaska.

During the long, fractured flight back from the Lucy field, Billy-Ray dozed, or tried to, but it was difficult, what with the wind buffeting the plane, the roar of the engines, the yells of the rig workers, who were passing round bottles, drinking to their success. The Hercules dipped and soared all the way back to Anchorage. Billy-Ray eventually managed to slip into the tiny crawl space between fear and dreams, and once he was wedged there he plucked faces from the

darkness – James Dean, wildcatter, standing beneath a cascade of
crude, Isobel lying beneath Sophocles, unmoving, Irochka looking
up as she held a loaf of the miracle bread, Wojciek Jancker placing
his pointed elbows on a bar as delicately as a cat. The final descent
into Merrill Field was greeted by whoops from the other oil men,
whoops that woke Billy-Ray. He caught a cab to the house on
Campbell Lake, which looked boarded up, which almost *was*
boarded up, shutters closed on the triple-glazed windows and doors
double locked. Billy-Ray forced open the front door, which had
warped a little, and dumped his bags in the laundry room. Then he
stood for a moment, looking around the open-plan ground floor,
which always had the air of having just been abandoned, as if someone had been there a few moments before and had left suddenly.
Every time he came back from a shift Billy-Ray felt as if someone had
been in the house; half expected to find footprints, damp towels and
cigarette butts in the ashtrays. Crossing the lounge, he dug about in
the cabinet, grabbing a highball glass before going to the freezer and
pulling out a frosted bottle of Finlandia. He switched on the boiler
and heaters and sorted through his mail at the breakfast bar – birthday cards, bills, flyers and junk – half listening for footfalls, and
then went upstairs to the bathroom.

This was always a weird moment – when he stared at himself,
examined his face. For weeks he would barely have glanced in a
mirror, and the face that stared back always surprised him –
bearded, long haired, slightly more battered than the last time,
scored by Arctic winds. And each time, he looked less like Siggy; his
memory of his brother's image was fading. Billy-Ray put the bottle
and the glass on the shelf by the tub and shaved himself thoroughly
as the tub filled. Then he shucked off his clothes, filthy with oil,
lubricants and the curious, fine dust of the Arctic, and slid into the
hot water, sipping the vodka. He closed his eyes and, as always,
was surprised by silence. No sounds; no bedrock screaming, no
thunder of flame, no pistons rocking back and forth. Silence. The
house in Anchorage was empty. This emptiness still had the power
to annoy him, even now, years later.

Isobel had come back from England after the quake, when the
shocks had finished, when the house was fixed up and the garage

rebuilt, when he'd spent weekends mending the fences and levelling the yard, and she'd announced that she wanted to move, wanted to live in Juneau. That was their first argument, their first real argument, when for days they hadn't spoken, then for days Billy-Ray yelled as Isobel stood, arms folded, watching him. But Isobel won in the end, as Billy-Ray knew she would. Women like Isobel always won; he knew he'd never lost the twinge of awe he felt when he first spoke to her, had never shaken off the sense that she was in some way superior, that she was always right. Billy-Ray also knew there was another reason Isobel had won and they moved to Juneau. All the time they were arguing, even when they slept in different rooms, Billy-Ray wondered whether she could detect Magde's smell (vodka, Monterey Jack and Dr Pepper) on his skin. Sometimes, when Isobel looked at him in a certain way, Billy-Ray thought she'd sensed it. So he caved in and let them go, let Isobel and Tufty move to Sitka Street. Over time, their lives bedded down again – Tufty enrolled in school there and Billy-Ray kept the house in Anchorage as a base for when he was working. When he finished his shifts out in the field, once he'd reported back to the offices, he flew down to Juneau and joined them. But he still both resented and loved the silence of the Campbell Lake house when he was there alone. And he *was* there alone – Siggy and Deet didn't bother him any more, didn't move around the rooms covered in blood and sea water. He hadn't seen them for a long, long time.

Billy-Ray climbed out of the tub, towelled down and dressed in old jeans and a sweatshirt, sorted out his bags, throwing most of the clothes away, shoving the rest in the machine. Then he sat for a while, tried not to think of what he was about to do, pretended he might consider going to bed, catching an early night. He sat there savouring silence, trying to convince himself it was sufficient recompense for loneliness. But after a while, Billy-Ray – who had been twice forgiven, who had been once absolved, who should have known better – picked up the phone and called a woman he had met in a bar a few weeks before. A slim, dark-haired woman who reminded him of Jacqueline, who'd mentioned her husband was often out of town, a woman who had given him her number as she made a movement with her mouth which he hadn't seen but knew had happened.

*

On a windy, bitter day in 1969, the oil men gathered in the Sydney Lawrence Auditorium in Anchorage for what must have been the biggest bran-tub dip ever. The sealed envelopes were opened at eight in the morning and by 5.30 over four hundred thousand acres around Prudhoe Bay had been leased by ARCO, Karbo Inc., Shell, Humble and BP. Between them, these companies – rolling in more money than many countries around the world – had spent $900,040,000. Alaska was, for the first time, in the black. Alaska was rich. Thekla Willoughby whooped as she watched the news in her house on Sitka Street in Juneau. It was all going to happen now – the new boilers, the new 4 × 4, the condo in Florida, all the things that money could buy. Lucca Barzini, who was also in Juneau, frowned as Thekla danced hugely, hugging herself in joy; Lucca frowned and reached for the telephone.

Billy-Ray Rickman, who had once watched a well being bored in the farmland at Bow Regard, who as a nine-year-old boy had rubbed the loamy till earth between his fingers, who had dreamed of exploring the world, began, then, to help in its destruction. The oil gushed, staining the frozen blue earth, creating a vacuum beneath the earth's crust, into which rushed more oil and gas, filling thousands of storage tanks. The bran-tub game had gone well after all – Karbo had bid on the leases running south towards Lucy and indeed there was a vast reservoir under there; the fat and tissue of long-dead sea creatures had risen through shales and conglomerates until they reached the Ivishak formation and there they stopped dead, waiting for Billy-Ray and his bit to release them.

There was one problem, however – the oil was there, stockpiling at the edge of the world, but how were they going to get it to where it was needed, the Lower 48?

'So, we got to choose a project and I chose pigs.'

Billy-Ray looked at his daughter. 'Pigs?'

'Yeah.' Frankie went to the table to fetch her exercise book.

'Why d'you choose pigs?'

'I dunno. I like them.'

'You ever seen one?'

'No, but I've seen pictures of them and I saw a wild boar once in the zoo. But it died.' Frankie came back to the sofa where she'd been sitting with her father. 'Look, I did all the drawings. Mom took me to the library and I copied them.'

Billy-Ray watched his daughter talking, thinking how much she had changed even in a few months. Sometimes he wondered about this, about whether he should be around more. 'Hey, they're really good.'

'Listen, this is what I found out.' Frankie read aloud, her voice stiff and formal. '"In olden times people kept pigs in their gardens. Sometimes in the cities, like New York, pigs were in the street and bit people and ate children."' Frankie looked up at Billy-Ray and smiled. 'It said in the book that the pigs pooped on people too, but I didn't think I should put that in.'

'Good call.'

'"Pigs are very good at smelling things and tasting too. But they can't see very well. They eat garbage. They came to America from Europe and there are more of them than any other animal in the world. Pigs are related to the hippopotamus and the peccary. The only native American pig is the collared peccary."' Frankie sighed. 'I wish I'd chosen something else to do, 'cos I can't find out any more but I can't change now.'

'I might be able to help you out there.'

'How come?'

'When I was a boy I lived on a hog farm. I helped to raise them.'

'Urrrgh! You must have smelled some.'

Billy-Ray smiled. 'Guess I must have.'

Frankie smoothed the pictures she'd drawn. 'Could you help? It's due Thursday and I have to write at least a page.'

'We should be able to manage that.'

Frankie fetched a pencil and wrote down what her daddy remembered about pigs. That they came in three types: lard, meat or bacon. That they didn't have sweat glands, which is why they rolled around in mud – to cool down, not because they were dirty. That some people thought they were related to the Devil because of their curly tails. That young pigs could be called piglets, barrows or shoats. Billy-Ray also told her that pigs were smart, smarter than dogs, but there was one thing they couldn't do. 'Guess what that is.'

Frankie looked at what she had written down. 'I reckon I got enough for a page.'

'Aren't you going to even try to guess?' This mattered to Billy-Ray.

Frankie shrugged. 'Um . . . um. Well, they can't fly.'

Billy-Ray smiled. 'More than that, honey – they can't even look at the sky.'

But Frankie wasn't listening, she was writing things out in her rounded script, and her father watched her fingers working, watched her frown for a while.

'Hey,' Billy-Ray said, 'you know what? I think you should go get some chips, because I happen to know that *Batman's* on TV in about two minutes.'

Frankie leaped up and rushed into the kitchen, opening and slamming doors, then ran back, jumped on the sofa next to her father, tearing open the bag and spilling the chips. The television blared in the corner as the two of them scooped up the spill and crammed chips in their mouths.

'It's only five o'clock, BR. We don't watch television until six.' Isobel stood in the doorway, licking her thumb, trying to rub away a black ink stain. 'And we don't eat crisps so close to supper.'

'Crisps!' yelled Frankie. 'She said "crisps"!'

'Who's "she"? The cat's mother?'

Frankie howled, fell on the floor, doubled over. 'Yeah – you're the cat's mother!'

'Ah, come on, Isobel – you can bend the rules a little.'

Isobel hated this, hated the way Frankie behaved whenever Billy-Ray appeared. The two of them seemed almost to gang up against her, and Billy-Ray always undermined her in some way. She tried to be rational about this change in her daughter – it was reasonable that Frankie would be pleased to see Billy-Ray, that she would want to spend as much time with him as she could. Isobel knew she was associated with school runs, trips to the doctor's for jabs, visits to the orthodontist, reading and school work, whilst he, Billy-Ray, was all about camping and hiking, shooting hoops and organizing softball games, fishing, barbecues and TV. Sometimes Isobel wondered whether she was jealous, but she couldn't work out of whom. She gave up and left them to it, went back to the study and began to write again. That afternoon Charlie Red-Wing had told her that a canning company had bought up leases on the Alexander archipelago and the waste from the factory was polluting the waters. The fish were dying, Charlie said, and families were going hungry.

Later that evening, once Frankie was asleep, floating in her marine bedroom, Isobel went into the den, switched off the television and woke Billy-Ray, who was sprawled on the settee, arm over his eyes, sleeping.

Billy-Ray yawned. 'What time is it?'

'Half-past nine.'

'Shit, I been asleep for hours.' He stretched, moved away from Isobel, worried she might catch a strange woman's scent, which was fresh, which was only a day old.

'That's fine. You've been working hard for months, you deserve a rest.' Isobel gave him an envelope. 'Happy very belated birthday.'

'Hey – forgot I was owed a present.' Billy-Ray tore open the envelope, found three airline tickets, a voucher for car hire and a sheet of paper listing hotel reservations. 'California?'

'Yes. It's five years late but better late than never.'

'Wow – that's great. What're the dates?'

'Seventh of May until the fifteenth.'

'Shit – I can't do that.'

'Why not?'

'I'm working then.'

'Can't you change it?'

'Nah.'

'BR, it's weeks away. You could at least try.'

'You don't understand – you *never* understand this. I gotta be there, it's my job.' Billy-Ray had already arranged to spend a few days with his latest lover, whose absent husband had a cabin out Valdez way.

'You always say that. I know it's your job, I know that. But I really do think that it would be good for the three of us to go away together somewhere new. Somewhere different, out of state. As a family.'

Billy-Ray sat up, stood, shoved his shirt in his belt. 'Well, fuck it, you should've told me. Told me the dates.'

'It's a birthday present. It's supposed to be a surprise.' Isobel's voice was mild, deceptively mild. Her husband, who was attuned to the weather, accustomed to sudden changes in temperature, felt the temperature drop.

'I'm forty fucking years old, Isobel. I don't need surprises.' Billy-Ray hated this. He glared at Isobel, sitting on the edge of the sofa, looking composed, looking beautiful, looking not so very different from the woman who, years before, had shot her favourite hunter and then dressed for dinner at the Coopers'. Billy-Ray fell in love again, as he had done a million times, as he did every time he looked at her. 'I don't need this, Isobel, not now.'

Isobel stood in one movement, stared straight back at her husband. 'At least try to change your plans, BR. You owe us that.' And she walked out.

She was always so fucking reasonable, that's what got to him. Typical fucking response. He fetched a beer, switched the television back on, turning up the volume. Rowan and Martin exchanged snappy one-liners as he drank and belched, not listening. Later, after he had snoozed again, he woke with a start, thought someone was in the room with him, but he was alone. He began to climb the stairs and stopped, noticing the study light throwing shadows on the floor.

'Isobel? You still up?'

Billy-Ray looked in the room to see Isobel sitting at the desk, making notes on a yellow legal pad. He moved over to her, stood behind the chair. 'It's late.'

'I know.' Isobel turned and looked up at him, taking off her glasses.

'Hey – when did you get those?'

'Last month. I'm suffering a degree of long-sightedness apparently.'

'Oh. They look good.'

Isobel smiled. 'Maybe.'

He moved his hands, put one on her shoulder. 'I'm sorry.'

Billy-Ray Rickman, his face in the shadow of the lamp, apologizing, always apologizing, but not as often as he had in the past. Not in the same way and not for the same reason.

*

Sitting on a bench out the back of Thekla's place, Charlie took a piece of smooth, weathered pine from a pocket, reached in another for a knife and began to whittle. For once, the rain was not falling on Juneau; indeed, the sun was warm enough to remind him of his childhood, when, of course, the sun had always shone.

'Hi, Charlie.'

He looked up and saw the Rickman girl, standing by the fence, dressed in some crazy outfit, wearing a Stetson and a pair of chaps made out of felt or something. Charlie patted the bench and the girl came into the yard, sat next to him. The two of them sat in silence, Frankie watching blond curls of wood fall at his feet.

'Funny how the wood's a different colour. Y'know, like the outside is grey but inside it's yellow.' Frankie picked up a shaving and pulled the long fibres apart. 'What're you making?'

'See if you can guess.' Charlie held up the snip of driftwood.

'Um – a whale?'

Charlie smiled. 'Too damn small. You ever seen a whale?'

'Yeah – when Dad and me flew over Glacier Bay last summer. Remember? I told you about it. When Dad took me over to Gustavus and we saw hundreds of whales.'

'Hundreds?'

'Well, maybe not hundreds. But we saw at least fifty.'

'Fifty?'

'OK – we saw maybe ten. But it might have been more – they all look the same, so there might have been hundreds.'

'Might have been one.'

Frankie considered this. 'No, it was more than one.'

'Dad home now?'

'Yeah. He came back last week.' Frankie picked up a handful of shavings, threw them in the air and watched them flutter.

'That's good.'

'Maybe.'

Charlie braced the wood against his thumb, twisted the blade and gouged out a deep, smooth U shape at the end. 'How come maybe?'

Frankie pulled out a pistol, the bright silver worn in patches, exposing white plastic. She shot Charlie in the chest and shoved the pistol back in the torn holster.

'How come maybe?' Charlie repeated.

'I dunno.'

Again, the two of them sat in silence. Charlie, a remnant of the Auk tribe of Tlingit Indians, had a face Frankie could watch for hours; it was like one of the lakes she saw from her dad's new plane – rippled but unruffled, alive but calm. 'Tell me a story, Charlie. Please.'

'What do you think?' Charlie held up the rough carving.

'A moose?'

'A *moose*?' Charlie manoeuvred the wood in his dry, worn palm. 'Many years ago, when the land was still moving and the seas boiling, a jealous father walked on the ice until he found his daughter and her husband. The father, who was angry although we do not know why, drew a knife, a long knife carved from a whale bone, with a point so sharp it could not be seen, and he killed the husband.'

Frankie sat still, hands resting on pistols, and listened to a story that had been told many times, the story of how the Great Sea Spirit came to be. When Charlie had finished, Frankie frowned. 'How come he didn't pull his daughter into the boat, instead of cutting her fingers off?'

'The legend does not say.'

'But that's not right. For sure he'd have pulled her in – especially in a storm. And there's no way he'd have cut off her fingers. He must have been a terrible father. Maybe he wasn't her father at all? Maybe that's it. Maybe he was just pretending to be her father.'

Charlie picked at a flake of pine, blew on the carving and smoothed it with his thumb. 'But there is some good in this. Because if the father had been a dutiful father, if he had not killed the husband and his daughter, then we would not have the Great Sea Spirit.'

'Charlie! You fixed that fencing yet? Hi, Tuf . . . hi, Frankie.'

Frankie and Charlie looked up, to see Thekla leaning out of the kitchen window, dressed in her housecoat, cigarette between her fingers.

'Hello, Mrs Willoughby.' Frankie jumped up and waved uncertainly.

Charlie stood and brushed down his sweater and jeans, brushed away the shavings and repocketed the knife. He held the carving out to Frankie.

'What is it?' Frankie asked, puzzled, turning the shape over and over in her hands.

'It is whatever you want it to be.' Charlie walked away, disappeared into the gloom of the garage.

When Billy-Ray and Frankie came in, drenched and dripping from an afternoon of fishing off the shingle a way up the Glacier Highway, it was to find Isobel sitting on the stairs, newspaper bunched in her hands. Frankie yanked off her parka, began to babble about the line that had snagged on an old child's pram, how she had pulled it to the surface and then the line broke and—

'Is this true?' Isobel asked her husband.

'What?' Billy-Ray shook his head, rain spraying from his long blond hair, soaking Frankie's T-shirt. Frankie squealed and picked up her sodden parka, tried to wrap it around her father, who tussled with her.

'Is it true?'

'Is what true?' asked Billy-Ray, laughing and pushing Frankie away gently.

Isobel stood up, waved the paper, looking down at Billy-Ray. 'The pipeline.'

Frankie skirted her father's hands, landed a punch in his stomach.

'Oooff.' He grabbed Frankie's wrists as she squealed, and turned her round in a half nelson. 'Watch it, you! Queensberry Rules, as your mom would say.'

'Is it true?'

Frankie yelled, drowning Isobel's voice but not for long. For the first time since he had known her, which was a long time, Billy-Ray's wife raised her voice, raised it so high she placed it on an unreachable pedestal.

'Frankie – go to your room or go and play with Minto. But leave us alone.'

Frankie, eyes wide, unblinking, twisted away from her father, struggled into her parka and ran out.

'Isobel! What's your problem?' Billy-Ray opened the door,

shouted after Frankie, but she just kept running. He slammed the door. 'What the fuck's got into you?'

'Is it true?'

'*What*? Is *what* true?'

'The pipeline.'

'The pipeline?'

Isobel handed him the crumpled newspaper, lit a cigarette as Billy-Ray scanned the front page, illustrated with a photograph of desolation. He shrugged and handed it back.

'Yeah – that's right.'

'You're going to build a pipeline from Prudhoe Bay to Valdez?'

'Well, I'm not fucking building it, am I? The industry'll pay for it and Alyeska, the pipeline company, will build it.'

'A pipeline?'

Billy-Ray shucked off his jacket, hung it on a peg. Kicked off his boots. 'What difference does it make? What difference does it make to you? So they build a pipeline. You got any better ideas?'

'What's wrong with shipping it?'

'For Chrissake, Isobel, goddam place is frozen up eleven months of the year. Do you realize where it is I've been these past years? I'm not exactly sunning my ass on a beach in Nassau.'

As the word 'Nassau' ricocheted around the hall, echoed up the stairwell, the knocker on the door was lifted and dropped. Billy-Ray, damp and fuming, swung around and yanked it open. Imagine his surprise when he saw Lucca Barzini standing on the step, lighting a cigarette with a match from a book, the old party trick as smooth as ever.

Minto and Frankie had been friends a long time, ever since the day, more than four years before, when Minto had not laughed as Frankie announced that her name was Tufty Rickman. Minto was a tall boy, wide in the shoulders, with intense blue eyes and hair so blond as to be white in sunlight. He had about him an air of permanent indignation, as did his whole family, which the residents of Juneau put down to sour grapes. Minto's family, the Thorenssons, were among the original residents of Juneau, a Norwegian fishing family, who had come west in the gold rush of the late nineteenth century, when the Tlingit chief Kowee had made the great mistake of bragging to two white hikers, Joe Juneau and Richard Harris, about a glittering mother lode of gold in a creek running off the glacier. Minto's great-great-grandfather had packed up the family home, sold his possessions and taken his wife and three children to Alaska. By the time the Thorenssons arrived, the gold had been panned out, so Grandfather Thorensson did what he knew best – fishing. Who needed gold when there was such an abundance of fish? More than that, he realized that what Juneau needed was a cannery so the silver gold of Alaska could be preserved and shipped across the world. Before he'd left Europe, Thorensson had heard about the closed vessel process, and he introduced this into the cannery he built at Elfin Cove on the Alexander archipelago. The building of the long wooden shacks, housing dormitories, vast kettles, tanks, belt lines and stock, was long and arduous. The Thorensson cannery was more than eighty miles from Juneau and it was difficult to lure workers to the construction camp. But the lack of gold in the hills meant men needed work, needed money, and so soon the timber was cut from the surrounding hills and the shacks began to grow, built up on pilings. The cannery, perched at the entrance to Cross Sound, at the junction with the Icy Strait, meant that the trawlers fishing the outer islands unloaded their cargo there, where it was convenient. The Thorenssons thrived; the cannery, it would seem, was a licence to print money. The family bought a long stretch of waterfront land in the young town of Juneau and Grandfather built three houses, ornate Victorian-style mansions with gabling, shutters, porches and imported stained glass. The Thorenssons represented the best of the new country as they speculated to accumulate. In the summer of 1912, Grandfather, now suffering from gout in his old age, was dragged from his four-poster bed to hear the news that the cannery had burned to the ground the night before; nothing could be salvaged. More, his small fleet of trawlers had been moored up, unloading (an appalling coincidence that they should all be at dock at the same time), and they, too, had burst into flames. In one fire-filled, riotous night, as the Chinese workers fled the blazing dormitories and huddled for shelter on the craggy shore, startled by the sound of exploding kettles, sickened by the stench of burning fish oil, the Thorenssons' fortune disappeared.

Minto's family had never recovered from this blow – the tendrils of the family's oral history wrapped tightly around each generation, feeding its indignation and resentment. Grandfather Thorensson had raged for weeks before dying of what appeared to be apoplexy – he was convinced that it was a conspiracy. Why would all his boats be in? The Indians had done it – uncivilized ingrates! First they had lured his family to this icy hellhole with lies, and then they had destroyed the inheritance he had laboured for so hard. His wife, brothers, grandsons and nephews listened to these rantings and believed every word, and those words were passed down. More than fifty years later, Minto still burned with resentment at this perfidy, would not walk along the two blocks of Egan Drive which passed the old family plot, where the grand mansions were now occupied by state legislators and government officials. Jesus, one of the old Thorensson homes was now a hotel, where the goddam Indians stayed when they came to moan during the oil hearings.

During late spring and summer weekends and evenings, Frankie and Minto spent their time fishing, wherever and whenever they could. Frankie would shoulder a backpack and walk the steep streets down to 11th and D Street, carrying rods and a bait box, to where Minto lived in a small frame house, with flaking rosemaling shutters. The two of them would set off for Egan Drive, or catch a bus out to the bay and drop down to the shore line wherever took their fancy. Once the bait had been hooked and cast, lines set, they'd open lunch boxes and chew on sandwiches as they talked, deafened occasionally by a blast from the cruise liners that occasionally churned up the channel. They always swapped sandwiches because Frankie liked jam and peanut butter, which she was not allowed at home, and Minto, surprisingly, liked the Marmite sandwiches Isobel made her daughter. (Lady Chalfont-Webbe sent three large jars of the thick, salt-tar-like substance every six months by air mail.) They spent hours together, staring at the moving blue palette of the water, talking about school, television, basketball, food – the things that mattered to them. When Minto once snagged a hook in the back of his hand, Frankie held it firmly, picked the barb out with steady fingers and, intuitively, licked the wound. When Frankie caught a chum too heavy for her line, when she wouldn't let it go, even as the line burned through the knuckle crease on her forefinger, Minto cut the nylon, looked her in the eyes and shook his head, before looking in his box for Savlon and a plaster. They never apologized, they never held grudges. It was a simple relationship; they were nine years old and they loved each other as long as each of them stayed the same.

So Minto said nothing when Frankie appeared at the house one evening, holding her parka tightly around her, her eyelashes plastered together in clumps with tears, her face pale. He looked at her for a while and then asked whether she wanted some ice cream.

Billy-Ray took some time to get over his surprise at seeing Lucca Barzini standing in his hallway. If he hadn't read the article about the Pulitzer he might not have recognized her but there was, he decided later, still something there, something that made him think of Cape Disappointment. If Billy-Ray was surprised, Lucca was dumbstruck. She stared at him, stripping lines and weathering away from his face, giving his shaggy hair a mental haircut, putting him by a fire in sand dunes as his hand stroked her breasts, twenty-three years before.

Isobel moved towards them, smiling, holding out her hand. 'Miss Barzini, how nice to see you again. Come in, please come in.'

Lucca stood in the hall as Billy-Ray closed the door, staring at her.

'Hope you don't mind me smoking?' Lucca asked, waving the cigarette, creating mares' tails of smoke.

'Not at all. I smoke myself. Lucca, please meet my husband, Billy-Ray or BR as I call him. Billy-Ray, Lucca Barzini.'

That was why she hadn't made the connection – Isobel had spoken of her husband only as BR. 'Pleased to meet you, Billy-Ray.' Lucca, who had already decided how to play this, held out her tiny hand, which Billy-Ray shook.

'Please come through. I must apologize for the mess, but Frankie, that's my daughter, has been on vacation so there's a lot of stuff spread around.' Isobel walked down the hall to the lounge.

Lucca and Billy-Ray stared at each other, until Billy-Ray shouted to Isobel, 'I'm gonna have a bath. Won't be long.'

Once in the bathroom, door locked, Billy-Ray sat on the edge of the tub and tried to order his thoughts. What was Lucca *doing* there? How had she met Isobel? Why was she even in Alaska? In Juneau? His thoughts, rather than ordering themselves, fractured into pieces like sunlight shattering on calm water.

Billy-Ray soon found out what was going on, as he sat and ate with Isobel and Lucca. Frankie had called to say she was eating at Minto's place and would be back later. Billy-Ray chewed his food, swallowed Amber ale and listened to the women talking, at first of nothing – hotel rooms, the cost of eating out, the cost of doing anything at all in Alaska, the ugliness of Anchorage. But then the talk turned to thornier, spikier subjects. At first, Billy-Ray didn't get the drift; Isobel and Lucca were talking in acronyms, meaningless strings of letters, but then he got it and began to understand.

'Excuse me,' he said, laying down his fork, turning to Lucca, 'are you saying that you work for the Alaska Federation of Natives?'

Lucca's eyes, as dark and intense as they had ever been, a legacy of her Italian grandmother, who had lived and died (as Deet had) in Salerno, turned to him. 'That's right – the AFN have invited me on board as an adviser.'

'But you're not an Indian.'

'No, I'm not a Native American, but I support their cause. I wrote a book—'

'I know. It won the Pulitzer. I saw the papers.'

Isobel looked at him and frowned – BR didn't care much for literature.

'Well, they need all the help they can get.'

Billy-Ray, lost in a maze of mounting guilt and fury, looked at his wife, not knowing what else to do.

'Lucca and I met at a seminar organized by the Legislative Council. She's been living out of a suitcase in the Alaskan Hotel. I suggested she might like to stay here for a while instead.'

'Which is very kind of you.' Lucca smiled.

'I've made up the room opposite Frankie's. I'm afraid it's on the top floor, but it has lovely views.'

'That's fine – I smoke so many of these I need all the exercise I can get.'

Billy-Ray excused himself the minute supper was done, went to the den and turned on the TV, not watching it, until he heard Lucca climbing the stairs to her room. Then he went in search of Isobel, who he found in the kitchen.

'What the fuck is going on?'

'I've asked a colleague to stay, that's all.'

'A colleague?'

'Well, yes. You could say we work together.'

'You *work* together?'

'Well, obviously, I'm not paid but I am working for the lobbying group.'

'Which lobbying group?'

'It's a coalition, if you like, of concerned parties – the AFN, ANSA, the Sierra Club . . .'

'The *Sierra* Club?'

'Amongst others.'

Billy-Ray grasped the edge of the worktop, stared at his hands, scarred from his days on *Viveka*, by snapped drill bits and flying cables, and breathed deeply. He knew he had lost his temper too often lately, knew he only had this one chance to make things clear. 'Isobel, the AFN are trying to stop the pipeline. No, no, don't say anything. Let me say what I want to say.' Isobel stopped washing up, dried her alarming hands and crossed her arms, leaned back against the sink. 'OK, Governor Udall has frozen the land claims – do you know what that means? Until they're settled, until this Native claims business is sorted, we can't do anything. We can't do anything with the oil.'

'Who's "we", BR? Who's "we"?'

Billy-Ray shook his head slightly, tried to dislodge the memory of Lucca asking him the same question. 'Look, Isobel, we reckon there's more than ten billion barrels up there. OK, so there are a few Indian villages in the path of where they want to put the pipeline, but they'll get paid off, they'll be relocated.'

'That's not the point.'

'What the fuck *is* the point?' Billy-Ray's voice began to rise. 'What is the fucking *point*?'

'It's their land.'

Billy-Ray reared backward, rubbed his face hard. 'You don't get it. And anyway, what the fuck's it got to do with you? You're not even an American.'

Isobel smiled faintly, enraging her husband further. 'They might say you're not exactly a Native American yourself, they might even argue that you're merely a second generation arriviste.'

'Oh, that's just great. So why don't we just give it all to the fucking bears? Just give it to the fucking *animals* that were here first?'

Isobel smiled then, began to laugh, finding the idea of letting the bears run the State of Alaska very appealing.

'Isobel, honey, don't you see? They take our money, ask for welfare, ask for heaters and snowmobiles and food and oil to be dropped way out in Stevens and Barrow and all those God-awful places. They say they need the land to exist but they can't exist on it any longer without us.'

'Why do you think that is?'

'Because we make their lives better, make them easier.'

'No, BR, that's not why they can't subsist any longer. It's because the oil companies and the government are taking their lands, polluting their rivers, shunting them into ever smaller spaces. There are dams built across spawning grounds, processing plants drawing water from creeks – do I need to go on? You know all this.'

'You don't get it—'

'No, BR, I don't think *you* get it. You used to get it. I remember at a barbecue somewhere, a few years ago, you said then that the Native Americans were here first, that we should respect them, ask them for advice. How many Natives does Karbo employ?'

'That's not the point.' Billy-Ray was back-pedalling, disturbed by the memory of his younger self being more even-handed, more tolerant even. He remembered that party, how he had felt when he danced with Isobel.

'The point is this isn't about cowboys and Indians, BR, it's not about emotions. It's about the law. This is about legal niceties which go back to 1867.'

'What are you talking about?'

'That's when Seward bought Alaska from the Russians. But there was no consultation, no title was drawn up through purchase or treaty. He never did buy the land. It still belongs to the Natives. Everywhere you and Karbo and ARCO and the rest prospect for oil belongs to the Natives.'

Billy-Ray tried to control himself, rolled his neck, cracked his knuckles. 'Isobel, you know this has all gone too far already. We're way past the point of return. No one is going to pull out because a bunch of Indians are sitting in fucking wigwams out on the tundra – d'you get what I'm saying?'

'Let the courts decide.'

Isobel was wrong, of course – it was all about emotions, and that was why, when Frankie came back from Minto's, her belly full of delicious fried chicken and ice cream, she opened the front door to hear the sound of her parents yelling at each other. She sneaked up the stairs and sat on the landing, her chin on her arms, listening to them, but she couldn't make out the words. All she could hear was a muffled sound: the sound adults make when they don't under-stand each other, the sound they make when they begin to stop loving each other. A sound like grief trapped in a submarine. Eventually Frankie climbed the stairs to her bed and didn't even notice the tiny, grey-haired woman asleep in the opposite room.

Over the next few months, as summer came and went, Fall arriving with the rain, Frankie heard a lot of arguments. The Rickmans didn't have a vacation that year – unlike the summer before, when Isobel and Frankie had gone to California, driving from San Diego all the way up to Monterey in the rental Mustang Isobel had chosen because she knew Billy-Ray had always wanted one. But Billy-Ray wasn't there; he, apparently, had work on the North Slope and couldn't get away. Frankie had loved that vacation, coming back with a tan and memories of sun, beaches, freeways and arching bridges, restaurants with decks and umbrellas, hanging over water. Alcatraz, the Wharf, ice cream, sea otters, clam chowder and choco-late, dark evenings, Spanish missions on the Camino Real. Strange acres of vineyards, which moved with them as the car flashed past. Frankie had loved it but she had missed her dad, wished he was with them. (Billy-Ray, staying in the cabin outside Valdez, had hated every moment of those weeks, hated himself, probed his guilt until it bled and scabbed and became resentment.) Sometimes, as Frankie mooched about on the docks, or went hiking with Minto, she thought about the California vacation and wished she was doing it again but this time with all three of them.

Indeed, sometimes Frankie wished she was anywhere but Juneau during those acrimonious months when Lucca stayed at Sitka Street. She never asked what was going on but her parents told her anyway. Whenever she and Dad were out in the car and had to fill the cans for the boat, Dad would remind her that they were using oil and gas to get where they were going. When Fall began to bite and the oil tanks needed filling, Billy-Ray remarked that without the oil they'd freeze. Whenever they cooked, drove out to Nugget Mall or saw an Alaskan Airlines plane fly in to the airport, Billy-Ray pointed out that without oil none of this was possible. One night after an up-and-downer with Isobel, Billy-Ray took Frankie into the den, where a huge map of Alaska was tacked to the wall, and he showed her where he worked, explained about the lake of crude beneath the surface, and then traced a line south down to Valdez, where his finger lingered. Whenever he looked at maps of the south-east coast, which was often, he thought of Urban, of that night when he and Urban had sat on the deck and watched the coastline slip by, as he had asked about the distant lights of Valdez.

'That's where the pipeline will run.' Billy-Ray looked down at his daughter.

'Right.' Frankie hated this, when each of her parents tried to get her onside.

'You see, you got to understand, Frankie, there isn't any other way of getting it out.' Billy-Ray swept his hand right to left across the map from the Yukon to Cape Hope, rustling the paper. 'All of this is frozen except for six weeks in June and July. The only way is to run a pipe down to Valdez, which is the nearest ice-free port. Do you understand?'

'Yeah.'

'It's not for us, not for Alaska, but for the Lower Forty-eight. Without it, America can't work.' Billy-Ray sometimes felt a little uneasy with this last statement – he knew, better than most, that the reserves under the North Slope, while they were vast, a veritable subterranean ocean of hydrocarbons, would, in the end, provide oil to match America's needs only for two, maybe three years. But, shit, that was no reason to leave it there untapped.

Frankie stared at the map. 'But . . . there must be things out there.'

'What d'you mean?'

'Bears and moose and otters and stuff. What happens if there's an accident? Will the bears drown?'

'No, honey, the bears won't drown because there won't be any accidents.'

'Promise?'

'I promise. Nothing will happen. It'll be fine.'

Isobel, who operated differently, rarely said anything directly, but when she did the words worked themselves under Frankie's skin. Lucca, Isobel and Frankie ate supper one night, Billy-Ray being away in Anchorage, and Frankie, who had spent a couple of hours next door in the garage with Charlie, retold a scrambled tale of a young girl who changed into a bear and when she went back to her village she was run out by the humans. A canoe wearing a hat had offered to save the bear-woman and she had climbed into it and all that happened was she and the canoe disappeared into the sun. Frankie laughed – the thought of a canoe in a hat!

'Do you know what tribe Charlie is?' asked Lucca.

'No, ma'am.'

'He's an Auk,' said Isobel, finishing her meal, closing the cutlery precisely.

'An Auk? That's interesting,' said Lucca.

'We're studying the Indians at school,' said Frankie, 'y'know, all about the different tribes. Mrs Grundie says that they all came from Russia or someplace. She said they came to Alaska first and then spread out everywhere.'

'That's right,' said Lucca, 'they did.'

'She said that they caused a lot of trouble when we all came, y'know, after the Civil War and all that.'

Lucca raised an eyebrow and looked at Isobel.

'Then she made us do this really weird thing – like a list we had to read and put crosses against. Can I show you?'

As Isobel made coffee Frankie went into the den and looked for the sheet of paper, came back and gave it to Lucca, standing by the older woman as she read it.

'We had to put a tick next to things we'd like to be near and a cross next to things we were scared of or we don't like.'

Lucca scanned the list, gave it to Isobel when she came back with the coffee, cigarettes and an ashtray.

__ a puppy	__ dark roads	__ a book	__ a church
__ a campfire	__ a strange man	__ a dead moose	__ a TV set
__ a gun	__ a hockey game	__ a live seal	__ a graveyard
__ Arctic poppies	__ a newborn baby	__ the teacher	__ ocean waves
__ a taxi cab	__ house on fire	__ a guitar	__ a cliff edge
__ a sick person	__ a river bank	__ roadkill	__ a storm
__ my grandfather	__ a moving snowmobile	__ a strange woman	
__ a brother or sister crying			

Isobel looked at the paper and frowned. Frankie had crossed a sick person, a strange man, a newborn baby, a book, roadkill and ocean waves. The teacher, grandfather and crying siblings options were left blank.

'Frankie, sweetheart, why haven't you checked these?'

Frankie looked at the list. 'Well, I didn't know what to say about Mrs Grundie, and I don't have any brothers or sisters, and my grandfathers are dead.'

'Grandfather's not dead.'

'One of 'em is and I never see the other one.'

'And why are you scared of books?'

'I'm not *scared* of them, I just don't like them much.'

Lucca smiled as Isobel pointed to the sheet of paper. 'And you've crossed the ocean wave. I thought you liked the sea, honey?'

'I do so like it. I like looking at it. And I like storms, y'know when there's lightning and all that. But I don't like big waves. One time Dad and I were out fishing in the boat and the sea got big and I didn't like it. Dad was scared too, I reckon.'

'Well, how interesting. Do you know why Mrs Grundie asked you to do this?'

Frankie sat back down and shrugged. 'She asks us to do lots of dumb things.'

'Frankie doesn't find the work at school particularly challenging,' Isobel remarked.

'Does Mrs Grundie say anything else about the Native Americans?' asked Lucca.

'Yeah. She says they're a . . . relict or something.'

'Relic,' corrected Isobel automatically. 'Do you know what that means?'

Frankie pursed her lips, gurned at her mother. 'Something, like, out of date? Kinda useless?'

'Frankie, these are *people* we're talking about. They're not relics, they live here. And they've lived here a damn sight longer than we have. How would you feel if strange people arrived here and threw us out of our house because they wanted it, or threw us off our land, asked us to leave Alaska?'

'I'd shoot 'em,' said Frankie.

'Why?'

'Because . . . because . . . because it's ours.'

'That's the thing, Frankie. Number one, it's not ours, it's theirs, the Native Americans'. And number two, it's a good job they're doing things a bit differently from you. They're not shooting at us, they're just trying to talk to us.'

'Mrs Grundie said they killed lots of us.'

Lucca, who could have explained in some detail the background to the clearances, the Trail of Tears and the atrocity of the Battle of Wounded Knee, elected instead to change the subject, asking Frankie what she and Minto were planning on doing that weekend.

Later, when Frankie was in bed, after she and Isobel had read through and annotated a press release from Alyeska that had been published that day, Lucca said, 'I know that story, the one Frankie told about the bear-woman.'

Isobel yawned, smothered it. 'Sorry. You were saying?'

'That story – it ends with the bear-woman being gang-raped by the sons of the sun.'

'Good God.'

'It's happened to all the Natives' stories – they've been stripped of meaning, sanitized and turned into fairy tales for our amusement. The true moral of the story is don't wander away from the tribe, don't mess with the animals, don't be seduced by thinking you're safe because if you do you'll suffer. Life was difficult and fragile, nature was terrifying, dangerous. And the markers of human life – the canoe, the village – were tiny when set against the forests, the oceans, the mountains.'

'They still are.'

'Yes – and I have a feeling that's the argument Alyeska will use, that when the pipeline is considered against the context of the size of the land, then it's no more than a strand of hair on a beach. Do you want me to leave? I can go back and get a room at the hotel. I realize that my being here is causing a few problems.'

'No, of course not. You're more than welcome. It will all die down.'

That night the three of them lay awake, Frankie trying to work out why it was wrong to shoot intruders, as Lucca ran through lists of meetings to be called, letters to be written, journalists she could contact. Isobel lay in her king-size bed, wishing Lucca were not quite so earnest and wondering how she had contrived to raise a daughter who was not afraid of fires and guns, storms and dark roads, yet who didn't want to be near newborn babies and books. She thought of her daughter and what she had said about her grandfather, about the paucity of her family, and Isobel wondered whether the time had come to say something. But it didn't feel right, not with the arguments that were going on, and she decided to leave it a while. It was very late when she finally drifted into sleep, wishing Billy-Ray would come home and they could stop arguing and start loving each other again.

Eventually, despite their best efforts, the inevitable happened: Billy-Ray and Lucca found themselves alone in the Sitka Street house. Frankie was in school and Isobel had taken an early flight to Anchorage for the day. Billy-Ray, assuming Lucca had travelled with Isobel, walked into the kitchen, dressed in pyjamas, scratching himself, to find the slight, grey-haired half-Italian standing by the coffee machine. Lucca turned and glanced at him.

'Good morning,' she said.

Billy-Ray waved at the smoke curling from Lucca's cigarette and crossed the kitchen to fetch some juice. He sat at the table, opened the previous day's *New York Times* and turned to the finance pages.

'Would you like a coffee?' Lucca asked.

'Yah.' Billy-Ray didn't look up from the paper.

'You have two sugars in that, with milk, if I remember right.'

'No. Just black.'

Lucca carried both cups to the table, sat opposite Billy-Ray. She drank and smoked and watched Billy-Ray, noticed that his hands shook a little, noticed that he wasn't reading.

'I've talked to Isobel and I'm moving out, I guess you'll be pleased to hear.'

Billy-Ray finally looked up at her. 'When?'

'I've taken rooms in a place off the Drive. I'll be moving tomorrow.'

Billy-Ray grunted, drank some coffee and flicked the pages of the paper. He was not going to be made to feel uncomfortable in his own place; he was not going to leave the kitchen first.

Lucca lit another cigarette and, despite himself, Billy-Ray was compelled to watch the matchbook trick; he'd never worked out how she did it. 'Look, Billy-Ray, I'm sorry if I've pissed you off. I didn't even know you were Isobel's husband and I certainly wouldn't have come here if I had known. I didn't move in to annoy you. But sometimes I get the feeling that you think all this is personal. Well, it's not.'

Billy-Ray raked his fingers through his thick, matted hair. 'To be honest, Lucca, I don't give a shit what you think this is about. Fact is, you've come here, into my house, and made trouble. You leaving here would be the best thing that happened to me in a while.'

Lucca looked at Billy-Ray and remembered driving in the Cord 812, through a wet, drizzly morning, heading for Seattle. Billy-Ray driving, his earnest, handsome, young face looking concerned as he tried to explain to her why it was important to discover unmapped places. Now Billy-Ray looked tired, looked arrogant and cynical, yet strangely unsure of himself. Lucca glanced at his trembling, scarred hands, tried to remember what they had done to her, how they had made her feel, and failed. She pushed back her chair, rinsed her cup at the sink.

'I'll call the Alaskan Hotel and see if I can get a room for the night.' Lucca wiped her hands, walked to the doorway and stopped. 'You want to know what I think? Well, of course you don't, but I'll tell you anyway. I think you're ashamed. I think you're ashamed of something and you don't know what it is. Maybe you got a lot of choices.'

Billy-Ray watched Lucca cross the hall to the stairs before looking back to the paper, still not reading a word. Ashamed? Later, when he came back from a trip to Nugget Mall, he climbed the stairs to the room at the back, under the eaves, and found it was empty, the bed stripped.

ARCO, Karbo, BP and Humble were still exploring the Slope but anything they discovered was ice-locked by the frozen land claims. The North Slope began to churn up, permafrost melting, tundra trodden underfoot, crushed under Caterpillar tracks; the Bering Sea became muddied and slick. Barges nosed their way through thick, near-frozen seas in the month and a half when it was possible, carrying supplies, tractors, cranes, rigs, cable, oxygen canisters, gas canisters and, of course, diesel fuel for the Cats. The network of gravel roads was spreading, the flames licking from gas burn-offs were roaring, lighting the days-long night sky; generators rumbled and rigs reared hundreds of feet high, staggering metal webs designed to bite.

Billy-Ray Rickman, now appointed Planning Manager, Karbo Inc., Alaska, sometimes wished for the same thing as Isobel, that the two of them would stop arguing – wished for this when he had time, when he remembered, when he could bear to think. Billy-Ray had so many thoughts in those days which he turned away from, literally turned away from, his head moving from side to side – turn your head and the patterns changed, have another drink, sleep with another woman, look at another chart, pull out a razor and a mirror and the thought patterns changed.

Still Karbo Inc. made sure it squeezed its money's worth from Billy-Ray, who was called to appear at congressional hearings in

Washington, DC, requested to liaise with engineers in Oklahoma and San Diego, required to supervise the design and start-up of the Karbo facilities in Prudhoe. All this as well as partying with the suits in Anchorage, in Dallas, New York, wherever. Billy-Ray spent more time in the air than he did with his daughter; spent more nights in hotel and motel rooms than he did in Sitka Street. The oil kept coming up, welling from the wounds in the earth and the sea floor, forced out by the pressure building beneath it, around it, but, until the claims were worked out, there was nowhere for the crude to go.

Those few years that followed the moment Billy-Ray felt the pulse beneath his boot-clad feet on his fortieth birthday, when he looked up into a paling sky to see the cataclysm of fire that signalled the gas burning off the oil reservoir beneath him, passed in a welter of conflict. Those years, which should have been his finest hour, when he was in his prime, flying high, respected and admired, were, when he looked back at them, a jumbled succession of cocaine-fractured acts. Unrelated acts, like the limbs of wooden marionettes, severed, strewn across a stage in a clatter, unmoving, immutable. Flying first class back and forth across the country, pampered by women who didn't even know his first name. Sleeping with women whose names he didn't know and didn't want to. Drinking and schmoozing with the great and good in restaurants up and down the east and west coasts, laughing, smiling, nodding agreement, trying to remember the sympathies of the various lobbyists, signing papers, snorting white powder which was like the strange dust he brushed off his Xtra-Tufs on the Slope.

Turning his head, filling his head, so he wouldn't think about why Isobel stopped being enough; turning his head so he wouldn't hear his father or Urban, wouldn't see Siggy and Deet. Turning his head so he wouldn't think of Frankie and fishing and walking the trails up behind Juneau, where he and Frankie had seen bears on the Lemon Creek trail, ten hours of slithering in mud and laughing, with no coke, no vodka, no beers or hookers, just laughing with Frankie, spying on bears, no dope, no liquor, just sitting on the boat at dusk by the Breadline hearing nothing, drinking coffee and watching the lures twitch on grey, ruffled waters as Frankie snuggled up to him and he put his arm around her because he loved her, no coke, no

ache, no panic, in the house at Halibut Cove, where they hadn't
been for years now, which must be full of spiders and crap and how
much fun they had had there looking for sea otters and seeing
whales' flukes flipping in Glacier Bay, Frankie going nuts, taking
hundreds of pictures which never came out, that never captured the
sense of tracking the clouds, skimming the waves, so close you could
see the barnacles on the flukes, and then climbing into the blue sky
with Frankie looking at the clouds, saying it was like another world
and hating yourself as you look at her smiling, braces catching the
sun, and so you do more lines, smoke more dope because – hey! you
can afford it and you're a long long way from home, a long long way
from Isobel which makes you take another toot, brush dust from
your tailored trousers because you can see her in your bed, see her,
long, slim, naked, blonde and lonely in your bed on Sitka Street and
whenever you go back there you know, you just know, you're sleeping with the enemy.

When Billy-Ray was working and Isobel had to go away with Lucca
for a meeting or a conference, Frankie either slept over at Minto's or
Thekla's. Isobel was never happy with this, which was curious,
given that she herself had spent most of her childhood sleeping in
dorms with strangers. But while she hated leaving Frankie, hated
waving goodbye and setting off for the airport, she knew it was the
right thing to do – there were greater things at stake than Frankie's
momentary discomfort. Frankie liked staying in the small, jumbled
Thorensson house on 12th, where the food was always 'poor', as her
mother would have said, where there was always a mess of brothers
and sisters and their friends, girlfriends and boyfriends. Lotte
Thorensson, Minto's mother, was a disagreeable woman without a
kind word for anyone. She stood in the kitchen – her domain – and
railed against the world, the Indians, the company her offspring
kept in a never-ending stream of inflected English. Frankie thought
she was amazing – her mother would never be so rude. When
supper (if it could be called that) was done, she and Minto would go
to his room or out down the pier, depending on the season. Minto's
half-basement room – which he shared with an older brother, Bud,
who was never there seeing as he'd joined the Marines – was

wonderful. The Thorenssons might not have much money but they sure didn't act like that. Minto had a hi-fidelity record player with headphones, a phone and TV of his own. The walls were covered in posters and pennants, the Red Sox vying with Bob Dylan and Woodstock. Frankie and Minto spent the evenings fooling round with ouija boards, playing knuckles and slaps, practising dead faces for poker, until they were told to go to bed. Minto had a bunk bed in his room and Frankie slept on the top, her nose inches away from the purple ceiling which Bud had painted.

Staying over at Thekla Willoughby's was a different proposition, an entirely different deck, as Minto would say, but Frankie still liked it, although she thought it was weird being able to see her own room from the bed in there. Weird being able to see her house, doors shut, windows blackened by darkness, knowing there was no one in there, that it was uninhabited, empty of life. Her room at Thekla's was the guest room, full of ruches and nylon, cute pictures of dogs and cats on the walls. All the colours matched, or nearly did, and there were posies of scented leaves everywhere. Frankie always opened the windows (even though she thought a bear might climb in) because she wanted to smell the sea as she slept. Sometimes she lay in the bed and tried to remember her room in Anchorage, but the room itself had disappeared and all she thought of was cold, ice and violence. Sometimes she wondered why Thekla was so fat, why she smoked so much, why she didn't do anything. OK, maybe her mom didn't work, didn't go to an office or something, but she did do things. She was always reading and writing.

The school bus dropped students at Main and 5th and Frankie had to toil up the hill that was Sitka Street, which followed the bends and curves of Gold Creek, to Thekla's house. Thekla always insisted she do her schoolwork before she was allowed to go out and meet Minto, or talk to Charlie, and that she be back by eight o'clock. So Frankie spread her books out on the table in the lounge and worked as Thekla sat opposite, smoking her Winstons, swiping at her ashy chest and swigging from cans of root beer. Frankie found her presence disturbing, annoying even, especially when Thekla took it into her head to ask questions.

'So what's your favourite subject, honey?'

'I like math. And art, I guess.'

'Math? Lord, that was one lesson I did not like. Never could quite understand it.'

'Dad helps me with mine, he's good at it.'

'Seems to me your pa can do just about ever'thing.' Thekla was a little in love with Billy-Ray.

'He can speak seven languages.'

'Lord – that's sure some talk.' Thekla had trouble speaking one.

Frankie sat back, pushed her hair out of her eyes. 'Tell me again about the photographs.' She went over to the fireplace, where two framed prints were hanging, ghostly prints, framed in ridiculous, moulded faux-gilt frames, photographs that looked as if they had been printed from thinned silver and mist.

Thekla smiled, shifted her huge hams and set her hands on her knees. 'Well, like I already told ya, honey, I reckon it's a load o' hooey, but some folks say that Fin is related to a guy called Richard Willoughby. He was born in Virginia but came up here for the gold rush. Did some prospecting, made a coupla claims, lost the money then set up a bor-dell-o' (Frankie loved the way Thekla said the word, dragging it out like warm toffee) 'in the town, right here. Or so they say. Anyways, he likes to move around a lot, do some explorin', so he sets off one June day for Glacier Bay – though it was known then as Muir Bay, I do believe. So there he is, with his dog sled and a few supplies and he finds himsel' a cave to stay for the night. Well, it's June twenty-first – and what's that mean, Frankie?'

'It's the solstice – longest day in the year.'

'Damn right that's what it means. Anyway, as the light begins to go, which is late, very late, Willoughby's sitting outside his cave and what happens?'

'He sees the Silent City. He sees the Silent City floating on the glacier.' Frankie said this while staring at the print, a pale, washed-out black-and-white photograph of a city such as she had never seen. Old, flat-roofed buildings, neat parkland, towering church spires, long windows with shutters, tall trees crowned with plump balls of leaves, iron balconies and a beautiful, swooping bridge hanging weightless over a deep gorge. Passing silently through the gorge was a tall ship, a three-masted schooner, skimming past busy docks.

And all of it, the whole vista, lit by stellate pinpricks of light, gas lamps burning late at night.

'That's right – that's what Richard Willoughby sees as he hears the hungry wolves howling. He sees a city. But when he goes home, back to Juneau, ever'body jus' laughs at him, they don't believe him. So what's he do?'

'He buys a camera from someone and goes back the next year, to the same cave, and he takes pictures and then he comes back here and he has them made into postcards.'

'Yup – and jus' about ever'one buys 'em. Shoot, people even come up from Outside to buy them and go to the cave to see the city, but no one ever does. And this Richard Willoughby – well, things don't go so well for him, or so they say. He was rich but no one believed him. Can eat away at a man, that can. So what happened in the end?'

Frankie, still staring at the fairy-tale city, said, 'The man he bought the camera from – he was just a visitor, he was an Englishman. And when someone from somewhere like Seattle saw the picture he said that the plate must have come from England. That Willoughby had mixed 'em up and printed the wrong one. This man from Seattle, he said he recognized the city.' This was the bit Frankie had trouble understanding – she didn't know whether it was a good ending or a bad one. 'He said he'd been there and that the English guy must have taken it before he left England and left it in the camera. He said that the Silent City didn't exist.'

'Which city did he say it was, honey?'

'He said it was a place in England, a place called Bristol in England.'

'And what do you think, sweetlips? Do ya reckon there's a silent city up there?' Thekla nodded out back, to where the glaciers extended icy tongues towards Juneau.

'I dunno.' Frankie frowned. She wanted to believe that the city was out there on the glacier – silent and beautiful – but also to believe that it really existed right then, that somewhere the city existed because she'd never seen anything like it and she wanted to go there.

The first time she told her mom and dad about the photos at Thekla's, over lunch one Saturday, when they'd both been away for a few days, when they weren't speaking to each other, when the silence was so thick Frankie thought she might suffocate, they were surprised into conversation.

'Hmm,' said Billy-Ray, 'could be it's true. I mean, there are times when you're deceived.' (And Isobel looked up from the *Juneau Empire*, looked at Billy-Ray over her glasses.) 'By the atmosphere, I mean. Atmospheric conditions can create illusions, hallucinations. People see oases in the desert, see things when they're snow blind, things that aren't there. Could be that he saw something – if it was the solstice, maybe. Hmm. Interesting.' Billy-Ray chewed the inside of his cheek. (Driving along the road outside Bow Regard, driving with Siggy, seeing a mirage, seeing water on a parched blacktop.) 'Happens.'

Isobel folded her paper, took off her glasses. 'I think it's a scam. I've heard about it but I can't remember who told me. I think this chap – Willoughby, is it? – knew exactly what he was doing.' Frankie felt herself relaxing a little, her neck felt longer, looser. Mom and Dad were talking. 'There's a word for it.' Isobel pinched the bridge of her nose, frowned, momentarily looked as she would when she was old. '*Fata Morgana,*' she said suddenly. '*Fata Morgana.* An act of Morgan. Good grief, I'd forgotten all this – um . . . the Straits of Messina, between Italy and Sicily. The Normans took the legend to Italy. The legend of King Arthur and his sister, Morgan le Fey. Illusions conjured up by Morgan to fool the sailors. Chimeras and sirens. Mirages and ghosts. Sometimes people want to believe, they want hallucinations, illusions.'

Der Geist. Tupilaq.

'But he could have seen it!' said Billy-Ray. 'Depends on the curvature of the earth, depends on the clarity of light, the inversion of hot and cold air, occluded fronts. Whatever. But he could have seen it.'

'Tattie bogle,' said Isobel suddenly, and smiled.

'What?' Frankie looked at her mother.

'I'd forgotten that too. In school, when something couldn't be explained, we used to say "tattie bogle". Socks that were lost, homework that had just disappeared, we'd tell the teachers it was tattie bogle. Something bad that was inexplicable.'

'Tattie bogle,' said Frankie, crossing her fingers so she'd remember to tell Minto.

Billy-Ray laughed, pronounced, 'Tattie bogle' in his best English accent.

'Maybe you're right – maybe it's a trick of the light,' said Isobel, and in those words she held forgiveness out across the table, held it out like a soft, warm wish which Billy-Ray could cradle in his scarred hands.

'Light would have to be good.' Billy-Ray looked at his wife and smiled.

'Hey, why not let's call Thekla and ask if we can go see them? See the photos?' asked Frankie, desperate to prolong the moment.

'Hey – let's.' Isobel raised an eyebrow, which Frankie knew meant she'd goofed again, word-wise. 'I can settle this once and for all.'

'Oh yeah?' asked Billy-Ray, looking at the line of his wife's ass as she stood.

'Oh yeah. You see, I know the city of Bristol. I used to visit there to stay with my first boyfriend and his family.'

Billy-Ray made as if to throw up and Frankie laughed.

Isobel called Thekla, who was delighted to have the Rickmans over, who was thrown into a frenzy of confusion by the thought of the two blond (lean) giants coming to her house, their tall (even leaner) daughter in tow, so she ran around the house shoving magazines under cushions, throwing empty beer cans in the trash, turning off the TV, straightening the sofa, yelling at the lump that was Fin.

Fin was the perfect host, even going so far as to move from the sofa to direct Isobel and Billy-Ray to the pictures. Husband and wife peered at the photographs, standing close, bodies brushing against each other, as Fin cracked open two cans of Amber, one for himself and one for Billy-Ray.

'Thank you,' said Isobel, taking Fin's, turning back to the image.

Fin looked at her long, aristocratic back and shrugged, went to fetch another.

'Well, it's certainly Bristol. Unmistakable.'

'How come?'

'The bridge – there's not another one like it. It's Bristol.' Isobel turned round, sipped the beer. 'Sorry, Frankie.'

Frankie frowned – there was something wrong here.

'That's not the point,' said Billy-Ray. 'The point isn't whether it's Bristol but whether the guy saw it. The point is – did Willoughby see it? Don't matter whether it's Baltimore, Boston or fucking Bombay – sorry, Thekla.'

'That's fine.' But it wasn't fine; Thekla was shocked.

The word made Frankie tighten again; she felt her neck grow harder.

'Look – the point is, did Willoughby experience something like a mirage? He could have done – it's the solstice, you have cold air, warm air, maybe it's cloudy, the precipitation levels are high. The sky could act as a lens . . . Bristol's what? Fifty degrees north? Maybe more? Fifty-five? Could happen, could happen. If there was no pollution, it could happen.'

In the silence that followed, the thin corrugated-tin sound of the radio in the kitchen could be heard – Thunderclap Newman's 'Something in the Air'.

'Well,' said Isobel eventually, 'one thing's for certain – even if it did happen, it won't happen again.'

'Huh?' Billy-Ray was busy thinking, trying to picture the curve of the earth over the pole.

'As you say, a mirage, a chimera like that would need an unpolluted environment. By the time Karbo Inc. is done, it'll be a miracle if any of us can see our hands in front of our faces.'

And Billy-Ray snapped to, looked into his wife's startlingly blue eyes, forgetting about the delicious feeling of her long legs around him, her thumbs working their way down his back, forgetting about how her lips felt on his neck, the English half-smile that made him shiver, the way her body unfolded for him. He slammed down the can of Amber, slammed it down so hard that foam oozed, like the oil on the North Slope, white foam, black sludge. 'Not here,' he said.

No, not here, Frankie agreed, as she watched Billy-Ray button his parka and walk out. Tattie fucking bogle, she thought, but she didn't say a word.

'We went up to Favourite Reef on Thursday,' remarked Frankie as Minto licked the black residue of Marmite from the corner of his lips.

'Dad and me flew up there late afternoon. Caught two halibut and some dollies.'

'Yeah? How much?'

'Not so big. Biggest halibut was maybe fourteen pounds.'

'That's small.'

'You ain't even caught one yet.'

This annoyed Minto, whose family did not own a floatplane, who could only drive up and down the coast or out to Douglas Island to fish, because they didn't have a boat either. The only places to catch halibut were out in deep water, by the Breadline or the islands, so Minto was stuck with cut-throat trout, coho, pinks, chums and dollies. Minto decided to keep the Snickers bars in his lunch pail for himself. Then he felt guilty because Frankie's dad had told him he could go with the Rickmans to the Salmon Derby out off Douglas Island on the boat and he'd never done that before.

'There was a fight last night in the bar.' Minto's father managed the Northern Lights bar way out on North Franklin and often came home with lurid tales of blood and bare bones.

'Yeah? What happened?'

'Couple of greenbacks got drunk and hit on some woman but her husband turned up.'

'Anyone cut up bad?'

'No – Pa went in with his bat and that was it.' Minto reeled in suddenly, thinking he'd felt something, but was disappointed.

Frankie looked at the bare hook. 'You gotta be quicker.'

'You telling me how to fish?'

Frankie stared at him with her green-blue eyes, same colour as the Gastineau Channel that bright day. 'Of course not. Sorry.'

''S OK.' Minto didn't know why he felt so prickly, like he was itching all over, like he was too big for his skin. He cut some herring, rinsed it in a bucket of sea water, forced the oily flesh over the hook. Once he was settled he asked, 'That crazy woman still with you?'

'Who d'you mean?' asked Frankie, who knew perfectly well.

'The Injun-lover with the grey hair.'

'Lucca? Nah – she's moved out. Got some rooms over near the Bay, but she still comes round to the house.' Frankie felt a bite, a tiny tug, and she yanked the line, stood up in one movement and began to turn the reel so fast the line screamed quietly. She knew the fish would try to turn its head on any slack but still she lost it, the hook and line flying out and looping, just missing Minto. 'Shit!' said Frankie.

Minto laughed, shoved her gently. 'So you still gonna teach me how to fish?'

Frankie laughed too, after a moment, then cut her bait and recast.

'So how come she's still hanging round? This Lucca woman?'

'I dunno.'

'Why's she here anyway? Pa says she's just a shit-stirrer.'

Frankie, who liked Lucca, who loved Minto, who didn't understand what was going on, why her mother and Lucca spent days in the Capitol Building, or holding meetings in the Sitka Street house, didn't know what to say. 'I don't think she is.'

'Pa said he read somewhere she was in Europe years ago. Fighting for the comm'nists. He said she wrote a whole book about the Injuns and how they need help. He says she's trouble squared.'

Frankie said nothing, began to reel in slowly, moving the herring slice around, trying to remember what her dad had said about making it come to life.

'He also said he thinks your mom's beautiful.'

Frankie smiled to herself then, because she knew it was Minto who thought Isobel was beautiful.

Minto could have stopped then, could have mentioned school buddies or asked what they were going to do that summer, maybe asked whether Frankie wanted to go hiking on Sunday. But he couldn't leave it alone. His family's history didn't *allow* him to leave it alone. 'Ma said this Lucca woman is gonna get us all bankrupted. Says she's gonna make sure the Injuns get everything and we all have to go back down south.'

Frankie still said nothing, confused by all the things she'd heard her parents arguing about.

Minto shrugged. 'I'm just surprised at your mother, is all. I mean, why's she friends with this woman? Mom says she should know better.'

Frankie suddenly began to reel in in earnest, kicked her bait box shut, emptied her bucket and shoved her jacket in her backpack.

'Just 'cos my mother's beautiful don't make her stupid. She knows what she's doing.'

Minto shrugged as Frankie walked quickly away down the pier, shrugged as if he didn't care, although the bottom had just fallen out of his day.

The citizens of Juneau, Alaska, knew the Rickmans were rich – why, they had a floatplane, a boat, a house in Anchorage as well as the house on Sitka Street, and it turned out they even had a cabin in Halibut Cove. There was a lot of talk about Isobel, about how she looked, how she acted kind of sniffy, but because she was well liked these characteristics were forgiven and, anyway, she was English. Rumours circulated about her being royalty, about her being related to the Queen, fuelled mainly by Thekla's flapping mouth. There was talk of a castle in England, filled with old paintings and statues. What people couldn't work out was why, if they had so much money, Frankie ran around looking like a hobo. In school she wore jeans, T-shirt and odd sweaters, most far too big for her (Frankie liked to borrow Billy-Ray's sweaters when he was away), and when she wasn't in school she wore jeans, T-shirt and odd sweaters that were far too big for her. No one had ever seen her in a nice skirt or a pretty dress; she even went to birthday parties in jeans. Her black hair was never styled, just cut whenever Isobel remembered. And she ran about with the Thorensson boy all the time, fishing, playing basketball and dodge ball, staying out late, hanging out at the Auke Rec Park. Come to think of it, Isobel never wore a skirt either, so maybe that was where Frankie got it from? And Frankie had that weird accent – clipped English with a dash of American – but the people of Juneau thought maybe she couldn't help that.

The people of Juneau talked a lot, not just about the Rickmans, but about everybody in town. And it *was* a town, a town that was drowning under an influx of strangers as the Native land claims arguments dragged on and on. The people of Juneau, who had lived a quiet life, in what they liked to think of as a friendly place, where everyone knew everyone else, whose parents and grandparents had known each other, talked a great deal in the diners and bars, in each other's homes, in the store, in the library, at the gas station, and as they talked the town split in two, yanked apart by those who wanted the pipeline and the oil and those who did not. Voices grew louder, glasses were thrown down and cracked, doors slammed as old friends walked away from each other, pulling on parkas and gloves and yelling. Those citizens who were smart enough watched the Rickmans closely, knowing that whatever happened to them was what might well happen to the State of Alaska itself.

The reason Frankie stayed out late, playing cards with Minto by street lamp, or skimming stones on calm waters, shooting hoops, racing round on snowmobiles, was because she didn't want to go home if both her parents were there. Why would she? All they did was argue all the time. If Isobel was there alone, Frankie went home from school and stayed home, spent the evening with her mother, talking and messing about. But sometimes she went back and walked in to find Lucca and others sitting in the den, talking in numbers and strings of letters, her mother making notes, and then Frankie'd sit in the kitchen, rush through school work, holler a good-bye and escape. That was bad enough. But the worst time of all was when Lucca was there holding a meeting and Billy-Ray came home, flying in early from Anchorage to find his house full of Indians. That time Frankie had been too slow to escape, had had to endure hours of rage.

'Shit,' Frankie told Minto, 'you should've heard them.'

'Was your pa drunk?'

'No, I don't think so. He did act kinda weird, but not drunk.'

Billy-Ray had been coked up to the eyeballs, had been in San Diego for four days, negotiating rig workers' contracts, and for four nights he'd partied. He wanted a bath and a bourbon, instead of which he came home to find his house full of Indians. He'd stood in the doorway, blue eyes glittering as the white powder burned, and he'd scanned the room.

Lucca glanced at him and went back to the papers on her lap. 'As I was saying, the Arctic Slope Native Association is worried that there will be insufficient compensation for loss of aboriginal rights to fish and exploit wildlife resources. What the state is taking here is the best land, as we know, and what are they offering? Ten million acres – which is insufficient even for subsistence living, let alone economic self-sufficiency. So I suggest—'

'And a billion dollars,' said Billy-Ray, who felt tall, blond and invincible, who felt like Thor, felt like a god.

'Excuse me?' Lucca's dark, hooded eyes turned to him.

'And a billion fucking dollars, which I reckon would be more than enough to buy some rods and a couple of wigwams.'

'You miss the point. The land is theirs. As long as the land and the Natives are one, their culture will survive; divide them and the culture dies. You cannot simply relocate people, you cannot take them away from their land, their heritage, away from what they have known for generations, and expect them to flourish.'

Isobel, who was taking notes, looked up and stared at Lucca, her eyes unreadable.

'Get real, Lucca – who gives a shit?'

'BR, stop it.' Isobel's voice made Frankie, who was sitting on the stairs, listening, her escape covered, shiver.

'What you got to realize is that it will happen – the pipeline will be built whether the Indians like it or not.'

Lucca flipped a match with a click of her fingers, lit a cigarette. 'I know that. What we're doing is trying to ensure that it's done properly. Ultimately it comes down to whether the State of Alaska controls the recovery of oil or whether the oil companies like Karbo control the State of Alaska and the fate of the people who live here.'

'I just spent four days working on the pipeline contracts – d'you realize that the average construction worker will be earning more than two thousand dollars a week? Think of the goddam economy, it will explode.'

'I have a problem with that. Where will the money be spent? Most of it Outside, where the workers live. They'll dig up the land, take their earnings from Karbo and BP and other companies and then get on a plane and spend it in Austin, Sacramento, Baton Rouge – wherever they come from.'

Billy-Ray was smiling, arms crossed, head cocked, smiling at Lucca. 'You have no idea what impact this will have, do you?'

'I like to think I do.'

'Well, I think you're talking out of your ass.'

In the corner sat a tall Native American, immobile but for his eyes, which scanned Billy-Ray's tailored suit and hand-tooled leather shoes. He stood slowly, unfolding until he was six inches taller than Billy-Ray.

'I lived in the Yukon Flats with my family. Seven years ago the white man came to look at our land. Then they built a dam and made a lake ten thousand square miles big. The fish died, the rivers disappeared, the animals fled. My family lived there for generations. They are buried, now, in a lake. My ancestors have been drowned. When the white man decided to stop the rivers he said that there was nothing there but a vast swamp uninhabited except for seven small Indian villages. He was wrong.'

The cocaine rush was fading and Billy-Ray's heart began to hammer although no one would have noticed this. Billy-Ray Rickman was scared of the Native men, scared by their appearance of calm, as if they knew things he didn't. He never forgot Urban saying that the Natives knew things he didn't, that he listened to them when they spoke. Billy-Ray looked away first, looked down at the toes of his highly polished shoes.

'You know the facts, Billy-Ray,' said Lucca, smoke curling through her hair in a shaft of sunlight. 'You know that Americans consume thirty-three per cent of the world's energy reserves. Six per cent of the world's population burns a third of its energy, all so we can double our GNP every sixteen years. Is that fair? What are you going to do when it all runs out? What are you going to do then? What's Frankie going to *do* then? What are we all going to do? Just keep digging? Keep tearing everything up so kids in California can cruise around in Thunderbirds, burning a gallon every eight miles? Do we keep throwing people off their land because we want to sit around wearing T-shirts at Christmas?' Lucca ground out her cigarette and grimaced. Stood up and faced him. 'I remember you telling me all those years ago that you wanted to explore, that when you were a boy you wanted to go to new places and find things and name them. I've been out to the Cook Inlet and I've been up to Prudhoe. I've seen the rigs and the wells, the tugs and tankers and crap that's all over it. Don't forget, Billy-Ray, I was the one who was with you when you saw the ocean for the first time and you loved it – blue earth, you called it. Always stayed with me. Blue earth. And now you're destroying it. Stealing it and then destroying it. What happened to you? You're buying up villages and lakes and rivers, even the sea itself. Is there nothing you think money can't buy? Seems to me you've sold your soul – how much was it worth, I wonder?'

Isobel frowned into the silence that followed Lucca's quiet voice stilling. 'I don't understand. How do you know these things about him?'

Lucca began to collect her papers together, tapping them on the table before slipping them into her briefcase. 'Billy-Ray and I met once, years ago. He was hitching to Seattle and I picked him up.' Lucca motioned to the Native men and they all stood as Billy-Ray stepped back. 'Isobel, don't forget Nixon's speaking tonight on the issue of federal government collusion with the energy corporations. Should be interesting.' She stood on tiptoe, kissed Isobel's cheek and walked out of the house, taking the Native men with her.

'That's when it got real bad,' said Frankie.

'How come?' Minto was bored with all this – Frankie was always yakking on about her parents.

'I don't think Mom knew that Dad and Lucca knew each other. She was really mad but I don't know why, I can't see what difference it makes. It's not like they were girlfriend and boyfriend or anything. I mean, it's not like they dated.'

Minto laughed. 'Oh yeah, like I can see your pa and Lucca getting hot – she's old enough to be his mother! Imagine balling that.'

Frankie, who was tossing stones into the choppy waters of the channel, looked up as a cruise ship blasted its horn and ravens clattered into the sky. She didn't want to tell Minto about the things her parents said to each other that night, and she really didn't want to tell him about how the next morning she and Mom had gone out to the car and found the windows covered in bumper stickers. The stickers were bright red and white and the message was repeated over and over on the glass: Let the bastards freeze in the dark. It took Isobel and Frankie two hours to scrape the glass clean and since then Frankie hadn't slept too well, knowing someone might be skulking in the garden, plotting, planning to break into the house.

'You ever wonder what you're gonna be?' asked Minto suddenly.

'What d'you mean?'

'Y'know – what you're gonna do when you're grown up.'

'Sometimes.' Frankie knew one thing she wanted to do – she wanted to find the Silent City.

Minto watched the cruise liner turning slowly to port. 'I don't want to stay here. I don't want to live here all my life. Y'know, the other day when Bud was back on leave?'

'Uh-huh.'

'We took the Chevy and drove up the highway. He let me drive the last bit 'cos he was too busy drinking a bottle of Wild Turkey.' Minto fell silent as the cruiser's horn blatted again.

'Yeah? And?' Frankie prompted.

'We went along Out the Road.'

'He let you drive right out there?'

'Yeah. Well, only the last bit. Maybe a half-mile. He showed me what to do.'

'That's cool. I reckon my dad might start teaching me soon, y'know, out by the bay.'

Minto wasn't listening; he just stared at the cruise ship. 'Thing is, it just stops. The road stops. I sat there with Bud guzzling down his whiskey and I was driving and the road stopped.'

'You *knew* that – we been out there before, lots of times – you knew that already.'

'I dunno. Maybe because I was driving it seemed different, getting to the dead end, knowing Skagway's only about twenty miles away and I won't ever get to drive there. You know? A whole different town, with different people and different places to go and I can't drive there. Sometimes I wonder if I'll ever fucking get out of here.'

Frankie looked at Minto's profile as he watched an Aztec on floats skim the waters, throwing up plumes of white foam, then glide to a halt and turn lazily towards the docks, as snow began to fall. Frankie thought how sad Minto looked.

1960

Over the torrid months of that summer, penned within the convent walls, Maggie watched her body metamorphose, change from the manageable to the unbearable. There was no one she could talk to, except other girls who were as ignorant of what was happening as she. No one sketched for her the anatomical concessions her body would make to accommodate the foetus; no one explained the effects of altered hormone levels, poor diet and enforced labour. Maggie, with the other Fallen girls, cleaned and swept, genuflected and prayed until their distended bodies gave up and they lay themselves down. Her belly scared her most, it was so hard, like the taut sides of her father's pigs, tight and lashed down. Her thighs chafed beneath her dress and sweat ran off her, making her skin slick as oil. Her face, when she had an opportunity to look at in a polished surface – mirrors were not allowed in the convent – was full, there was a suggestion of another chin, even her eyelids seemed pouchy. And all the time she was plagued with cravings for things she could not have – chocolate, crisp bacon, bananas – and dust. This last she didn't understand, was vaguely disgusted by, but still she'd sweep her fingers over shelves and chair-backs, furtively licking the resulting grey curl.

By the middle of September, Maggie was bloated, so swollen she thought her skin would tear, and she was relieved of her duties and sent to the small hospital at the back of the convent. She was due any day and she lay in bed examining her body, watching it for signs of imminent birth. The skin of her belly was by then stretched so thin it was nearly transparent, and she could make out the shape of the baby, could see its elbows, full of hard, angular bone, jabbing her under the ribs, beneath her huge, blue-veined breasts. When he kicked – and Maggie was sure it was a boy – she hated it, hated the feeling of being punched from within. She lay in the airless, dim ward, believing she loved her son-to-be and yet hating him, hating him for bringing her to this. Maggie had always known she was attractive to others, and had known why. And now she was reduced to this thing, this mass of fat and water and blood. Her hair was thinning, her gums, racked now by gingivitis, were too tender to touch. She needed to pee all the time, which meant hauling herself to her swollen feet, almost rolling off the bed, slipping on shoes the laces of which she could no longer tie, and shuffling to the toilet. The worst thing was the acid, the reflux, which meant she could not sleep, could only doze sitting up, her back pressed against the hard iron railings of the bed head. The only change that was bearable was in the weather, which broke suddenly as storms came in from the west. The ward, then, was almost dark, even at midday, but Maggie didn't care. She listened to the rain beating on the corrugated roof and was grateful the endless sweating had ceased.

In the first week of October her due date passed and the baby dropped, all nine pounds of it dropped into the bowl of her pelvis, pressing harder on her bladder, and Maggie was scared, then, that when she sat in bed she was crushing him in her lap. She tried to heft the mound when she walked or stood, cradled it in her arms, fingers laced beneath it, and she tried to lift it to take the strain from her back. Days and nights passed as her skin stretched farther and Maggie's world shrank to a single thought. And then, one morning, as she stood outside the toilet door, her hand on the jamb to take some of her weight, her eyes closed, rocking slightly, it happened. A small, bloody plug fell from her and her waters gushed out. Maggie opened her eyes in surprise, looked down to see her dress stained dark, her shoes wet, as the waters kept coming. She tensed, tried to stem the fluid, but it ran and ran. She was embarrassed by this, embarrassed by standing there, legs open, bucketing water, embarrassed and terrified, and she looked up to see her sister, Mary, watching her, dressed in a simple white habit, her bare feet blue with cold.

1971

On the morning of 18 December 1971, Richard Nixon sat at a large polished desk in Congress as cameras flashed and he signed into law the Alaska Natives Claims Settlement Act. It had taken one hundred and four years but finally the Native Americans were to be given recompense for the theft of their land, the forfeiture of their livelihood, the death of their culture. Was it enough? Nine hundred and sixty-two million dollars pocket money and forty-four million acres of land? Was it enough recompense? The oil companies whooped and cheered, thought of the miles of pipe stored in Valdez and pictured the thread running across a beach. Tricky Dickie smiled his treacherous, disturbing smile, safe in the knowledge that the recording tapes were rolling in the Watergate building.

As it turned out, the oil companies whooped too soon – sure, they'd brushed aside the Native Americans, paid lobbyists to persuade Congress to settle the claims, lined many pockets, back-handed, glad-handed, back-scratched, palm-greased and seduced the Alaskans into thinking the oil was rightfully theirs. The Native Americans took the money and the land and fell silent. The next chorus of voices came from the environmentalists, the Sierra Club, the Wilderness Society, Friends of the Earth . . . a chorus that rang in the ears of the executives of Alyeska as one from a Greek tragedy. Lucca Barzini and Isobel Rickman were still singing loudly.

'My mom says you were all shafted – well, she didn't actually say that but that's what she meant.'

Charlie looked at Frankie as she clumsily whittled a piece of drift-wood, frowning, her tongue sticking out as she shaved the end. 'Why am I shafted?'

'She and Lucca reckon you all should have stuck out for more. What d'you reckon?'

Charlie stared at the snow-covered mountains, sitting immobile, weathered hands on aching knees. 'I reckon the world's going to hell,' he said after a while. Charlie didn't really understand any of it, the way it had worked out. Now, it seemed, he had to prove his Native American ancestry in order to own shares in a land that was his, when his ancestors were all around him. What Charlie wanted to say was that it hadn't felt good to have two white women fighting his cause, that it made him feel worthless. He didn't want to tell Frankie that he drank cheap liquor every night until he fell over because it was better than thinking of voices by a fireside. He didn't want to tell Frankie that he sometimes thought of ending this, of walking out on to the ice fields, walking away from the town with nothing and joining his family, his family who lived in the stones and the forests and the sky and the glaciers. That he wanted to walk out there and lie down because he felt powerless. 'If you cut here and here you can hollow out the middle.' Charlie pointed to the wood with his brown finger, spatulate nail grimed with oil from fixing Thekla's car.

'Why d'you reckon the world's going to hell?'

Charlie shrugged. Seemed to him the whole place was a mess, full of people and cars and planes. When he was a boy, living in the village on the west side of Admiralty Island, life was simple. The men fished in canoes, the women tanned leather and collected berries and fruits, they had potlatch and ceremonies of celebration. The salmon ran, the eagles soared as orcas passed by; the bears feasted and so did the humans. He remembered sitting by the fire at night as the elders told their tales, elaborate myths that prepared the young and appeased the dead. His grandfather often told of the time in '98 when the gold rush started for the Klondike, speaking of how the white man arrived in cardboard shoes, thin shirts and open jackets, mad with earth-lust. How these men, and some women, set off into the foothills and on up to the passes through the mountains, heading for the Klondike, not knowing where it was, or how far it was, not knowing that they would die soon. His father remembered how the white men had come to the villages on the coast seeking help, looking for guides, for porters. At the same time that these white people arrived, a Spirit Bear had appeared in the creek at the back of the village, a pale bear with white fur and curious blue eyes. An omen that could not be ignored. The Spirit Bear stayed by the village for years, its albino face showing itself each summer as the fish ran. Only once the white man had discovered zinc and lead by the village and opened the Treadwell mine there did the bear leave. Some of the Native men had gone with the white men who asked for help, only to return with tales of trails winding up through the mountains, a thin black line of black on white as men, women and horses fought their way through ice and across crevasses, driven by greed, by snow-blindness, by gold-blindness beyond the point of exhaustion. The returning Native men spoke of the dead lying frozen by the trail, half covered by snowdrifts, stripped by passers-by of leather boots, jackets, shovels, buckets, knapsacks and bed rolls. The dead were left in the snow, near naked, their empty palms turned up, facing an uncaring sky. 'We thought them foolish,' Charlie's grandfather had said in the light of the fire. 'We thought they were foolish and mad and that they would leave.' But seventy years later they were still there, thought Charlie. They *were* mad and they *were* foolish but they were still there. It was his village and his family that had disappeared. 'Money does not put things right,' Charlie said. 'It cannot replace the dead.'

Frankie frowned, said nothing, kept scraping at the wood. She was carving a bear, standing on its hind legs. Holding it out, she turned it admiringly. 'What d'you think?'

'Not bad. Good.' Charlie watched Frankie brush her long hair from her eyes. The garage was warm, snug in the snowstorm coming in. 'Why don't you see Minto any more?'

'I do. Sometimes.'

'But not often?'

'Sometimes.'

'Maybe you had an argument?'

It was Frankie's turn to shrug. 'Maybe.' But they hadn't had an argument, they had simply drifted apart. Frankie wasn't sure why Minto didn't want to see her, why he hung out with a different bunch of people, but he did. He even looked different, with long hair curling over his collar, wearing jeans and a black leather jacket he borrowed from Bud's wardrobe.

Charlie often saw Minto as well, when he walked back to his room on Egan Drive, saw the big, blond boy smoking cigarettes and swigging from a brown paper bag, surrounded by older boys, a few girls flirting on the edges of a fluid circle of boredom. The Thorensson boy, who watched Charlie pass with icy eyes. Minto knew Charlie was an Auk, that Charlie's family had fished in the waters around Hoonah and Tenakee. Charlie knew Minto blamed his village for setting the fire that had raged through his family's cannery and the fleet at dock. Minto stared at Charlie and with his blue eyes and pale hair the boy reminded the man of the Spirit Bear. An omen that cannot be ignored. 'Perhaps it is right that you don't see him.'

Perhaps it was right, thought Frankie, but it didn't stop her feeling lonely.

The citizens of Juneau, who were still talking, still yelling at each other, had by then forgotten how to cut the Rickmans some slack, how to tolerate difference. The way they began to look at it, the Indians and the Greenies were stopping them getting their money, and there was this weird, tall Englishwoman and her crazy daughter mixed up with both of them. No wonder Frankie felt lonely.

Isobel gradually became aware that Frankie had fewer friends. She lifted her head from the textbooks and reports on congressional activity one day to realize that Frankie was still with her, that her daughter hadn't been out for weeks, staying, instead, at home, watching TV and kicking her heels. Isobel was nonplussed. What to do? She thought about it and decided that she was pleased Frankie no longer saw Minto – for she, too, had seen Minto hanging out drinking and smoking, sitting on the hoods of cars that had radios blaring rock music. What to do instead? Isobel decided to distract Frankie from her loneliness and she did manage it in some ways; she remembered the mantra of love, food and stimulation (in that order) that had sustained both of them during the grim years of living in Anchorage. Isobel made time, punching gaps like sucker holes in her days and weekends. She took it upon herself to go river fishing with

Frankie, amazing her daughter with her skill, amazing herself with the effortless recall of the switch of a wrist as her father's hand rested on her shoulder. She went to the school to watch Frankie play basketball, took her skating when she could. They'd catch a movie on Friday nights and go on to Belle's Pierpoint for a burger, fries and Coke as a treat. Isobel even took Frankie down to the shooting range out past the bay and amazed her daughter all over again. Frankie watched her mother wrapping her huge hands around the stocks, or holding shotguns loosely, as if they were extensions of her long arms, and then snapping to and blasting perfect scores out of distant silhouettes. The first time this happened, the men in the neighbouring alleys stopped their firing to watch Isobel's round. When the final echoes of a single rifle firing had died down, a bearded guy in a check shirt spat on the concrete floor and looked at Isobel, who was reloading.

'Reckon you can do that again, lady?' He crossed his arms high above his dung gut and squinted up at her.

Isobel pressed the restart button, turned and winked at Frankie as the paper clipped on wire shuddered to the farthest station, at six hundred feet, and Isobel heard the sound of shattering clay as a popinjay stood next to her on a distant Cotswold ridge. 'Let's try something else,' she said. Selecting a .38, she turned to the target and shredded the bull's eye, barely touching its circumference.

'Shit,' said the fat man.

The other men there broke into reluctant applause as the target rattled to a stop and Isobel unclipped it. The way they looked at it, she might mix with the fuckin' Indians and tree-huggers, might talk like an asshole and look down at 'em all, but, hey, you had to admit the lady could shoot.

Sometimes Isobel lay in her bed, hating and missing Billy-Ray equally, and she thought of taking Frankie, taking the plane, taking the money and running, running all the way back to Highbury, England. But she knew she could not leave. Juneau's pastel houses, the soaring mountains, glittering, turquoise glaciers, forests and creeks, the view over the green-blue-purple channel and beyond to the fractured, churning coastline – all this kept Isobel there, trapped her. And yes, trapped was exactly how she felt – by the rain, by the dead-ended road, by her inability to fly, the steepness of the streets, the sloughing avalanches that closed the few miles of road available, the darkness, the looming rock face behind the house. Isobel, Minto, Thekla, Fin, nearly everyone in the capital of Alaska experienced this warping, emotional schizophrenia – what kept them there was that which would sometimes make them mad. Frankie felt this too, this profound emotion, which was not love for the landscape but, rather, an approximation of it.

In the end it was Billy-Ray who saved Frankie from her moping. He saw her one day, during her summer vacation, when she was thirteen, sitting in the den with the drapes closed against dazzling sunshine and the TV on. He watched her, unseen, and saw that she wasn't really watching the screen. Frankie wasn't doing anything.

'Hey,' Billy-Ray said, 'how about coming up with me and seeing where I work?'

'Huh?' Frankie turned her unfocused eyes on him.

'How d'you feel about flying up to Prudhoe and seeing what I do?'

'Flying how?'

'Just you and me. We'll fly up there together. It'll take a few days.' And Frankie smiled.

Billy-Ray chartered a de Havilland Beaver with radial engine (his Super Cub was too small for what he had planned) and a few days later they flew out of Anchorage heading for the North Slope. This was new territory for Frankie, new territory for most people. The de Havilland buzzed above endless marshland, the plane shuddering, shifting in the thermals and winds. Occasionally Billy-Ray spoke into the mike as he pointed out settlements – Wasilla, Willow, Talkeetna, flat, grey towns strung out along the highway. Frankie barely spoke, her eyes glued to the ground below or scanning the sky, the uninterrupted miles and miles of sky. Mounts McKinley, Foraker and Silverthrone appeared to the west and Frankie was no longer aware of the noise of the engine, of the shifting in unexpected directions. She didn't speak, she barely breathed. There was nothing in her view but cloud, ice and rock. And then there was the sky – the ever-changing sky, as the earth twisted on its axis and the two of them flew north, towards the pole, in a mess of cables and fibreglass, moving with the sun on what would be a never-ending day, moving with it, skimming the earth.

That night they stayed in a hotel in Fairbanks. After they'd eaten, Billy-Ray settled Frankie in her room, made sure she was asleep before locking the door and going out. He walked around the town for a while, crossing the streets to avoid gangs of listless Natives hanging round, faces blank, breath sour with stale alcohol. Billy-Ray needed films for his camera and he went to the Co-op store on 2nd, where the air reeked of fried onions, perfume, coffee and pop-corn, only for the girl to tell him they had none, nor did they have any batteries or shampoo. Chewing gum, looking bored, she announced, 'The pipeline guys came through – y'know, Alyeska? Bought up all them. Happens all the time. Last week we ran out of burgers and soap.' Billy-Ray went across the road, decided to have a beer in the Flame Lounge, which was a gloomy hole. He sat at the bar and ordered a Bud – which cost a dollar! A whole fucking dollar! – and looked around himself. Men sitting at tables, eyes glazed, hanging on to their cans and glasses as if they were the only things they could believe in. Riggers, pipeliners, truckers and boomers dressed in Stetsons and Western shirts, wads of bills burn-ing holes in their pockets, looking desperate, looking bored, looking half alive. Billy-Ray felt a touch on his elbow and turned to see a young Native girl, maybe sixteen, maybe less. 'Wanna come home with me, mistah?' Billy-Ray shook his head, shrugged her off and finished his beer. As he walked back to the hotel on 4th and Cushman, a Native staggered out of a liquor store, shouting, waving dollar bills. He tripped and fell, cracked his head on a waste bin. Billy-Ray pulled his jacket close, was startled by a wolf dog which threw itself against the glass of a 4×4. Neon flashed feebly in the daylight at midnight, promising girls and entertainment, as men hitched their trousers and stepped inside. Billy-Ray checked Frankie's door when he got back, checked it was closed and locked, then unlocked it, crept into the room and slept on the floor by her bed.

As they waited for clearance the next morning, Frankie watched a Hercules freight aircraft lumber down the runway ahead of them, kicking up dust as it roared. She didn't know (but Billy-Ray could have told her) that Hercules planes, each with a payload of nearly fifty thousand pounds, had been taking off every hour from Fairbanks for the past three years, heading north for the oilfields. Frankie watched the earth recede as Billy-Ray took off and headed west, at a thousand feet, so low Frankie could see the houses of Stevens Village, sitting, now, on the edge of a vast, strange lake, which seemed out of place. (Billy-Ray could have explained this, too – beneath the reservoir, drowned by the dammed waters of the Yukon, were the ancestors of the tall Indian.) A couple of hours later, unaware that she had crossed the Arctic Circle, Frankie looked ahead and saw, stretching for hundreds of miles, left and right, fading to the horizon, an unbroken line of mountain peaks, clearing the curvature of the earth, folds of slate grey and velvet purple, disrupting the pale blue dome that hung over her.

'Gates to the Arctic,' said Billy-Ray's voice in her ear, and her father turned to her and smiled. His daughter looked, he thought, as he must have done when he saw the Pacific for the first time.

'Chandalar, this is Beaver 2475. What is your weather, please?'

'Beaver 2475, this is Chandalar. Weather. Sky clear, temperature sixty-eight, wind oh-thirty at twenty. Altimeter oh-oh-two.'

Billy-Ray smiled again, began to climb – the Gates were open. The Beaver shook and rattled as the thermals fought the aerodynamics of the wings and the huge tyres' drag factor changed in the thinning air. Dietrich Pass, at nearly five thousand feet, opened up before and beneath them. Frankie stared at the mountain walls growing tight and tall around them, rising above them, indifferent, cold and treeless. Down below, a ribbon of blue-green melt water flowed north towards the coast, mirrored by a white line that followed the river's course. The peaks began to slide away, became foothills, and then they were through the pass, still following the river. Scanning the suddenly flat and featureless horizon, Frankie frowned as the plane buzzed north. The Slope stretched nearly two hundred miles to the Arctic Ocean, mile after mile of permafrost and tundra, laced with filigree creeks and rivers, lakes, melt water, thawing ice. What was confusing Frankie was the horizon: there seemed to be three of them, three horizons fading like steppes in shades of blue, silver and grey. As she stared, the horizons came into focus, fell into place. First there was the edge of dull, brown tundra, then the strip of ocean, which disappeared beneath the white, rippled ice sheet covering the pole, and above that a pale, flat sky. The horizon line between ice and sky was almost impossible to distinguish.

The engine's drone changed pitch and the Beaver descended towards a mess of huts and gravel heaps, rigs, cables, trucks and pipes. Fumes belched from exhausts as front-loading Cats, cranes, flat-beds, utilities, 4 × 4s and trucks crunched around the Karbo headquarters; gas escaped from the enormous field trapped beneath the tundra and burned off in roiling, smoky flames, the carbon particles drifting due west, leaving a faint smudged line against the sky. Once the Beaver had taxied to a halt and edged its way in to dock amongst a swarm of other light planes, Billy-Ray switched off the engine and stretched as Frankie looked around. Confused by being able to see the edge of the world, a little scared by the hard-hatted, bearded men yelling and cursing all around her as they wrestled with machinery, she stayed close to her father as he slapped backs and yelled greetings. Again and again he pushed Frankie gently forward to shake hands with a worker and she'd shake then shrink back against her father. Billy-Ray showed her to her room, one among many arranged in a three-storey building that had been barged from Seattle. Billy-Ray wanted to show Frankie the camp, but she said she was tired and wanted to go to bed. Lying in her featureless room, where the light never faded, she found it hard to breathe. All she wanted was to climb back in the Beaver and fly into the sun, just like the planes had done when she and Billy-Ray and Isobel had watched them taking off from Merrill Field in Anchorage all those years before.

For three days Billy-Ray flew or drove Frankie around the camps and drilling sites on the Slope, showing her the Christmas trees (nothing but a mess of metal, a stunted growth of valves and stopped pipes) which capped well heads, the rigs that were boring new wells. Development was taking place all around the Operations Center, where bright red pilings were being driven into the tundra to support three-storey buildings housing computers. Frankie was stunned, overwhelmed by sound, despite the ear defenders she wore – pulverising Cats, roaring helicopters, light planes, freight planes, arc welders, distant explosions as depth charges fired, saws, grinders, drill bits screaming. One day her father flew her north to Karbo's rig near the port, which was drilling out under the Beaufort Sea, and whilst Billy-Ray went into the offices Frankie skulked around the rig, the lower part of which was closed in, shrouded against the bitter wind. Walking round stacked bags of drilling mud and untidy piles of pipe and cable, the only sound the rumble of encased machinery, Frankie could see no one. She watched long, grey stratus clouds roll in over a peaceful, damaged sea and shivered. In the evenings they showered and then met in the dining area of the Operations Center, which was painted in kindergarten colours – bright blue, pink and yellow. As they ate Billy-Ray talked statistics at Frankie, talked work with the men who joined them, drawing diagrams on napkins, his voice rising as they discussed pipeline strategies, as they argued about how to get the damned pipeline built. Frankie tried to block out the muzak that played constantly as she watched Billy-Ray. He was, she realised, proud of what Karbo had done.

It wasn't until they were flying back south, leaving the midnight sun behind and flying into shadows, on the journey home, that Frankie remembered something her father had said. She adjusted the mouthpiece, turned to look at Billy-Ray, who smiled at her.

'You said that Karbo and the others—'

'BP and ARCO.'

'Yeah – you said they'd all been building for three years.'

'That's right – well, four, if you include the time we spent drilling on the east field.'

'But how come? How could they be building?'

'What d'you mean?'

'Well, they weren't allowed to – you know, all the stuff about the Native Americans and all that? All the stuff Mom and Lucca are doing? How could they build?'

Billy-Ray smiled again but not for the same reason. 'Frankie, honey, those Indians were never going to stop it. They only got what they wanted because we wanted them to have it. Without us they'd be dead in the water, with no money, no land, chewing whale fat or whatever it is they do.'

'But that's not right.'

'The Indians did damn well out of it.'

'Charlie said the world's gone to hell.'

'Charlie's a miserable bastard.' Billy-Ray grimaced, checked the instruments.

Frankie stared at the clouds – high cirrus, whipped by freezing winds. 'What about the environ . . . environmental – you know, what Mom's doing now?'

'They'll be OK. We're doing all these studies – working with them. That will be OK.' Billy-Ray began the climb to the Atigun Pass, which led to the Gates of the Arctic.

Frankie felt inexpressibly sad. Watching the crags of the peaks harden, as the russet red, gold and autumnal green of the tundra faded, she knew her mother would never win. No one would. Not the Indians, not the Greenies, not even Lucca would win. Frankie had seen the metal monster chewing up the earth and sea, she knew how loud it was, how big it was, how it flattened and blitzed and never stopped. Tattie fucking bogle, Frankie thought, but she didn't say anything.

Why did Billy-Ray do this? Why did he take Frankie to the North Slope? He did it because he wanted to spend time with his daughter, because he wanted to draw her back to him. He knew there was a struggle taking place in Sitka Street which he thought, sometimes, would never be resolved. There were nights when he lay next to his wife and he wondered about many things. Billy-Ray, who was forty-five, knew he had probably lived more than half his life, knew that it had been an unusual life, and also knew that at some point he had lost control of it. What had happened to the Reichmann gene that prompted planning, endless planning? Prompted rectitude and fidelity? Maybe it was the coke or the vodka or the money – he didn't know. But sometimes he wished Isobel would roll over and wrap her arms around him, rest his head on her shoulder and stroke his greying hair and tell him it would all be all right. There were nights when he lay awake and tried to remember how to say 'I love

you' in seven languages but he had forgotten how. So he decided to
draw his daughter back to him and planned the trip north, to
Prudhoe. He wanted to show her how minimal was the damage
done, how insignificant the pump stations and pipeline and well
heads would be in the vastness that was the North Slope. Perhaps if
Billy-Ray had spent more time with Frankie before, he would not
have misjudged her. Because, as it turned out, rather than showing
her insignificance, he showed her escape. Frankie went back to
Juneau and decided she was going to fly; she was going to earn herself a pilot's licence and she was going to fly into the sun.

In the end, of course, Billy-Ray was right. In the end, all the meetings, seminars, lobbying and surveys and environmental reports
amounted to a hill of beans. Isobel and Lucca, indeed everyone
involved in trying to slow the destruction, had wasted their time.
When Frankie went to high school that Fall, with memories of the
blue dome hanging above her, the members of Opec met with the oil
companies to negotiate the price of a barrel of crude. Five days later,
when Nixon requested millions of dollars in aid for Israel, the cost of
oil rocketed by seventy per cent and the Western world convulsed.
Those convulsions could be felt from Norway to Texas, all the way
from Venezuela to Prudhoe Bay. Congress voted to bypass the
National Environmental Protection Act and the wraps came off the
Japanese pipeline which had been stockpiled for years at the terminal in Valdez.

THE REGANS

Sean Regan died on a cloud-ragged, blowsy summer evening, as a gentle wind blew over the peninsula, warmed by the Gulf Stream which had flowed all the way from Mexico. He lay on his blood-rust-stained mattress and dreamed himself away, having had enough of this world. Sean faded quickly after the diagnosis – he had cancer of the spleen and the red and white pulp of that organ was corrupting, cancer cells spreading as fast as spilled whiskey. Sean Regan was not yet fifty and he had been poisoned by the radon that permeated the land.

For a few short weeks that summer, Sean Regan took to his bed before dying and was waited on for the first time in his life. He no longer had to fuss with clothes and washing, no longer had to look at his yellowing toenails and scraggy thighs. He lay down and he let his mind fly. And where did it fly to? Sean Regan (shaman? priest?), with his skate-wing face and ossifying skeleton, finally allowed himself to dream. He left the peninsula, he left the land itself, riven as it was by bombs and bullets, maimed bodies lying in the streets of Belfast as young boys schemed revenge and British soldiers stalked the streets, and Sean Regan flew. He did not fly as a dove or an eagle or a phoenix, for he was none of these things. He flew as a crow, a raven, because that was what he would have been. Scavenger, a scavenger all his life, living on the pickings of other people's lives. He lay in his bed in Ballysod and he took flight.

What might he have been? What might Sean Regan have been if the accidents that were death and birth had happened differently? If he had been born a hundred miles south, on rich loam land? Or by a deep bay with a sound harbour, where waters squirmed with fish? What would have happened if he had not met and married Annie?

Or if he had been born into a home where there were both books and time? Would he have been an artist or a poet? He might have spent his life wrestling with words on the page, or carving them into stone.

During his last days, Sean Regan refused food and water, managed to cut the cord along which the pain flowed from his body to his mind and released himself to ponder possibilities, to face for the first time the fact that things might have been different because it no longer mattered. He felt weightless, ecstatic almost, as he flew away, the tips of his blue-black wings brushing against possibility. For hours he might consider the harsh beauty of the sheer, razoring cliffs of Blacksod Bay when the falling sun hit them just so; or the movement of tall grass in high wind, undulating as if it were singing. Imagined himself, young and tall, his unseamed face long and pensive, walking the honey-blush corridors of Trinity, thinking pure thoughts. Sean Regan, his face made almost beatific by peace, lay dying as his wife sat by him, flicking beads. He was unaware of the priest entering the dingy room, unaware of the last rites being administered, as he dreamed himself into an attic full of babies and saw himself kneeling by a cot, holding the foot of a black-haired, blue-eyed baby girl. Perched on the foot of the cot was a raven, head cocked, and in its beak, as thick and dangerous as a broken mussel shell, was clamped a butterfly.

1974

It was over, the fight was finished, and everyone knew it. Once Alyeska began gouging an eight-hundred-mile trench, eight feet wide and eight feet deep, across Alaska, people began to settle. The arguments and spats weren't forgotten but they dimmed in the memory; the longer the memory, the longer the pipeline, the less the arguments seemed to matter. Yet some endings are indiscernible; sometimes it may not be until years later that it becomes evident that a distant point in time was an ending of sorts. The slipping away as gradual as the movement of the planets, the retreat of the tide, the melting of glaciers.

It was over, the fight was finished and everyone in the Rickman house on Sitka Street knew it too. Frankie knew it because the house fell silent, there were no more meetings chaired by the chain-smoking Lucca, no more nights of sitting on the stairs, listening to her parents ripping up conversations. Even her mother's Remington fell silent and Frankie missed the sound of her irregularly syncopated typing, her occasional cries of 'Bugger!' Frankie was relieved but something troubled her, something she couldn't identify, because on the face of it everything was fine. School was cool, she did well in class, and she played basketball on the team. She fished with new friends, who seemed easier to find now the pipeline was started, and sometimes she stayed at their houses for sleep-overs. These evenings weren't as much fun as playing slaps or jacks with Minto, or trying to give each other tattoos with needles and ink, or just sitting on the dockside watching water with him. But Minto had broken the cardinal rule and he hadn't stayed the same, he had changed so she didn't love him any more. Or she didn't think she did. When she wasn't fishing or playing or listening to music on her new record player, Frankie was flying, either in Billy-Ray's Super Cub, with Billy-Ray piloting and talking her through what he was doing, or, when he was away, Frankie flew in her mind, her imagination taking her out over the Slope, or skimming her over lakes. She checked aviation books out of the library and committed the flare of a wing or the angle of a strut to memory, and soon she could identify any small plane at dock or in the air. Frankie lay on her bed, in her watery room, and looked at the clouds scudding by, dreaming of being sixteen.

Lucca Barzini and the ecology groups left for Washington and New York, where they intended to harry Alyeska, knowing the huge corporation would try to evade regulation. They packed their bags and flew away, leaving Isobel Rickman behind, like a lone survivor on the deck after a storm. The house seemed huge, seemed far too large to accommodate her plans and aspirations. And just what were they anyway? Isobel took to walking around her yard at night again, just as she had ten years before, smoking and thinking, staring at the night sky, at the mountains. Isobel Had Enough – Will Someone, Anyone, Collect? She'd stand and stare at the golden-lit windows of the houses around her, wonder at the lives being lived behind them, wonder about the quality of those lives, about the quality of her own life. This confused her, this last thought. Because even if she tried to imagine how her life would have been if she had not married Billy-Ray, if, for instance, she had married the boyfriend in Bristol (who had been, after all, from her own class), she still could not imagine what she would be *doing*. She had been so ill prepared for life – do the things you're good at, her father always told her. But what was she good at? Isobel wondered as a cloud bank came rolling in, shutting out the stars one by one. Shooting, riding, skiing, fishing, eating, drinking. She couldn't do anything useful. She stood in her yard, listening to rain spatter on shingled roofs, listening to the swollen waters of Gold Creek racing to the ocean, and she felt trapped. By the dead-end road, by the coastline, by the glaciers. By Frankie. Twice a week the ferry docked, loaded and then sailed away, heading for Bellingham in the Outside, and Isobel watched it every time, watched it heading south.

Billy-Ray, like Frankie, noticed the silence in the house. More than a silence; a silence like a bank, like a dyke, like a tall, smooth dam, holding back a great weight. Billy-Ray was not often in Sitka Street but when he was he felt this weight pressing against him. One night, after he'd spent hours in the study looking though construction reports, he yawned, stretched, realized he was cold, and went looking for Isobel. He saw her, out of the kitchen window, smoking, staring at the sky. Opened the door and shivered.

'Hey, what you doing?'

Isobel looked over at her husband. 'I'm watching the ferry.'

Billy-Ray joined her in the darkness, jigging a little, trying to warm himself as he looked down the slope of the yard, down to the Gastineau Channel. 'You know they call it the Vomit Comet? Goes all the way out to the Aleutians, out to Umnak Island. Gets pretty rough out there. But it looks pretty, even if it is a rusting bucket. I've never seen it at night before.'

'Well, you're never here.'

Billy-Ray, who was tired, who was content, who wanted warmth, decided to say, 'I'm taking Frankie out tomorrow, up to Glacier Bay. If you want to come, I can change plans. I can arrange a pilot to take the three of us.'

'No, thank you.'

Billy-Ray blew on his hands, rubbed them together. 'Why don't you come in? I'll get a fire going.'

Isobel watched the ferry and asked in a voice as neutral as blank, white paper, 'Do you see Siggy and Deet any more?'

'What?'

'Do you still see Siggy and Deet? Remember? You called me that time in England because you kept seeing them.'

The ferry blasted three minor notes which twisted up the valley.

'No. No, I don't.'

'Why not?'

'I don't know.'

'Is it a good thing? That you don't see them? Do you think it's a good thing?'

'I don't know. I think so.' Billy-Ray looked at Isobel, at her profile, which wasn't so different from the first time he met her. 'That's a weird question.'

'Maybe, but you knew the answer.'

Later, when they were lying in bed, Billy-Ray was too scared to touch his wife, even to wrap his arm around her. Too scared, too, to fall asleep.

'I miss you,' Isobel said into the darkness.

Billy-Ray waited until he knew Isobel was sleeping and then he slipped from the bed and walked quietly down the stairs, through a silent house. He opened a bottle of beer and sat in the kitchen in a pool of light, hands flat on the table. For once his mind wasn't turning over problems about refrigerated below-land pipes, gabion and concrete mats or pig launching/receiving facilties. Instead, Billy-Ray closed his eyes and rode the sleep piling up in him. He found himself walking alone across a featureless landscape in harsh sunlight, the grass beneath his feet short and dry, struggling to thrive. He looked up and saw a small pyramid pile of rough stones. He walked over to the cairn and began to turn the stones, stones that had been in place for a long time, stones that were well bedded down. He turned the stones with his scarred hands and beneath each one he found an unpalatable truth he had ignored.

Beneath the first he found Isobel's loneliness. He'd known for years that Isobel was lonely, that she was unhappy, but she was always there, when he came back, she was there. Nothing changed; Isobel stayed, as he knew she would. And he'd taken it to mean he was forgiven because she stayed. Because the house was clean, the yard tidy, the refrigerator full, supper on the table, year after year. Isobel loved Frankie, made sure she was happy and healthy, took her to meets, played with her, talked to her, made sure she was content. And they both stayed, so surely he must be forgiven?

Beneath the second stone he found a question: why did he work so hard? Stay away so much? Because he was always trying to make money, trying to catch up with Isobel and her trust funds, her private wealth; he was still trying to be the provider, and he knew he never could be. Sometimes waves of fury would wash over him because Isobel was a better shot, a more accomplished rider, a more successful fisherman. Because she had learned her skills at leisure, for leisure. Whilst he had learned them because he needed to, to kill vermin on the farm, to put food on the table.

Another stone and beneath it he found infidelity. Found the fact that he played around, that he had sex with women he'd known for a day, women he'd known for an hour. Why did he do these things? Because he'd never lost his awe of his wife. The way she stood, the way she moved, something about the tilt of her head, the gravity of what she said, made him feel small and unwanted. Isobel never lied, never deceived. No matter how often he took her, no matter how often he shouted and cursed, he never felt he'd won. Yet when he came back home – hung over, coke-blasted – there she was. She stayed. But he knew that it was her sense of duty now, rather than love, which kept her there. He could only have it all because she was prepared to have so little of him. When he'd spent that week with Magde, all those years ago, the first time he'd considered having it all, he'd known Magde was grateful, grateful to have him. By the way she had wrapped her arms around him, touched his scar, he'd known she was grateful. Magde made him feel needed. Isobel never made him feel that way; Isobel made him feel need.

A June day in Minnesota, when the world was younger, when men rode horses and women baked miraculous bread, a boy was told by his mother to go to his father, who needed him. He went and he found his father trying to dig holes in the hard, packed earth. The boy was told by his father to go to his mother, who needed him. He went and when he found her she disappeared.

Billy-Ray turned another stone, which was so old it was lichen-spotted and mossy, and beneath it he found a list – Magde, Lucca, Jacqueline and one other whose name he'd forgotten. A list of the women he had known before he married Isobel, women who had mattered in some way, women who had changed him.

The last stone – and beneath it was the thought that one day he would come back home, his skin having soaked up the scent of yet another woman, and Isobel would not be there. Isobel would be gone. What did this thought do? It made Billy-Ray feel need.

The kitchen door creaked and Billy-Ray opened his eyes and turned, thought he saw Siggy standing outside the pool of light.

'Are you OK?' asked Isobel.

*

Billy-Ray changed after that night; he stopped snorting lines, cut down on the booze and made it back to Sitka Street as often as he was able. He tried to remember how it had been before (before what, exactly? Before the North Slope, Isobel could have told him), how their lives had been, and he suggested going to the movies, trips to Halibut Cove, vacations to the Outside. He took Isobel and Frankie out to eat, the three of them went fishing, spent time hiking together. Prompted by the dream memory of turning stones, Billy-Ray became more careful, of himself and his wife; no one would lure him away from Isobel; he would come home for the rest of his days and find Isobel still there.

But then, one sleet-drenched night in New York City, Billy-Ray climbed out of a cab outside Karbo Inc.'s head office on Madison Avenue, already late for the AGM. He jogged into the lobby and as he stood shaking rain from his hair, slapping at the sleeves of his coat, he smelled it: tobacco, Chanel and vanilla, a long-forgotten perfume. And Billy-Ray was lying in a bed at the Ritz Hotel in London, years before, making love.

Jacqueline, who was standing by the elevator doors, saw Billy-Ray looking for her and she smiled. Why was she there, in the lobby of the Karbo Tower? Because Sir Sidney had bequeathed Jacqueline his legacy of a chain of petrol and service stations and, as a shareholder in Karbo, she had an interest in the corporation. She also had an interest in Billy-Ray Rickman. Always had.

JACQUELINE COOPER

Sir Sidney's will to live took Jacqueline by surprise – he lived for many years after her first having worried about his imminent demise. His cough and stoop remained the same as he grew older; his skin grew more pale and wrinkled, he lost what little libido he had enjoyed and his odour changed to something unidentifiable, but his presence in the house could still be located by the curious, dry hacking followed by a fumbling for a handkerchief. But in the end he began to fail, his heart began to fail him. Sir Sidney Cooper, who had had an uneventful yet financially profitable life, simply faded away; he died in much the same way as he had lived, quietly and diffidently.

It took Sidney failing to make Jacqueline realize how fond she was of him. She realized this when she chose, if not to nurse him, then to sit with him, to *be* with him during his last months. She spent most days in his suite of rooms, Sidney propped up on pillows, occasionally reaching for oxygen, Jacqueline sitting in a wing chair by his bed, and she read articles from the paper, helped him complete the crossword, helped him eat and drink. When he needed to visit the bathroom, when he was still able to walk, she held his arm and helped him lower himself on to the seat. Their relationship, she realized, ran deep enough for him to not object to this; his pride was not sufficiently injured for him to object. And she knew this was because while she may have been Jackie Olivetti from Albany, Sidney was not so far removed from humble roots himself. As he grew weaker Sidney regressed, wanted nothing more than nursery food – Marmite soldiers, boiled eggs and suchlike – and the two of them would eat from the same tray, feeding each other spotted dick, forkfuls of cottage pie, spoonfuls of ice cream.

Eventually Sidney slipped too far away from Jacqueline to provide any company at all, yet still she sat with him. She would watch him labouring to breathe, occasionally wiping his face with a damp flannel, and she thought that he had been a good husband; he had been caring and generous, attentive when the situation demanded it and discreet when necessary. Had he known about her infidelities? Had he known about Billy-Ray and all the others? Jacqueline didn't know but reckoned he probably had and in that weird way the English had he'd decided to ignore them. What was it? Discretion being the better part of . . . valour? Maybe. Jacqueline sat most afternoons, holding Sidney's hand, and thought it was the least she could do, because, when she looked back at the past years, he'd treated her well. They'd had good holidays together, spent many quiet, comfortable weekends at Sherston Park. They had lived together at Jarman House for years, essentially enjoying some kind of harmony. Jacqueline held Sidney's hand and she wondered about his first wife, what she had been like. Remembered Miss O'Toole telling her how things were done in Lady Cooper's day. Jacqueline remembered the succession of gardeners and maids they had had, often thought about Maggie Regan and wondered why she had never come back to work for her; she was surprised by that, had always assumed she'd open the door one day to see Maggie standing on the steps, baby in one hand, suitcase in the other. Jacqueline sat and watched and thought about the embassy dinners, the gallery openings, the parties, and was grateful to the dying man because he had invited her to be a part of a life she barely deserved.

Sir Sidney's funeral was a quiet affair, held in the Yorkshire village where he had been born. Jacqueline had never been there before and was appalled by the poverty she saw in the nearby cities and towns, and she returned to London as soon as decently possible. She expected nothing, thinking that she had shared in enough of Sidney's good fortune already, knowing that he had left everything to his two sons from his first marriage. Sitting in the solicitor's office off Southampton Row, where Sidney's will was read, she was stunned to find that while the sons had been left a great deal, her dead husband had chosen to bequeath her the petrol station chain.

She allowed herself a small smile when she heard this, because she realized then that Sidney had indeed always known about Billy-Ray.

Jarman House was one of the bequests to the younger son, and Jacqueline bought an apartment in Victoria and leased offices in Belgravia, from where she ran her newly acquired business. She had always known the values of both time and money and how to spend them, and she proved to be an astute businesswoman, doubling the revenues in two years. Jacqueline worked hard, finding she liked it, liked work. No more afternoons to fill, no more empty mornings. Her evenings were filled with engagements, her nights with a succession of lovers. She had never been happier. She had long ceased to worry about the slipping of her skin from her bones, the paperiness of her upper arms. She looked in the mirror and saw a woman who had made herself, who had caught the chances thrown at her and run with them. But then the bombs began to explode on the streets of London (she missed the explosion at Harrods by moments) and Jacqueline sat in her office, assessed her assets and decided that the time had come to go back to New York.

One squally, gusty evening as she waited for an elevator in the Karbo offices on Madison, she saw a man she knew too well jog into the lobby. Watched him slapping at his wet raincoat, and she knew that she had been right to come home.

1976

Strangely, it was death which also eventually saved Isobel, the death of her father in the early summer of 1976. Lord Chalfont-Webbe's demise made the front pages of the broadsheets in England – he keeled over in the House during a debate on capital punishment, in a state of mild intoxication as his heart gave up the struggle. Isobel flew back to England for the first time in years, her heart aching because she had loved her father and she had not seen him often enough and now she would never see him again. She travelled to Highbury and was stunned by the opulence of her childhood home, felt awed by its dimensions and value. For it had been left to her, in its entirety, with the proviso that her mother remain there if she wished. But Lady Chalfont-Webbe did not so wish; she wanted to move to the house off Sloane Street.

Once the funeral was over Isobel spent days riding through the estate and walking around the house from room to room, noting the wealth on the walls, in drawers, in well-hidden safes. She walked in the formal gardens with her young nieces and nephews (her sister, Victoria, was, like her mother, a stickler for convention, and had provided a titled landowner with an heir and many spares). Isobel rode and she walked and she thought. She mourned her father and then she remembered what she was good at; she called in the money men and spent hours with accountants and bank managers, consultants and solicitors. The arrangement she arrived at was tortuous, spiked with arcane legal points, but it sufficed. Isobel mortgaged and remortgaged, sold a number of oil paintings by minor European artists, arrived at an agreement with the National Trust over the management of the house. These negotiations took weeks, and after a while, despite the familiar beauty of the English countryside in summer, Isobel found herself thinking of Juneau, of the glaciers and creeks, the jagged mountainsides she could see from her bedroom window. She began to miss Frankie's company. When she climbed into the chauffeured car that would take her to Heathrow, she had in her luggage the papers and documents detailing the finer points of the trust fund of the charity she had established for the protection of aboriginal rights.

Isobel arrived back in Juneau at the end of August and was not surprised to see Frankie and the apparently reformed Billy-Ray waiting at the airport to greet her. Was not surprised to find herself hugged and kissed, have her hand held all the way to the waiting cab. Nor was she surprised when Billy-Ray carried her cases, ran her a bath and announced that when she was ready he was going to cook up a storm on the barbecue. As Billy-Ray, who was nearly fifty and looked forty, who was tanned and looked loose limbed, his blond hair longer than it should have been, whose eyes were clear and untroubled, who was still the sexiest man Isobel had ever seen, as Billy-Ray cooked, Isobel wandered around their huge garden, dotted with stands of aspen and birch, all the way down to Gold Creek, which ran along the back of their property. Beyond the creek the mountains rose up, and when she looked at them Isobel smiled. The weathered granite, streaked with the stains of age, was now more familiar than the dry-stone walling of the fields around Stow-on-the-Wold. She was home. Alaska, finally, was home. It had taken nearly sixteen years but Isobel felt she was home. Looking back up the slope, through the trees, to the barbecue, oily smoke roiling skyward, she watched Billy-Ray and Frankie fooling around, bumping hips and singing from a song sheet Isobel didn't recognize. She watched Frankie move, watched the way her legs bent and dipped, the way she pushed her hair back as she turned the cobs; just like Billy-Ray. Isobel wondered whether the time had come to tell Frankie, whether that night would be the time. Pushed the question to the back of her mind, as she always did. What, really, was the point?

Over steaks and caribou sausages, corn and slaw, Isobel told her husband and daughter what she had done.

'You *gave* it away?' asked Billy-Ray, a fork in one hand, a napkin in the other. He thought of the porch, of the ballroom, of the stables and parkland and marbled hall, the fireplaces and and and . . . 'You gave it *away*?'

'No, I haven't given it away. It's held in a covenant and trust fund.'

'You've given it away?'

'No, BR, I haven't. I'm simply using it as collateral to set up the charity. That's all.'

'But what happens . . . when . . . when Frankie, y'know. When, y'know, when—'

'When I die? Well, I'm only thirty-nine, so that might be a while yet. But anyway, Highbury will eventually revert to my nephews.'

Billy-Ray frowned. 'Surely you can leave it to whoever you want? It's your choice. You can leave it to Frankie.'

Frankie laughed. 'I don't think so. That place is weird.'

'No,' said Isobel as she looked at Billy-Ray. 'I can't.'

'Well, that's OK by me,' said Frankie, trying to spear corn. 'Place is like the Addams family or something.'

'I can't, BR.' Isobel put down her plate. 'And anyway I wouldn't. It's difficult to explain. It's my family home. It's been ours for generations.'

Later, when they had cleared up and gone to bed, Isobel wasn't surprised that Billy-Ray made love to her. Made long and careful love to her. When it was done, when Billy-Ray had wrapped an arm around her waist, tucked his knees into the back of hers and fallen asleep, his breath warming her shoulder, Isobel lay awake. She was wondering how she could tell him that when she'd said 'I miss you' all those months before, she hadn't meant that she wanted him to cook for her, take her to the movies or carry her luggage. She'd meant that she missed Billy-Ray Rickman, popinjay. The Billy-Ray who saw ghosts.

Charlie was old, Frankie realized. Not old like Mom or Dad, but old old. His face was seamed, his eyelids drooping, and his hands shook as he carved wood. Yet there was still something about Charlie which drew Frankie over to Thekla's place whenever he was there, drew her almost against her will. She'd sit, long legs folded beneath her, watching him as he turned wood.

'It's my sixteenth birthday next week and guess what?'

Charlie barely heard her, barely registered the sounds. He was feeling lonely and he thought he could hear the ice fields calling. 'What?'

'Guess what I'm getting for my birthday present.'

Charlie blew air, flexed his aching fingers. 'How would I know?' People had so much these days it was difficult to know why they wanted more.

'Mom and Dad are getting me flying lessons. I'm going to learn how to fly. I'm going to get a pilot's licence.'

Wiping a hand over his face, Charlie thought about this. Now young girls took to the sky, flew like birds, like ravens. The white man might indeed be crazy but he was still here. 'Reckon you'll like that.'

'Tell me a story, Charlie. Any story.' Frankie felt so young around him that she still wanted stories – about fish that walked, rivers that ran with gold, mountains carved by the angry slash of a bear's claw.

'I have no more stories.'

'Ah, c'mon, you know lots of stories.'

Charlie rubbed at his knuckles. 'I am tired.'

This was Frankie's first encounter with a polar change of direction, like the throwing of a magnetic switch, when she became, suddenly, responsible for someone who she had always thought would protect her. 'Maybe, when I get my licence, we could go to Glacier Bay? You and me? Charlie? We could fly over and count the whales. See if there are ten or maybe hundreds. Or maybe just one. You and me, we could do that.'

But Charlie didn't hear Frankie, Charlie was sitting by a fire with his father, listening, remembering. Then he turned his face to the girl. 'I do have something to tell you but it's not a story. First I need to know, do you still have the carving I gave you? The wood that can be anything you want it to be?'

'Yes.'

'What is it you want it to be?'

'Right now? It's a cloud.'

'That's good.' Charlie nodded, scraped back his long, grey hair. 'I will tell you something but, as I say, it is not a story. It is something my grandfather used to tell us by the fire. When the white man came. My grandfather would tell this as if it was his own, which in a way it was. It is all of ours. It is yours, too. It is something the Great Chief Seattle told the white man.' Charlie Red-Wing, Auk, Native American, cleared his throat, looked to the distant mountains, seemed to speak in a voice as old as the world itself.

'"When the last red man has perished from the earth and his memory among white men shall have become a myth, these shores shall swarm with the invisible dead of my tribe, and when your children's children think themselves alone in the field, the store, the shop, upon the highway or in the silence of the woods, they will not be alone. In all the earth there is no place dedicated to solitude. At night, when the streets of your cities and villages shall be silent, and you think them deserted, they will throng with the returning hosts that once filled and still love this beautiful land. The white man will never be alone. Let him be just and deal kindly with my people, for the dead are not altogether powerless".'

'Well, hi there, Frankie! How you doing?' Thekla Willoughby, who had joined a fitness club, hauled herself out of the car and waved, the sweat stains on her T-shirt showing dark.

'I'm fine, thank you, Mrs Willoughby.'

'I see that ladder by the house, Charlie, but you still sittin' here like you chained to the earth.'

Frankie looked at the old man she had known most of her life. 'You don't have to do this, Charlie,' she whispered. 'I can ask my mom, she knows things that you can get, y'know, money you can get, from the government.'

Charlie, whose ancestors had walked the ice bridge from Siberia, who had seen rainbows in pure snow, who had seen blue in all its forms, smiled and took Frankie's hands in his, rubbed their palms with his hard, whorled thumbs. 'You and me – maybe one day we will fly together.'

Thekla was breathing heavily by the time she reached them. 'I'm about to git myself in the shower, believe me, but I jus' thought you'd want to know, Frankie, what I heard in town. Well, seems like we got ourselves an al-bi-no bear. Few hikers saw it last night out by Lemon Pass. How 'bout that?'

Charlie stood, but slowly, so slowly, and passed a hand over his heart. The Spirit Bear – an omen that cannot be ignored.

'What a mornin'!' said Thekla, plumping down on the bench that Charlie had vacated. 'I have had a mornin' from hell. God forgive me.' Thekla crossed herself, dabbed at the sweat at her temples. 'First, the truck stalled at Capitol and West Seventh and would *not* start again. Can y'all believe it? Coupla guys gave it a shove and rocked it an' then it was OK, something about the belt. Anyway, then I get to the mall, and guess what, honey?'

Frankie wasn't listening; she was watching Charlie climb the ladder, so slowly, the ladder shifting.

'Well, I got myself the groceries for the week – y'know the sorta thing – got me a coupla carts – and then realize I ain't got my purse. Lucky they know me but means I got to go straight back down there and sort this out. Then the fitness class – like I say, a morning of it.'

'My mom says bad luck always comes in threes.' Frankie watched Charlie reaching for a gutter.

'So that means I got somethin' else comin'? Lord. Hey! Charlie! Careful there.'

Thekla hauled herself to her feet as Frankie watched Charlie seemingly reaching for the sky.

Triplets, London buses, darts, clover leaves – all these things come in threes. Bad luck, kismet, karma, fate, destiny – all these come as they should.

1977

The stewardess gave Billy-Ray the message three hours into the flight from San Diego and he headed straight for a phone after landing in Anchorage.

'Frankie? What's the problem?'

'Dad? You gotta come home.' Frankie was crying, trying not to and failing.

'Frankie? What's the matter?' Billy-Ray wondered whether now was the time he would go home and Isobel would not have stayed.

'Mom's been arrested.'

'What? *What* did you say?'

'Mom's been arrested.' Frankie gulped, wiped roughly at her mouth. She was at home alone, the lights off, drapes drawn, sitting on a hard chair by the phone. She'd been waiting for Billy-Ray to call for nearly four hours.

'Why? What's going on? Is she OK?' A car accident?

'She shot Minto,' and Frankie began to howl, drew her knees up to her chest and howled.

Isobel and Frankie drove back from the game along Out the Road with the radio blaring, Frankie singing along to Thin Lizzy's 'The Boys Are Back in Town' at the top of her lungs as the sun began to drop behind the islands. An eagle cruised unseen yet keenly felt thermals and the channel waters looked scoured clean, the surf bubbling at the tip of gently rolling waves impossibly white. Evenings like these . . . well, they were precious, Isobel thought. They reminded her of why she'd stayed, why she hadn't turned and walked away. She and Frankie were going to swing by Dietrich's to pick up some fried chicken and then pig out in front of a fire. Isobel smiled as Frankie hollered and slapped her thighs to the rhythm.

'Hey, Mom, meant to tell you – Mr Franz, y'know, the basketball coach, he says I can't go to hoop camp this summer, because I'm a girl. He says only the boys can go. Pisses me off, y'know? I'm a better player than any of 'em and I can't go.'

Isobel remembered having to watch and applaud potential suitors during her debutante season, knowing she could outshoot and out-ride them all. 'Have you told him that?'

'Yeah, 'course I have, but it don't make any frigging difference, apparently. I mean, he knows I'm the best player but he won't let me do it.'

'Ask him again, don't let it go. And tidy up your language.'

Coming into town, near the Glacier Avenue junction, Isobel was slowed by a trooper waving his hand. The junction was closed, an ambulance spinning red and blue light on the shabby buildings, transforming them. Five squad cars were slewed across the road. Isobel felt compelled to stop, although she couldn't have said why. She yanked on the handbrake, motioned for Frankie to stay in the car and walked over to the trooper, pulling her jacket around her against the chill.

'Excuse me, Officer, can I ask what happened here?'

'Indian's been shot.'

'Do you know the victim's name?' A premonition, that was why she'd stopped.

'Not yet. An old guy, a drunk by the smell of him.'

'Did anyone see what happened?'

The trooper sighed, took off his hat, rearranged the band and reset it. 'Guess you'll hear about it anyway. Yeah – we do have some witnesses. They say they saw the Thorensson boy causing trouble.' There was no need to ask which one. 'He took off after a couple of shots were heard. Cleared a couple of walls and disappeared. He knows the trails round here, could be difficult to find him. Plus he could steal a car. We already know that.'

'Thank you, Officer. Good luck.' Isobel walked slowly back to the car. What to tell Frankie?

'What's going on, Mom?'

'There's been an argument. Someone was shot.' Isobel started the car and drove to Dietrich's.

Once Frankie was in bed, Isobel checked the TV news, tuned into the local radio station, and at midnight came the confirmation: Charlie Red-Wing had been shot at twenty minutes past eight that night and was DOA. The police wanted to question Minto Thorensson, who was armed and considered dangerous. Still Isobel wanted the drama to play itself out before she told Frankie. Slipping on her jacket, she stepped outside, lit a cigarette and looked up at the stars. Not a cloud, no rain for two days. Why on earth did Minto do it?

Minto did it because he was mad at the world. He was mad and drunk on a stolen bottle of Jack Daniel's, with a bellyful of poppers and purple hearts exploding in him. He sat in the shadows of a corner store on Egan Road, drinking, dreaming of driving as far as he wanted to, when he saw Charlie shuffle past, on the way home to his room, a brown paper bag in his hand. Minto stood up, matched Charlie step for step, walking so close Charlie could hear his breathing. Charlie would not stop or turn up an alley. He was no sable brave but he *was* an Auk and he belonged there.

When Charlie reached his boarding house, Minto turned, standing between Charlie and the door.

'What you got there, old man?'

Charlie looked at Minto, looked into his bloodshot, pale blue eyes and said nothing.

'Hey – I'm talking to you, old man. What you got there?' Minto grabbed the bottle, tore off the bag. 'Oh, so you Injuns are drinking Thunderbird now? Kiddy liquor. Doncha know it's bad for you? Very bad for you.' Minto dropped the bottle on the sidewalk, where it smashed. Still Charlie said nothing, didn't move, even when Minto closed in.

'Where d'you get the fuckin' money to buy liquor? Look at you, you look like shit and you can still buy a drink. Know why you look like shit? Because you are shit.'

Charlie wasn't even blinking. He knew what would happen, had known it the moment he felt the Spirit Bear boy following him. Minto would shout and then he would boil over with rage and, when Charlie didn't move, didn't answer, Minto would draw the gun he had stolen from his father's bar and shoot Charlie just above the heart. Which is exactly what did happen.

The poppers were still firing Minto, pumping his legs, moving his arms, wiring his brain. He sprinted away, up over a wall, across a yard, over another wall, dropped down into brush and ran up to the tree line, lost himself. Minto ran because he'd done what he'd wanted to do all his life and it didn't feel good. It didn't feel good at all. He stumbled on a trail he recognized and slowed to a jog, a stitch pulling at his torso. He jogged as if he knew where he was going and then he realized he did know where he was going. His brain felt as if it belonged to someone else. He was going to see Frankie. He could still remember how her tongue felt on his hand, how she had made him feel better once she'd pulled the barb from his hand. Minto was going to climb into Frankie's room and wake her up and she would make it feel right.

The moon wasn't quite full, missing a sliver, a nail paring, but strong enough to throw moon shadows, Isobel noticed. A dog bark. A distant car engine. A sound. Isobel stood stock still, listening. Water being scuffed. The sound stopped. Isobel relaxed, dropped the butt of her cigarette and ground it out. Another sound. Shading her eyes, she made out a shape way down by the creek; she watched the greyness, the way it moved. She had tracked prey often enough to recognize a predator. Moving silently, Isobel slid away in the silver night, slid as far as the garage, reached up to a tin on a high shelf, found the key and unlocked the cabinet. Loading the rifle, she noticed a tremble in her hands, in her murderer's thumbs. She snapped the rifle to and slid back out into shadows. The shape made its way up the gentle, wooded slope rising from the creek, reached the edge of a clearing and crouched. Isobel drifted into shadows, down into tree cover, and moved silently towards the sound the shape was making.

Minto was a way away from the house, a few hundred feet, he reckoned. He could see Frankie's light was off but her window was open and he thought he could get up there. It was late, no one was around; he could climb the drainpipe and then he could tell Frankie what he'd done. It still didn't feel good. He suddenly reared up out of his crouch, sprinted across open ground, reached the clapboard wall of the house and was swallowed by deep shadow.

Isobel heard branches thrashing ahead of her, swivelled left and ran to the edge of the trees, saw the grey shape weaving across open ground before it disappeared into darkness. She stood stock still, like a hunting dog, rifle half raised, and she waited, saw a flash of white. Isobel lifted the stock, nestled it into her shoulder, raised the barrel, sighted along the bead.

Minto began to shin up the drainpipe, the poppers forcing his thigh muscles to brace his weight against the wall as his aching hands inched upward. He was a long, long way from Isobel, but that didn't save him.

Frankie, who'd been woken by the sound of branches thrashing and thought it was maybe the albino bear down by the creek, or even the madman plotting in the driveway, had got up to have a look. She stood at her window, worried by sounds of panting and scratching, and so it was that she caught a tiny, web-like silver flash in the corner of her eye, turned in time to see a tall, blonde woman, rifle to her shoulder, firing at moon shadows.

The shock waves of the case spread far and wide, exciting comment as far away as Stow-on-the-Wold, in England. The people of Juneau were surprised by this – an intruder had entered the property, no doubt with intent to steal, murder or worse, given the history of the dead boy and the fact that he was armed. Mrs Rickman had the constitutional right to defend herself. Two hearings in the Court House and that was that. The only remarkable aspect to the case, the people of Juneau thought, was that it was a hell of a shot. The good old boys at the shooting range raised their eyebrows when they heard, shook their heads and whistled. But, when they thought about it, it figured. The lady could shoot. Minto was buried and mourned by few, other than by his mother and, of course, Frankie.

Isobel was calm and controlled throughout the investigation and the hearings. She was photographed, looking cool, looking composed, leaving the police station, entering the Court House. She refused to give interviews, she wouldn't discuss that night, not even with Billy-Ray. 'You know what happened,' was all she would say to him. It was when Billy-Ray was away that she would lie awake sleepless, replaying the detective's question over and over.

'Mrs Rickman, could you see who you were shooting at? I mean, could you make anything out?'

Had she known it was Minto? Isobel wasn't sure. At first she'd thought it might be the Spirit Bear, but if she had thought that she would not have shot it. Then she had seen the shock of near-white hair – had she guessed? Isobel didn't know.

'No,' she had said to the detective, because she couldn't be sure.

'Hell of a shot,' the detective had said.

At school, Frankie found it difficult – kids and teachers didn't know what to say to her. 'How's it goin'?' and 'Hiya' were about as good as it got. The new friends she had made melted away and Frankie found herself alone again, walking the long corridors, sitting in the refectory, standing by the lockers in the sports hall, alone. She'd arrive home and go straight to her room, because she didn't know what to say to her mother. What *could* she say? Her mother had killed Minto, who had killed Charlie. Frankie sat on her bed in her room, headphones clamped to her head, legs crossed, eyes closed, and she tried to work out how to feel. In her hands she held the carving that could be anything she wanted it to be. It was no longer a cloud; now it was escape. And then, on her sixteenth birthday, Frankie went down to the docks, clambered into a Piper Super Cub and began to learn how to escape.

The work on the Trans-Alaskan Pipeline was relentless: gravel piles turned into roads overnight, Cats and Euclid haulers groaned and strained as they remoulded the landscape; seventy thousand people were strung out along the tundra and sub-arctic mountain ranges, digging, welding and burying. But Billy-Ray tried to make it home more often, tried to make it back to Sitka Street as often as possible during that time. It was difficult, the time wasn't right – but then, when would the time be right for your wife to blow away a sixteen-year-old boy?

In an attempt to try to stitch his family back together again Billy-Ray arranged a vacation and he took the three of them down to San Diego. For a few days, it worked, the sun worked its magic. They sat in silence a great deal of the time, a not uncomfortable silence, one that betokened the fact that there was, really, far too much that could be said. Billy-Ray was still aware of the smooth, tall dam protecting the silence, and he didn't want it to burst. Frankie and Isobel were still careful with each other, their occasional, short conversations light footed, as if they were walking on bruises, but they were talking, and as the Rickmans walked back from a restaurant to their hotel one balmy night, Frankie slipped her arm through her mother's and smiled.

Isobel and Billy-Ray had talked for a long time about what they could do to try to recompense Frankie for her losses, and they decided that a week doing the two things she enjoyed the most might help – flying and fishing. So the Rickmans flew from San Diego to Santo Domingo in Baja, on a Twin Otter Billy-Ray chartered with a crew, landing on a dirt strip and staying for a night in the small Mexican village, before flying on the next day to Cabo San Lucas at the tip of the peninsula. At Billy-Ray's suggestion, the pilot asked Frankie whether she wanted to sit up in the cockpit and he answered all her questions, talked about the differences between single engine and turbines, distracting her from thoughts of absence.

There were few people on the cape then – the tourists and flotillas had yet to arrive – and the rooms Billy-Ray found in a dilapidated hotel were clean but shabby. As the evening drew in, the three of them walked through the town and found a bodega, where they ate blackened tuna and grilled sardines with pinto beans and corn fritters, all washed down with cold beers. Isobel sat back, lit a cigarette and watched Frankie talking to her father about what the pilot had told her, moving her hands, using knives, fish bones and matches to map out pilots' imagined disasters on the tabletop. During this time Isobel had a permanent twist of guilt turning in her stomach and she could think of no way to stop it turning because she knew that Frankie had loved Minto. She watched her in the candlelight and tried to think of something she could say to bring her daughter succour, wished she could erase her memories of hearing Minto falling. Wished she could talk to Frankie the way Billy-Ray did, but she never had and never could. Would she ever tell her? Isobel began to doubt it.

When they'd finished their hot, bitter coffees, Billy-Ray left them to go in search of a local captain to arrange three days' game fishing. But he spoke no Spanish, and it was not until he found a raddled

Englishman, slight and stooped, who had lived in Cabo San Lucas for decades and owned a thirty-six-footer that he could sort it out.

For three days Isobel lay on the beach, reading and thinking how much she wished they had undertaken this trip five years before when it might have done some good, when it might have made a difference, as her husband and daughter went out into the deep waters of the Sea of Cortez.

'See,' Billy-Ray said to Frankie as they nose-hooked mackerel and put them back in the tank, 'the Sea of Cortez is like a continuation of the Aleutian Trench – some of the deepest waters in the world out here. Plus you get the temperate waters, y'know, on the Pacific side, meeting a tropical sea, trapped in here. It's called a temperature break, apparently.'

'You need to stop talking and start looking,' remarked Captain Scott. 'Look for birds, debris, breezing fish. Where you see those, you'll find the big ones. And look for blue water. There's a saying round here: *el único uso para el agua verde es cuando no hay agua azul.* The only use for green water is when there is no blue water.'

So Frankie looked for blue water.

'And get rigged up for trolling. Penn thirty-W with an eighty-pound line will be OK for you, and I think we'll use the *petrolero* plumas today. You might want to try local style too. Finish your main line with a perfection loop tied to a big snap swivel – don't use a Bimini, just snap on a leader. Pre-rig some two-hundred-pound monos on that. I'd say best to start with a ten-inch skirt.'

Billy-Ray – who had once been able to speak in many tongues – found himself foundering in a language swamp. He had no idea what the man was talking about, tried to translate but was stumped.

Captain Scott looked at him, and there was something about the set of his mouth which reminded Billy-Ray of Urban's expression during the first few days out of Seattle on *Viveka.* 'You done much fishing?'

'Well, yeah. Sure I have, but never done game fishing like this.'

'The principles are the same. Let me show you.' The way Captain Scott looked at it, the man was paying him whatever they did. He let the boat drift and it rocked in a moderate swell as he set the reels and showed them the different lures, talked about when to use dead, live or artificial bait. When he was finished, when Billy-Ray and

Frankie had set up two rods each on the outriggers, the lures lying three boat lengths back, with two more lying off the corners about a wave's length shorter and a short teaser in the bubbles, the captain opened up the throttle and they cruised towards Gordo Banks at nine knots.

Captain Scott may have been raddled but he knew how to fish, and he certainly knew *where* to fish. For once Frankie didn't look at the sky, at the clouds, the distant skyline. She looked at the fighting chair, swivelling gently in the swell, and imagined how it would feel to be belted into it, yanking on the rod. Then she watched the lures skimming and jumping in the wash, watched for birds, fins and tails, Minto and Charlie forgotten. A lure disappeared and the rod curved as a fish was hooked and dived, the reel spinning as Captain Scott slowed and the boat sank a little. He locked and hefted the rod, touched the line with a fingertip. 'Yellowfin, I think,' he said, 'a big one. Could be near a hundred pounds.' And Frankie felt something like a golden splash burst in her chest. They returned late that afternoon to dockside with a haul of yellowfin, dorado, black sea bass and spearfish. Frankie's best catch was a twenty-eight-pound roosterfish, and Billy-Ray had pulled in the yellowfin, after a long fight, at eighty-seven pounds. Isobel was required to listen to hours of Billy-Ray and Frankie recounting how they'd pulled in, interrupting each other, gesturing, speculating how it might be to pull in one of the big game fish. Isobel nodded and smiled, relieved to see Frankie relaxing, unfurling almost.

On their last day – by which time Billy-Ray and Frankie were setting the rods without help, judging for themselves when to toss live bait, finding it easy to spot tailing billfish – Frankie found out about pulling in the big one. She was scanning the wake of the outriggers, saw the flash of a dark triangle, the suggestion of metal in the blue water. Shouted, pointed, and Captain Scott came down, looked along the line of Frankie's finger and immediately rigged a Senator with a four-hundred-pound line, baited with a seven-pound tuna and 12/0 Mustad hook, which he set from mid-stern, in front of the fighting chair. Then he said, 'That's a monster. See the size of the dorsal?'

'What is it?' asked Billy-Ray, shading his eyes against the dropping sun.

'It's a black marlin.'

Billy-Ray watched the billfish chasing as the boat moved up to ten then eleven knots. 'Friend of mine once said they can come in at sixteen hundred pounds – that right?'

Captain Scott shrugged. 'You hear stories. I've seen an eight-hundred-and-forty-pounder winched up in San José. An extraordinary sight. They say someone brought in a thirteen-hundred-pounder at San Jaime but I didn't see any photos and you would think there would be some. Perhaps twenty, thirty years ago it was possible, but now there are more boats I'm not so sure.' He looked back at the tailing marlin. 'But that's a trophy right there.'

Thirty years before, on a different boat, in a different world, Urban Svensson had told Billy-Ray his dream of drinking tequila and fishing. Billy-Ray surprised himself by smiling at the memory.

The bait disappeared and the boat shuddered, slewed a little.

'Got you,' muttered Captain Scott.

Billy-Ray sat in the fighting chair and opened up his shoulders, flexed his neck. Wrapped gloved hands around the rod. Two hours later the billfish was still fighting and Billy-Ray was beginning to hurt, his damaged thigh aching. When he'd first started hauling in and playing out they'd caught glimpses and the captain had whistled but Billy-Ray and Frankie had no comparisons they could make. But then, as Billy-Ray leaned out, spun frantically and hauled in with a few bursts, the marlin rose up and tail-walked across the waves, thrashing with fury, its bill cutting the sky, and Frankie stepped back, although the fish was still eighty, maybe ninety feet out.

'Jesus!' yelled Billy-Ray, relaxing his grip for a moment.

'Fuck!' said Captain Scott. 'Sorry, Frankie.'

"S OK,' she whispered, watching the colossus dance on the tiny, finny feet of its tail.

Do this in remembrance of me.

'How heavy d'you reckon?' Billy-Ray shouted above the engine as the captain revved and pulled a little at a few knots.

Captain Scott shook his head. 'I really don't know – but it's much bigger than the San José catch.'

Another hour and Billy-Ray was beginning to cramp. He'd pulled the marlin in another fifty feet and the fish was zigzagging, working the line, which Billy-Ray was sure was going to break. The captain motioned for Billy-Ray to move, they manoeuvred and he took over the rod, slipping into the chair and belting up with practised movements. Captain Scott was nowhere near as strong as Billy-Ray, but he was professional, he was wily, he wore the fish down, promising freedom and then slamming the marlin in another direction as it ran. Billy-Ray, his neck stiff, his hands bruised, watched Frankie following the captain's every move as he steered the boat, watched her eyes flicking from the chair to the fish and back again.

'You want to try?' Billy-Ray asked. 'Frankie? You want to sit in the chair? Just to feel it?'

'I don't know,' she said.

'I'll help you.'

'I don't think it's a good idea for the girl to do that,' said the captain in his clipped English accent, which always sounded strangely formal.

This annoyed Frankie. 'Yeah, I'd like to. But you got to help me, Dad, promise?'

Captain Scott glanced over at her – she was tall, taller and broader than he was, maybe five ten, big, muscled shoulders. 'OK, but I take no responsibility – it's your decision.'

Frankie slipped into the seat and fumbled with the belt, her hands shaking. She pulled on the gloves, put her hands where the captain showed her and listened (but didn't hear) as he told her how to pull, in which direction and for how long. She had never been as nervous; she touched the belt, checked that the clasp was tight shut. Then the captain flicked the switch and the line screamed as Frankie was yanked and slammed forward, the belt chafing her belly.

'Shit!' she yelled as Billy-Ray came up to the chair, locked the Senator reel and helped Frankie pull back, gradually releasing his grip. It took her a while – she was at first overawed by the weight, the *gravity* of the fish – but she began to understand the rhythms of the fight, the giving and taking, the dance of death. The bill, as sharp and serrated as fear, slashed at air and water. Frankie wasn't sure whether she'd brought it in at all, but she loved the curve of the rod, the glittering water, the chaos of foam and the silver filament flashing in the light. Billy-Ray slipped away to fetch his camera and took a shot of her, her face set, eyes squinting in the sun, bare feet against the back board, thighs straining as she hauled. He lowered the camera and looked at his daughter; she reminded him of someone, looked like someone he used to know. Who was it? He slipped the camera in his pocket, frowning. He needed to pee and went down the hatch to the heads, and it was whilst he was unzipping that it happened.

The marlin, which was enraged, which was demented with pain and confusion – it was, after all, a predator, unused to being strung along – dived, kept diving and then reared up with searing, heart-straining speed and suddenly there was slack where there had been tension. The silver line of filament looped, flew in the wind and tangled around Frankie before slamming taut again as the marlin turned, wanting to head back to the banks, back to the *bajos*, to cruise the deeps. Frankie, shocked by the sudden slack, hadn't reacted, hadn't reeled in fast enough, and as the sixteen-hundred-pound black marlin dived again, it took with it the ring finger of her left hand.

Frankie didn't see her finger flying away but as she listened to screaming nylon the pain hit her in the chest, in the same way as the golden burst. Later she had faint, skittering memories of Captain Scott revving the engines, thudding over the eleven miles back to the coast, radioing ahead as her daddy tried to stem the flow of blood. Frankie would not look at her hand, never looked at it, never saw the pale bone and curve of a bare knuckle. She was loaded into an ambulance and bounced over the mountainous roads to La Paz, medics hooking her up to bags of blood. She drifted in and out then, and as she lay there rocking with the motion of the tyres turning on uneven dirt, she knew it had happened because Minto hadn't been there to cut the line. She knew that if Minto had been there he would have cut the line, looked her in the eyes and shaken his head.

Billy-Ray and Isobel were stunned by this loss and each began to wonder whether they were in some way cursed or jinxed, but they never said anything to each other about this. About the sense of being damned in some way. They flew back to Juneau, taking it in turns to hold Frankie's undamaged hand, and bunkered down in Sitka Street. Billy-Ray knew why he was being punished, he'd always known, and he consoled himself with work. Isobel couldn't fathom this fresh blow, this latest absence. She tried to rationalize it, tried to think of it as just an accident, but she couldn't shake the notion that it was a sign. If Charlie Red-Wing had still been alive she would have asked him because Charlie knew all about signs, knew how to read life. But Charlie was, of course, dead, and so Isobel, too, lost herself in work. Of the three of them, Frankie seemed to care the least. The way she saw it, she hardly used the finger, and anyway, pilots sat in the left seat; once it healed, it would be fine. The only thing that got to her was that the recovery time meant it took her months longer than it should have to get her Single Engine Sea licence.

By May 1977 the Trans-Alaskan Pipeline was nearly finished. Three years, eight billion dollars, fourteen airfields, seventy-three million cubic feet of gravel and thirty-one lives later, Alyeska was preparing to pump the first oil. Billy-Ray Rickman was sent to Prudhoe Bay for a last trip down the pipe's eight-hundred-mile length. He flew in over the tundra, the Haul Road running straight as a die below, cutting the state in half. Sprouting off the highway now were the pump stations and construction camps, resting on shunted gravel, surrounded by dammed sluggish rivers and streams. Billy-Ray knew that beneath the tundra, beneath the Bering Sea, were other fields and pools, that prospectors were out there, core-sampling in Endicott, Kuparuk, Milne Point; lines were being slung over hundreds of square miles of ice and permafrost. But for the first time he felt no desire to be back out there, judging the curve of the earth, felt no desire to stand in winds with a chill factor of minus a hundred and thirty-five discussing the viscosity of a reservoir. Billy-Ray, who was a year off fifty, had had enough.

For three weeks he was flown or driven to each camp, each station, where he met with Karbo engineers to talk about thermal expansion and tie-in temperatures, special burial refrigerated pipes, magnesium ribbon sacrificial anodes, the zigzag formation of the pipe which allowed for earthquakes.

'Got a lateral movement of eight feet – it can withstand anything up to nine on the Richter.'

'Eight feet?' Billy-Ray looked at the engineer, looked out of the window of the prefab hut at flat, unending tundra. Running above it was the pipe, heated and cooled, moving laterally and vertically. Eight feet? Billy-Ray remembered his stumble through Anchorage after the quake, remembered the exhaust of a car grinning at him, the demolition of downtown stores, the Chugach Range jumping as the Pacific plate moved thirty-three feet. He frowned, swallowed, ached for a cigarette. 'Where you from?' he asked the man.

'Kansas, originally.'

Happy Valley, Coldfoot, Prospect, Old Man, Sourdough – Billy-Ray moved south, following the pale thread of the Haul Road, which became the Richardson Highway at Fairbanks. The names of the camps reminders of when white men had travelled there before, hoping to mine a different gold, dressed in cotton shirts and thin boots, escorted by native men. Billy-Ray knew that most of the miners had died, of hunger, of cold, all killed by earth-greed. Leaving Tonsina Camp, he arrived at Pump Station 12, increasingly uneasy and out of sorts. He sat in the rec room, smoking, watching the roustabouts and boomers playing pool, watching TV, eating piles of steaks and fries, doughnuts, ice cream, handfuls of supplements, staring into space, dreaming of spending their scads of money in Phoenix, Detroit, Salem, Jacksonville.

'Hi there, how you doin'?' A man Billy-Ray vaguely knew sat next to him, began to wolf down fried chops and potatoes.

'Fine. You?'

'Great, just great. We're nearly done. Heard today they reckon it'll be June twentieth when they flick the switch. June twentieth and we'll be in business and I can get the fuck out of here.'

Billy-Ray remembered who the man was, what he did, and asked, 'What's the predicted line fill now?'

Swallowing and wiping his mouth with his hand, the man said, 'Nine million sixty thousand barrels, give or take.'

'Right.' At any time, once the switch had been flicked, there would be more than nine million barrels of crude in the pipe. Eight feet? Billy-Ray made his excuses and left. Only to lie sleepless in an air-conditioned room that looked exactly the same as the room Frankie had slept in, in Prudhoe.

The next day he was driven down to Valdez, having decided to bypass the Sheep Creek Camp. It was more than ten years since

Billy-Ray had spent time in a lover's cabin outside the town and he recognized nothing. After the earthquake the town had been re-located and a grid of roads built, but the roads were nearly empty, plots left undeveloped because there was more money to be made throwing up temporary accommodation for the terminal workers. Workers who caught the ferries that ran to and from the new Valdez to the old cannery town of Dayville on the opposite bank, where Alyeska was building the terminal for the pipeline. A thousand acres of pipes, valves and holding tanks more than sixty feet high which could contain more than half a million barrels of oil. Four berths where tankers would dock and load simultaneously, cranes manoeu-vring the vast crude oil loading arms. Billy-Ray tried to focus on what he needed to do, set his briefcase on the hood of a car and looked at the list of meetings he had planned for the afternoon, but he could barely think for the racket of flapping helicopters, the roar of bulldozers and the straining diesel engines of dumpsters dealing with the detritus all around him. Smoke drifted down the Narrows from fires burning in the construction site, stinging Billy-Ray's eyes as a high-speed ferry roared past, its cargo a group of men in hard hats. A man in a dark suit strode towards him, hand extended, mouthing something Billy-Ray couldn't hear.

Later that same day Billy-Ray found himself, as arranged, on the deck of a tug refurbished by Karbo to provide transport for its exec-utives in the Sound, no matter what the weather. That afternoon the weather was, to say the least, changeable. Billy-Ray left the terminal dock with the sun splashing on pale blue water; twenty minutes later he couldn't see his hand in front of his face for fog. He felt dis-oriented, undone, confused. The local ferry, *Bartlett*, passed to port, its horn mournful, and Billy-Ray was spooked – if the Wave could make a sound, that was what the sound would be. Then suddenly the fog cleared and Billy-Ray could see that he was in the Valdez Narrows, and he sucked in his breath: rocks were crowding him, crowding the tug; it felt as if they were crowding his *heart* – because he knew that Alyeska planned to have twenty-one 150,000-tonne oil tankers a week moving through the Narrows, to collect the crude which would never stop flowing, from the Bering Sea along the pipe to the termi-nal. More than that, none of the Seven Sisters – indeed, none of the shipping companies – was required to supply ships with double hulls. Billy-Ray could hear the voice of a Grumman Goose pilot echoing down the years, yelling as the waters in Valdez Narrows rocked two hundred and thirty feet up the sides of the fjord.

As the tug chugged its way south, through the Narrows, into Prince William Sound, Billy-Ray began to wonder, began to wonder about an idea he really, really couldn't entertain: the idea that he might have been wrong. He had worked on the North Slope on and off for nearly twenty years – the thought of the oil finally flowing should have been cause for celebration. Instead, as the tug turned and laboured back towards Valdez, passing the cacophony that was the Marine Terminal, Billy-Ray heard another old but familiar voice. For twenty years he had done everything Karbo had asked of him, had done it as he ignored the Wave, the angriness and the mad-eyed wolverine at his shoulder. But perhaps he had been wrong?

If each man looks at what he does – well, it's nothing. But together they can make a storm.

Billy-Ray had never been so glad to fly into Anchorage, to be away from the bedlam of construction. He caught a cab downtown, because he had to swing by the Karbo office, drop off some papers, and he sat in a stupor, imagining his first drink in his A-frame house, sitting in the den, looking out over Campbell Lake. But driving into town, along 4th, it was as if he was seeing Anchorage – seeing it clearly – for the first time: the banks, First National, Alaska Bank of the North, Bank of Commerce, all of them set up to deal with the new money, and where did it all go? Outside. Bail bond offices, pawn shops, liquor stores, gun stores, massage parlours, men staggering drunk along the street, auto accidents, pick-up trucks blaring country music, Baptist churches, a McDonald's being built, Natives rolling out of the Montana Club and Goldie's, bars open twenty-four hours a day. Anchorage had become a mad house, full of soldiers and hookers, boomers and hopers, all wanting to head north and grab themselves some money, flocks of ravens burgeoning everywhere, scavenging on rich pickings. Charlie had been right – the world had gone to hell. Billy-Ray told the cab to wait, dropped

off the papers and headed straight back to the airport to catch the
last flight to Juneau.

On 20 June 1977, Billy-Ray chose not to be at Pump Station 1 when
the thick snake of crude began nosing its way along the pipe, heading
for Valdez Marine Terminal – a journey of nearly five days. (A journey
that took longer than it should have done because someone at Pump
Station 8 forgot to throw a switch when the oil came online, and the
mechanical back-up failed. A spark flared and the station was blown
apart, killing a man. Thousands of gallons of crude oozed out on to
the tundra as men in hard hats ran around, flapping like headless
chickens.) Instead, Billy-Ray chose to be in Juneau on 20 June, to go
to a science fair at Frankie's high school, where she was presenting
a paper. Blood had been Frankie's project for that semester and
Isobel told Billy-Ray that Frankie had spent weeks making posters
and planning experiments for the talk, that she'd even invited the
Red Cross to park a van outside the sports hall so visitors could
make donations.

Billy-Ray and Isobel ate lunch together before leaving for the
school. They sat out on the deck behind the house in warm sunshine,
eating salads, cold meats and bread, washed down with Olympia
beer. Isobel read the papers with a slight frown, groping for the bottle
on the table without looking up from the page. Billy-Ray watched his
wife of seventeen years and wondered whether to tell her that he
thought he might have been wrong about the pipeline, but something stopped him. These days Isobel seemed increasingly distant,
seemed to be drifting away from him, but so slowly that he didn't
notice any movement. She spent her days in the study, hammering
out letters to foreign governments, calling embassies and consulates,
trying to establish schools and clinics in the wildernesses around the
globe. When he came back from a business trip, she no longer sat
with him as he bathed, no longer massaged the small of his back.

'I'm going to quit Karbo next month,' he said quietly.

Isobel looked up, took off her glasses. 'I beg your pardon?'

'I'm quitting next month. I'm getting out of Karbo.'

'Why?'

'I've had enough. I don't want to do it any more.' Billy-Ray looked up at the blazing sky, was dazzled. For the first time in a long time, he considered the possibility of not having it all. Considered giving Jacqueline up and not having it all. Could he do it? 'I'd just like to sit in the sun, maybe read, definitely go fishing. I've been away too much, for too long. I want to spend time with you and Frankie. I can always do consultancy work. And I reckon the time has maybe come for us to move. I've had enough of snow and rain – we could move to the sun somewhere. California, maybe.'

Isobel looked at her watch. 'We should go. Frankie's presentation is in forty minutes.'

Frankie, dressed in jeans and a T-shirt too big for her, stood in front of a board covered with images of red cells, platelets and wounds and talked about blood. About its properties and composition, the fundamentals of circulation, diseases associated with blood and Mendelian laws concerning heredity.

'There can be many problems associated with blood and heredity. For example, Alexandrina Victoria, a daughter of the House of Hanover who became Queen of England, married her first cousin, Prince Albert Saxe-Coburg-Gotha, and gave birth to nine children. These children married into other royal families but unknown to the men of the monarchies of Spain and Russia, Victoria's daughters had an X-chromosome with a recessive sex-linked factor and, as a result, the male heirs suffered from haemophilia, the Christmas disease. The boys could not produce factor-nine blood protein. This meant their blood didn't clot and if they were cut or injured they could bleed to death.

'King George III was an ancestor of Victoria's. People thought that he was mad. In fact, he suffered from porphyria – he didn't have the porphyria molecule which combines with iron to form haem, the basis of haemoglobin. King George wasn't mad, it was just that his blood was too thin.

'There are lots of diseases of the blood which can be inherited – thalassaemia and sickle-cell anaemia, for example. Other diseases carried in the blood come from infections – malaria, bilharzia, Weil's disease, Lassa fever and sleeping sickness for example.

'In the early part of this century a man called Karl Landsteiner discovered that there were four main types of blood – O, A, B and AB.

This meant that blood transfusions could be done properly because people were given the right type of blood, because their blood type was matched. It has also been discovered that some races have a particular blood type. Blood type B appears most often in eastern Europe, whilst type A appears in Finns, Norwegians and Irish. Interestingly, the rare Rh negative type is highest in the Basques. Among Native Americans blood type O is found most often. This blood type is known as the universal donor, because nearly everyone can receive it. Type AB is called the universal recipient.

'I have discovered that there are many myths and legends about blood – about Aphrodite, the Goddess of Love, being born in the waves, which had been dyed red by the blood of Ouranos. There is the story of Moses turning the waters of the Nile to blood, and the legend of Dracula. There is also the belief that red wine at mass becomes the blood of Christ.

'In Aztec mythology, there is a god called' – and Frankie smiled, because she couldn't pronounce the name properly – 'Huitzilopochtli, the Sun God. He was reborn every morning as the sun came up and, like many gods, he needed sacrifices made to him so he would rise again. These sacrifices were whole human hearts and bowls of human blood. The reason I liked this myth was because his name' – and again Frankie smiled – 'comes from "huitzilin", which means hummingbird. His mother had him after carrying a ball of hummingbird feathers in her chest, apparently. The victims of the sacrifices were prisoners and dead warriors. After the sacrifice, the warriors became part of the sun for four years and after that they were reborn as hummingbirds. Which I think is kinda neat.'

Frankie lowered the sheets of paper she had read from and invited the audience to visit the Red Cross stall, where they could look at slides of samples taken from different vertebrates, have a blood test to determine their own type, and then maybe they'd consider donating blood?

Isobel had hardly listened to a word her daughter said, focusing instead on the missing digit on her left hand – so obvious, the wound still red raw. She wondered whether Frankie was aware that she often rubbed it? Billy-Ray, however, did listen closely and was proud – the paper was a straight A-grade.

'I didn't know that haemophilia was called the Christmas disease,' Billy-Ray remarked as Frankie tore open a spike pack, then swabbed the tip of his thumb.

'Only haemophilia B.'

'And what was that, um, thala something?' Billy-Ray liked the feel of his daughter's fingers on his hand; they were cool and sure.

'Thalassaemia.'

'Strange word – wonder where it comes from?'

Frankie pushed her hair back, stabbed her father and collected a couple of drops of blood. 'Apparently it comes from the Greek for "sea", because people thought most of the sufferers were from around the Mediterranean. But now we know that it's a global problem.'

Who's 'we'? Billy-Ray wondered. He looked at Frankie's hand. Wondered whether to tell her that he was quitting Karbo, that they might be moving soon. Wondered whether she would be glad. 'I'm sorry about your finger,' he said instead.

'So am I,' said Frankie. 'It itches sometimes. Something to do with synapses and nerves, my science teacher told me.' She looked at her father and smiled. 'It was a hell of a fish though, wasn't it?'

A monster, tail-walking on the waves towards her. A Fish God, demanding sacrifice.

'Damn right it was. A mythical fish, a *legend* of a fish. Biggest damn fish in the world.'

'And we nearly brought it in.'

'*You* nearly brought it in.'

'It doesn't matter, Dad. It doesn't matter.' And Frankie beckoned Isobel over, tearing open another surgical spike.

It took a while, took a few hours. First, Frankie won the Science Prize, and the Rickmans decided to celebrate this by dining out on imported lobster. Frankie was allowed some white wine, which she sipped as she listened to her father telling her about the places north of San Diego where he thought it would be good to live, listened to him describing how the sun shone, the surf was always up and they could go camping, maybe buy a little place out on the coast for weekends. Frankie noticed that her mother was smoking more than usual, noticed that she didn't join in, didn't follow the thread of the conversation.

It took a while, took a few hours.

They drove back to Sitka Street and Frankie put the science trophy on the shelf, slotting it in among all her sports prizes. Settling in the den, Billy-Ray and Frankie watched reruns of M*A*S*H and the *Tonight Show* as Isobel tried to complete the crossword. Billy-Ray, his stomach full of exotic meat and fine wine, felt content. Felt relieved, tried not to think of the oil oozing, nosing its way south across a dangerous wilderness. Ready to go to bed, Frankie stood and stretched, kissed her parents goodnight. As she reached the door, Billy-Ray, still watching the TV, not looking at her, said, 'Hey, Frankie, there's an envelope on your bed. Suggest you look in it,' and Isobel looked puzzled. In the envelope was the deed to the Piper Super Cub, which was now owned by one Frances Rickman. Frankie thundered back down the stairs, dragged Billy-Ray from the couch and danced around him. Billy-Ray couldn't help laughing. 'Well, I don't use it enough now.' Frankie whooped, she yelled, she went back to her room and waited until she heard her parents going to bed before celebrating by lighting the joint she had hidden in her closet. Leaning out of the window (looking out over the clearing that Minto had crossed, poppers firing), she inhaled deeply, frowned and blew.

It took a while, took a few hours.

Lying on her bed, feeling mellow, listening to Blondie's 'Man Overboard' on her headphones, she flicked through photographs of floatplanes landing and taking off across the world – from lakes and glaciers, pontoons and lagoons. She giggled quietly, felt an urge to devour a slab of chocolate. Giggled again as a thought, small and silver as a smelt, wriggled between the cracks of her euphoria.

Billy-Ray had type B blood; she had AB. Isobel's was blood type O.

Triplets, London buses, darts, clover leaves – all these things come in threes. Bad luck, kismet, karma, fate, destiny – all these come as they should.

2000

There's a woman knitting, a gorilla, a coastline crowded with icebergs, an Aristotelian profile and a teddy bear, but then there are always teddy bears. Frankie leaves the balcony, steps into her tiny kitchen, smaller even than a galley, cracks open a bottle of Tiger beer and checks the clock: ten minutes to kill. On the television, soundless, wordless, George Bush moves his thin lips, the caption telling her that he is demanding that Al Gore back off and concede defeat. Frankie swigs a mouthful of freezing beer. It's amazing – turns out Americans can't even count any more. Katherine Harris, mouth painted like a slashed wound, walks into a room thousands of miles away in Tallahassee and Frankie flicks the TV off, goes back out onto the balcony. Her apartment is on the tenth floor and the balcony faces west, high above the shanty huts in the compounds below. She scans the streets, sees washing drying on the brown-and-silver corrugated roofs, shirts with arms akimbo, creased, nearly burned by equatorial sun. She looks down, watches the crowds heading home, cycles and motorbikes weaving between men pushing carts, women balancing laundry baskets on head or hip. Ten to six – the sun will set in seven minutes. The woman in the rocking chair has stopped knitting, has morphed into a hammerhead, drifting with intent towards the gorilla. The balcony, like every structure in Malé, is tiny; there is only room for a small stool, and only if Frankie sits at an angle can she lean against the wall and put her long, long legs up on the rail. Which is what she does most evenings, with a bottle of Tiger and one of the five Marlboro Lights she allows herself each day. Which is what she is doing right now, as she watches the clouds moving north, colliding, swirling, making faces, teddy bears and uninhabited islands. Another ritual, begun many years before, when she'd sat on Billy-Ray's lap on the gallery of the cabin in Halibut Cove and they made pictures of the sky. It's an illusion that the temperature rises as the sun falls, but nevertheless the fireball, the fire *storm* that's falling so fast she can see it move, seems to sear the air before it drops below the horizon. Frankie watches it intently, hoping to catch the green flash but it doesn't happen. In five years she's seen it only four times, the emerald explosion on the edge of the ocean that races left and right before fading as the sun disappears.

Frankie finishes the beer, stubs out her cigarette and steps back into the living room, a small, white box twelve feet square. The room is plain, painted white, a few photographs of sea and sky on the walls, the wooden carving that can be whatever she wants it to be the only ornament. Picking up the phone, she flicks through her diary, finds the number and dials, stares out at the darkening sky. It takes a while, takes many minutes and many conversations with distant operators, but eventually she's patched through and a familiar voice comes on the line.

'Frankie? Is that really you?'

'Happy birthday, Mom.'

'Well, this is something of a miracle, I have to say.'

'You having a good day?'

'I'm having an . . . interesting day, shall we say. We had an outage last night and I've been trying to replace the vaccinations we lost because the generators didn't kick in. They have to stay below freezing and it's eighty-six in the shade here.'

'Well, today at three o'clock it was a hundred and three here. Beat that.'

Isobel laughs. 'I don't know how you can stand it.'

'It's fine. Kept promising myself air-conditioning but I never got round to it. How are you, Mom?'

'I'm fine, busy as ever. The school's finished and the clinic opens next month. I can't believe I'm sixty-three. It doesn't seem possible.'

'Well, no doubt you're looking good on it.' Frankie licks the scar where her ring finger should be – sometimes it still itches, which drives her crazy. How can an absence itch? 'Listen, I've only booked ten minutes on the line. Are you going back to England for Christmas? I only ask because I could meet you there.'

'I wasn't planning on it but I can be. I will be, if you're going to be there.'

'My contract here finishes on December nineteenth and I thought I'd fly to London. I've got a couple of things I want to do there.'

'In that case I shall make sure I'm there. I'll aim to be back before you and meet you at the airport. It will be lovely to see you, it's been far too long.'

'Two years. It's been two years, Mom.'

'Has it really? Good Lord, I suppose it must.'

Frankie glances at the television, is reminded by its blank, grey face. 'I saw Dad yesterday.'

Isobel says nothing, stares unseeing at a Coca-Cola truck kicking up dust as it races down the road to Lake Victoria.

'I don't mean I actually saw him, I mean I saw him on TV. Remember I said we get CNN here now? Well, there he was, standing in the background when they were interviewing Bush.'

'Was she with him?'

'Nope. He was just standing there with all the other suits. Are you getting the news? I mean, d'you know what's going on? With the election?'

'We sometimes manage to pick up the BBC World Service, but they say there are a lot of solar flares at the moment and that seems to cause interference. I gather that there's a recount.'

'Yeah, well, I reckon we all know what's going to happen.' Frankie jams the phone against her neck, rubs at the raw-looking skin on her hand. 'So we'll meet up in London next month?'

'How did he look?'

'He looked . . . he looked,' Frankie shrugs, 'he looked very sleek. He looked the same as he always did. Mom, you know what Bush is saying?'

'What's he saying?'

'He wants to drill in the wildlife refuges, in Alaska.'

'Oh, Lordy. Is nothing sacred?'

'D'you reckon that's why Dad was there?'

'I don't know, Frankie, and I don't care. And neither should you. Anyway, this is costing you a fortune.'

Frankie shrugs again. 'Mom, how far is Bristol from London?'

'Not far, maybe a two-hour drive. Why?'

'Can we go there? At Christmas?'

'Why on earth do you want to go to Bristol?'

'Remember Thekla's photos?'

'Yes, I remember.'

'Maybe you could look up your old flame.'

'Pardon?'

Frankie smiles. 'I remember you telling me you knew Bristol because your first boyfriend lived there.'

'Well, he's no doubt by now a happily married pillar of the community.'

'You have one minute left,' the voice of an operator breaks in.

'So what you doing tonight, Mom? How you going to celebrate?'

'Ruble and I are driving overnight to Nairobi. We have to collect medical supplies. I'll be back the day after tomorrow.'

'Well, you certainly know how to have a good time.'

'Write to me and let me know all your movements.'

'Will do. Happy birthday, Mom. Be careful.'

'And you. I look forward to—'

The line falls dead and Frankie stares at the mouthpiece for a moment before replacing it. The room feels hollow, more silent than it had been before, feels like a beach after a storm, empty and surprised. Frankie fetches another beer, fighting the desire to drink something stronger, fighting the desire to find a flat surface and drink herself far away, drink herself to oblivion. She returns to the balcony, leans on the railing and watches as weak, pale blue neon strips flare over the streets. Watches a 747 taking off, rising slowly, roaring. Frankie is trying not to think of her mother sitting in the cab of a Land Rover at dusk, preparing to drive through the African night, a night that Frankie always thinks darker, more malevolent than any other. Does not want to think of her mother juddering across dry river beds, rocking in potholes, chain-smoking, squinting into blackness, trying to anticipate danger. Surely her mother should give it up soon. Give it all up and go home. Play golf, take tea, visit galleries. Do whatever women of a certain age and disposition do.

Frankie opens Coetzee's *Disgrace*, glances at it, puts it back on the table. She turns on the television, leans against the wall and watches the silent images scroll. And there he is again, sleek Billy-Ray Rickman, looking as if there is nothing he could wish for, looking as if he has a hard, cold curl of butter in his mouth, looking as if he has no wounds, no scars. Frankie watches her father, whom she has not seen for eleven years, and as he walks out of frame she notices he is limping.

Eleven years before, on the twenty-fifth anniversary of the Alaskan earthquake, the *Exxon Valdez* grounded at Bligh Reef and a thousand feet of metal shuddered, groaned and ripped apart. Three days later Billy-Ray Rickman flew to Valdez in an Alyeska floatplane and stepped on to the dock at the Marine Terminal with a headache and a hard hat. It had happened; the unthinkable had happened. And who'd have fucking thought it? Not an earthquake, not a tsunami, not the Wave roaring up the Valdez Narrows – instead a few beers and bourbons. Billy-Ray, his heart jumping, his head pounding, looked south down the Sound, expecting to see a wave of thick, viscous crude, all eleven million gallons, barrelling towards him. An Alyeska engineer, sleepless and unwashed, walked over.

'What the fuck happened?' Billy-Ray was nearly shouting.

The man rubbed his face and shrugged. 'It's a fuck-up.'

'Where was the fucking response barge?'

'It was out of service. Needed maintenance.'

'Shit.'

The engineer looked down at the scarred planking of the dock. 'To be honest, wouldn't have made a difference anyway. Plus we just got a radio call – the dispersants aren't working.'

'What about the skimmers and booms?'

'Don't have enough.'

Billy-Ray, speechless, helpless, looked around the terminal, looked up at the sky. Ran his hand through short, grey hair. 'What are we going to do?'

The engineer shrugged again. 'Pray.' The man walked away, but so slowly, his feet dragging. He'd been awake for seventy-two hours, during which time he'd twice been flown over the slick. The engineer knew there was nothing to be done; if the dispersants weren't working then there was nothing to be done. He'd seen the blanket of crude, moving gracefully, moving with the swell, like a dancer, shimmering, almost, in sunlight. Beautiful, it had looked strangely beautiful; beautiful and endless and uncontainable.

Billy-Ray watched the engineer's retreating back, bowed by defeat and tiredness, and began to walk towards the administration block. A floatplane caught his eye, a Cessna 185, bobbing on the swell, its tag a swirl of bulbous red letters sprayed behind the prop: Tattie Bogle. As the crude in the ruptured tanks of the *Exxon Valdez* oozed from ragged tears, worming its way upward through the waters of Prince William Sound and sea otters began to gasp, Billy-Ray Rickman stared at the plane. Tattie Bogle? A tall, tanned woman with short, spiked black hair threw open the cockpit door, stepped down on to the dock, checked the mooring rope, yawned and stretched. She glanced over, saw Billy-Ray and froze, back arched, mouth open.

Frankie is lying in her bed, curled into a ball, hands tucked beneath her chin, unaware of the faint, rhythmic tick of the fan whirring above her. She's breathing deeply, eyes closed, dreaming her mother's journey with her; she is not sleeping but drifting. If Frankie drifts, then her mother will live, will not be corralled by bandits, will not be left raped and broken in the bush. If Frankie sleeps, her mother will be in peril. The glow in the Land Rover's cab, lit by the dash and the headlights flashing on baobab trees, the red tip of her mother's cigarette – Frankie can see it all. The flank of a wildebeest, the unblinking eyes of a lioness. Frankie can do this, she can float away and dream others' lives and yet remain within herself.

As she travels with Isobel, along the Great Rift Valley, Frankie thinks, too, of a tall blonde woman with a gun and of Minto falling. She hears the thud of a sixteen-hundred-pound black marlin diving, remembers stabbing her father and collecting his blood.

Billy-Ray watched as his daughter fell out of her stretch, shrugged on a fleece and faced him. She stood unmoving, looking ready to run.

'Frankie.' Billy-Ray walked slowly, almost warily, towards her, as if she were a young deer in his sights. 'Frankie.' He watched her watching him as he stood in front of her. Almost as tall as him and looking much older than the last time they had seen each other. 'What are you doing here?'

'I came back up to fly the clean-up workers out to the beaches.'

'Right.'

Frankie's mouth was working; she was chewing the inside of her cheek, a tic he had forgotten.

'You said this would never happen. You promised me it would never happen.'

Billy-Ray had nothing to say. 'I'm sorry.'

'Don't apologize to me. Try saying sorry to the Native villagers, the fishermen. Try saying sorry to the birds and the whales and the otters. They're beginning to pick them off the rocks. The birds can't fly, they're drowning in oil. The otters are suffocating in crude. The coastline, the beaches are covered. Just who are you planning on saying sorry *to*? The fucking oil companies, because they can't ship any more for a while? Have you flown over it yet?'

'I just got in.' Billy-Ray couldn't look in Frankie's eyes.

'It's like nothing you've ever seen. What are you going to do about it? What's Exxon and Alyeska going to *do* about it?'

'Pray.'

Frankie zipped her fleece, pulled on gloves. 'Looks like Mom and Lucca were right all along, doesn't it?'

'Frankie, this should never have happened—'

'I know that. But it has and you're all already three days too late. You want to know something? You can't fucking buy your way out of this one. This is one thing money really, really can't buy.'

Frankie walked away, turned her back on her father and walked away. Billy-Ray never saw his daughter again but he caught the expression on her face before she turned to go: utter contempt. Tattie fucking bogle, Billy-Ray thought, but he didn't say anything.

Half-past three in the morning and Frankie slams her door, trots down the stairs and out on to the street. It's thirty degrees, the coolest it ever gets in the capital of the Maldives, the coolest and darkest. Frankie has not slept, has lain on her bed, travelling hundreds of dusty miles with her mother, and now she knows Isobel will be OK. She bends her leg, stretches her thigh muscles, her heels digging into her buttocks, holds her muscles there, at the point of pain. Her hand rests against a door, her favourite door, a dark, scoured blue which reminds her of the light at twenty metres down the reef. The houses have no numbers, only names to guide the traveller, and behind the blue compound door there are family homes called 'Aston Villa', 'Tomato', 'Love Nest' and 'Swastika'. Her hand always rests against the plaque on which 'Swastika' is written, covering it. Frankie always wonders, as she stretches the muscles of her buttocks, what goes on in the house called 'Every Night', what doings there are in the house called 'Cheese'. Then Frankie begins to run. Every morning, Frankie runs for thirty minutes wherever she is. She runs fast, runs as if she has somewhere to go, as if she is late, as if someone is, somewhere, waiting for her. In five years she has run along every street in Malé a hundred times. Every alleyway is familiar: she knows where dogs lurk, where chickens will scatter, squawking, where potholes hide beneath puddles in the rainy season. Frankie runs; it's what she does.

Malé is tiny, not even two kilometres square, and there are more than sixty thousand people crammed on to this speck of coral. There is no space to spare, no private space to defend. And yet, when she reaches the sea wall, Frankie can see all the space in the world, an endless vista of sky and ocean, a surfeit of air and surf and moonlit clouds all around her. Malé – crowded yet limitless. At her back she can feel the weight of thousands snuffling and turning in their beds, breathing heavily in the hot air.

At night, when the streets of your cities and villages shall be silent, and you think them deserted, they will throng with the returning hosts that once filled and still love this beautiful land.

Frankie passes the harbour twice on her daily run because passing the harbour makes her feel less lonely. Even at this time, the dead of night, when the undead walk and the lonely sprint, there are people at the harbour. Dhonis are coming in, fishermen tossing the plump, silver bodies of skipjack and yellowfin tuna on to the dock, like expectant grenades. Teashop owners stand tall, stretching outside their shops, jigging their torsos as Frankie runs past, waving casual, brown hands when they see her. Men with barrows stacked high with sour gourds, betel leaves, bananas, melons and arreanut weave their way down to the bazaar, lean, thin shanks working, pushing heavily loaded trollies. Some of the workers on the docks are gaunt and twisted, their heads swollen, overlong limbs like twigs, and Frankie knows this is because they suffer from thalassaemia, a fact she learned many years before.

Routine, which often saves the lonely, is easy in such a place. A small coral island, surrounded by the Indian Ocean, where the day is always twelve hours and the night the same. Every day, every night, the same. Each of more than a thousand islands is similar, coral rings within atolls, turquoise lagoons, white sand, covered in brush, palms and sea grape, surrounded by infinite blue sky. Frankie can tell the time to within a few minutes by glancing at the shadows on a familiar wall, by looking at the sun slanting over mosques, by sensing a rise in temperature. She wears no watch and yet knows when her thirty minutes are up, and she jogs back to the apartment block, drenched with sweat, wet as if she has been caught in a storm. She showers, drinks tea as she dries, and then dresses in her uniform of starched, white short-sleeved cotton shirt, knee-length dark blue shorts, black leather belt, watch and reef shoes; she slips shades in her breast pocket, along with two pens. Picking up her pilot's case and an overnight bag at 5.05 (routine, routine), she walks down the stairs to the taxi which will take her to the airport, a man-made strip of garbage and tetrapods a couple of kilometres away.

Two long flights that day – south to Daahlu Atoll, back to Malé via Rangali, then a late afternoon drop to Veligandu and an overnight stop, leaving at 6.15 the next morning with a large party. Frankie checks in at the office, collects her manifest and flight plans, picks up documents to sign concerning the end of her contract, and walks out to the taxi dock. The planes are lashed, a line of de Havilland Twin Otters, moving on the water, bumping the boards of the walkway, their undersides white and blue, yellow livery above. Frankie is flying with Jan, a Dutch guy, as co-pilot, and they run through the checks as dawn breaks and the tourists clamber aboard, all of them sweating, made disgruntled by long-haul flights from cold northern cities. The steward loads the luggage, balancing the weight, as Frankie fires first the left and then the right prop. As the Otter motors slowly to take-off point, Frankie runs the last checks, pushes the stick, Jan's hand resting on hers, and the plane lumbers, a little skittish, until it reaches the step and then breaks away, water sluicing off the pontoons. A few clouds, which Frankie skirts as the plane ascends, engines chuntering, and then she levels at sixteen hundred feet. Relaxes a little, scanning the dials, noting down time and data on the flight report. Only seven passengers, plus luggage; she calculates the flight time at an hour and twenty.

And then Frankie looks around. *This* is what it was all for – all the arguments with Billy-Ray and Isobel about not going to college, the hundreds of hours spent flying over waterways and ice fields, the evenings spent studying for her SES and twin engine endorsements as her parents fought over what little was left of their life together. This is what it was all for – so she could spend her days flying over coral rings, passing the gulls' wings of dhonis' sails, seeing dolphins' curved backs and the black mass of hammerheads beneath the water's surface as massive leatherbacks cruised in lagoons. To fly between the clouds, so close she could touch them.

The giant manta eases itself away; such an unlikely creature, a silky black tablecloth flapping lazily, tail swishing. The tourists in the bar, watching the film, are rapt, flinching as one as a close-up of a moray eel appears. Frankie has seen the film more times than she can remember, so she sits alone at the bar, nursing an orange juice.

Just as she had known he would, the young guy with the tattoo and the Oz-blond-surfer look comes over and sits on the stool next to her.

'Can I buy you a drink? To say thank you? I was one of your passengers over here this afternoon.'

Frankie shakes her head. 'I've got an early flight tomorrow morning, so I won't have anything, thanks.'

'You been doing this long?'

'Five years. My contract ends in a couple of weeks.'

'Must be an amazing job.'

He's handsome – young and probably very dull, but handsome. 'Yeah, it is.'

'So, d'you fly every day?'

'No, we do five days a week, get two off.'

'What d'you do for holidays? I mean, this whole place is like a holiday, which must be weird.'

'I dive a lot. From here it's real easy to get to the Philippines, Australia, Thailand, Bali. And, obviously, I do some diving here, but a lot of the reefs are dying.'

'I thought you looked fit.'

And Frankie looks at him, looks right at him and wonders whether to have sex with him. It's been quite a while, after all. 'This your first time here? In the Maldives?'

'No, I've been before. Spent a couple of weeks last year in Lily Beach, but this place seems really fit. I've come with my brother.'

And she knows what he wants. Watches the way his mouth hangs open as he breathes. Decides against asking him to her room. 'Well, have a good time.'

The boy looks surprised. 'I can't place your accent,' he says, anything to keep her there. 'Where you from?'

Frankie pockets her cigarettes and lighter. 'I don't know,' she says, and walks out of the bar.

Frankie Rickman travels light. She drags a rucksack from the cupboard of her tiny Maldivian bedroom and packs a wet suit, a change of clothes and a wooden carving, which is no longer a cloud or escape; it has now become a question. After five years of flying the atolls that is all she has – a carving and a question. They are all she has held on to, in her years of flying the ice fields of Alaska with hunters and hikers, the keys and coastal waterways of Florida with fishermen, the corn fields of Kansas and Iowa dusting crops, the towering cumulonimbus of the west coast with meteorologists in search of the perfect cloud, the perfect Kelvin-Helmholtz spiral; and the coral rings of the Maldives in search of solitude.

In all the earth there is no place dedicated to solitude.

Sitting on her balcony, with a Tiger beer and a Marlboro Light, Frankie spends her last evening in Malé watching the sun set, watching the sky pale and then darken, falling down through shades of blue, the restless ocean swaying beneath it – a world streaked with aquamarine, azure, midnight, plum and cobalt, beneath a sky of lapis lazuli and violet. The moon rises and she follows the backlit clouds rolling inexorably across the horizon. The constellations of Orion and Scorpio wheel slowly above her, dazzling, as she tries not to think too much of the future. She climbs into bed but does not sleep. At three o'clock Frankie runs her last worn path around the worn streets, which are beginning to sink under the weight of buildings and cars.

Frankie showers, dresses, closes the door and hands the apartment key to the owner. Walks down the stairs and into a taxi, which takes her to the airport, where she checks on to a flight to London, England. A place she hasn't visited since she was a child, when her mother ran away from the moving earth. A place where she sat on her mother's shoulders and waved to Jacqueline Cooper, her tiny hand turning like a wink.

The Silent City sprawls out across a plain below them, far from silent. The sounds of car horns, sirens, the grinding of gears, the growling of diesel engines float up to Frankie and Isobel as they stand on the bridge, suspended high above the muddy river, which has carved a deep, steep-sided gorge. What Frankie sees is a city, with high-rises, stadiums, industrial estates, malls and car parks framed by low, green hills; graffiti sprayed on the rock faces of the gorge. She feels like crying – for nearly thirty years she has waited to stand on this bridge and all she can see is the cancer of concrete.

'I have to say, it's changed a lot since I was last here,' says Isobel. 'Mind you, that must have been nearly fifty years ago.'

'I don't recognize anything.'

'The bridge is the same.'

Perhaps her memory is playing tricks with her? Frankie drifts a little, becomes her eleven-year-old self, standing in Thekla's lounge, Fin hovering nearby with a beer, as her parents argued. She is sure that there were tall trees, terraces of houses cascading down to the river, iron balconies and flat roofs.

'We should visit the *camera obscura*. If I remember rightly, you can see a panorama up there.' Isobel points to a curious round building on top of the Downs.

Mother and daughter climb the stairs of the sandstone building, emerge into the lightless room at the top, and on the wall is projected an image of the Silent City. And there are the terraces and parklands and spires, the black-and-white tin canopies suspended over balconies, the towering beech and elm trees. The pinhole camera that throws the image seems to have stripped out the roads and high-rises, and Frankie is looking at a silvery, silent Victorian cityscape. The room, dark and cold, becomes a camera, the walls the film. Frankie stands in the path of the light source, and the city is imprinted on her face.

'This is amazing,' she says, and smiles. 'It's not an illusion, it does exist. Whether Willoughby saw it or not.'

Frankie, who has not driven for five years, sits in the passenger seat as Isobel negotiates the Gordian knot of roads leading to the motorway that will take them back to London. The Catherine wheel of cars at roundabouts, the never-ending stream of metal which passes them, unsettles Frankie, who is still trying to shake off memories of lagoons and leatherbacks, who is getting used to the idea of driving for miles and knowing there are miles left to drive. Driving a road that leads somewhere, a road that is not a circle. She thinks of Minto, thinks of his despair that he would never drive to Skagway, and she glances at her mother's murderer's thumbs, wrapped around the steering wheel, cigarette smoking between her fingers.

'What are you going to do now?' Isobel asks, putting her foot on the accelerator and nudging the needle up to ninety.

Frankie swallows and grips the seat. She is still unused to speed. 'I don't know. There are a few possibilities but they don't really appeal to me. I heard of a few options to buy planes – there's a Cessna one-eight-five, with STOL, takes two to three passengers with a seven-hundred-pound payload, hardly used, for sale in Florida. It's fifty thousand dollars but I can manage that. I guess I could go back to the States and work for the National Parks, or set up in Anchorage and run parties to Denali and all that shit. I dunno. Feels like going backwards or something. Of course, the best money's working the oil rigs, but I don't think so, somehow.'

'I can understand that. You could come back with me, work for the charity, or Oxfam or something similar. You wouldn't earn much, but money's hardly a problem.'

It wasn't money which kept Frankie away from her mother, it was fear. She thought of the pitch-black African night sky, the rusting fuselages of craft littering the banks of runways, thought of the etiolated black limbs of limp children, the upturned empty palms, the endless dust plains, where no rivers flowed, where no water gushed into crystal lakes. 'You're going back, then?'

'Of course. There's still so much to be done. It will never end, I know that. What we do makes a near-insignificant difference. In January I'm going to Nigeria. We've finally got permission to build a compound outside Ibiapukiri.'

'Where?'

'It's on the Bight of Bonny.'

Frankie is confused. 'The bite of bonny?'

'Ibiapukiri is a town on the Niger delta, not far from Brass. Mangrove swamps, lagoons, tributaries. Malaria, yaws, yellow fever. The usual. Illiteracy, high infant mortality rates, AIDS.'

'Sounds charming.'

'All compounded by oil pollution in the delta. Brass is where the oil storage facility is, surrounded by old, poorly maintained pipelines. There are hundreds of spills every year, and the locals try to burn it off. It's in the water, in the crops, in the soil. They can't grow anything any more, so they're going hungry too.'

'It never stops, does it? No matter how far we go, no matter how far away you and me go, there's always the fucking oil. It never stops. Y'know, in the Maldives the atolls are beginning to disappear. Did you know that? The rise in sea level – they're only a couple of metres high. What does anyone care? After all, it's just a bunch of brown people sitting on a bunch of coral.'

'You heard that Bush won the election?'

'Yeah.'

And both of them picture sleek Billy-Ray Rickman limping out of the frame.

Frankie chews at the inside of her cheek, looks at her mother's profile – lean, gaunt, almost, but still beautiful in a pale grey way.

Isobel Rickman, driving too fast, smoking too much. Frankie looks at her own hands, still deeply tanned, resting now on her thighs. Small hands, with long, tapering fingers.

'Do you ever think of Charlie?' she asks her mother.

'Of course I do. Every day. I called the clinic in Kenya the Charlie Red-Wing Hospital. The locals love the name.' Isobel begins to pull out to overtake a lorry, and a BMW flashes her, forces her back in lane. 'Bugger.'

'You ain't allowed to say that.'

'And you ain't allowed to say ain't.' Isobel smiles.

'Do you ever think of Minto?'

Isobel lights another cigarette, checks her mirror, pulls out again. 'Sometimes.'

'What do you think when you think of him?'

'I think of the Spirit Bear.'

As they approach London and the motorway reduces to two lanes, Isobel slows down and Frankie stares out at the Christmas lights flickering in the office blocks of Chiswick. It is dark and cold, the outskirts of the city are ugly; she is reminded of Anchorage. She is reminded of so many things; sitting next to her mother, being reminded of so many things.

As they sit in a traffic jam on the Earl's Court Road, Frankie turns up the heater and says, 'Do you remember that carving Charlie gave me? The carving that can be anything?'

'Of course I do.'

'I still have it, I take it everywhere, wherever I move. Do you want to know what it is right now?'

'What is it?'

'It's a question.'

'What's the question?'

'Why did you wait so long to tell me I was adopted? Why did I have to ask?'

Isobel turns to her daughter, her face flushed by red neon flashing nearby, and for once she does not look cool, does not look composed. 'Because it didn't matter. It made no difference. I loved you as if you were my own.'

'You don't know that.'

'I *do* know that. The time to tell you never seemed right. And then it seemed to matter less as the years went by.'

'Maybe to you.' Frankie touches the raw skin on her fourth knuckle. 'It matters *more* to me as time passes. The other day, someone asked me where I was from and I told him I didn't know. And I don't.'

'Frankie, you know you're loved, which is more than many people are. Which is more than the orphans in Ibiapukiri are.'

'This isn't about them.'

'I'm sorry.'

'I need a drink.'

'We'll be home soon.'

'I thought,' Frankie fishes a cigarette out of her mother's pack, opens the window a crack, and a cold draught snakes in, 'I thought whilst I was here, I might try to find my birth parents. I assume I was born here. I don't want to piss you off, but I'd like to know.'

Isobel frowns.

'I went on the Net when I was in Malé, and I know they've got all these databases now, which makes it easier, in a place called Somerset House. And the British government has changed the law so it's easier to find stuff out.'

Isobel pulls the car over to the kerb, flicks on the warning lights and ignores the cascade of car horns that greets this. 'Frankie, my love, you won't find them. You were an orphan.'

'But I could still dig up some information.'

'No.'

'What d'you mean, no?'

'You won't find anything.'

'How can you be so sure? I mean, I can look up some papers. There must be papers—'

'There aren't any papers. Frankie, there aren't any official papers.'

'Why not?'

'Because your father bought you. He bought you from a baby farm.'

Frankie says nothing, stares into her mother's blue-blue eyes, thinks, Tattie fucking bogle, but she doesn't say anything.

Was there really nothing people wouldn't buy? Nothing they wouldn't sell?

2000

Billy-Ray Rickman lives now in a fabulous Spanish-style villa in Santa Barbara, California, with his second wife, Jacqueline, née Olivetti. The house boasts the latest computer technology; polluted air is filtered and ionized, temperature remotely controlled. He has a pool, a hot tub and a sauna, he drives a Maserati and he owns a seventy-foot yacht. Billy-Ray has a diverse portfolio of shares, a small but rapidly appreciating collection of art, and apartments in New York and Dallas, houses in the Bahamas and Cape Cod. He has a personal trainer, a well-equipped gym and a finely toned, permanently tanned stomach. At weekends, he and his wife occasionally invite friends to join them on the yacht, and they cruise the channel islands. Or, perhaps, they drive down to Palm Springs for a few days of golf. Twice a year they visit the Virgins and the Bahamas, Christmas they spend at the Cape, after a week in New York City, visiting galleries and taking in the shows. Billy-Ray Rickman, who is now seventy-two but looks fifty-two, has everything he ever desired. He has money, he has power, he has the ear of the President. He also has nightmares, wakes every night, whimpering. It is Deet who keeps him awake, sitting at the end of his bed, his chest shattered, seemingly drenched not with blood but oil. Deet sits there and keeps his brother awake.

Billy-Ray Rickman has no one to whom he can leave his oil-soaked bounty. This is not his only regret but it bothers him because when he dies the Reichmann genes die with him. Billy-Ray now understands why Isobel decided to leave Highbury to her nephews and nieces in her will – it is theirs, their bloodright. Jacqueline was forty-three when she stood by the elevator doors in Karbo Towers, watching Billy-Ray being transported to a room in the Ritz by the scent of tobacco, Chanel and vanilla. She was forty-five when they married. Jacqueline is still beautiful, she still knows how to deal with time, but she cannot give him children.

Sometimes Billy-Ray sits in his landscaped gardens, in the shade of a wide-spreading flamboyant, smoking cigars, turning lead crystal wine glasses in his hands (Jacqueline will not allow him to drink vodka) and he wonders at his regrets. He regrets that he never said goodbye to Lucca Barzini, that he was rude and surly and churlish the last time they met. Lucca taught him how to make love and he never thanked her. He regrets the fact that he got off the Greyhound bus in Missoula because he couldn't bear the thought of seeing his mother being lowered into the ground; more, that he lied about this to Urban. He regrets the day that Isobel and Frankie surprised him in the Campbell Lake house – Frankie had brought Isobel with her on her first solo flight to Anchorage and they had wanted to surprise him. And they had because it turned out he always had to have it all. (I'm forty fucking years old, I don't need surprises.) He had looked up from Jacqueline's naked body to see Isobel's retreating back and Frankie's shocked blue eyes.

Sometimes Billy-Ray tries to work out when, exactly, he lost control of his life – not that many would suggest that he had, if they saw him sitting in his garden, sipping fine wine, looking like a man who makes his own luck. Billy-Ray regrets that the last time he saw Frankie was on the dock of the Valdez Maritime Terminal as a thick oil slick blanketed Prince William Sound and she looked at him with contempt. He misses Frankie and he misses Isobel. He still misses Siggy, after all these years he still misses Siggy. Somewhere along the line, as he bored into the earth and ocean, digging his own pelf-well, he lost them all.

And then there is the regret that never fades, never changes. A boy standing on a porch, sending up a prayer. *Bitte, Gott, lass es Dieter sein.* Had that boy been cursed? Been damned? Billy-Ray has everything he ever wanted, there is no more that he can possibly desire, and yet he looks around, at his house and pool and cars, and he feels damned. Because the price was too high; Lucca had been right and the price was too high. Sometimes he thinks he should have gone out with the Svenssons, should have gone fishing with them

that summer, instead of going to the Kenai and beginning to destroy
the thing he loved.

When it's hot, when the temperature soars, Billy-Ray dozes in the
shade, exhausted by his sleepless nights, and he drifts back to Blue
Earth County. He can feel the water of Home Lake on his palm,
smooth as silk, can recall the smell of miraculous bread and the softness of a horse's underlip. Small things – the woof and weft of life.
Billy-Ray now knows that if all he remembers of his father is Oliver
smiling in the afternoon sun as he tells his son that pigs can't look at
the sky – well, that's fine. Hot *placki kartoflane*, the comfort of old,
worn jeans, his mother laughing when the lights were turned on in
the church and the stained glass burned like fire. Small things.
Simple things.

As the evening light creeps across the lawn, Billy-Ray sometimes
thinks it is, perhaps, right that the Reichmann family grinds to a
halt with him. Because he has spent his whole life trying to have it
all, making sure he was never found out, and he hasn't been. But
Deet knows, and that is why he sits on the end of his brother's bed,
sabotaging his sleep.

1960

The Mother Superior was kneeling on the slate floor, thanking God once more for the break in the weather – the stunning heat of August and September had made life very difficult. Tempers had shortened in the convent as the mercury rose; even the brides of Christ, it seemed, could have enough of a good thing, and the vow of silence had been broken many times. For weeks, the Mother Superior had prayed for rain and little else. The giant oaks surrounding the serrated railings had begun to creak, then wilted and lost their leaves after sucking the last drops of moisture from the parched ground. The Mother Superior had as much love for living things as the next person, but the fact was that the convent buildings were beginning to shift, lifted by the swarming roots of the trees. She knew she couldn't have the oaks felled because there would be uproar among the locals. But she had begun to consider the possibility of poisoning the roots at night – the perfect crime. A month before, however, she had woken to the sound of rain on the snug, well-maintained roof, and she had smiled. How apposite that it should happen on the Sabbath. She was beginning to think her Maker had gone a little too far, however; the early, light rains had become a relentless, never-ending stormy gale, sweeping in from the west.

The Mother Superior did not, in fact, have much to send up thanks for – despite the rain, despite the papal edicts emanating from Rome, she had a sense of impending doom. She knew that Outside things were changing, and not for the better if the numbers of fallen girls arriving at the gate were anything to go by. She'd even heard that Outside they were thinking of producing a pill that stopped the girls falling with child. They would then be able to fornicate with impunity, going unpunished. What was happening to the world? The world, it seemed, was on its way to hell. The Mother Superior sighed, shifted a little, and was then surprised by a touch on her shoulder. Even after all these years, she had not become used to the silent, barefooted approach of her charges. She hauled herself to her feet and followed the nun from the chapel.

'She has started,' said Sister Mary.

The Mother Superior was soaked to the skin, buffeted by wind and disgruntled by the time she threw open the door to the small hospital. There, before her, was one of the Fallen, thighs open, a mess of pink, wet tissue gasping, groping for something, she knew not what. Above the sound of the incessant rain she heard a cry, an odd, muffled scream. The baby was already breathing, howling in the echo chamber of the birth canal. And then, thank God, the plastered web of black hair appeared, skull pulse beating. Innocence. The Mother Superior grabbed at the head, tried to pull, but then there was the cord. A knot, two snips and she was ready to be on her way.

'Clean her up,' she told the nun, and then disappeared, fighting a gale, innocence locked in her arms.

Sister Mary looked at her own sister, lying there on nothing but a wooden plank, covered in shame. Maggie moaned as Sister Mary listened. Maggie began to bleed as Sister Mary watched. Handsome husbands and Czechoslovakian castles? Sister Mary didn't think so. The blood began to flow as the placenta ripped, tearing from the womb in pieces. Sister Mary had seen her sibling often over the past months and had not acknowledged her. Had seen her sitting in the gardens, skirt hitched up, bare legs there for all to see. Unashamed. Unrepentant. Mary had clear memories of their shared childhood, could remember Maggie sitting out on the wall, sunning herself, thinking, no doubt, of doing filthy things with the Maconnell boy. Maggie reached for her hand but Mary batted her away. She remembered Maggie saying she wasn't going to have babies and she smiled. The engorged arteries and capillaries of Maggie's womb burst and began to bleed as Maggie slipped into a coma. Mary looked at her sister's pale, sweaty face and remembered how beautiful Maggie had been, always turning heads and being talked to as she, Mary, dragged along behind. Well – look where beauty got you. Look where lust got you.

Once it was over, Sister Mary rearranged the body, lifting heavy legs and limp, muscled arms, and looked at Maggie for a last time. Lying in the middle of the red-stained sheet, her blue-black hair wild, she looked white as alabaster, cold as marble. She looked like the victim of a catastrophe. Covering her dead sister with a coarse blanket, Mary began to pray for her soul, her muttering the only sound in the ward, other than the whispers of wind.

1960

The riddle of Isobel's marriage to Billy-Ray Rickman, which niggled at Jacqueline Cooper for months, was finally solved on the evening of their wedding. The Coopers were, of course, invited, being close friends of both the groom and the bride. Jacqueline watched Isobel, six feet of satin and composure, huge hands hidden by a bouquet, walk down the aisle to join Billy-Ray Rickman at the altar. She tried not to stare at Billy-Ray but found she had to – he was, after all, the man for whom she might – *might* – have given it all up. The reception, a lavish bacchanal held in the grounds and ballroom of Highbury, was blessed by fine weather, unusual for late October. As Jacqueline stood in the line to be greeted by husband and wife, she felt for the first but not the last time that perhaps the time had come to go home, back to New York. She felt estranged, alien among all this ritual and ceremony. As Billy-Ray leaned forward to kiss her cheek, he asked whether she would spare him a moment later that afternoon.

'Thing is,' Billy-Ray said, when he caught Jacqueline alone in a quiet spot in the gardens, 'I need to ask a favour. I'm really sorry, but I can't think of anyone else to ask.'

'What is it?'

Billy-Ray lit a cigarette with the worn brass lighter that Jacqueline remembered, and said, 'Isobel can't have kids.'

Jacqueline frowned – this was not what she had expected to hear. 'Right.'

'When she had that accident – remember? Last year? She had a riding accident?'

'Yes.'

'Well, there was a lot of damage to her abdomen and she started haemorrhaging one night and they had to operate.'

'Yes.'

Billy-Ray stared down at his shoes. 'They found she has a condition – something to do with her septum? It's bicornuate or something. It's one of those things that you don't know you have. Y'know, everything seems normal. Anyway, the thing is, because of that she can't have kids.'

'Right.' Jacqueline waited. She remembered how Billy-Ray operated.

'Well, we want to adopt but there's all this crap about papers and nationalities, because I'm American and we want to live out there, so they're saying we can't do it here. I'm going back in a few weeks and I need to sort this out.'

'Yes.'

'Look, I remember you telling me once about some woman who worked for you who could help with this kind of thing. I can't remember exactly now, and I know it's not kosher or anything, but I don't care. I just want to get this wrapped up. I can pay, I'll pay anything. I'm real sorry to ask, but I can't think of what else to do.' Billy-Ray looked at Jacqueline, his face hopeful and handsome.

'Call me Wednesday morning.' Jacqueline ground her cigarette out on the immaculate lawn and walked away. So *that* was it – it didn't matter who Isobel married because she couldn't produce a Chalfont-Webbe heir.

Just as Sean Regan had done, Billy-Ray climbed into the attic of Constance Wycherley's house as rain fell on the roof slates like a lullaby, and in the soft yellow light he thought the babies there were glowing, like angels.

'I'll leave you here a while,' said Constance Wycherley. 'Take as long as you want – it's not a thing to be rushed.'

Billy-Ray nodded. Once alone, he moved from cot to cot, all five of them, and he knelt to look into wavering eyes, his fingertips brushing the tiny palms that were held out to him. He wanted a boy, a boy he could go hiking with, shoot hoops with. A boy he could teach to seduce a muskellunge into taking bait, to calm a horse by stroking its underlip. The rain grew stronger as time passed and Billy-Ray kept moving from cot to cot. How to tell? How to choose? He was on his knees, his trousers snagging on the sawn wood of the floorboards, and he stopped to tidy a blanket, gently picking up a soft, warm foot. Instead of tucking it in, Billy-Ray Rickman kneeled by the black-haired baby with the blue-blue eyes, and stroked the little foot, touched each toe as the baby drooled and suddenly smiled, revealing spit-glistening pink gums. And Billy-Ray knew. He sensed someone at his shoulder, smelled brine and the scent of a Lucky Strike cigarette, heard the sound of a sheet being pulled back, and he knew.

Constance Wycherley, who had climbed back up the stairs to ask whether he'd care for some tea, found Billy-Ray smiling; found the big American on his knees, smiling.

'She'll be a beauty, that one, you mark my words.'

'It's a girl?' said Billy-Ray, but he couldn't stop smiling as the foot grew warm in his hand.

As he left the lonely house, surrounded by windswept hills, the rain heavy now, blowing in his face, Billy-Ray jogged to his rented car in darkness, a bundle in his arms. It had taken hours to fill out the counterfeit forms, to provide fictitious details of his and Isobel's lives, to wait for the ink to dry on forged birth papers, to count out the many banknotes, but it was done. Nearing the car, he heard a cry, a mad, hawking sound. He made out a shape on the roof of the car – a raven in the rain. Billy-Ray covered the baby's head with his hand, afraid. The bird seemed to look at him, shiny black head turning as its eyes glittered. A squawk, a wing flap and the raven nodded, wheeled away.

2000

Decades later, on a different continent, in a different world, Billy-Ray dozes in his garden, the Californian sun pale in a smog-tinged sky. Suddenly he jerks awake, wipes at his mouth, says, 'What's that?' He had dreamed of a tall, black-haired girl he once knew, tall and beautiful and muscular, a girl who once plied him with vodka. He followed her up long, winding stairs to a rhomboid room and she bit his shoulder when she came, on the bed in her room beneath the eaves on New Year's Eve, 1959, a snowstorm flying around the turrets of a tiny castle.

He remembers now, he remembers the name missing from the list hidden beneath his lichen-covered stone. Magde, Lucca, Jacqueline and

'Maggie,' Billy-Ray Rickman whispers. 'Maggie Regan.'

The ice bridge that Charlie Red-Wing's ancestors crossed is long gone. That glittering span stretching across the frozen shallow sea melted thousands of years ago, as Charlie's people moved tentatively across an albino landscape, a white earth. The span thawed and flowed into the shallow Bering Sea, which is no longer shallow, which is rising because the earth is warm, much warmer than it should be. The tongues of glaciers that licked down valleys, that spread from ice fields covering mountain peaks, some larger than European countries, are retreating. Ice sheets split in half, float south and melt. Clinking bergy bits play their haunting music for a moment and then disappear. The oil that has been pumped from beneath that sea has been burned and the residue wraps itself around the world as a blanket, trapping the sun's rays. The cold waters flow south, on the Kurisho, Somali and Gulf Stream currents, to be heated and then return in the gyres. But now there is too much water flowing south; it is drowning valleys and coral atolls, flooding estuaries and deltas as swollen rivers spread over plains baked hard by the sun during rainless days.

Sedna (or Arnaknagsak), the Great Sea Spirit, broods in her watery kingdom of Adlivun. She has watched the slaughter of sea otters by the Russian promshlenniki, watched the corpses fall through water. She has seen seals drown in oil, walrus coated in crude. She has not seen the blue-grey, meaty bulk of the blue whale for tens of years, but she has seen the hammerhead, the minke, the grey whale harpooned, thrashing in pain until worn out, and then she has watched as men swarm over the still-living beasts with flenses, knives and cutlasses. Fine, flimsy nets drift in Adlivun, drift across oceans, spread forty miles long, and Arnaknagsak has watched as dolphins, whales, sharks, turtles all writhe and drown. New lands appear in her kingdom as islands sink beneath the lapping waves. Sedna no longer hears the voice of the shaman, no longer hears his praise and regrets. The Moon Spirit and the Air Spirit tell her of other things and she knows the Wolf and the Great Lynx are nearly gone, and the Eagle is powerless. Only the Raven is left, birthed by a woman who swallowed a feather. The Raven – hero and trickster, thief and buffoon – is still here, has spread across the world, living in cities, on far-flung deserted islands. Perhaps there is salvage?

When the Great Sea Spirit is angry, insufficiently propitiated, she will send a dead spirit, a malignant tupilaq, to unsettle the mortals living on the ice shelf.